NIGHT OF THE KRAKEN

MARK L'ESTRANGE

SEVERED PRESS
HOBART TASMANIA

NIGHT OF THE KRAKEN

To my darling Rachael, for the good times.

NIGHT OF THE KRAKEN – PROLOGUE.

The creature moved swiftly through the water, propelling itself forward with its massive tentacles. Often, it would allow itself to drift along with the current, catching any sea life which happened to cross its path. But tonight, their strength was no match for its powerful thrust. The creature drew water into its mantle cavity and shot it through its siphon, propelling it forcefully through the water.

Tonight, it had a purpose!

It had tasted human flesh for the first time almost a week ago. A small fishing vessel caught unawares in a storm. The meagre crew hurled into the dark water, thrashing about wildly to keep themselves afloat.

The creature had never seen humans at such close quarters before. Content mainly with life beneath the waves, it had on occasion raised itself from the depths at night when there was no light shining upon the surface of the water, to take in some air and see the stars. A couple of times, usually in very deep water, it had glanced a passing ship or liner in the distance, but they were too far away for it to make out any occupants, even with its exceptional eyesight.

The unfortunate members of the overturned fishing boat had been another matter. One of them had injured themselves quite badly, and the smell of the blood had attracted several sharks to the area.

The creature had seen them off with a fierce glare from its bulbous eyes before turning its attention back to the men. The blood tasted sweet in its mouth, different to that of anything it had eaten before. The temptation was too great. One by one, it had dragged each swimmer towards it huge beak-like jaws and crunched them clean in half before devouring the rest of them whole.

That flavour of blood, bone, and flesh still lingered in the creature's mouth.

And it could not wait any longer before tasting it again!

***

"Cappy" Jackson staggered across the street from the Fisherman's Arms, raising a grateful hand to the honking horn of the van that had to swerve to avoid him. Once on the pavement, he braced himself against the iron railings, breathing in the cool sea air. After a moment, he climbed over the top bar and jumped down onto the beach.

The tide was out, and picking up a deckchair from the pile by the sea wall, *Cappy* began to make his way over the wet sand towards the sea line.

The moon was almost full tonight, and glistened in silvery silhouettes across the rolling water in the distance.

When he was about thirty feet from the water's edge, *Cappy* set up his chair and slumped into it, his weight causing the wooden stands to sink deeper into the slush.

He took out his hip flask and saluted the water before knocking back a slug of dark rum. The liquid warmed his insides as it slipped down, protecting him against the night chill.

For someone who had spent his entire life in and around the sea, first as a sea scout until he was old enough to join the Navy, then later having grown weary of travel, as a fisherman, he was at his most content with a belly full of booze gazing at the sea in total solitude.

Over the last five years, having turned seventy, "Cappy" had started to gently slow down and pace himself more. He had sold his big boats, keeping back the smallest and easiest to maintain, which he still used whenever he felt the need to be back on the open water. He had been a resident of Skullen Bay all his life, and still lived in the cottage he had been born in. The locals had called him "Cappy" – short for captain, due to his service record and the sea captain's hat he always had perched on his head – for so long now that he was willing to bet none of them could remember his name was actually Stuart. Not that he minded; the term was used as an endearment and he had always liked it.

He was a character in the village, and everybody knew and liked him. A confirmed bachelor, he had been no stranger to the ladies, and in his service days lived up to the old tradition of having a girl in every port. Having never settled down, he had the luxury of keeping his own hours without being answerable to anyone, and that had suited him fine. Never having regretted not marrying or having children, he was content to spend his remaining days fishing, drinking, and charming newcomers with his tales of the deep. Even tonight, he had only paid for two of the six pints of strong ale he had consumed in the pub. The rest were all purchased for him by enchanted listeners directed by his hosts to his special corner where he always sat in the rocking chair, donated to him by a local furniture maker in return for several fishing trips over the years. Even the regulars never seemed to grow tired of his tales. And there were so many that some believed he would never have to repeat the same story twice in a year. Pete, the pub landlord, knew that "Cappy" helped bring in trade with his stories. And for the cost of a large glass of dark rum at the end of the night, both parties found the unspoken arrangement mutually equitable.

A low cloud scudded across the moon, masking its glow.

"Cappy" took another long swig from his flask before replacing it in his pocket, and taking out his pipe. He had always preferred a pipe. For one thing, it seemed to fit his overall persona, and secondly, it didn't leave an ugly yellow stain around his beard.

He sucked on his empty pipe and contemplated lighting it, but then he felt his eyes growing heavy and decided it was best not to. He calculated that he still had a good few hours before the tide would turn back, plenty of time for a short doze before turning in. With the sound of the distant waves lapping, "Cappy" slipped into a peaceful oblivion.

***

The creature raised its head just above the water level, just enough to allow its eyes to see the land. Cautiously, it surveyed the area. The tide was on its way back to shore by now, and it had waited until it was sure that there were no vibrations in the water signalling passing vessels. Seeing that all was still, it lifted its enormous head. Closing off its gills, it opened its lungs, freeing them to take in pure oxygen. It breathed in deeply, easily adjusting to the lack of water. It savoured the moment. It had been under for a long time and this was a welcome break. Turning, it scanned the beach and the sea surrounding it, its night vision allowing it to pierce the darkness.

Then it stopped. There in the distance, it made out the shape of the man slumped in the deck chair. It waited. Not moving. Trained not to draw unwanted attention by years of stealth and camouflage both under and on top of the water.

It waited until it was sure that the old man hadn't seen it.

The tide was now only about twenty feet from where the man sat sleeping. The creature shifted its eyes back and forth, scanning the horizon once more. Nothing moved.

Slowly, it began to propel itself forward until the water beneath it gave way to solid sand. Using its eight huge tentacles to drag it onto the shore, the creature approached the slumbering "Cappy" undetected.

Once it was within reach, it thrust out two of its tentacles and secured them around the sleeping figure and its deck chair, clamping them together in a tight embrace.

"Cappy" barely had time to register what was happening before the monstrous tentacles crushed the life from him, splintering the wooden chair and his bones in one swift action.

"Cappy" was dead long before he had a chance to look back into his killer's eyes.

The creature slid back into the water, taking its meaty snack with it.

Within seconds, the water had swallowed it entirely.

CHAPTER ONE

Caitlin Howard lifted back her arm and threw the tennis ball as hard as she could. She watched as it bounced along the sand up ahead finally rolling down to meet the tide, her golden retriever, Honey, bounding after it, barking excitedly.

Caitlin stretched her arms above her head, locking her fingers together. She took a deep breath allowing the sea air to fill her lungs. She felt totally at peace.

Since moving to Alton at the beginning of the summer, she had started her ritual of bringing Honey to this area of the beach every morning at 6 o'clock. The deserted beach allowed Honey to race along the sand with abandonment, without Caitlin needing to concern herself with her dog annoying any other users.

It often surprised her that no one else seemed to be out this early, especially in a seaside location. But secretly, she was glad for the privacy.

Honey arrived back, sliding to a halt at Caitlin's feet and dropping the ball in front of her. The dog sat back, wagging its tail in anticipation. Caitlin tried to throw it farther this time, allowing herself a longer interval before Honey retrieved it; her arm was starting to ache with all the effort.

Having completed her degree in Marine Biology, Caitlin had initially sought employment within her chosen field, but after several unsuccessful attempts, she resigned herself to taking a job in admin just to start paying back her student loan. Within two years, she was bored to tears. The monotony of the hum-drum office procedure and wretched futility of office politics was causing her to age before her time. Already, she was in the alarming routine of having dinner in front of the telly most nights before falling asleep watching whatever rubbish was on after the news. All her colleagues ever talked about was boyfriends/girlfriends, make-up, reality television, and going out.

She sorely missed the intellectual stimulation of the academic environment she was used to. The daily challenge of learning new and exciting things and staying up till all hours discussing and critiquing with like-minded mentally stimulating peers.

Now, she felt as if her brain was stagnating!

It was after a chat with one of her friends from university that she decided she had to do something to give herself a sense of purpose once more. She enrolled part-time in a Masters Degree course, and though she found the physical challenge of trying to study after a day's work exhausting, she found the experience of returning to study mentally stimulating.

It was during her first year that she met Rob. Rob was using the university library to research his PhD, and they seemed to hit it off immediately. They moved in together far faster than Caitlin would have usually contemplated, and at first, everything was wonderful. But soon the cracks began to show. Rob was not only extremely untidy, but his hygiene habits left something to be desired. Having always lived in shared accommodation or student digs, Rob thought nothing of inviting a gang of his old buddies over to the flat for an all-night drinking session, ignoring Caitlin's pleas that she had to be up at six for work.

Rob still lived off his student loans plus money his parents gave him, so his time was mainly his own. He was in no hurry to finish his degree as the end scenario involved the potential of having to get a job, and that was not high on his priority agenda.

Eventually, after a huge row, Caitlin moved out. She ended up in a tiny studio flat, much smaller than the flat they had shared, but in devoting herself to her studies, she decided she would be spending more time at the library than at home, so she did not let it get her down too much.

Once she had passed her Masters, Caitlin decided that she would once again seek relevant employment in her chosen field with renewed vigour.

She managed to secure herself a place on *The Calypso Rising*, a huge vessel equipped with the very latest technology for studying the underwater habitat and its occupants. The captain, a man called Stoker, had named his ship after the legendary Jacques-Yves Cousteau's most famous ship *Calypso*, and he loved to tell stories of the time he had spent with the great man on board his ship in the early eighties.

The position advertised offered eighteen months at sea for pure research and Caitlin loved every minute of it. She made some good friends during her time on board, and followed some to another opportunity for more research, this time involving just a year on board.

This second venture was not as exciting as the first. For a start, the vessel was much smaller and the conditions quite cramped and claustrophobic. The equipment too was much older and far more unreliable than the cutting edge machinery available on *The Calypso Rising*. Worse still, she began an imprudent relationship with one of the crew after a drunken night of strip poker, which she ended two weeks later. In truth, she knew she should have done it sooner, but she kept chickening out until she could finally bear it no more. They had absolutely nothing in common, and though the physical aspect was good, it was not enough by itself for her. But working together in such confined conditions and seeing each other multiple times a day did not allow for a very conducive parting. The man was clearly upset by the break, and Caitlin did not know what he was telling the other crew members about her, but the stares and whispers made her feel very uncomfortable. She decided to focus solely on her work and keep her other activities to a basic minimum.

The year could not end soon enough.

From there, Caitlin found a research post in Birmingham, but the contract was only for six months and was not renewed. From there, she applied for a few research assistant posts, but most of them were short-term due to the lack of funding.

She stayed in Birmingham for a while until all avenues seemed exhausted, then she eventually found herself back in London, living in another tiny bedsit, and working for an agency until things improved – if they ever did!

The job as Curator of the Alton Maritime Museum had not immediately appealed. Especially when she saw how little they were offering in terms of wages. But she went along for the interview and instantly fell in love with the place. Compared to the hustle and bustle of city life, a few years by the sea certainly appealed. The lack of wages was certainly made up for in terms of scenery and accommodation.

The job came with a flat above the museum, and it was at least four times larger than her present dwelling and much more tastefully decorated.

Having checked with the town council who ran the museum that pets were allowed, Caitlin picked Honey up from a dog sanctuary a few miles outside town. She had always wanted a dog, but due to her younger sister's allergies, she was never allowed one as a child.

Now with the beach across the road from her lodgings, Caitlin could take Honey for a run three times a day to wear her out. And since finding this little nugget at Skullen Bay, it also gave them both a bit of variety. Honey was a gorgeous animal, friendly, playful, loving, and great company.

The museum still closed half day on a Wednesday, so in effect, Caitlin only worked four and a half days a week. Her staff worked on a rota which covered all opening hours including Saturday, but Caitlin said she could always step in if they were ever short staffed. She had a lovely little team who were all locals and took great pride in their work, and they all made a great fuss over Honey.

As the months passed, Caitlin began to feel more relaxed and content. She found the quaint old-fashioned charm of the town and the easy-going manner of its inhabitants most congenial.

She closed her eyes and took in a deep lungful of sea air, then held it a while before slowly releasing it. She felt completely relaxed.

Honey's bark brought her back from her reverie. She looked down at the eager canine who had returned with her ball and what looked like an old hat with a broad plastic rim at the front.

Caitlin nudged the hat with the toe of her deck shoe, reluctant at first to touch it. The hat lay upside down on the sand. Caitlin could tell it was soaking wet with a few strands of seaweed clinging to it, so presumably Honey had found it in the sea. The tennis ball was inside the upturned headgear, and Caitlin surmised her clever pouch had managed to somehow get the ball inside it and carry them both back to her. Certainly, Honey seemed very proud of herself and deserving of a stroke.

Caitlin leaned down and ruffled the dog's coat. "Good girl, Honey, good girl." She retrieved the ball and threw it once more into the distance, the dog bounding off in pursuit.

She bent down and picked up the cap, deciding it was not too disgusting to handle. It looked to her like an old sea captain's hat. It was dark blue with a broad navy band around it, and a dark plastic peak. There was a very distinctive emblem on the front which looked like a ship's anchor with a chain wrapped around it. Caitlin studied the insignia closely.

"'eel not be needin' that agen."

Caitlin turned around, startled.

The stranger's voice from behind had taken her completely by surprise. She had not heard anyone creeping up behind her on the soft sand. She looked at the man before her. She estimated he must have been in his mid-to-late sixties, very shabbily dressed in an old raincoat which was at least two sizes too big for its wearer and some baggy trousers tucked into wellingtons.

The man wore a beret slightly tilted on his head, and his face wrinkled, scarred, and unshaven had been burned by the sun.

Caitlin gulped. "Sorry, I didn't see you there; you took me quite by surprise."

From behind, she could hear Honey bounding back towards her, barking at the stranger as if to warn him away from her mistress. Caitlin was immediately comforted by the dog's presence. Honey, the ball now forgotten and left behind, began to move in on the stranger, sniffing around him.

To her surprise, the stranger went down on one knee and started patting and stroking the dog. Honey seemed to like the attention and moved around excitedly, rolling in the sand on her back, her tail constantly wagging.

Caitlin sighed. Some attack dog you'd make, she thought to herself.

The man carried on playing with Honey. "That be old *Cappy's* 'at you got thur. 'e ain't got no use fer it now."

"Oh really," answered Caitlin, allowing the hat to dangle from her finger. "Why's that then?"

The old man looked up. "'Cos 'e's dead." The man rose to his feet, and after looking around, leaned in so he could whisper to Caitlin just in case anyone else might hear what he was saying. The fact that they were the only two souls on the beach obviously had not registered with him. "The monster got 'im."

His words did not register with Caitlin immediately. Her focus was on not making it too obvious that she found the combination of his pungent his body odour and the stale smell of whiskey on his breath, repulsive. Caitlin felt her stomach heave. She slapped a hand over her mouth, pretending to be shocked by the tramp's words.

He moved back slightly, and the air started to clear. Once Caitlin could breathe deeply again, his words came back to her.

"A...A monster you say?"

"Yus it were. A big black ugly monster crept out of the sea and ate him." He pointed to an area behind where Caitlin was standing. She looked over; there was nothing there to suggest anything whatsoever in line with what the tramp was saying.

Caitlin decided it was time to go. Honey, now realising that the stranger no longer wished to play, and deciding that he was no threat to her mistress, barked once then set off down the beach in search of her ball.

Caitlin held out the cap towards the man. "Would you like to see that your friend's relatives get this?" she asked, timidly.

The tramp shook his head. "No point, missi, ain't got no folk, least none 'round 'ere." He pointed towards the top end of the beach. "You could always ask in the pub over thur...They knew old *Cappy*." He laughed to himself. "They knew him very well."

Caitlin thanked him and made her goodbyes. She walked back towards the road, whistling to Honey who bounded behind her. When she reached her car, she looked back. The old tramp was collecting driftwood and had his back to her.

There was no sign of life at the pub across the road, which was hardly surprising at this hour. She did not wish to seem rude or uncaring, so she slipped the soggy cap into a box she had in her boot, carefully removing the books she had packed in it first. She slipped the box into a large plastic bag she had also left in the car from an earlier shopping trip. At least this way, she could mask off the smell and stop it leaking water onto her boot carpet.

She opened the back door for Honey who jumped in and lay down, exhausted from her morning workout. Before climbing behind the wheel, Caitlin looked back once more to the beach. The old tramp was standing at the water's edge. From this distance, it appeared to Caitlin as if he was calling out to the water – or something in it. Gesturing wildly with his arms, the old tramp was lost in his own world. Caitlin slid into her seat and headed back into Alton.

CHAPTER TWO

Dan Savage stood on the deck of his boat *The Lady Anne* and surveyed the growing crowds of holiday-makers walking along the beach. Many were here merely for the sun and the quaint atmosphere of staying in a working fishing village, but others – the ones that Dan was interested in – were checking out the prices of the tours and trips on offer at the tourist hut.

This was Dan's third summer at Skullen Bay, and so far it was working out to be his most profitable to date. Though Dan was not a resident of Skullen Bay, the majority of the locals had begun to accept his presence.

Jake Johnson, or "Big Jake" as he was known locally, did not like Dan because he felt he was stealing his customers. Jake had the largest boat for rent on the Bay, and certainly it was a beauty to behold, but Jake also charged the highest prices for his services, and at the end of the day, he could not guarantee that his customer's catch would be any bigger or better. And those who just wanted a relaxing couple of hours taking in the sights could do just as well on one of the smaller cheaper vessels, saving themselves some money into the bargain.

But Big Jake was a bully. At six-foot-five and a little under eighteen stone, with his bushy black beard and grizzled appearance, he was a serious force to contend with, and over the years, he had used his imposing size and boorish manner to ride roughshod over the rest of those working in the industry at Skullen Bay. It was well known throughout the village that Jake had forced several locals out of the business altogether, but they were all too scared of him to make any official report. Jake felt as if Skullen Bay was "his".

A local boy, born and bred, everyone knew Big Jake and knew to stay out of his way rather than cross swords with him.

That was until Dan arrived. Dan ticked all the boxes in Big Jake's "reasons to dislike someone" list. For a start, he was not a local, which in itself was a hanging offence to a local boy like Jake. Furthermore, he was not prepared to adhere to Jake's strict pricing policy which ensured that the others along the Bay could not undercut Jake and lose him customers. And thirdly, and by far the most serious of all his crimes, he was not prepared to allow Jake the first pick of the day.

Dan could just about make out the form of Big Jake, as usual sitting on the deck of his boat, waiting for his first customer of the day to come to him. The operator sitting in the tourist kiosk knew better than to not speak of Jake's tours in glowing terms.

Tammi MacDougall Dan's chief (and only) engineer climbed up on board, wiping grease from her hands with a red-and-white spotted bandana. She blinked in the sunlight like a cave dweller emerging from a winter's hibernation, and pulled her baseball cap further down over her face to block out the glare.

"All ready, Captain?" asked Dan, glancing over his shoulder.

"Aye," replied Tammi in her broad accent. "They'll no catch us today."

Tammi had worked for Dan for a little over five years. They had met in a bar in Amsterdam when Dan had accidently knocked into a man and spilled his drink. The man was already tanked and clearly trying to show off in front of his friends, so he was not prepared to accept Dan's sincere apology.

The drunk looked about ready to land his first punch when out of nowhere, Tammi leapt to Dan's rescue, wedging herself between them and staring straight up at the drunk, challenging him to start. At barely five feet, and weighing no more than six stone, Tammi was hardly what could be described as an imposing figure. But the drunk must have seen something in her eyes which told him he was about to get his arse kicked by a woman, because he suddenly backed away, mumbling to his friends about not fighting with a woman.

They hit it off straight away, though the attraction was not physical, at least not for Tammi. Tammi was a lesbian and made that clear from the start. But she was also a fantastic mechanic and knew her way around boats as if she was born to it. As a child, she had been brought up by an uncle and aunt after both her parents had been killed in a car accident. Her uncle was a fisherman, and from a young age, Tami spent every spare moment she could on the boats with him, learning all she could about the workings of the craft.

Dan knew her story, at least as much of it as she cared to reveal. She had grown up in a relatively small coastal town in Scotland where the residents thought that a scandal was putting the water in the cup before the milk. Most of them would not have known what a lesbian was, and if told would have doubtless gone running to the nearest priest to arrange an exorcism.

Tammi had always known that she was different. Growing up, she had few friends because she did not seem to share any of their girlie interests. Most of the girls she knew at school could not understand why Tammi would spend her weekends up to her elbows in oil and dirt, working in sometimes claustrophobic conditions with sweaty smelly men with tattoos all over their bodies. It was something which Tammi could not explain to their satisfaction, so she just stopped trying.

Tammi's sexual relationships were virtually non-existent in the town, so she had to travel further afield where the locals' minds had expanded beyond those of the smaller holdings. Through the internet, she found several clubs that catered to her tastes, and these intermittent sporadic encounters were enough to quell her frustration, but not enough to quash it all together.

Then she met Scarlet. Scarlet had recently moved to town with her husband to help run his parent's family business. Her husband, Scot, was a burly man, who spent most if not all of his spare time in the pub. His parents had run a large fish stall and delivery service in the town for as long as people could remember, and because of Scott's habit of waking up too hungover to drive, Scarlet had started delivering and collecting while he stayed in the market.

When Tammi and Scarlet first met, there was an instant attraction. Though Scarlet had never previously confessed to herself any lesbian tendencies, she had a curiousness which meeting Tammi made her want to explore.

They met whenever Scot was in the pub – which afforded them ample opportunities. As time passed, they grew closer together until finally they agreed that they wanted to be together exclusively.

By now, Tammi's aunt and uncle had passed away, leaving her the small stone-built cottage she had lived in since moving in with them. Tammi and Scarlet both know that the town would never accept their relationship, so they decided that they would sell up and move somewhere more accepting.

The night Scarlet decided to tell her husband, he beat her so hard she ended up in hospital with cracked ribs and internal bleeding.

When Tammi heard, she went straight to the hospital, barged her way through the medical team ignoring their objections, and burst into Scarlet's room to see her lover lying in bed unconscious, her face a mass of cuts and bruises, and a dozen or more tubes emanating from beneath the covers and leading to several machines which beeped in and out of sequence.

Tammi stood there with her mind in turmoil. She blocked out the commotion the doctors and nurses were making and focused on her lover.

Suddenly, she was aware of another voice from behind her. She turned and there was Scot, standing in the doorway, drunk as usual, and spitting obscenities at Tammi and his wife.

Tammi leapt at Scot like a child jumping into its parent's arms. The force of the impact took Scot by surprise, and falling backwards, he smashed the back of his head against a metal cabinet. Tammi did not notice or care that Scot was not moving. She pounded her fists into his face and body without mercy until two burly hospital porters managed to pull her off.

Scot was dead. The impact from the fall caved in his skull.

While Tammi was in custody, news reached her that Scarlet had died as a result of her injuries. Tammi could not feel guilty for what she had done to Scot; in her eyes that was justice. All she could do was grieve for the loss of the love of her life, and the life they should have spent together.

Unfortunately, her lack of remorse for Scot went against her at her trial. Whilst friends and family painted a picture of a loving, caring husband and son, Tammi sat expressionless, gazing into space, almost unaware of what was happening around her.

She received six years for manslaughter, and was released after three for good behaviour. For the next three years, she was legally on parole and had to report in weekly, then monthly, then quarterly for the final year. After that, Tammi continued moving from town to town, job to job, one-night stand to one-night stand, unable to find anything to fill the void left by Scarlet.

Meeting Dan had been a turning point for her.

Working for him had given her back a purpose in life. Though it would never be the same without Scarlet, she was content. They respected each other's privacy, and neither of them was judgemental.

Though Tammi had made her sexual orientation clear from the beginning, they had slept together on a number of occasions. Tammi would always remember the look of shock and amazement on Dan's face the first time she knocked on his cabin door in the early hours and asked if he would mind her using his body for an hour or two, as she was fed up with masturbating.

Since then, they had a sort of unwritten rule between them. If one of them felt horny and there was no one on the horizon, they would ask the other for a favour. But whoever did the asking had to accept if the other person was not in the mood, then that was that! So far, neither had denied each other in time of need.

They gave each other support, space when they needed it, consideration, and most of all, respect.

"Coffee, Captain?" asked Tammi, scanning the growing number of beachgoers.

"Great, just give me five minutes, I think I see our first customers of the day approaching."

***

At six o'clock that evening, Dan was hosing down the deck. They had had a steady stream of customers all day, most just wanting a round trip taking in some of the sights, an hour out and the same back. Then late afternoon, some visiting fishermen asked to be taken out to try their luck. The only thing Dan hated about fishermen was the smell their catch left behind, which if not treated that same evening would leave an odour which ingrained itself into the woodwork, taking days, sometimes weeks to clear completely.

Below deck, Dan could hear Tammi swearing to herself as she wrestled with the craft's inner workings. Earlier that afternoon, one of the gears had stuck. Tammi had managed to release it, but she wanted to check it out properly before they finished for the night.

By seven, they were both exhausted and ready for a drink and a good dinner. They elected to eat at a small restaurant that some of the locals had recommended. It was a little off the beaten track, but away from the touristy sites, so a table was always guaranteed. It served good old fashioned English fare: steak and kidney pudding, toad-in-the-hole, bangers and mash, fish and chips. All served with bread and butter, and a choice of peas, baked beans, or for the connoisseur, mushy peas.

The food was scrumptious. The only thing the restaurant lacked was an alcohol license. The owner was a large buxom woman in her mid-sixties who had run the place since its conception. She was a permanent presence in the restaurant; in fact if you did not know she owned it, you would have thought that she just worked there. When asked, she told Dan that she used to be licensed, but that she decided it encouraged the wrong kind of customer, so five years earlier, she decided not to bother renewing it. Trade had not decreased; she had merely swapped the previous rabble for a much more sedate clientele.

After dinner, they headed for the local pub for a nightcap.

The Fisherman's Arms was as picturesque and welcoming as you could ever wish a pub to be. The front of the pub sat on the pavement, affording patrons a breath-taking view of the sea in the distance.

They found a table at the back, not far from the rocking chair one of the locals was usually to be found in, relating tales of the sea from days gone by.

Tonight, it sat vacant.

Dan sat with his back to the bar, placed Tammi's bottle of ale and her glass in front of her and took a long gulp of his own pint, leaving the glass only half full when he stopped.

"Needed that?" asked Tammi, smiling as she poured her drink.

"You can say that again," Dan answered, wiping any lingering foam from his mouth. "That was a good day. A few more like that will not come amiss."

"Were any o' them repeaters?" asked Tammi.

"The first bunch said they might come again before they go back. The fishermen seemed happy enough with their haul, but I heard one of them grumbling about the cost."

"Huh," Tammi huffed. "They'll no find anyone else cheaper 'round here!"

"Yea, that's what I thought. Well, let them find out, they'll soon be back."

The bar was reasonably full for the time of night, and general buzz from conversations blended into a single level of noise and commotion.

Just then, Dan heard the pub door opening and the noise level seemed to taper off slightly.

"Now there's someone I would n'ee throw out ma bed fer fartin'," said Tammi in a low voice, so only Dan could hear her.

Discreetly, Dan turned to see who Tammi was referring to. The girl who had just walked in was slight in build and not much taller than Tammi. Dan estimated she was anywhere from early to late twenties, and though none of her clothes were particularly revealing, they clung to her ample figure, showing every perfect line and curve.

Her blonde hair was tied back in bunches, and from what Dan could make out, he had to agree with Tammi's earlier statement.

Once she had the barman's attention, she placed a carrier bag she brought with her onto the bar. Dan watched her talking to the man, who looked inside the bag before gesturing to a man sitting at the other end of the bar. The barman accompanied the young girl to him, and they waited whilst the other man surveyed the contents of the bag.

Dan saw the girl look up and over towards them; he turned back in his seat before she caught him staring at her.

He and Tammi moved in closer and whispered their appreciation of the young girl. Though Dan had recently turned forty, he was in very good shape for his age. His dark hair had not yet started to lose its natural colour, and he still had plenty of it on top. Always a keen swimmer, he had been a lifeguard in his younger years during which he developed a lean muscular frame which had stayed with him. His permanent tan from working outdoors also helped to enhance his overall attractiveness.

Yes, Dan Savage could still punch above his weight. And if he ever managed to get a chance with the girl at the bar, he was more than up for the challenge.

"I think she likes me," said Dan, taking another sip of his beer. "Did you see her looking over here?"

Tammi laughed. "In y'ur dreams old man. She's well out o' y'ur league!"

"Rubbish." Dan shrugged his shoulders, sitting upright in his chair. "I'm in excellent shape...The shape I'm in."

Tammi's laughter quickly changed. "Dan," she hissed, beneath her breath.

Dan did not immediately pick up on her demeanour.

"Dan!" Louder this time, but still under control.

Dan looked up just in time to register Tammi's facial expression before he felt a huge rugged hand clamping down on his shoulder.

The noise in the bar died down to a low mumble.

Before Dan could turn, he was hoisted from his chair by Jake Johnson and dragged back against the bar wall.

Dan looked up at his assailant. Jake's nostrils were flared and his eyes burned with rage. Dan surmised this was not going to be a social call.

"Hi, Jake, how have you been, can I buy you a drink, big man?"

Jake moved in closer. Dan could smell the whiskey on his breath.

From behind Jake's frame, Dan could see three of the lackeys who always shadowed him awaiting their orders. He knew that two of them were the sons of Maggie Clive, a local B&B owner and also his part-time lover.

Then he saw Tammi starting to rise, her empty bottle grasped at the neck.

Dan looked at her without trying to give the game away. His look said, "No!"

Tammi hovered, not willing to sit idly by while her boss was being threatened but still conscious that she did not want to spring into action unless it was called for. Her past could so easily catch up with her!

"You've nicked my customers for the last time!" Jake spat the words out through gritted teeth. He now had Dan securely by his shirt collars and Dan could feel his feet starting to lift off the floor.

Dan resigned himself to the fact that things would soon grow ugly. He knew he was clearly outweighed and outsized by the massive man, so he planned on making the first move. But what he really needed was an equaliser. Something like a snooker cue would do nicely, but from his present position, access to anything remotely suitable was negated.

Dan decided to try and stall for time. "Are you sure we couldn't just sit down and have a drink and talk about this?"

Jake sneered. "By the time I am finished with you, drinkin' will be all you can do as you won't have no teeth to eat with!"

Dan began counting in his head. On five, land the first punch and hope he lets go, he thought.

As he reached four, a voice from the back of the bar called out.

"Leave it alone, Jake!"

Dan could just make out that the voice came from the man the gorgeous blonde with the bunches was talking to.

Jake took a deep breath. Without turning to face the man, he called back. "This ain't your business, Seaton, just leave it alone."

"Then don't make it my business, Jake."

Jake stayed put, still hoisting Dan above the ground. He was breathing hard, looking directly into Dan's eyes. A few endless seconds passed before the big man let go of Dan's shirt.

Dan straightened himself out, Jake still only a few feet in front of him. He looked up at Jake and shrugged his shoulders, smiling. Jake took a half-step forward and began to raise his fist. But then thought better of it and stormed out of the bar, his henchmen just behind him.

After a moment more of silence, the noise in the pub carried on as before as everyone returned to their conversations. Dan and Tammi slumped back in their seats. Without saying a word, Dan downed the rest of his pint, placing the empty glass in front of him. "Needed that!" he said, breathing out hard.

"For a wee moment there, I thought we were going to have some fun," said Tammi, smiling.

"Fun like that, I can well do without, thanks."

Tammi went to the bar to get refills. Dan took himself over to the man who had saved him to say thank you.

He was still talking to the blonde and the barman when Dan approached, his hand extended. "Thanks for that, I thought I was a gona' there. Dan Savage."

"Oswald Seaton, Sgt. Oswald Seaton of the local constabulary." The man shook Dan's hand. "I'd advise you to stay clear of Big Jake; his temper often gets the better of him."

Dan held up his hands. "Don't worry, I plan to." He extended his hand towards the woman next to the officer, realising this was too good an opportunity not to introduce himself to her.

"Catlin Howard, how do you do."

Dan indicated to the carrier bag he had watched her hand to the officer earlier. "A souvenir from the beach?" he asked, playfully.

"Caitlin smiled. "No, not as such. My dog retrieved it this morning on the beach and I think it belongs to a regular here."

"Aye," said the barman, "That's old *Cappy's* hat, sure enough. It's odd, but in all these years, I don't think I have ever seen him take it off."

"And you say your dog found it on the beach this morning?" asked Seaton. "And at what time would that have been?"

"About six thirty maybe." Caitlin looked a little sheepish. "The thing of it is, I was approached by a tramp – well, I think he was anyway. And he said that he had seen this Cappy lose it when he…" She trailed off, looking around to make sure no-one else was within earshot.

"When he what?" asked the officer.

"When he was taken by a monster from the sea!" There was stunned silence for a moment from the three men, before the barman and officer Seaton burst into laughter.

Caitlin could feel her cheeks starting to redden.

Dan, though looking at her quizzically, did not laugh. Caitlin from her expression was clearly not impressed by the other two men's reactions, and Dan seriously wanted to impress her.

Finally, Dan asked, "What sort of monster did he say it was?"

Caitlin looked at him, gratefully. "He said it was just a big, black monster that crept out of the sea and grabbed Cappy."

"Oh, that must have been old Sam Cleary," said the barman, drying tears from his laughter. "You don't wanna be takin' any notice of 'im, 'es proper barkin'."

Caitlin sighed. "Well, I just thought that if he was drunk at the time for example, he might have witnessed an assault and just imagined the assailant had crept out of the sea. Of course, I wasn't sure if there was anything in it. Mr. Cleary was a tad inebriated when I saw him this morning, but as he said that Cappy was a regular in here, I thought I would bring you his cap just in case he was in here and had lost it during the fight."

"Yes," Dan spoke up, "now you come to mention it, I've seen him every time I've been in here." He looked at the barman. "Doesn't he sit in that old rocking chair at the back and tell stories, or something?"

"Well yes," said the barman, thoughtfully. "Come to think of it, e's usually in 'ere by now."

Sgt Seaton turned the cap over in his hands, studying the band. He himself knew that Cappy virtually lived in the pub, and it was true what the barman had said for he too had never seen him in public without his famous cap on.

The officer turned to Caitlin. "I'll tell you what, miss, I'll keep hold of this, and Ted," he looked at the barman, "you let us know at the station if Cappy turns up. If he hasn't by tomorrow, I'll see if we can get any sense out of old Sam."

"Good luck with that one," said the barman, smiling.

"How can I get hold of you should I need an official statement please, miss?"

"Oh, I'm the curator at the Maritime Museum in Alton. I live above the shop, so to speak."

They parted company after their goodbyes, and Dan went back to Tammi and his beer.

"You took your time!" she grinned. "I saw you chattin' up that blonde bird, filthy git!"

Dan lifted his pint. "For your information, we were discussing a mutual interest in all things maritime...And early morning walks along the beach"

"You denny even know what an early morning is." Tammi laughed, and took a swig from her bottle.

CHAPTER THREE

Cheryl Wright pulled off the motorway, turning left at the next round-a-bout, and she headed through the town towards the coastal road. She glanced at the clock on her dashboard. The traffic had been heavier than usual, but it looked as though she had still made good time. Another twenty minutes or so and she should be there.

She reached across the seat and retrieved the water bottle from its holder. Checking the road ahead, she slipped the straw between her lips and drew heavily.

Must be properly hydrated for this one, she thought to herself.

Cheryl had been on the game more or less for the last fifteen years. She still shuddered inwardly when she remembered her early days in the business; the result of fate rather than design. At twenty, she had been a promising student halfway through her English literature degree and destined for a first. That was until the head tutor she was having an affair with carelessly managed to get himself crushed under the wheels of a juggernaut.

They had mutually agreed to keep their liaison a closely guarded secret. Him because he had a wife and family, not to mention his position, to consider. And her because if the truth came out, then the more suspicious amongst her lecturers, like Mr. Watson who had raised more than a few eyebrows at her submissions which were too good to be true considering her lack of attendance, might demand an investigation. That would doubtless reveal the poor examples she had submitted for her lover to grade. In some cases, when he was the only lecturer for the subject, she hadn't bothered handing anything in at all, knowing that she would still end up in the top stream.

Group work was the worst. But her lover had guided her as usual and given her the best arguments to put forward, thus deceiving her colleagues into thinking she had actually read some of the books they were working from.

But it all changed when he died!

She had just finished her second year, with the big one to go. Conscious of the painful fact that she would now have to work for her grades, she buckled down as much as she could during the summer holidays instead of enjoying the student high jinks she had promised herself.

Failure was not an option!

Her parents had always been adamant of what they expected from their three children. When her elder brother, Adam, announced that he intended to become a musician instead of following their father into the law, her parents disowned him. Cheryl kept in touch with him through e-mail mainly, and let him crash at her flat when he was in Bath with nowhere to stay. Admittedly, he hadn't made the splash in the industry he was hoping to, but she still admired him for having a dream and following it. Something their parents would never understand.

This, in turn, seemed to goad their parents to put even more effort into ensuring that Cheryl did better, and did not disgrace them. Their youngest, Kevin, was already two classes ahead at his private school, and well on his way to achieving all that their parents desired.

Unlike Adam, she had no dreams other than to marry well and live an easy life, so she picked English as her degree subject because she believed it would be the easiest academically because of the lack of exams. But, boy, was she ever wrong on that score!

Within the first couple of months, she was already starting to struggle with the workload expected. Finally, her head tutor – soon to be her lover – summoned her to his office. It was quite clear from his initial observations that he felt it would not be in either of their interests for her to continue studying at his university, unless she could guarantee a vast improvement in a very short space of time.

The harshness of his words and the realisation of her position caused her to burst into tears right there in his office. To her surprise instead of just passing her a tissue, the tutor stood up from behind his desk and came and put his arm around her.

Cheryl had certainly not expected that!

She did pride herself on having the foresight to dress as inappropriately as possible for the meeting, showing off as much leg and cleavage as a certain level of decency would allow. But that was only as a rouse to distract the tutor's attention and potentially fluster him enough to forget the reason he had summoned her.

Thinking on her feet, Cheryl saw an opportunity and grabbed it. She pulled the tutor down by his tie until their lips met. She kissed him hungrily, sliding her tongue inside his mouth before he had a chance to object. He responded in kind, bombarding her with slippery, slobbery kisses.

Cheryl had to forcibly stop herself from gagging. But she decided then and there to cross a line which she hoped in the end would lead to a far greater good.

They had sex there in his office.

Afterwards, Cheryl made it clear to him that she was prepared to make this a regular occurrence, but she needed his help to get her through the next three years in return. She could see his mind working as he considered the offer. It didn't take him long to decide. After all a fat, bald-headed, middle-aged tutor with a frumpy wife was not offered sex on a plate by a gorgeous eighteen year old every day.

Luckily for Cheryl, their encounters did not occur as often as her lover would have liked, due mainly to their lack of feasible accommodation. Cheryl was living in a house-share with four other students, and obviously her tutor's family home was off limits. They did use his office a few more times, but then he became concerned that others might get suspicious seeing her entering and leaving too often. So after several very uncomfortable quickies in the back of his car, he found a Travel Lodge far enough out of town so as to avoid discovery.

For Cheryl, the sex was awful, but at least it was quick. And in her opinion very much worth the effort when she saw the kind of grades she was receiving in return.

But his accident had changed all of that. Unable to cope, even with all the time and energy she put into studying during the summer break, Cheryl fell at the first hurdle. Her first essay of her final year did not even garnish a mark in double figures. Mrs. Lang, who had stepped in to cover the position left vacant by her lover, would doubtless not succumb to an offer of sexual favours – even if Cheryl had been that way inclined.

It was over!

When the realisation hit, Cheryl had nowhere to turn. Her parents had paid for her tuition and kept her topped up with rent and spending money, and she knew that if she pulled out of her studies, they would disown her just as they had done to Adam, leaving her to a life of potential poverty and no inheritance to look forward to.

Her only option was to lie and say that she was still continuing at university. At least that would buy her some time to come up with a plan. And the tuition fee for her final year would be returned, giving her some extra cash to help sort her out.

By mid-year, she still had not come up with a possible solution. Her only plan so far was to keep up the lie and keep taking the money.

Fooling her parents hadn't been as difficult as she had imagined. She told them that she and a group of fellow students were going to boycott the graduation ceremony in protest at one of their class being expelled for sleeping with a tutor, when the tutor was allowed to keep their job.

Her parents were not happy, but accepted Cheryl was standing up for a principle. She managed to acquire a very impressive forgery of a graduation certificate from the web, and due to her missing her graduation, her parents paid for a private photographer to take her portrait in cap and gown.

For a while, Cheryl made the pretence of applying for a host of graduate opportunities, each time acting totally dejected in front of them when she received a fake rejection letter which she herself had written.

Frantically, whilst keeping up the bravado, she was trying to secure any employment which might pay similar to what a graduate could earn. But the pickings were all too meagre. And she seemed cursed by having female interviewers, not even allowing her the option of trying to flirt her way into a job.

Her salvation – such as it was – came from one of the students she had house shared with. They had always got along and so kept in touch after graduation. She was also the only person whom Cheryl had trusted to tell about the affair with her tutor, after his accident. Her friend in return confessed that she had done some escort work to help make ends meet, and boasted about how much she could have earned had she a mind to.

Though initially reluctant – a casual affair with one bloke was one thing, but with a different man every day – Cheryl eventually called her friend and asked for some details about the agency she worked for.

The woman representing the agency on the phone sounded terribly posh, so Cheryl was quite surprised when she turned up for her interview only to find the head office – only office – tucked away in a filthy cut through behind some derelict shops in Kings Cross.

The man who interviewed her was painfully thin with very sharp features and a hook nose. He reminded Cheryl of one of those old-time spivs from the films. His lanky jet black hair was greased back behind his ears, and he leered over the desk at Cheryl's legs whenever he asked her a question. The agency charged its clients £150 for the escorts company, of which Cheryl would only get £25, so it was up to her to extract whatever else she could from the punter, however she could.

"That should be easy for a nice looking girl like you," the spiv laughed, revealing two rows of nicotine-stained, very crooked teeth.

Her first client came through the next day. He was a regular according to the spiv, who liked different girls whenever he was in town. His company had put him up at one of the more exclusive hotels in London, so at least Cheryl surmised that the surroundings would be nice.

He wasn't all that bad looking either, so Cheryl turned on the flirting as soon as she was inside his room. He offered her £100 for sex, but she managed to convince him without too much effort that her clients paid her a minimum of £150.

For the next five years, Cheryl stayed with the agency. She soon gathered a list of regulars who would always ask for her, and she was happy to see the ones who paid the top rates for her services. She was earning between £250 and £500 a session, depending on what her client wanted. More if they wanted her to stay overnight. As far as her parents were aware, Susan was now working for a firm of HR consultants in London and part of her job included travelling all over the country, which accounted for the nights she stayed away with clients. This also helped explain the days when she did not go into work, claiming it was time her firm owed her.

She discovered over time that she had a knack for acting out S&M fantasies, and this naturally brought in even more money from the requester. And for her, the best bit was most of them did not want sex afterwards. A hand-relief at most, but some seemed happy to complete the task themselves whilst she was demeaning and humiliating them.

Then greed took hold of her. Even though she was making more money than she could have possibly believed, picking and choosing her clients to suit herself, and now comfortably set up in her own flat with a car and a beautiful wardrobe full of designer apparel, it was not enough!

She had begun to resent the agency taking such a huge cut of her earnings, especially as now she was established and could rely solely on her client list to keep her in the manner she had become accustomed to.

She decided to contact some of her regulars who had previously given her their business cards with their mobiles on them. Just the top spenders, she realised how suspicious it would look if suddenly all her clients stopped calling the agency.

At first, her plan worked marvellously. She offered to split the agency fee which by now was £200 with her clients. That way they saved £100 and she made another £100 clean profit. Everything was falling into place.

One night, there was a knock at her door!

The spiv had long ago been *bought out* by an eastern European family whom Cheryl had found out on the grapevine, also had side lines in people smuggling and money lending. The two gorillas in black leather jackets standing on her landing had been sent by the agency. Somehow, they had discovered what she had been up to.

They both pushed themselves in and slammed the door. Before Cheryl could react, one of them slapped her so hard she fell back on the floor. Her assailant straddled her, allowing his considerable bulk to rest on her stomach. Then he leaned down and clamped a large meaty hand over her mouth.

Through her tears and with her mouth closed off, Cheryl could barely breathe. The man on top of her said something to his partner in their language, and the other man began opening Cheryl's drawers and cupboards, discarding her belongings on the floor.

Dresses, shoes, coats, everything landed in a rough pile, having been checked over by the intruder.

Eventually, there was nothing left to search. The man looked at his partner pining Cheryl down and shrugged his massive shoulders. The man on top of Cheryl removed a flick-knife from his pocket and clicked the blade open. Cheryl tried to scream, but he clamped his hand even harder across her mouth.

He brought the point of the blade down to within a centimetre of Cheryl's eye. She closed it automatically, but he screamed at her in broken English to open it again. Cheryl did as she was ordered and stared up at the cold steel through bleary tear-stained eyes.

"Now," he said, looking down at her. "Where's the fuckin' money, bitch?"

He partly released his hold on her mouth, allowing Cheryl the chance to reply. She knew exactly what they meant, and she did not feel in a position to prevaricate or try and bargain with them, so she indicated towards the corner of the room.

"Over there...Under the lamp."

Her assailant said something to his colleague, and the other man strode over to the other end of the room and snatched up the lamp. Turning it upside down, he found a large envelope taped to the base. He ripped it off, throwing the lamp to one side, smashing the bulb in the process. Having seen the contents of the envelope, he held it up, smiling at his comrade.

The man on top of Cheryl turned his attention back to her. He leaned in closer, the point of his knife now dangerously close to her eye. She could smell the vodka on his breath, mingled with what seemed to her like raw onion. He licked his lips, leaving them wet and shiny. Cheryl could not move under his bulk. She could barely breathe between stifling her sobs and the fact that his hand still covered her mouth.

There was no way she could scream. And even if she could, she doubted her assailants would let her do so without slitting her throat there and then. She meant nothing to them. Less than nothing!

Her attacker started to speak, his thick accent and guttural tone menacing.

"You fucken 'hoore, theenk you gonn' steeel from us?" As he spoke, spittle sprayed from his lips landing on Cheryl's eyes, nose, and forehead. Cheryl coughed involuntarily behind the man's hand. She felt the bile rising in her throat, was convinced that she was going to vomit any second.

The man slowly began to trace the edge of his knife over the contours of Cheryl's face. Not hard enough to pierce the skin, but enough to leave a temporary white mark. His partner laughed as he shoved the envelope he had retrieved with the money into his inside jacket pocket.

"You theenk you prity face gonna' save you?" Her assailant clicked his tongue, shaking his head. "Men still fuck 'hoores in my country with ugly face." He stopped moving the knife around Cheryl's face, and placed the tip on the edge of her nose, prodding gently. Cheryl could feel a fresh flood of tears running down her cheeks.

"You listen 'hoore, you do this ageen' I slice you preety face up bad, then smuggle you back to my country and you work as 'hoore, fuck night and day...No fucking money!"

Cheryl tried to nod as best she could.

The man removed the knife, unlocked the blade, and pocketed it. He took his hand away from Cheryl's mouth, allowing her to finally take a deep breath. Her face was still speckled with his saliva, but with his weight still pinning her arms down, Cheryl could not wipe it away.

From nowhere, the man slapped her face hard with the flat of his hand. Cheryl yelped pathetically. Before she could recover, he slapped her other cheek with the back of his hand. Cheryl cried softy, not wanting to antagonise the man any further. She was afraid of what might come next.

After a minute, the big man hoisted himself off her. Turning, he spoke to his colleague who patted his jacket pocket in reply.

Neither of them said another word to Cheryl as they left.

That incident was enough to make Cheryl revaluate her situation. Without even realising it, the *agency* had become her pimp, and she knew now how seriously they took their business.

She had to get out!

Cheryl did not leave her flat for three days until the bruising had gone down. She knew that she could not carry on seeing her present clients unless she did so through the agency, the alternative risk was just not worth it. Plus, she did not know who she could trust...Someone had tipped off the agency about her little arrangement!

She stayed with the agency for another three months whilst she plotted her escape. She decided that she would have to leave London altogether if she intended to carry on with her business. She knew that her chances of finding a proper job that paid anywhere near what she earned was highly unlikely. And the thought of taking a poorly paid job and moving back in with her parents did not bear thinking about.

Eventually, she upped sticks and moved to a small town just outside King's Lynn. She had visited the town on several occasions during her childhood when they visited her father's sister. She was long dead now, but the place still held a familiarity which Cheryl found comforting.

She told her parents that she was moving because she had accepted a promotion and had to relocate, and they were very proud.

She set up her own website, advertising her services as a dominatrix, and managed to rent a two-story house with a convenient basement which she converted into a dungeon.

Over the next ten years, she established herself with a full complement of regular clients, and eventually saved enough to buy the house outright.

At thirty-six, she now had a very comfortable, in her mind, enviable lifestyle, with three or four foreign holidays a year, a new car every two years, a wardrobe which could match most footballer's wives, and best of all, she had actually come to love what she was doing.

Her clients – which she had carefully chosen over the years from the thousands who flooded her website – were all polite, well-mannered businessmen, who acted as discreetly as she did with their comings and goings, so not to raise too many questions. She had allowed word to spread that she was a personal therapist who used her house as an office, and only saw private clients. This seemed enough to stop the curtains twitching, or anyone whispering behind her back in the high street.

Not all her clients, however, wanted to be tortured in the dark confines of a dungeon. Several had outdoor fantasies which involved anything from camping scenarios, to being beaten up in a school playground, and one who paid her to half-drown him once a month at the local swimming pool.

But Cheryl had come to love the variety and imagination of her clientele.

Best of all some of those with the more "bizarre" requests had admitted to her that she was the first person whom they had trusted enough to confess their little caprices to, and how liberated they felt when she acted them out for them.

That was one of the reasons she was happy to go the extra mile to help these poor frustrated men to realise their dreams.

Such was the reason for tonight's little adventure to Skullen Bay.

Cheryl swung her car into a vacant slot. The other two or three cars parked in the marked-off area were all empty. She glanced at the clock on her dashboard; it was almost midnight. Cheryl retrieved the water bottle from its holder and drank heavily, draining it. She could feel her bladder starting to fill. Good stuff, she thought.

Exiting the car, she walked around to the boot. The sea air was cool and refreshing after such a hot day. She decided that her miniskirt and T-shirt would be warm enough without needing a jumper. Lifting the boot door, she balanced on one foot and removed her white converse, throwing it in the back. She took out one of her dark green wellingtons, and balancing against the car, pulled it on. She did the same with her other foot. She was about to close the boot when she remembered something. She sighed deeply. It would have been much easier before she put on the wellies, but she could not be bothered to remove them again. So, having glanced around to make sure the coast was still clear, she bent down and removed her knickers, easing them over her boots, and then discarding them in the car before slamming the boot shut.

Cheryl walked down the familiar path to her meeting place under the abandoned peer. Halfway down, she could see the shadowy figure of Cedric Hardcastle waiting in eager anticipation for her arrival. This would be their fifth meeting in as many months, and so far, Cheryl had learned that Cedric was in the import/export business, dealing mainly in meat, and lived in the next town along from the Bay with his wife and three sons. His wife did not understand him…Apparently.

Cedric smiled broadly as Cheryl approached.

"Hi babe," he said, with his familiar greeting. He handed her an envelope crammed with £20 notes. Cheryl did not have to count them; she knew the full amount would be there.

"Thanks," she replied, gratefully, easing the envelope into her tight-fitting skirt pocket. They talked casually for a while. Cheryl was always conscious of not revealing too many personal details to clients, but some of them seemed eager to spend half the night telling her everything that had happened in their lives since their last meeting.

Eventually, Cheryl decided it was time to get into character. Cedric was warbling on about some deal he had pulled off and seemed mighty pleased with himself for doing so. Cheryl cut him off in mid-sentence by placing her hands on her hips and forcing her soft features to form a severe and stern look.

This was the beginning! Cedric knew the rules – it was his game. She stood there, looking him up and down for a moment without speaking. She could see Cedric was already starting to grow excited, but she did not dwell on his swelling.

Cheryl, hands still firmly placed on hips, circled Cedric whilst he stood there motionless, barely breathing.

Finally, when she was back in front of him, Cheryl broke the silence.

"You really are a pathetic excuse for a man, aren't you?" It was said more as a statement of fact rather than a question which needed answering. Cedric looked down as if in shame, his eyes not being able to see past his rising bulge which obscured his view of the bottom half of his body.

Cheryl sighed. "God, what a useless worm you are…I should just crush you beneath my feet and leave you to die in the sand!" As she spoke, Cheryl twisted one of her booted feet into the sand. She noticed Cedric's eyes following her movement, his gaze now fixed firmly on her feet. "In fact," Cheryl continued, "you are not even worthy to be called a worm…No living creature could be as worthless as you!"

She walked over to one of the old pier's support frames and picked up the shovel which Cedric had left there earlier. Striding up to him until she was only inches away from his face, Cheryl held out the shovel.

"Now dig yourself a hole little man, and make sure it is big enough for me to bury you in!"

Whilst Cedric dug, Cheryl walked slowly back and forth, surveying his work. The sand was wet and compacted quite tightly in places, so by the time he was finished, Cedric was sweating profusely, his T-shirt and nylon shorts clinging to his body.

Cheryl walked over and looked down into the hole. That'll do, she thought.

She ordered Cedric to climb in the hole. Once he had crammed himself in, Cheryl began the task of filling in the sand around him, until he was packed in tightly. Only his head was now visible above the sand.

Cheryl took a quick breather; the exertion of the task she had just completed reminded her she needed to renew her gym membership.

Cedric looked up at her, an Amazonian giantess who could kill him with just one stamp of her mighty foot.

Cheryl moved forwards until she was almost directly over Cedric's bald head. Taking aim, she allowed a huge globule of saliva to drop from her full height until it splashed on his upturned face. She waited until the discharge gathered momentum and began to slide down his cheek before aiming another one directly in the same spot.

For the next thirty minutes, Cheryl walked back and forth in front of Cedric's head, abusing and belittling him constantly, threatening to commit all manner of humiliating and degrading acts upon his defenceless dome. Several times, she emphasised her words by placing a boot on top of his head or in his face, and smearing sand all over him with her sole.

As she worked, she could feel her bladder pressing harder and harder against her pelvic bone. All that water had done the trick. Finally, she placed one foot on each side of Cedric's sand-speckled head and squatted down low enough so that she was only inches from his dome. Breathing deeply, she let out a shooting stream of warm urine which rained down all over Cedric, washing away some of the sand she had trodden into him.

It was a relief to finally empty her bladder. She had held that in for too long!

A combination of the powerful force of her stream and the fact that Cedric's head was clean shaven meant that whilst she worked, she felt subtle specs of her wee peppering the insides of her legs. She made a mental not to wipe herself down with wet-wipes before getting back into her car.

Cedric was breathing heavily, his tongue licking hungrily around his mouth, trying to savour the taste of Cheryl's urine. Cheryl tried not to look. Once the act was over, the moment was not hers to savour.

Eventually, Cedric let out a huge sigh of contentment and smiled up at her.

"Thanks babe, that was wonderful, as always."

Cheryl smiled back. "You're welcome," she said.

She collected the discarded shovel and began the laborious task to digging Cedric free. The wet sand had compacted even more now, especially where she had been walking and standing over him.

From behind, she could hear the sound of the water lapping the shore. The tide must be coming back, she thought. Better get a move on, don't want the poor sod to drown. Cedric's eyes were still transfixed on her feet, watching every move of her wellingtons as they squelched as she moved.

Cheryl stood up to take a breather.

Then Cedric screamed!

It was not the sort of noise she expected to emanate from a man. It was high, piercing, almost a shriek.

Cheryl looked down. Cedric's face was twisted into a macabre of fear. He was looking past Cheryl at the sea.

Cheryl turned. Shovel raised in anticipation to fight off whatever Cedric had seen.

Then she saw it too!

The creature was only about thirty feet away from them, sliding itself along the ground, using its massive tentacles to gain purchase on the wet sand.

Cheryl's mind raced.

She had always considered herself a very practical girl. She did not believe in UFOs, or Bigfoot, or even in the Loch Ness Monster. And she certainly did not believe in sea monsters.

BUT HERE WAS ONE, LARGER THAN LIFE, AND COMING STRAIGHT FOR HER!

She had almost forgotten about Cedric. His screams shook her from her panic-induced reverie. She turned back to face him. Cedric was screaming at her to dig him out. She could tell from his strained expression that he was trying to get himself free, but the sand was packed too tightly to allow him much movement.

She was his only chance!

But the creature was coming!

She glanced over her shoulder. It was only twenty feet away now and she estimated she had all of ten seconds to get away...Nowhere near long enough to dig Cedric out!

She looked back down at his upturned red face for a moment. He knew instinctively what she was thinking. He mouthed the words "No" and "Please" without actually making a sound. All Cheryl could do was whisper "Sorry" in return, before running back up the beach; away from the hideous gargoyle slithering towards the pleading Cedric.

Cheryl tried to block out Cedric's cries as she ran, not daring to look behind until she reached the comparative safety of her car.

Breathless, she turned to look back. In the shadowy darkness, she could just make out the overall mass of the thing which was now sliding its way back towards the sea, Cedric's crushed body held tightly in the folds of one of its might tentacles.

She watched until it had disappeared from sight, swallowed up by the encroaching water.

Cheryl stood there for several minutes, still not able to fully come to terms with what she had just witnessed. Looking down the beach now, there was no evidence of the horror that had just occurred.

What to do? she thought.

A man had been brutally murdered in front of her eyes…But who would believe her story? The police would probably just brand her a nutter. And if the papers got hold of it, well, she could certainly do without their prying eyes camped outside her house.

And innocent of any premeditation or not, just how complicit were her actions in causing Cedric's death!

Could she end up in prison?

She shivered involuntarily. What could she do?

Cedric was already dead; she reasoned she could not have saved him and would have doubtless ended up sharing his fate had she tried. The thought eased her guilt slightly.

No one knew they were meeting tonight. She doubted very much that he had told his wife – unless they had an extremely open relationship. His only contact with her might be her number on his mobile, but it was a pay-as-you-go one she had bought on purpose, just in case she inherited a stalker at some time in the future.

She decided to leave before someone saw her, and try and deal with her guilt from the safety of her house.

Poor Cedric! She did not actually know what kind of man he had been, but she knew he did not deserve to die like that.

Cheryl climbed into her car and quietly pulled away from the curb, using the vehicle's electric feature rather than the petrol option to ensure she made as little noise as possible.

Halfway home, she remembered that she had forgotten to wipe the splashed pee from between her legs before getting behind the wheel.

CHAPTER FOUR

Sgt. Oswald Seaton set out early the next day to try and find Sam Cleary. He knew from experience that there was no good time of day to speak to the old man. It all depended on how much he had had to drink, and as that was a twenty-four-hour mission with Sam, it was always hit and miss at best if you found him coherent.

Seaton was convinced that there had not been a serious crime committed, but it was odd that old *Cappy* did not turn up for his usual quota at the Fisherman's Arms the previous evening. Don Sykes, the pub landlord, had called Seaton at closing time to confirm that *Cappy* had not been in. There were other pubs in the area, and several more in the town, so he could have dropped in to any of them in theory, but it was the discovery of *Cappy's* old cap by the young lady from the museum that caused Seaton to suspect that something was amiss. *Cappy* never took it off!

A visit to *Cappy's* cottage revealed nothing out of the ordinary. There was no sign of a break-in or a burglary even though the old man never locked his door. But the fact remained that he was not there. Seaton was aware that *Cappy* often still went out with the fishing boats if he had a mind, so there was a chance he would come back later in the afternoon. But the officer could not help thinking about his hat. Locals had often joked with him about buying a new one, but Seaton himself had heard *Cappy* say on more than one occasion that he intended to be buried in it.

Seaton parked the patrol car opposite the pub and walked along the beach towards the harbour at the far end. Along the way, he checked under the tarpaulins of all the boats moored on the sand banks as possible sleeping places for Sam. He had already called the Hostel – another of Sam's resting holes when the weather was bad – that morning, and been told that Sam had not checked in. Therefore, it was a relatively safe bet that Sam had spent the night on the beach.

He walked towards the last group of boats before reaching the harbour. He was about to look under the first tarp when he heard a loud snoring coming from somewhere at the far end of the line. He honed in and found Sam fast asleep underneath the cover, clutching a half-empty bottle of red wine. Several discarded bottles of similar spirits were scattered around the beach near to the boat, and Seaton could easily guess who was responsible.

The combination of alcohol, bad body odour, and expelled rectal air assailed his nostrils as he pulled back the cover. Seaton waved his arm in front of his face as if to clear the stench; meanwhile, Sam remained blissfully unaware that his cover had been breached. Seaton considered leaving Sam for now, as judging by the look of him he was probably going to be of no use as a witness right now. The alternative was to either take him down to the station to sober up, which would mean him stinking out the patrol car. Or, he could try and find him later when there was every possibility that the tramp would be in an equally incoherent condition.

Seaton bent down and shook the old man by the shoulder. Sam murmured something unintelligible and turned over, still asleep. Seaton tried again, more forcefully this time. Sam eventually sprang to life, flailing his arms and shouting abuse. The bottle fell from his clutches and rolled away down the belly of the craft. Before he even looked to see who was attacking him, Sam grabbed for his bottle. Once he had secured it, he looked up and saw Seaton.

"Bloody hell, what did you 'ave to go an' do that fer?" he raged, squinting in the early morning sunlight.

"I wouldn't have done it if it wasn't important, Sam," replied Seaton, removing his police hat and scratching his head. "Now, what's all this about *Cappy* being attacked by a monster from the deep?"

Sam shuffled himself in the boat until he was sitting almost upright. He opened his mouth to speak but a raging cough came out instead. The officer winced as Sam tried to catch his breath. Once the raking had stopped, Sam un-stoppered his bottle and took a long swig from it.

When he'd finished, he drew in a deep breath and let out a loud belch.

"Charming!" said Seaton.

The old man wiped his mouth with the back of his sleeve, and scratched the four-day-old stubble on his chin.

"Come on, Sam," said Seaton, impatiently, "I'm not standing here for my health."

Sam looked up at him. "You bin talkin' to that young lady I saw here yesterday, ain't yer?" He chuckled to himself, holding his hands out in front of him. "Lovely pair o' knockers she 'ad, did yer get an eyeful?"

"Never mind the size of her tits, what about *Cappy*?" Seaton was fast losing his patience with the old drunk. "Or would you rather come down to the station and give an official statement?"

"All right, all right, where's yer sense o' humour?" Sam took another gulp of his wine and then cleared his throat. "It were a couple of nights ago, I was here, jus' getting' comfortable, when I saw *Cappy* walkin' down there towards the sea." He pointed to the far end of the beach. "The tide wus out o'course as it wer so late, but it were definitely 'im."

"And how much had you had to drink by then?" Seaton asked, sarcastically.

Sam looked at him and scowled. "Do yer wanna know what I saw o' not?"

"Okay, okay, just get on with it."

Sam hoisted himself out of the boat, and carefully found his footing on the beach. He steadied himself against the side of the craft to stand up, carefully placing his bottle in his raincoat pocket. He gazed out to sea. "It came from the water, big and black it wer, with huge arms and legs fifty feet long. It grabbed poor old *Cappy* and took 'im down with it," he turned back to face Seaton, "and that were the last I saw o' 'im."

The office looked out to sea, his hands on his hips. Sam's story sounded like the ramblings of a drunkard or a madman – or a combination of both. He had known Sam since he first took up post in Alton seven years ago, and he had to admit the old man had never spun a yarn like this before, at least not that he had heard of. And he could not get away from the fact that the lady had found *Cappy's* hat.

But he needed some corroboration before he stuck his neck out on the word of an old drunk.

Seaton turned to leave. "Thanks for that, Sam; I'll be in touch if I need an official statement."

The old drunk laughed. "Ahh you don't believe old Sam, do yer?" Seaton turned back, the old man's eyes though bleary through sleep and alcohol appeared to be sincere. Sam shook his finger at the officer. "Believe me or not, we'll never see old Cappy again!"

Seaton stood there for a moment thinking. Naturally, he did not believe the old drunk had actually seen a monster. But then what could it have been? He would have given anything for old *Cappy* to suddenly turn up demanding to know where his hat was. But in the meantime, what action should he take?

In his reverie, Seaton did not notice Sam sidle up beside him.

"An' there were another one las' night."

Seaton spun around in shock. "Another one, what?" he demanded.

Sam pulled back slightly, almost losing his balance. "Another sacrifice, that's what!"

The officer pulled a puzzled expression. "Now what are you going on about…Sacrifice!"

"Aye," said the old man, trying to keep his balance on the sand. "Last night, I saw a woman bury a man in the sand down there by the pier." He pointed to an area at the far end of the beach where the remnants of the old dilapidated pier still stood in defiance of the elements. "She buried him up to his neck, an' left him there for the monster…He wus a sacrifice I tell ee."

Now his story was becoming far too incredulous for the officer to believe. Still, it was his duty to investigate crime, so he still had the onus on him to prove that Sam was talking rubbish through the drink. Not that he believed for a moment that there was anything in his tale about monsters rising from the depths, but he could not ignore the sincerity in the old man's voice.

He turned back to Sam. "And did you recognise either the woman or the victim?"

Sam shook his head. "Not from round 'ere. At least I'd never seen either of 'em 'efore."

"Would you be able to give a description to a police artist?"

The old man rubbed his chin, the bristles rasping against his callused palm. He thought for a second or two more. "Nah, probably not. It were too dark."

Seaton let out a long sigh. There was absolutely no credibility if Sam as a witness. If he launched an investigation at this stage based on what Sam was telling him, he could set himself up as a laughing stock.

He decided just to ask his officers to keep an eye out for *Cappy* and leave it at that for now. Before he turned again to leave, Sam grabbed him by the arm. "Any chance of a few quid fer breakfast?" he asked, breathing an intoxicated lungful of stale air straight at him.

Seaton pulled away. "Only if you promise to brush your teeth before we next speak." He shoved his hand in his pocket and pulled out his loose change. Surveying it, he dropped three pound coins and some silver and bronze into the tramp's outstretched hand. Sam grinned and did a false spit on the money before stuffing it in his trouser pocket. Seaton winced. "And try and spend it on food this time!"

***

The beach had been packed with holiday makers all day, and Dan and Tammi had made three round trips of the bay by tea time. There was still plenty of opportunity for more customers to come forward, but Dan was feeling lazy and could not be bothered with spouting off his usual chat-up spiel to bring the punters in.

He had tried to wake early so that he might be able to catch Caitlin walking her dog. But Tammi had been right in her assertion; he was a nocturnal animal and not much good in the early morning. He would have to make more of an effort if he wanted to get chatting to the museum curator.

Tammi climbed up on deck, wiping her hands on her dirty overalls. She squinted, shielding her eyes with her hand as she surveyed the beach. There was plenty of time to take in at least another party before calling it quits, but like Dan, she too was feeling lazy and in need of something to lift her spirits.

She jumped down from the platform leading up from the engine room and landed softly next to Dan's chair. Her oil- and grease-stained pumps, which had once upon a time been brilliant white, hardly making a sound when she made contact with the boat's wooden floor.

"Hey, Boss, any chance of a wee early night?" she asked, optimistically.

Dan turned away from the sun's glare to face her. "You feeling tired too?"

Tammi laughed. "No, just the opposite, I'm meeting someone in a club tonight."

Dan smiled. "Oh I get it, you want me to sling my hook?"

"Well, it would make life easier for me. And besides, you could always hook up with Maggie, you haven't seen her in a while, have you?"

Dan pondered the idea. Since last night, he had only had Caitlin on his mind, but right now, she was just a fantasy, and one which might not ever come to fruition. Maggie, on the other hand, was far more of a certainty. They had known each other for years since he had stayed at her B&B when his boat was in dry dock being repaired. She was fifteen years older than Dan, but still in fine shape. She was always well presented, hair and make-up just right, and living by the sea all her life she had a perfect all over tan; Dan could attest to that. They had what Dan liked to think of as an "understanding".

Tammi's suggestion certainly appealed. The thought of Maggie's bronzed, toned, naked body pressed against his in the throes of passion was already making him excited. He decided it prudent to call ahead. Though there were no strings attached to their relationship, Dan did not want it to seem as if he was taking her for granted by presuming she would be free to drop everything for him on the spur of the moment.

He knew Maggie was a free agent, and during his intermittent visits, was not surprised to find she was seeing someone else. After all, she was a very attractive woman, and not just for her age, but in general.

Whilst he was on the phone, Tammi used their only bathroom to freshen up. The club she was heading for was almost ten miles away, but it had been worth it last time. She had found it on the internet, and because of the area and the location, had expected it to be a bit of a flash in the pan, but it had been going now for over a year and was definitely popular with the local gay and bi-curious scene.

The woman she was meeting tonight had hooked up with her on one of the dating applications she used via her mobile. She had told Tammi she was in a relationship with the father of her two boys, but that they were not a full-time item and she often craved female company. It sounded promising.

She met Dan in the corridor outside the bathroom waiting for his turn.

"Well?" she asked, expectantly.

Dan gave her the thumbs up, a silly big grin on his face.

After he had showered, Dan dressed himself in a pair of light shorts and a polo shirt. It was going to be a warm night so he did not bother with a jacket.

As he was about to leave, two men and a young woman approached his boat. Dan estimated that they were probably all in their early twenties, and both men were carrying huge boxes of equipment strapped to their backs.

The girl walked forward and called up to Dan. "Excuse me," she said, politely, "we were wondering if we could hire you to take us out on the sea tonight?"

Dan jumped down to join her. He could not help noticing how her tight T-shirt and hot pants accentuated her pert little figure. He nodded acknowledgement to the two men behind her before turning his attention back to her.

"I'm really sorry," he said, apologetically, "but I'm afraid I have closed up for the night." He could see the disappointment on the trio's faces. "If you like, I could save a particular time spot for you tomorrow," he offered.

The girl had begun to pout, and the look suited her. Under other circumstances, Dan would have gladly accepted the commission, but tonight was a night not to miss. Maggie was a sure thing and he could already sense the feel of her velvet skin against his. It would take more than the offer of a kind smile to move him.

"Unfortunately, we only have tonight," the girl continued, half the pout still there, "we have to go back to Uni tomorrow. We're trying to film a documentary for our course and you were recommended to us by the guy in the tourist box,"

"Oh I see," said Dan. "Well, under other circumstances, I would be only too pleased to offer you my assistance, but as I said, I have closed for the day, I am meeting a good friend in town." He felt he needed to hammer the nail home.

The girl turned sullenly to look at her two companions. Dan saw one of the shrug his shoulders, the other looked completely non-plussed.

From the far end of the beach, Dan saw Big Jake appear from across the road.

Thinking quickly, he raised his hand and signalled for Jake to come forward. When Jake noticed the gesture, he remained on course, surprised that Savage would be trying to get his attention. When Dan realised he was not going to change course, he waved more frantically, making the situation clear.

Jake, puzzled, turned towards Dan's boat. Still suspicious for the reason behind the gesture, he strode purposefully with a scowl on his face.

Jake walked up behind the two men and stood with his hands placed firmly on his hips. Dan, without the slightest hint of sarcasm in his voice, spoke over their heads to the big man.

"Jake, my old friend, these lovely people would like to hire someone to take them out tonight to make a documentary film. Interested?"

The girl turned and smiled at Jake, the gesture waning when she noticed him still glaring at Dan. "We're happy to pay, though we have no idea what the rate should be," she offered. "Would £100 be acceptable?"

Jake switched his gaze to the girl at the sound of the offer. He rubbed his chin thinking. "'ow long you want to be out fer?" he asked, his voice gruff and unfriendly.

"Oh only a couple of hours at most," the girl offered, confidently.

"What's all that equipment?" the big man demanded, indicating the loads carried by the two men. "If you damage my boat, you'll have to pay extra!"

The girl looked sheepishly at him. "They're just camera and sound equipment. We won't need to even attach anything to your craft. It's all hand-held or free-standing."

After a moment more, once Jake had decided that this was not a wind up instigated by Dan, he nodded his agreement. The girl thanked Dan for his help and the four of them all walked away in the direction of Jake's boat.

Dan called out to their receding backs. "You're welcome, Jake old son, anytime." Jake did not bother to respond.

Dan found Maggie sunbathing in her garden. The bikini she was wearing barely covered her ample figure. The white lycra fabric complimented her deep tan, marvellously. When he opened the gate, she did not stir. As he drew closer, he realised she was asleep.

He stood there for a while, watching her chest rhythmically moving up and down, focussing on her nipples which protruded through the flimsy fabric. He crept over to her lounger and kneeling, planted a gentle kiss on her exposed belly.

Maggie woke with a start. Seeing Dan, she smiled. "Oh, it's you." She put her hand out and pulled him towards her. "Come here, lover."

Dan joined her on the lounger, their combined weight making the frame creak. The garden area was off bounds to her guests, and the high hedgerows which surrounded it afforded them some well-needed privacy.

Their lips locked, tongues encircling each other's. Dan let his hand slip down to one of her breasts, squeezing it gently through the fabric. He felt her nipple stiffen as he rubbed it with the underside of his thumb.

Maggie moaned softly. Her hand slid down his torso until it came to rest on the bulge in his shorts. She stroked him, expertly. Her slender well-manicured fingers encircling him, squeezing, releasing then moving up and down his shaft with practiced grace.

Now it was Dan's turn to moan.

The sound of someone approaching from behind the hedge brought them back to reality.

"Come on," Maggie whispered, "let's go upstairs and really get this party started."

Maggie's bedroom was the largest in the guest house. It was a modest business, but she had built it up from nothing and was rightly proud of her achievements. The room had a super king-sized, four-poster bed dominating it, with frilly drapes hanging down and matching pillows against the headboard.

The duvet felt cool to the skin as they both fell onto it in each other's embrace.

Dan left his shorts on the floor and allowed Maggie to lift off his polo shirt for him. Once he was naked, he began kissing her from her feet up her legs until he reached her bikini bottoms. She lifted her bottom off the bed and allowed him to remove them. Once they had been discarded, Dan moved in and used his tongue to enter her moist cleft, swirling it round and licking the top of her opening until he brought her to ecstasy.

Maggie cried out in pleasure. Reaching down, she grabbed hold of Dan's head in her hands and pulled him towards her face, her mouth searching for his. She could feel his throbbing erection pressing against her belly. She stroked his back, sliding her hand over his bottom and around to his penis. She eased him to the front of her opening and guided him in. Both of them gasped in unison as he slid himself inside her all the way for the first time.

Their bodies became one as they moved back and forth. A two-headed creature lost in the throes of pleasure. Dan managed to hold off until he heard Maggie come again before releasing his load. Once he had finished, he stayed inside her as they lay together bathed in a thin sheen of perspiration. Maggie wrapped her legs around his back as if fearing he might try to exit. Their tongues continued to explore each other's. The taste of her post-coital skin was heady to Dan. Soon, he was ready to start again.

CHAPTER FIVE

Jake Johnson sat in the wheelhouse of his boat scanning through an old porn magazine one of his crew had picked up on his last visit to the continent. He leered at the pictures of mostly naked young girls cavorting over various cars, vans and bikes, as well as an array of very lucky young men. Jake flipped open the centre fold revealing a double-page spread of the girl of the month, a leggy blonde with obviously dyed hair, wearing nothing more than some tasteful jewellery strategically placed around various parts of her anatomy. The girl was languishing on a brand new Triumph motorbike, and the angle of the shot left little to the imagination.

Jake wished to himself that the magazines on the top shelf over here were more like the ones they sold abroad. England had far too many rules and regulations about this sort of thing for his liking. If a beautiful young girl was happy to pose stark naked for his pleasure, then why should the authorities care? Probably a bunch of big fat interfering bitches with hairy armpits on the panels, he thought. No one would pay good money to see them naked!

He glanced out of the window to the front of his craft where the three students were busying themselves setting up their equipment. They had asked him to bring them out just far enough so that they could complete their filming without any land or passing vessels in sight.

The young girl was bending down, attaching something to a wire. Her behind stretched the fabric of her tight jeans almost to breaking point, and Jake wondered what she would look like naked. He drooled, licking his lips at the thought. Perhaps when they reached port, he would get her alone and offer to pay her back the money she had given him if she was willing to do him a little favour. He imagined her lithe young body naked, covered in perspiration, sliding over every inch of him, her tongue searching, kissing, licking, nibbling her way down his naked torso towards his manhood. Jake felt himself go hard. He had to fight an immediate urge to go out on board and throw the two male students into the sea so he could have the girl all to himself, now!

But he knew he would have to bide his time. Perhaps if he started talking to her on the way back, he could make up some story about his life at sea that might peak her interest. If he said it was for her ears only and that he did not want anything put on film, maybe she would dismiss the other two back to their lodgings and stay on board with him. The thought made him harder.

Once alone, he would bring out some of his excellent dark rum, and before she knew, it the girl would be putty in his hands. She certainly did not look strong enough to fight back after a double of the good stuff.

Jake's mind was set. He would put his master plan into action on the return journey. For now, he would just play the congenial host and plant a few seeds of interest.

Checking his reflection in the mirror above him, Jake licked his hand and smoothed it down over his greasy, lank hair. He repeated the operation for a stubborn follicle which refused to stay down. Giving up, he grabbed an old baseball cap from its perch on the back wall and pulled it down over his head. After checking his profile, he smelled his shirt. It had the distinct odour of stale fish and sweat. But then he had been working all day, what could the girl expect?

He thought for a moment. Did he have a spare one downstairs? He decided it was worth a look. Sticking his head outside the cabin, he called to the students, ensuring that he only made eye contact with the girl. "I'm just poppin' downstairs for a bit, I won't be long. Will you be alright up here on your own?"

The girl acknowledged him, but before she could answer, one of the men did. Jake ignored him and kept his eyes on the girl, smiling to her as if it had been her with the answer after all.

Once below, Jake found a couple of old shirts he had put there for emergencies. Checking them, he discovered that neither smelt any better than the one he had on. He looked from one to the other, trying to decide if it was worth bothering to change.

There was a shower room along the corridor which was hardly ever used, and he wondered if it might be worth him using it, but reasoned even with a clean body, the smell from his clothes would still permeate through. He managed to find some deodorant and sprayed himself all over. The cold icy blast made him shiver. He undid his trousers and aimed the nozzle of the can between his legs, careful not to let the spray get too close to his privates. By the time she gets down there, she'll be too pissed to care about the smell, he thought, chuckling to himself.

Belching loudly, Jake could taste the aftermath of his wife's fish stew. Good as it was on the way down it left a lot to be desired on the way back up. Remembering that there was a bottle of mouthwash in the shower room, Jake made his way along the corridor. A quick rinse and a gargle would do wonders in the love stakes.

Up top, Sharon Post bent over to brush her hair before flinging her head back and re-brushing it straight. She had washed and conditioned it that afternoon as she wanted it to shine and look healthy when the lights caught her on camera. She checked her makeup in her compact mirror, and re-applied a few minor touches of blusher and lipstick. Perfect!

She turned to the student behind the camera. "Ready for me, Gary?" The man stayed behind the lens as he lifted his thumb up.

The man with the sound boom checked his readings to ensure that the girl's voice would be clearly heard over the sound of the creaking vessel, as well as any noise from the sea. Once he was happy, he looked at her. "Where do you want me, Shar?"

The girl thought, nibbling on her thumbnail. "I thought that I would stand with my back to the sea, right at the pointy end," she indicated behind her.

"The bow," said the cameraman, sarcastically.

"Whatever!" replied Sharon, pulling a face. "Then if you can pan the camera around as I speak, we should be able to take in a complete panoramic view which will hopefully give us the isolated almost eerie feeling I'm going for." She turned back to the cameraman. "What do you think?"

Gary nodded in response. "Good with me." Turning to Ron, the sound technician, he said, "Can you hold the boom over my head from behind, and sweep it across as she walks by?" The man nodded. "Keep it about two feet above her and it shouldn't get in the way of the shot."

"Will do," replied Ron, ensuring that he had adequate cable to spare.

Sharon moved towards the bow, pushing a few tousled strands of hair off her face. The wind coming in from the sea was quite strong and she considered tying her hair back for the shoot. Then she remembered she had done that earlier when they completed their narration on the beach, and she wanted to go for a different look on the night shoot.

She held her microphone between her legs and settled her hair again whilst the boys sorted out their positioning.

The boat rocked gently on the waves, adding depth to the atmosphere of the setting. This was going to finish their production marvellously. They had spent three days on this project – in accordance with their university's instructions. During that time, they had interviewed several key members of the fishing community in the town. A local fishmonger and a fish and chip shop owner. Poor Gary had been up before dawn to catch the fishing vessels, heading out to sea twice, as he was not happy with the lighting on the first take.

This night shoot should just about clinch the deal.

Sharon had wondered if it might be worth trying to film some extra footage interviewing their captain. But she decided he was a very tedious individual who only managed to slur out a few syllables at a time before tripping up over his words. No perhaps not, after all, she thought. Now the first boat owner they had approached might have been a different matter. Handsome, good looking, erudite, even quite eloquent in his own way, what a pity she could not persuade him to take part.

Once they were all in position, they were ready for a first take. Gary turned on his camera and waited a few seconds before calling, "Action."

Sharon smiled at the camera, took a moment to mentally remember where she was up to in her script, and began. "Though fishing in the North Sea is concentrated mainly in the southern part of the coastal waters, since the early nineteen eighties, the numbers of fish caught there has declined by almost one million on an annual basis. This, experts claim, is as a direct result of over-fishing, though other factors like the introduction of non-indigenous species, industrial and agricultural pollution, trawling, dredging, offshore construction, and heavy shipping traffic have also contributed to the decline…"

"Hold it a second." Gary looked up from his lens. "The backdrop's not reflecting any of the light onto the camera."

Sharon shrugged, "What's that mean in layman's terms?"

Gary held up his hands to elucidate. "The lack of daylight, stars, passing vessels or land in the distance makes it look as if you are just standing on a model ship in a studio. We need some sort of background and the sea is just too dark."

Sharon turned and looked out across the sea. Gary was right; she had never seen it so black and ominous looking. The low cloud blocked the starlight, and it was hard to make out where the water and the sky joined in the distance.

"So what do you suggest?" she asked, turning back to face the boys.

Gary thought for a moment, and then said. "If we change places, Ron and I can stay at the back with our backs to the water…"

"You mean the bow!" Sharon winked at Ron who laughed back.

"Yeah, yeah very funny," replied Gary smiling in spite of himself. "Then you can walk in front of the wheelhouse as you talk, and end up at the door. We could always ask the captain to come into the shot at the end taking control of the wheel."

Sharon looked over to make sure that Jake was nowhere in sight. "I'd rather not if you don't mind," she whispered.

The boys re-shuffled their equipment to set up camp in the bow. Sharon re-checked her appearance and added a touch of lip-gloss for the camera. She worked out where she was going to walk and how many words she could get in for each step. She attempted a few poses leaning against the wheelhouse to accentuate the overall professional image she was trying to project. She glanced behind; she was glad Jake had disappeared. He gave her the creeps. The thought of him appearing behind her from his vantage point sent a shiver through her, which she shrugged away.

Gary and Ron had re-set their equipment and were ready to start again.

Sharon positioned herself and made sure that her microphone was on.

Ron raised the boom to the correct height, as Gary counted down mentally before calling out, "Action!"

As Sharon opened her mouth to start speaking, a large, slimy, black tentacle swung over the side of the boat and knocked both men into the water.

Sharon's mouth was still open in anticipation. Her brain could not register what had just happened. She stared for a moment at the place where the two students had stood seconds earlier.

Then she screamed!

Jake heard the scream from below. He had been busy rinsing out glasses to share his rum with Sharon. He waited a moment, listening, wondering what it could have been that made her scream like that.

Then a thought struck him. Perhaps those lads fancied their chances with his girl and were trying it on. Well, he wasn't having any of that!

Leaving the glasses and bottle carefully placed on the table, Jake took the stairs two at a time as he heard Sharon scream again and call for him. She was in trouble and needed him. This was going to work out better than he had expected. He would give both those lads a taste of what a real man can do and show the girl how he protected his women. Then he would chuck the boys in the drink to swim back to shore and he could get on with the business at hand.

By the time Jake reached the deck, Sharon was almost hysterical.

When she saw him, she ran straight to him and clung to his chest, sobbing uncontrollably.

Jake looked about the deck; the two men were nowhere to be seen. He turned to check behind, ensuring that the girl was still locked in his embrace. He liked the feel of her body against his. She was soft, warm, and smelled lovely.

For a moment, Jake wondered if the two students had jumped overboard when they heard him approaching, afraid of the beating he was going to give them for daring to try it on with his woman. Or had fallen over the side fighting over who was going to have the first go with her. Either way, they were no longer on board.

Jake hugged Sharon tightly. "There, there, it's all over now, Jake'll look after yer." He began stroking her long blonde hair, lowering his face until his nose was just above her head; he breathed in deeply and smiled. He could already feel himself stirring. Sliding his hands down her back, he pressed her pelvis against his erection and moaned.

Sharon immediately pushed him away. She was strong for someone her size, Jake thought, but still no match for him. If she wanted to play hard-to-get, that was okay with him too. He liked it that way!

He remembered the previous spring when he and the two Clive boys had delivered some machine parts down to Cornwall. They decided to make an event of it and went on a bit of a pub crawl. That dirty little slut they picked up was so wasted she didn't even know what they were doing until they were back aboard the boat. Then she decided to play hard-to-get and started bellowing and shouting to be let go. They had to hold her down while each of them had their turn with her. Jake smacked her to keep her quiet. Maybe he had been a bit too rough with her, but she deserved it making all that noise.

They carried her back ashore in the early hours and left her on the beach before setting off home. She was still alive as far he knew, and they had spent a fortune buying her drinks all evening, so what did she have to complain about!

If this little beauty wanted the same treatment, then so be it. Jake knew that that was what some women liked, he'd read about them in the Sunday papers. Well if that was the case, Jakey-boy was her man.

He made a grab for Sharon, but she was too quick for his clumsy advance. Jake grinned down at her. Where did she think she was going to run out here at sea?

As Jake moved towards his prey, Sharon began pointing frantically to the bow of the boat. She was mumbling something incoherent through her tears, but Jake could not understand any of it. He looked over to where she was pointing, convinced it was a trick. All he saw was their equipment lying on the floor.

Sharon was sliding down the side of the wheelhouse, her arms crossed in front of her, until she sat there clutching her knees with her arms.

Jake had had enough; he was determined to get to the bottom of what was going on. The girl's histrionics were starting to get on his nerves. Bending down, he grabbed her by the arms and hoisted her to her feet. Sharon fought back feebly, still blubbing.

Jake shook her violently. "What the bloody 'ell is goin' on 'ere?" Sharon looked up with glassy eyes, but did not respond. Jake lifted his hand and struck her hard across the face, hard. Sharon yelped in pain. "Now pull yerself together an' tell me what the 'ell happened?"

Sharon tried to get herself under control. The big man was holding her so tightly she could feel his fingers digging into her soft flesh. She looked back over to where her fellow students had stood moments earlier. Her mind tried to form the words to describe what she had seen, but it could not.

Eventually, all she managed to say was, "Overboard."

Jake released her and walked over to the bought to investigate. If those two idiots had fallen overboard, that was their hard luck. He would call the coastguard and leave it to them to sort out. He had more important fish to fry.

Jake leaned over the side of the boat and stared out to sea. There was no sign of anyone in the water, and straining, he could not hear anyone calling for help. Perhaps the girl had struck them with something when they tried it on and sent them both overboard. If that was the case, Jake could use it to his advantage. Tell her he was duty bound to report her to the police…Unless of course they could come to an arrangement.

Jake turned back. Sharon was still holding herself and sobbing. Jake walked over and tried to put his arm around her shoulders, but she shrugged him away. He knew he needed to calm her down. She would be no fun like this.

He waited until he sobs subsided, then asked, "Are you sure they both went overboard?"

Sharon looked up at him. "Yes, of course I'm sure. Something knocked them both over the side."

Jake frowned. "Something... What thing?"

"I don't know, it was like a big sea snake or something, it just swept over the side and knocked them both in the sea. It all happened so quickly I don't know what it was, but when I looked over the side, I couldn't see either of them, or the thing that took them."

Jake walked back to the bow; Sharon followed him, tentatively keeping him between her and the edge of the boat. She let Jake look over the side for a minute before she joined him. There was no sign of either Gary or Ron, or of the thing which claimed them. In her mind's eye, she saw the incident again and again, but it all happened so suddenly that she was beginning to doubt her own recollection.

She scanned the water's surface for any sign of movement. She could hear the water lapping at the side of the vessel, but there was no visible evidence of anything being in the water.

She grabbed Jake's cuff. "We need to report this, quickly. Get the police or the coastguard out here to make a search."

Jake held out his hand. "Now wait a second, if they went over here, the current wouldn't have carried them off just yet, why aren't they calling out for help?"

"I don't bloody know. Perhaps whatever took them over, took them under as well, and still has them!" Sharon was almost screaming by now.

Jake felt himself losing control of the situation. "Look, wait 'ere a second, I'm going to get a torch. We need to make a thorough search before we go alertin' the authorities." He glared down at Sharon with a malevolent gleam in his eyes. "An' if this turns out to be some kind o' stupid student prank, so help me..." He didn't finish; A.) Because he did not know what to threaten her with, and B.) Because the trailed off sentence seemed to have even more of an effect at conveying menace.

Sharon clung to the boat as she watched Jake make his way back into the wheelhouse. She gripped the side tightly with both hands as she continued surveying the water. She still could not believe what had happened to her two friends, even though she had witnessed the incident herself. She began to wonder what sort of reaction she would receive from the authorities when she told them her tale. She could not say what it was that had taken the boys, because she did not know what it was. All she could do was describe it, and even that was not much of a description.

Jake glanced out of the window at the girl whilst he searched for his torch. He was sure it was here, he had used it only recently. He bent down on his haunches to rifle through the junk in the cupboards beneath the dashboard. Pushing aside old magazines, cans of lubricant, an assortment of rags, tools and brushes, he finally located what he was after. Jake tested the beam to make sure that it was working. Once he was, he stood up.

The girl was gone!

Jake walked back out on deck, looking around him, but there was no sign of her. He walked over to where he had just seen her standing a moment before and looked over the side at the water. There was nothing there. Surely, if she had just fallen or jumped in, she would still be visible beside the craft. Flailing, splashing, waving, shouting, something!

Instead, all he could see was black water. He shone the torch's beam down to survey the surface. Nothing moved.

Now Jake really began to suspect a prank. He took his torch and carried out an immediate search of the rest of the boat, convinced he was going to find the three of them hiding in a corner somewhere, trying not to bust a gut laughing at the poor dumb fisherman. Well, he was certainly going to kick some butt when he found them. The girl's too. And then he was going to drag her down stairs and she was going to help him work out his frustration.

The search proved fruitless; there was no sign of any of them and nowhere left on board for them to hide. Jake stood on deck scratching his head, his hat moving backwards almost toppling off. Now this was weird. Where had they gone to?

The obvious answer was overboard, but how? The sea was calm, and there were hardly any waves; certainly none big enough to cause someone to lose their balance and fall in.

Jake thought for a moment about what the girl had said. Something about a large sea snake. Jake laughed to himself. Stupid bitch was probably high on something, all these fucking students were. They spent all their money on substance abuse and booze instead of books, and still managed to come away with qualifications that guaranteed them a job for life without ever breaking a sweat. Well screw them. If they started hallucinating about sea monsters and threw themselves overboard, what was that to him? Why should he care?

Still. he thought, it was a shame about the girl, he could have had some real fun with her before she dived over and then no one need be any the wiser. He wished now that he had forced her to go down with him instead of pandering to her imagination and looking for the torch. Damn it, he could have had her by now! He would probably have been able to play with her all night while the drugs took effect, and she would have been none the wiser.

Too late now, he thought.

Jake considered calling the coastguard. He needed to report this mess, even though it would mean hours of questions and God knows how much paperwork. Then they would want to check the safety of his vessel, and now he came to think of it, he had not got around to fixing that faulty catch on his gangway since his last warning. He had been meaning to, but they would not believe him. Anything to harass a poor honest fisherman!

Perhaps he would not report anything. After all, no one had seen them leave the harbour. No one knew that he had even taken them out. Except maybe Savage; he had been the one to introduce them.

Jake thought. Savage did not actually see them leave together. Jake could always say that they argued over the price, or he suspected them of taking drugs so refused his services. No one need be any the wiser. After all, they were not locals, so who could say where they disappeared to.

It was then Jake noticed the student's equipment lying in the footwell. He would have to get rid of all that overboard too, otherwise he could be asking for trouble if his boat was searched.

Jake picked up the camera Gary had been using to film Sharon. It looked very expensive. Not that Jake was an expert, but if this gear had been supplied by the university, then it could well be worth a small fortune.

He turned the camera over in his hand, and then checked the case Gary had brought it on board in. There were no markings of any description save the manufacturer's emblem. Nothing to denote ownership, anyway!

Jake mulled over his options. He could take this stuff out of town and pawn it. Give a false name and address and just pocket the money. No one ever needed to know. The other option was to throw it overboard, but what a waste that would be.

He looked around, as if concerned that another vessel might have snuck up on him and seen him holding the evidence. But there was not another craft in sight. Not even a ferry on the horizon.

Jake took one final look overboard before collecting up the equipment and taking it below deck. He would hide it there until the morning, then leave early to sell it off.

Once Jake had secured the items, he returned to the wheelhouse and headed back to Skullen Bay.

***

Tammi and her date lay sound asleep in her bed on the Lady Anne wrapped in each other's embrace. The woman, whose name was Geraldine, had made it clear to Tammi from their first drink that she wanted to sleep with her. Initially, the plan was that they would go back to the boat, make love, and then Geraldine would catch a cab home. But a combination of their vigorous exertions and the bottle of Jack Daniels they bought on the way back resulted in them both falling asleep straight afterwards.

A sudden jolt from underneath the vessel caused them both to wake with a start.

Tammi rubbed her eyes. "What the hell was that?" she asked, rhetorically.

Geraldine sat up with a start, suddenly conscious of the fact that she had stayed longer than she initially intended. Forgetting momentarily about the judder from below, she scrambled to locate her watch from the nightstand, squinting to read its face.

Tammi, her instincts trained, grabbed the large spanner she kept under her bed and placing it on the sheets, quickly pulled on her clothes. Geraldine, suddenly feeling vulnerable, pulled the covers over her naked body. She watched as Tammi slipped on her trainers and grabbed the spanner.

"What is it?" asked Geraldine, her voice quivering with fright. "Has someone broken in?"

Tammi stood up, her body tensed. "I dunny know," she replied, trying to sound calm. "But you stay here while I take a wee look."

Geraldine reached out and grabbed Tammi by the wrist. "Please don't leave me here, I'm frightened!"

Tammi patted her hand. "It'll be fine, probably just some kids messin' aboot." She leaned over and kissed Geraldine on the mouth. "Just wait here, I'll nay be long."

Geraldine watched Tammi slowly disappear up the stairs from her cabin to the upper deck. Geraldine was beginning to wish she had not fallen asleep and left the boat once they had satisfied each other, as she had initially intended.

Now she was in fear for her life! She imagined masked men lying in wait for Tammi to appear before bashing her over the head and throwing her overboard.

Then what?

They would come in search for her. Find her, and have their evil way with her before assigning her to the same fate as Tammi.

She tried to check herself. This was not an American crime show; this was a tiny fishing village on the southeast coast of England for goodness sake. Things like that did not happen here!

Or did they?

Geraldine strained to listen for Tammi's footsteps on the boards above her, but there was only silence. Unable to sit still, she began scrambling for her clothes, pulling her jeans on in such a hurry that at first she did not realise that they were inside out. She scrabbled around on the floor for her shoes, standing on one leg at a time to slip them on. She did not bother to look for her panties or bra; there was no time. She wanted to get off and onto terra firma.

Once dressed, she grabbed her handbag and stood still for a moment. The boat rocked gently on the waves, and she listened intently for any sound that might give her an indication of what was happening above. Still nothing!

Part of her felt that she should wait for Tammi to return. It would be the decent thing to do. But part of her wondered what she would do if Tammi did not return; then it might be too late for her to make good her escape.

Deciding that discretion was the better part of valor, Geraldine crept towards the staircase. The boards beneath her feet creaked loudly on her third step. Geraldine paused and cursed to herself. Anyone above was bound to have heard her. She waited, holding her breath. There was still no noise from above.

Carefully, she removed her shoes and decided to carry them until she was safely away from the boat. As she ascended the wooden staircase, the door above her flew open. Geraldine fell backwards with a start, just catching the banister post to steady herself and stop her sprawling backwards on the floor.

Tammi walked down the top three stairs. "Are you alright?" she asked, concern in her voice.

Geraldine heaved a sigh of relief. "Yes, thanks." She could feel her cheeks flush, embarrassed that she was prepared to leave Tammi alone in the face of danger. "Did you find out what it was that made that noise?"

Tammi shrugged. "Nope, nothing goin' on up top. I've checked all over, there's definitely no one else on board. No sign of a break-in either." Tammi walked down to the bottom step and realised that Geraldine had dressed. "Are you leavin' then?" she asked, trying to hide the disappointment in her voice.

Geraldine smiled. "Yes, I should have left ages ago really. I need to be home when my sons wake up."

"Okay," replied Tammi, understandingly.

"Do you know where I could get a cab around here?"

"Aye, I've got a wee card upstairs. Give 'em a call and ask them to meet you outside the *Fisherman's Arms*, I'll walk you over there and wait with you."

"Thank you." Geraldine moved closer and Tammi reciprocated. They held each other tightly for a moment, kissing passionately, their hands exploring each other's now familiar body.

"Will you give me a call next time you're free?" asked Tammi, expectantly.

"Of course I will," replied Geraldine, pulling Tammi towards her and searching out her eager mouth, again.

CHAPTER SIX

The distant sound of a vacuum cleaner roused Dan from his slumber. He opened his eyes focussing on the patterned ceiling of Maggie's bedroom and stretched himself to life. On the bedside table was a note in Maggie's handwriting, with one word on it: "Breakfast".

Dan smiled when he recalled the previous evening. After making love, they had fallen asleep in each other's arms. They awoke at nine thirty, and both feeling hungry, Maggie suggested that they go out for dinner. Dan treated her to her favourite Chinese restaurant, and between them, they polished off three bottles of wine.

They took a detour so they could stroll along the beach. The cool night air a blessing after such a hot day. In the distance, Dan thought he saw Jake's boat returning to the harbour. He surmised that those students he had introduced him to must be returning from their shoot. He did not bother to linger; Maggie was drunk and giggly and using him to keep herself upright as she tripped for the umpteenth time.

They returned to Maggie's B&B and managed to make it to her bedroom without waking any of her guests. Dan felt tired and drained from such a long day, but Maggie seemed to find a second wind and pushed him onto her bed before jumping on top of him. She undressed him slowly, kissing his bare flesh as she exposed it. By the time she removed his shorts, Dan was fully at attention. Smiling at his erection, Maggie slipped out of her dress and climbed back on the bed, taking him gently in her mouth. Working him up and down with practised skill, Maggie brought Dan to the point of explosion before climbing on top of him and sliding him into her.

They made love with a passion and agility that belied Dan's exhaustion. Eventually, they fell asleep, and Dan did not stir until the morning.

He showered and made his way down to the dining room. Most of Maggie's guests had finished their breakfast, and Maggie's two waitresses were busying themselves clearing away. Dan looked around the room and offered a friendly smile to those who remained seated. Over at a far table sat Maggie's two sons, Stan and Gerry, both leaning towards each other deep in conversation. When Gerry looked up, Dan acknowledged him and received a half-raised eyebrow in response.

Maggie was not exactly proud of her offspring, but as she had told Dan in the past, they were still her sons so she loved them as a mother should. According to her, they were the image of their father, a wasteful drunk who never earned an honest living, who she had finally kicked out when he raised his hand to her once too often. She had not seen him since the boys were toddlers, and hoped she never would again.

Stan was thirty-five and his younger brother thirty-two. Before working for Big Jake, both boys had scrounged a living in various capacities, working around the harbour in Alton. They had both always loved the sea and the rough trade and heavy drinking that was associated with it. But Maggie was firm with them. Sons or not, they had to toe the line whilst they lived under her roof. She would not tolerate them getting in trouble with the police, and on more than one occasion, she had made them both sleep on the boat for spending the very modest rent she charged them on booze. Maggie was not a big fan of Jake's, but at least working for him gave her sons a regular wage.

Maggie appeared from the kitchen and placed a full English in front of Dan. Dan smiled up at her and discreetly patted her rear. "Thank you, I could do with this," he said, appreciatively.

"Coffee?" Maggie asked, gently touching the back of his hair.

"Please, strong and black."

Maggie returned to the kitchen while Dan tucked into his bacon and eggs.

***

When Dan returned to his boat, Tammi was on deck, scrubbing down. She stopped when she saw him. "Hey, boss, gude night?" She knew the answer by the smug look on his face.

"Oh yes, wonderful," replied Dan, smiling. "And how did yours go?"

Tammi stood the mop to one side and walked over to meet him as he boarded. Leaning against the railing, she shoved her hands in her overalls. "It was wonderful, until about one o'clock this morning when something barged into the hull."

Dan's brow furrowed. "What!" He swung himself on board. "Was there any damage? Did you see what it was?"

Tammi shook her head. "I checked everything out when it happened, and again this mornin' in the daylight. There's definitely no damage internally, no sign o' leakage or splinterin', definitely no knock-on effect to the engine or the on-board computer."

"What was it, do you know?"

Tammi shook her head again. "Nope, whatever it was it must have been a fair size though, bloody well nearly threw me ute a-me bed."

Dan was puzzled. "Wonder what caused that then? something drifting in the water, an abandoned craft maybe?"

"Well if it were, there were no sign o' it when I looked overboard. I was thinking we might get the tanks sorted and have a wee look underneath afore we set ute today, what d'yer think?"

Dan thought for a moment. "Might not be such a bad idea. It's encouraging that you can't find any sign of leakage, but it couldn't hurt to double-check."

While he was talking, Maggie signalled behind him. Dan turned to see three men dressed in Hawaiian shirts and shorts carrying fishing equipment and a cool box approaching their gang plank.

The tallest of the three covered his eyes, shielding them from the sun before calling up to Dan. "Hi there. We were wondering if we could hire you to take us out fishing for the day."

Dan turned back to Tammi. Without speaking, he was asking her for her opinion. Did she think it was safe to go out, or should they double-check the outside of the vessel from underneath first? Tammi took a moment to decide. She had already completed all the pre-sailing checks and the *Lady Anne* was sound. Plus, a full day's sailing would be easy money for their labours. She nodded in response.

"Climb aboard, gents," said Dan, bending down to help the men with their equipment, "the fish await you."

***

Sgt. Oswald Seaton sat in his office in the Alton Police station, outing the finishing touches to his report – such as it was – after his conversation with old Sam Cleary. His training had taught him to always report the facts as best he could remember, but how anyone could take anything Sam said with anything other than a huge pinch of salt was another matter.

Seaton re-read it for the third time that morning. He decided that two re-writes was more than enough time wasted, and closing the file, stood up and placed it in on one of the metal filing cabinets lining the wall on one side of the room.

Opening his office door, he walked down the corridor towards the front desk. Constable Ralph Carmody sat flicking through the local paper. He straightened up when he heard Seaton approaching and folded the paper neatly, placing it on one side.

The desk was immaculate, as it always was when Carmody was on duty. Not that the others were untidy, but Ralph believed fervently that everything had a place and there was a place for everything.

It was a quiet morning, which was just the way Seaton liked it. He had been a policeman now for almost thirty years, and would soon be entitled to his full retirement pension, should he wish to apply for it. But he loved his job, and at the age of fifty-three, having never married and with few interests and hobbies, he saw no immediate reason to consider hanging up his helmet and boots just yet. All his liaisons since joining the force had been with female colleagues, but he had never felt the need to make things official. Perhaps he had just never met the right person?

Had he have still been working in London or Birmingham where he had initially been stationed once he completed his training, it might be a different matter. Though he was born and brought up in London, he had never been a fan of the big city. The crowds, the noise, the dirt and pollution, pounding the streets day after day, night after night, breaking up fights, having drunks throw up on your uniform with startling regularity, being abused, spat at, and generally left feeling totally unappreciated by those he was sworn to protect.

After he had passed his sergeant's exam, Seaton landed a desk job in Norwich, which was far quieter than what he was used to, but it still had shades of London he would rather leave behind. His transfer to Alton seven years ago came at just the right time for him. By then, he had lost all passion for the job, and was seriously considering early retirement when this vacancy arose.

As soon as he saw Alton, he fell in love with the place. He loved being by the sea, meeting friendly, cheerful people on a daily basis. There was the odd troublemaker of course, but that was to be expected. Big Jake Johnson for one. He could be a handful, and sooner or later, Seaton knew that the big man would cross the line and end up on an official charge. But by and by, the majority of the town were ordinary civilised working folk.

Living above the station was an added bonus. He had always rented because of the nature of the job and the fact he had grown accustomed to moving around so much during his career. But now, he felt truly settled. The station at Alton had originally only had one constable who had been in the job all his life and reported back to Norwich. When he finally retired and moved to Spain, it was decided that due to the growing size of the town and the surrounding villages, that a larger force was required.

Seaton was the first one appointed to the district, closely followed by Constable Joe Green who had moved his family down from Leicester. Ralph Carmody was a relatively local boy from Great Yarmouth whose partner had family in the town who they lived with.

Young Sally Poole was fresh out of training academy, and like Seaton, had originally lived in London. At just under six foot tall with the impressive shoulders of a regular swimmer, she was an imposing sight in her uniform and a welcome addition to the team. She was very worldly for her tender years, and had passed through the academy with flying colours. She could take a joke with the best of them – vital in this organisation – and she could dish it out by the shovel full when required.

Seaton felt very protective of his young charges. He often wondered if they were his surrogate family. He was always invited to their get-togethers, Christmas and birthday parties and the like, and he was an honouree uncle to Constable Green's two young children. He liked to think that all his officers looked up to their superior, but at the same time, did not just see him as their boss, but also as someone they could turn to in times of trouble.

Seaton walked up and stood beside Ralph. "All quiet on the western front?" he asked, cheerily.

"All quiet, Sarge," replied the officer, unconsciously standing to attention.

"No word on *Cappy* yet, I suppose?" asked Seaton, optimistically.

"I am afraid not, Sarge; Joe and Sally are still out making inquiries though." He studied his superior's expression. "Are you getting worried about him?"

Seaton ummed. "Not worried, exactly," he replied, sounding nonplussed, "but it's all rather odd that no one seems to have seen him for the last couple of days. Especially when you consider he's spent every evening for as long as anyone can remember in the same pub."

Ralph thought for a moment, then offered, "Well, we've checked out all his other known haunts; there aren't that many of them to be sure. We're still asking around at the harbour. Chances are, he was taken on board as crew for one of the larger vessels. It's not unusual for them to be out for days at a time."

"True," agreed Seaton. Ralph could see he had not convinced his superior.

The main door to the station opened and Sally and Joe entered, removing their caps and wiping perspiration from their foreheads. "It's a hot one out there today," announced Joe, looking at his watch. "And it's not even noon yet."

Sally immediately picked up on her superior's pensive mood. She walked over to the desk before speaking. "Anything up, Sarge?" she asked, genuinely concerned.

Seaton smiled back. "Not really, it's just..." He trailed off, gazing into space for a moment before addressing his team. "Come on, you lot, I need a quick word with you all in private."

The three constables followed Seaton into his office. They exchanged concerned glances, wondering if it was bad news from headquarters. Downsizing was uppermost on their minds; the big boys were forever talking about cutting the size of operations, especially somewhere like Alton where the crime rate was so low.

Once they were all seated in the closed office, Seaton slumped down behind his desk, not quite sure how to begin what he was about to say without sounding completely foolish.

He made a pretence of straightening his tie before he began. "Look, I know what I am about to tell you is going to sound completely barking, but it doesn't feel right to me holding back the details."

Now the constables were really worried.

Seaton rested his elbows on his desk, interlocking his fingers. "I spoke to Sam Cleary yesterday morning concerning *Cappy's* disappearance; I told you all he spoke to that young lady from the museum when she found *Cappy's* old hat on the beach."

There were nods of agreement. "Well, anyway," he continued, "old Sam has it in his head that Cappy was...Now don't laugh...Grabbed by *"something"* that emerged from the water."

His statement was met with stunned silence.

Before his team had a chance to answer, he jumped back in. "Now I realise that Sam is a drunk and more often than not incapable, but we still haven't managed to find Cappy and that in itself is quite unusual."

He waited for a response.

Joe spoke up. "Er, did he say exactly what it was he saw coming out of the water?"

"Not exactly." Seaton looked at each of their faces. "Yes, I know how ridiculous this all is, but bear with me." He took a deep breath. "Sam reckons that some kind of big, black monster came out of the sea and grabbed *Cappy*. And not just that, he also told me that he saw another man being buried down by the old pier night before last, and he reckons it was some kind of human sacrifice, and the victim was also grabbed by this...This monster!"

Seaton could see his audience was having a hard time buying his story.

It was Sally who broke the ice. "How much credence do you want to put in old Sam's story, guv?" Her voice had a nervous edge to it which made Seaton feel even more conscious of what he was saying.

"I have no idea at this moment, Sally, I just feel that I need to lay out the facts for you all." He waited a moment more to see if anyone else wanted to offer an opinion, before continuing. "Sam said he saw this monster take *Cappy*, fact!" He started counting on his fingers as he rattled off his information. "He also said he saw this other bloke being buried like some bloomin' human sacrifice, then being pulled out of the sand by this same creature, fact! *Cappy* is still missing, fact! Sam may be a drunk, but in all my years here, I have never known him spin wild yarns like this, fact!"

Joe had an idea. "Okay, so regardless of what he actually saw, or says he saw, who is the other bloke then? We haven't had any other missing persons reported!"

"True," replied Seaton, relieved that they were not treating him like someone who needed sectioning. "But if there is any truth to what he says, this other bloke could be from anywhere, not necessarily a local."

"Yes, but guv," chimed in Sally, "monsters from the deep, human sacrifices...It all sounds a little far-fetched, don't you think?"

"I agree," replied Seaton, "but the fact remains that his statement is now on record," he pointed to his filing cabinet, "and regardless of what the truth eventually turns out to be, I wanted you all to know what he said, just in case…" He trailed off and shrugged his shoulders, unsure of how to finish his sentence.

None of the young officers laughed or even smirked. They would not have been so disrespectful. But it was still hard for them to fathom out where to go from here.

Seaton, understanding their apprehension, spoke up again. "Listen, everyone, just so you don't think I've got sun stroke or dementia or something," there was a smattering of titters at his humour, "I do not believe in sea monsters. The Loch Ness Monster…Maybe, who can say, but in general, no! The abominable snowman, UFOs…"

"Now hold on, Sarge," Joe jumped in. "You can't deny the photographic evidence from –"

"Yes, yes thank you, Constable Green," Seaton cut him off in mid-sentence. There was another smattering of laughter from his colleagues. Seaton continued, "Human sacrifices, well we've all read the Sunday papers, and as coppers, we should appreciate that there are enough nutters in this world to make most things possible. So I just want you all to keep in mind what old Sam said, and if by chance you overhear anything in the town, no matter how weird it might sound, bring it back and let the rest of us know."

There was murmured agreement amongst the constables.

Seaton relaxed. Now the worst was over and he still felt his dignity was intact.

"'ear, Sarge," Ralph suddenly piped up. "What if we get a similar story from someone with more credence than Sam?"

Seaton sighed. "Then, my old son, our troubles will really begin!"

CHAPTER SEVEN

Dan strode across the beach on route to the Fisherman's Arms. They had had a good day all-in-all; the three fishermen had been very fortunate in their endeavours, and that in turn made them happy and generous when it came time to pay for the day's services. Dan surmised from their conversations that they were all in business of one sort or another, and fishing was their passion. They left promising repeat business which was always a good way to end the day.

After clearing up, Dan felt as if he had earned a couple of pints and the best meal the pub could offer. Tammi was not tempted and opted for something from the freezer on board and an early night to catch up on lost sleep.

They had decided that depending on how business was tomorrow, they would have their tanks re-filled and investigate the outside hull of the boat for any damage sustained after whatever it was crashed into it the previous night. Tammi had kept a keen eye on everything whilst they had been at sea, and fortunately, there was no sign of any leakage anywhere. But even so, it would be worth checking just for their peace of mind.

Dan felt very lucky to have Tammi on his team. Good crew were hard to find at the best of times, and when you had to live and work with the same person day in and day out, they had to be special or else you would wind up wanting to kill them. He reflected that he did not tell Tammi often enough how grateful he was to have her on board. Then again, he hoped he showed his gratitude in other ways. It was almost as if they were equal partners rather than the boss and his staff member, and he hoped Tammi realised that.

In truth, Dan realised that he relied on Tammi more than he knew. He was nowhere near as efficient as she was around machinery, and her constant attention to detail had probably saved him countless trips to the supply house. Not to mention what she had saved him on repair bills over the years.

He made a mental note to make a point of showing his appreciation more often in future.

As for tonight, he could not help wondering if that gorgeous girl from the museum might be in the pub. He had promised himself an early morning to see if he could catch her walking her dog on the beach, but this might be a better option. He was glad he had taken the time to shower before heading off for the pub. Normally, it would not have made much difference, drinking among the other fishermen and boaters who had probably all been sweating for the best part of the day out at sea. But if Caitlin was there, it would definitely have been worth the effort.

As he crossed the road and entered the pub's courtyard, Jake Johnson emerged from the pub door, pulling on his coat as he walked. He seemed oblivious to the fact that Dan was standing a few feet away from him, so as he turned to leave, Dan called after him.

"Hey, Jake, how did you get on with those students last night? Was it worth the trip?"

Jake looked back once he realised someone was calling to him. When he saw it was Dan, he scowled. "What?"

Dan sighed; what a miserable so and so. He moved closer to Jake so that he could hear him more clearly. "I asked how it went with those students I put your way last night."

Jake's face flushed, then he re-composed himself almost immediately. "Nah, they were being a pain in the arse, so I told them to fuck off!"

Dan was surprised. "Really? They seemed nice enough to me. I thought I was putting a nice bit of business your way."

Jake turned on Dan as if he was about to hit him.

Dan tensed, ready to defend himself. He could not understand the man's hostility, certainly not under these circumstances.

Jake suddenly relaxed, realising he was over-reacting. Dan's inquisitiveness had caught him off guard. He had set out early that morning and pawned the student's equipment at a pawn shop he knew up the coast in Cromer. He did not receive as much as he might have done selling the stuff privately, but the shop owner was known amongst a certain group of society, above all else for his discretion.

Jake tried to relieve the tension he had caused; the last thing he wanted was Dan getting suspicious he had something to hide. "Thanks for trying, Savage, but you know what kids are, want something for nothing." He turned back and left before Dan could answer.

Dan watched Jake depart. He felt instinctively that something about the big man's story did not gel. Jake could be evasive at the best of times, and Dan was used to man's economy with words when it came to answering a question, especially one he did not like being asked.

Dan decided it was not worth wasting time over for now, at least.

Hopefully, he would have more luck in the conversation area with Caitlin in the pub.

***

Amy Friar was bored with her existence. She could not bring herself to refer to it as her "life" because as far as she was concerned, she had not been given a chance of experiencing anything as magical as a "life".

She had worked full-time in her father's fish and chip shop since leaving school at fifteen. Prior to that, she had worked there every Saturday and most evenings after school since she was thirteen. It was no surprise to any of the teachers at her comprehensive in Alton that she failed every exam she ever took. Her having to put in so many hours for the family business left little time for homework, or anything else for that matter. Now at the tender age of nineteen, she felt as if she had stagnated, with nothing to look forward to in her near future.

Her father, Harry, had never believed that education suited ordinary folk, as he was fond of saying. He was proud of having left school at fourteen and working his guts out until he was able to purchase his own business, and making a very decent living out of it. As far as he was concerned, so long as you could add and subtract, no one could ever take advantage of you; and in business, that was what counted.

Amy's mother had left them when Amy was two. Her father was not averse to telling her that she was an accident which neither of them wanted, and that he had only kept her because ultimately he knew she could work for him for very little.

Her mother had suffered from deep post-natal depression, which caused her to abandon baby Amy twice, before finally leaving home for good. Initially after her mother left, Amy was handed from pillar to post by a succession of relatives in the town whilst her father worked all hours. Eventually, on recommendation, he paid an old spinster in the town to look after his daughter on a more permanent basis, though he did make the effort to see her when he could and always on Sundays when the shop was closed.

Harry Friar was not a cruel or wicked parent, but he wasn't a natural father either. Luckily for Amy, he grew into fatherhood over time.

The old lady was very good to Amy. But alas, all that unbridled love manifested itself in the woman over-feeding the needy youngster to the point where she became obese.

Starting secondary school just made things worse. The school uniform was dark brown, and having a name like Friar and being the size she was resulted in her nickname being "Tuck". Added to that, once she started to help out in the chip shop, the cloying atmosphere caused her hair and skin to become oily and greasy, and spots became a permanent fixture on her chubby face.

Her glasses didn't help matters either. In this day and age of super-thin lenses, her prescription still called for "Coke-bottle" wide rims, without which she could barely see anything unless it was right in front of her face.

But for all that she was still a pretty child, and most of her friends agreed that if she could lose a bit of weight and get her skin to clear up, she could be quite stunning.

However, her overall appearance still gave her an inferiority complex which she could not shake. And this, in turn, made her put herself on offer to virtually any man who gave her a kind word or even smiled sweetly in her direction.

As a result, Amy Friar had gained a bit of a reputation around town, which had cost her more than just a few of her friends. True, she had sex with several of her friend's boyfriends, but in her defence, she did not know who they were at the time. Sex was very important to Amy. For a brief moment, it was the comfort of being wrapped in two strong arms, feeling the warmth of their naked body gliding against hers. Feeling their breath on her cheek and tasting the moistness of their probing tongues. But even so, Amy would still not have allowed her urge to destroy a friendship. She would never try and chat-up a friend's other half. In truth, they had all come on to her, then lied to their girlfriend's when caught out saying that Amy had led them on. As if she could!

More fool them, she thought, for having believed their unfaithful partners, but the end result was always the same; she would be another friend down with the possible knock-on effect of losing others through association. And in a small town like Alton, friends were important.

Amy slammed the till drawer and glanced up at the clock. It was almost 11pm, just one more hour to go. Her father insisted on keeping the shop open until midnight on Fridays and Saturdays because he knew how much extra business was there for the taking come chucking out time.

Amy hated the last hour the most! All the drunks, young and old, pouring in the door, pushing and shoving, fighting in the queue, belching loudly, challenging each other to fart the loudest, offering £5 and £10 notes soggy with beer and spirits so that the stench came off on Amy's fingers. And, of course, there were all the smutty remarks she had to contend with. In truth, she didn't mind it so much when one of the younger, more fit men cracked a joke, no matter how crude some of them were. But it was the old ones she hated. Especially the fat bald ones with half their teeth missing and you were spoilt for choice for them in this town. Most of them were fishermen who had come ashore at noon and gone straight to the pub, only to remain there until now. Still reeking of rotten fish, sweat and booze some old enough to be her grandfather, they leered at her over the counter, making suggestive drunken remarks as if they stood a chance.

Her father thought it was all good fun, and had even suggested that it was her presence which brought such punters in.

She hated her father for being such a miser that he insisted to staying open to pander to such idiots. Not to mention the fact he refused to pay for extra staff to cover the late shifts.

Amy did not wish her father's demise to come any sooner than nature intended, but when it did finally happen, she swore to herself she would never set foot in the shop again. Being his only heir, Amy knew that he had left her the business, but she had already decided that she would either hire staff to run it, or sell up altogether and move somewhere where she – and her reputation – were unknown.

Yes, the compensations of working for her father were definitely few and far between. She had her little car, which she loved, and the freedom to do what she wanted on Sundays. But other than that…

Then one of the rare "compensations" joined the end of the queue.

Amy looked up and felt her heart skip. She had seen him in here before, though he was not local. She assumed he was one of the labourers a local landowner had drafted in to build his extension. There were about a dozen of them, all staying at a local B&B whilst they completed the work.

She was pretty sure his name was Pete, having heard one of his mates calling him that on an earlier visit. Amy stole a glance while she was wrapping a portion of sausage and chips. Her eyes roamed over his body. He was wearing tight jeans which emphasised his tiny butt and a white T-shirt which showed off his perfect six-pack.

As Amy's eyes drifted up to his face, she realised he had caught her checking him out. He gave her a broad smile. She felt her face flush as she tried to return the compliment, before focusing back on the task at hand.

As Pete moved steadily closer, Amy could feel her whole body starting to shake. She had to play it cool. She knew men did not like girls who were over eager.

Then he was standing right in front of her. Amy felt her heart in her throat, almost making her want to cough. She managed to stifle it.

"Yes, love." She smiled, flushing again. "What can I get for you?"

Pete ordered for all his friends. Amy wondered if he had asked to do that, or one of them had suggested it as a wind-up. It was obvious to anyone looking on that Amy had the hots for him.

While her father began preparing the order, Pete paid. As Amy counted back his change to him, he leaned in closer. "What time do you get off work then?" he asked, smiling.

Amy tried as best she could to keep her cool.

She glanced up at the clock. "In 'bout twenty minutes," she replied, nonchalantly. "Why?"

"Well, I was wondering if you fancied a walk along the beach, clear the cobwebs?" Amy stole a glance at his friends at the back of the shop. There was plenty of nudging and sniggering going on, and she wondered if this was all a cruel joke. Pete certainly sounded genuine. Or was it just her hoping that he was!

Amy began wrapping his order. "That would be nice," she replied, pretending to concentrate on adding the salt and vinegar. "I often go for a stroll after being stuck in 'ere all day."

Pete leaned on the counter. She could smell his aftershave, she liked it.

"So do you fancy going for a walk tonight with me?" He obviously wasn't shy, but Amy liked the fact that he also didn't sound too overconfident.

"Okay, then," she smiled, handing over his order. "I'll meet you outside the *'Lots-of-Fun'* arcade when I'm done 'ere."

"Lovely." Pete grinned, showing off a set of perfectly white teeth. "I'll look forward to it."

After closing time, Amy left her father to finish tidying up whilst she slipped upstairs to the flat they shared above the shop. She splashed some water on her face and applied her make-up. She could have really done with a shower, but she was afraid if she took too long that Pete might not wait around. She changed her clothes, pulling on a light summer dress, and doused herself with perfume to cover any odour of grease which might be lingering.

She took a moment to check herself out in the full-length mirror. She wished she could ditch the glasses. She had tried contacts, but due to her prescription, they were very awkward to put in and take out, and she had always been a bit squeamish about anything being too close to her eyes, so she went back to her glasses.

Pete was sitting on the low wall outside the amusement arcade as promised.

When Amy saw him she waved, trying not to look over-enthusiastic. She glanced around looking for his mates, still half-suspecting that this was a wind-up. But there was no sign of them. Still, she thought it best to play it with caution.

"Where're your friends?" she asked, casually.

Pete shrugged. "Not sure, gone off for a lark in one of the arcades, I think." He looked around. "They stay open late around here," he observed.

"Yea, during the summer season they do. During the winter, most of 'em stay shut. It's only the tourists that make it worth 'em keepin' open."

"Oh, I see." Pete looked back at Amy. "I like your dress." He smiled.

"Oh, thanks." The compliment took her by surprise, but at least he was trying. "I usually only wear dresses on Sunday as it's me day off. It's not worth making the effort in the shop; they'd only be ruined."

Pete laughed. "Yes, I suppose so."

They both looked about them in an uneasy silence. Neither of them quite sure what to say or who should make the first move.

Finally, Pete spoke up. "So where do you fancy going for this walk then?"

"Well," replied Amy, glad that he had moved things along, "it's nice an' quiet up at Skullen Bay this time of night."

"Where's that?"

"About three miles up the coast road," replied Amy, signalling and pointing in the general direction.

"Oh," said Pete, surprised. "Sounds like a bit of a trek."

"Me cars round the corner," offered Amy. "It'll only take a couple of minutes in that."

"Now you're talking," said Pete, putting his arm around her shoulders and giving her a gentle squeeze.

On the drive up the coast road, Pete's hand strayed on to Amy's knee. She giggled as he gently slid it under her skirt and up her thigh. She could feel her knickers slowly becoming damp through the flimsy fabric. When Pete noticed she was wet, he slipped a finger under the band and expertly began to arouse her.

Amy began to squirm. This was so nice; she could feel herself starting to orgasm. Her eyes closed in a moment of euphoric bliss.

The mad honking of the approaching lorry brought her back to earth.

Amy swerved to avoid the vehicle, realising she had strayed onto the wrong side of the road. Pete fell back in his seat, his quest suspended for the time being and replaced with the task of preparing for a crash. He crossed his arms in front of him and closing his eyes, pressed himself hard back into his seat, awaiting the impending impact.

Miraculously, Amy missed the lorry. She swerved around it then back on to the wrong side of the road, before finally bringing the vehicle under control and travelling in the right direction.

Pete let out a long gasp.

"Oh my God," he yelled, his voice higher than before.

"That was your fault," Amy retorted, slapping him on the arm.

The slap caught Pete by surprise. "Ow!" he yelped, rubbing his arm. "Why do I get the blame? You seemed to be enjoying yourself as I remember."

Amy laughed. "'at's not the point."

Relaxed after their near miss, Pete leaned over and put his hand back on Amy's thigh.

She slapped it away. "No, bad boy. You can wait 'til we get there. It's only over the next ridge!"

Pete reluctantly removed his hand and sat around, facing the front, his bottom lip protruding in a false pout.

They parked up overlooking one of the more remote parts of the bay. Once she had applied the handbrake, Amy turned towards Pete and they began kissing and fondling each other without saying anything.

Amy could feel herself getting aroused again. Pete had one hand massaging her breast, and the other snaked under the band of her panties, gently stroking her moist passage with his middle finger. Amy moaned softly. She could feel herself starting to orgasm. She pulled Pete in closer as her passion mounted, forcing her eager tongue into his mouth, prodding, searching, meeting his in a challenge for supremacy.

Amy let out a soft moan. Pete felt her climax. He continued surveying her with his finger, plunging in deeper, trying to cover her entire chasm.

Amy slid her hand down between Pete's legs and squeezed his erection through the tight denim of his jeans. Now it was his turn to moan. Amy smiled at the look of anticipatory contentment on his face while she rubbed her palm up and down his shaft slowly, then faster, then slowly again before squeezing the throbbing bulb at the end of his penis.

Pete, suddenly aware that he was about to explode in his underwear, moved Amy's hand away and lifted her skirt whilst simultaneously slipping her panties down her thighs.

She stopped him

"Nah, not here, Pete. Not in the car, it's too cramped and awkward."

Pete's face registered a moment's disappointment. "Where then, babe?" he asked, almost pleading.

Amy nodded past him. "Down there on the beach; there'll be no one around at this time. I've got a towel in the back we can spread on the sand."

They made their way down towards the water's edge, the wet sand giving way under Amy's weight, seeping over the rims of her sandals and becoming wedged between her toes. She hated that feeling and wished now that she had worn her trainers instead. But the sandals were very pretty and they showed off her feet. She had always been proud of her feet which belied her size by their elegance; especially when she could be bothered to paint her toenails.

They laid out the towel and Amy removed her dress and underwear, giving Pete a complete view of her ample proportions. Though she was on the big side, Amy had never really been ashamed of her body, regardless of some of the cruel remarks she often heard in passing. And besides, she knew that a lot of men liked larger women – she had been with several of them already.

Amy folded her dress into a neat pile, and placed her handbag on top to stop it blowing away. She went down on all fours and turning herself, lay sprawled on the towel. The soft fabric felt soothing and comforting against her back. She brought her knees up until she had one foot flat down on either side of the towel, her legs parted, invitingly.

Pete had ripped off his T-shirt and flung it to one side. He did not bother to remove his jeans, merely pulled them down to his knees along with his boxers. Amy could just make out his erection in the dim light. Having left her glasses in the car, everything was still a bit of a blur, but she knew that he was ready. She would have preferred more foreplay at this point, but she didn't want to tease him. And besides, he had already let her come once, so it was her turn to repay the compliment.

Pete joined her on the towel. She felt him prod her just above the pelvis. He was kissing her neck and squeezing her breasts. Amy stroked his bare bottom, then slid her hand underneath and guided him inside her. They both moaned in unison.

For ten minutes in the cool night air, their bodies joined as one. They jerked and wobbled up and down until with a shudder Amy felt Pete explode inside her. He stayed inside her for a while, exhausted. The warmth of their shared intimacy caused a thin film of perspiration to form between them, lubricating their flesh while they slid up and down, and leaving a sticky residue once the performance was over.

Pete withdrew and slumped down beside Amy, breathing hard. Now that she was uncovered, Amy suddenly felt the cold rush of the sea breeze enveloping her, causing her flesh to goose pimple. She missed the warmth of Pete's body, and wished he had remained inside her a little longer. She had often pondered why it was most men felt the need to extricate themselves immediately having juiced. One of her friends once told her it was because they were afraid of becoming stuck inside like some animals did. Then the only release would be to have a bucket of water thrown over them. Amy had laughed at the time. She could not imagine anyone getting stuck inside her, regardless of how big they were.

After a moment, Pete sat up, leaning on one elbow.

"Babe, I just wondered, we are alright...Aren't we?"

Amy looked at him, puzzled. "Alright, 'ow do you mean?"

A sudden cloud of concern crossed Pete's face. "I mean, we are covered, yeah?"

"Covered, 'ow?" Amy knew exactly what he meant, but continued playing dumb.

Pete was starting to feel embarrassed. "I mean, I've got some in me wallet, but I sort of got carried away, so I wanted to make sure that you...Took something?"

Amy could not contain herself anymore; she burst out laughing. "It's okay," she said, giggling. "I'm on the pill if 'at's what you wanted to know."

Pete was obviously relieved. He lay back down expelling a long breath.

Amy shivered. The sea breeze was growing stronger, but she was in no hurry to cover up. She edged closer to Pete and pulled one his arms around her. He took the hint and moved in for a cuddle.

Amy closed her eyes and focused on the sound of the water lapping at the beach. The gulls had all turned in for the night, so the only other sounds to reach her ears were from an occasional car passing above, and the distant intermittent wail of a ship's horn out at sea.

She felt totally relaxed after another arduous week at work. This was the perfect way to unwind. Tomorrow being Sunday, she would take a long drive along the coast road and find a good spot for lunch. She wondered if it would be worth asking Pete if he wanted to tag along. They could stop off at one of the trail parks and go for a long walk in the woods – taking the towel, naturally.

She felt herself starting to drift off.

Suddenly, Pete screamed!

The sound shook Amy out of her reverie. She opened her eyes and sat up, focusing through the darkness. Pete was blocking her view, scrambling, trying to stand, his feet failing to make purchase on the wet sand; twice he fell back on his knees. Pete screamed in frustration, grabbed hold of his jeans and boxers and tried to pull them up as he rose.

It was only then that Amy could make out the dark shapes climbing up the beach towards them. Though somewhat out of focus, they looked like huge snakes striking out, their frenzied flailing bodies slapping against the wet sand, allowing them to slither further up the beach towards them. And behind them, the snakes seemed to be dragging something even more monstrous closer to the lovers, to seal their fate.

Amy's mind raced. She still was not sure what she was looking at, but whatever it was, she knew she did not want to be there anymore.

As she tried to lift herself up, Pete, still struggling with his pants, fell forward on top of her, his left knee jamming hard in her belly. The force knocked the wind out of her, and Amy fell back holding her stomach.

Pete leapt over her, and as Amy rolled on her side, she could see him running up the beach.

He's leaving me! Leaving me to face this thing on my own! Bastard!

Then, as if remembering his partner, Pete turned back and half-slid, half-ran towards her. Amy stretched out her hand to him, but Pete ignored it. Bending down next to her, Pete riffled through Amy's handbag until he found her car keys. He grabbed them, dropping the open bag back on the sand.

Amy could not believe what was happening!

Not only was Pete willing to leave her behind, he had the cheek to try and use her car to make his get-a-way.

Amy rolled back. The nearest snake was only a few feet away from her foot. She instinctively pulled it back and tried to shift herself back. Her breathing was coming easier now, Pete's blow finally wearing off.

She could hear Pete scrambling frantically behind her. Amy pushed herself up on her knees and grabbed her dress and bag. She could not force herself to look behind her, but she could hear the snakes sliding closer, and the huge apparition behind them had starting to make a low hissing, slurping noise as they dragged it forward.

Amy could feel their presence close behind her. She threw herself forward up the beach, only gaining a few feet. She could see Pete in front of her, still trying to gain ground without much success, his feet almost running on the spot as he flicked sand behind him.

Amy stayed on all fours and thrust herself forward again. Moving like an overgrown drunken crab, she managed to make headway and was soon almost side by side with Pete. He looked over at her. His eyes bulged in a half-apologetic, half-scared witless type of stare.

Just then, an enormous snake shot forward and wrapped itself around Pete's leg. Pete shrieked. Turning on his back, he tried frantically to kick it away with his free foot, but it was to no avail.

The creature had a firm hold of its prey, and was not likely to give it up so easily.

Amy froze in fear and panic. She turned and watched as Pete was dragged kicking and screaming towards the huge bulk which the snakes had been dragging behind them. But now Amy's eyes had focused enough so that she could see that they were not dragging it, they were attached to it – it was part of whatever these things were!

The huge blob opened its plate-sized eyes, glaring red fury at Amy's slumped form. Two more of the creature's tentacles had wrapped themselves around Pete, and he was almost now at the blob.

Amy could not watch. Yet she could not compel herself to turn away either.

Pete's next scream spurred her into action, and she frantically continued scrabbling up the beach. The sand beneath her feet became encrusted with shingle, cutting into her soles and making her squeal in pain as she ran. She slipped, regained her balance and moved forward, slipped again, this time grazing her knee on a sharp jagged rock protruding from the sand. She felt the creature upon her, taking advantage of her cumbersome attempt at escape. She could almost feel the heat of the creature's fetid breath on her back, imagined one of those menacing tentacles just about to envelope her in a hug of death before dragging her limp body back towards its ravenous mouth. She fell again. Defeated and too exhausted to try anymore, she lay slumped on the ground, waiting for death.

After a few seconds, she turned and looked back. The creature was nowhere near her. She squinted to try and get a better view, and could just make out a mass tangle of tentacles and Pete's body flailing wildly in their clutches.

Amy, spurred on by the realisation that she still had a chance of survival, took in a deep breath and thrust herself forward up the beach on all fours. Finally, she came to rest against the railings which separated the beach from the pavement.

Gasping for breath, she turned back. Through the haziness of her blurred vision, Amy could just make out the huge blob and its snake-like appendages moving over the wet sand back to the sea.

Pete's cries had ceased, and through the darkness, she could not tell if he had been left behind on the sand or not.

She waited until her breathing came easier. The blob was nowhere in sight, but neither was Pete, as far as she could tell. She looked around in the hazy darkness but she could not see anyone nearby.

Amy turned back towards the beach and called for Pete. There was no reply.

She climbed through the railings and leaned against her car to steady herself while she slipped her sandals back on, dusting the soles of her feet as she did so.

The streets were completely deserted. She could just about make out some lights shining from the houses in the village, but she decided she would rather not disturb anyone at this hour of the morning, regardless of the circumstances. And besides, leaving the lights on did not necessarily mean that the occupants were awake. Often people left the lights on overnight for security.

She knew that there was no use trying to search the sand for her car keys. And besides, Pete might have taken them with him–wherever he was now!

What's more, Amy did not want to take the risk of that "Thing", whatever it was, emerging from the waves again and coming after her.

She found her mobile in her bag and called her father, straining to make sure she hit the correct contact number. She wondered what he would have to say when she told him her tale of the night's events.

CHAPTER EIGHT

The phone on the bedside table burst into life, shattering the pre-dawn silence. Oswald Seaton glanced at the clock; it was 2:15am. He knew that whatever the news was, it would not be good. Grabbing the receiver, he rubbed the sleep from his eyes.

"Alton Police, Sgt. Seaton speaking,"

On the other end was a very frantic Harry Friar. As he relayed the tale his daughter Amy had just told him, Seaton felt the blood drain from his face. He sat up straight, shifting back until he was resting against the wooden headboard. He knew that Harry Friar was not the kind of person to play practical jokes, his daughter perhaps, but if there had been any doubt in Harry's mind that she was not in earnest, he would never have called the station, especially not at such an hour.

The more Harry spoke, the worse the situation sounded to Seaton. Unlike old Sam, Amy was a much more reliable witness, and one he would have to give credence to. That, and the fact that Harry was saying that a young lad was also killed by the thing from the water, meant he could potentially be the third victim – if Sam was to be believed – so far with very little action from the local police force, for which he must take responsibility.

Seaton had never heard Harry sound so agitated. The usual gruff voice had been replaced by a ninety-mile-an-hour squeak which rose dramatically in pitch at the end of each sentence. When Seaton realised that Harry was starting to repeat himself, he cut him off.

"Look, Harry, are you calling from your place?"

"What...?" the man seemed momentarily confused, as if losing his train of thought had thrown him completely. "Yes, I've been trying to calm Amy down; she's been hysterical, poor darlin'. Her brand new car is still up there and she's too scared to go and collect it, even with me, she's refusing to go anywhere near that place again, even says she wants us to move away from the area, and who can blame her?"

Seaton started to get out of bed. "Alright, Harry, listen, just do what you can to keep her calm and I'll be over as soon as I can, alright?"

"Yes, okay mate, oh my God this is terrible, what the hell is that thing?"

Seaton sighed. "I've no idea, mate, just stay with her and I'll be over soon, okay?"

As Seaton dressed, he considered calling his team together. A report like this – especially added to the ones from Sam – needed a thorough investigation. He would probably need to report the incident to headquarters, not to mention calling in the coastguard, and if the papers got hold of it, it did not even bear thinking about.

Looking at the clock again he decided that it might be more prudent to see what Amy Friar had to say once she was coherent, and by the sound of it, that could take a while.

Seaton arrived at the fish shop half an hour later. He parked around the back of the shop; not that he expected many people to see his official car parked in the high street at this hour, but the sight of it might cause gossip he could do without.

He found Harry and Amy sitting at the dining table in the living room at the back of the shop. Harry had his arm around his daughter whilst she tucked into the most massive portion of fish and chips Seaton had ever seen. The fish itself took up half the dish with each end hanging over the plate. There was a massive dollop of mushy peas covering the chips and a second plate next to it with even more chips piled up high.

Amy barely acknowledged Seaton entering the room; far too busy concentrating on her food. Her cheeks were still stained from tears, and there was a mountain of crumpled tissues scattered around the table, next to a half-empty box.

Seaton sat himself down opposite her. He took out his notebook and pen, hoping that Amy would take the hint and stop eating long enough to make a statement, but he soon realised that that was not going to happen.

He decided to soldier on regardless. "Now, Amy love, your dad 'ere tells me that you had a bit of a fright down at Skullen Bay last night, do you want to tell me about it?"

The girl looked up at him as she shovelled a huge fork loaded with chips into her mouth. She began talking while she was chewing. Seaton concentrated on his notebook. "I went up to the Bay with this bloke 'oo comes into the shop, 'e 'aint local or nothing, but 'e asked me out and I liked 'im."

"I'm always tellin' her about goin' off with blokes she don't know," Harry piped in, "but you know what girls 'er age are like."

"Dad, leave it out!" Seaton looked up just in time to see a globule of ketchup trickle down the girl's chin as she talked. Realising that she was oblivious to it, Seaton reached over and handed her a fresh tissue from the box.

"You can say leave it out," Harry retorted, his face starting to flush, "but one of these fine days, my girl, you'll go too far with one of 'em blokes, and' end up Gawd knows where!"

Seaton tried to bring the conversation back to his reason for being there. "So, Amy, what was the name of this lad?"

"Pete...some'ink, I think 'e did tell me, but I've forgotten now."

"And 'oo can blame 'er after what she saw." Harry gave his daughter a comforting hug. "You tell 'im what you saw, girl."

At last, thought Seaton, trying to look concerned.

Amy put down her knife and fork and wiped her mouth with the back of her hand. "Well," she began, "we wus on the beach up at Skullen like I said, and we were jus'…" she glanced quickly at her father, "…sort of 'avin' a cuddle, you know? Anyway, all of a sudden this bleedin' great thing comes out the water an' grabs 'im. Dragged 'im into the sea…It were orrible!"

She dived back into her plate before Seaton could say anything more.

Just then, an alarm started to beep from the kitchen area of the shop. Harry excused himself and disappeared through the adjoining door.

Seaton continued. "Okay, Amy, this thing you saw, can you describe to me what it looks like?"

"No, not really." She shovelled in a huge piece of fish. As she crunched down on crispy, freshly prepared batter, Seaton noticed mushy peas oozing out from the sides of her mouth and slopping back onto her plate.

Seaton winced. "Why's that then?" he asked, hoping in vain that she might not answer until she had finished masticating.

"Well I didn't 'ave me glasses on, an' I wus runnin' away from it up the beach an' trippin' an' fallin' a lot, an' by the time I reached the road, it were gone like."

"And the boy?"

Amy swallowed hard, and her eyes began to swell again. "Well, it got 'im, didn't it? Grabbed 'old of 'im and took 'im back in the sea wiv it!"

Seaton saw a new tear streak its way down her cheek. He reached over to grab a fresh tissue for her. Just at that moment, Harry re-appeared carrying something on a plate. He placed it next to Amy's dinner with pride.

"There you go, babe, jus' what the doc ordered."

The tears were now forgotten. Amy stared at the object on the plate, and then looked back up at her father. "But, Dad, I said a large bar," she wined.

Harry sighed. "Oh, I'm sorry, princess, you did too. Tell you what, you finish that one and I'll make you another, 'ow's that?"

Amy was not impressed by her father's solution, but seemed to accept it. Begrudgingly, she returned to her food.

Seaton looked over, curious. "May I ask what that is?" He pointed to Harry's latest production with his pen.

Harry smiled. "Fried *Mars* bar, speciality of the 'ouse. Want one?" he offered, congenially.

Seaton held up his hand. "Thanks all the same, Harry, not sure my cholesterol would cope." He turned back to the girl who had now started on the chips from her second plate. "So Amy, tell me, do you know where this Pete boy lives?"

Amy thought for a moment thinking, then replied, "I know that it's a guest 'ouse somewhere 'round 'ere, I think 'e said it was called The Pigeon Coup, or The Pigeon's Nest, or some'ink like that. He said there were a bunch of 'em staying there from the same building firm. Their guv'nor put them up there while they're working out at the Grange, building some'ink for the new owner."

Seaton copied all this down. "Well that's very helpful, thank you, Amy, I should at least be able to make some inquiries there tomorrow." Seaton turned to a fresh page. "Now getting back to this creature you saw, I know you said you didn't have your glasses on, and that you were running away from it, but is there anything whatsoever you can remember about it? The shape? The size, maybe? What colour it was?"

Amy thought again, her fork stopped halfway to her mouth, a couple of chips fell from it and landed back in her plate. She didn't seem to notice. "Well," she offered, eventually, "it had bloomin' great big like arms or some'ink, you know." She looked at Seaton, expectantly. "Like what an octopus has!"

"You mean tentacles?" offered Seaton.

Amy's eyes lit up. "Yeah, that's it, like wackin' great tentrickles." Her best effort, Seaton decided not to bother correcting her. "Only a hundred times bigger an' thicker than anything what I've seen before; Ooohhh 'orrible they were." She shivered involuntarily. "Yer won't get me goin' back there again!"

"She doesn't even want to come with me to collect 'er new car, like I told yer over the phone. Who can blame 'er? Little mite." Harry gave his daughter another comforting squeeze, and she smiled back at him with a face covered in discarded ketchup and mushy peas.

When Seaton arrived back at the station, it was almost 4:30am. The sun had started to peek through the eastern sky as he pulled his patrol car into its allotted space. He had too much going on in his mind to consider returning to bed. He might have taken Amy's story with a pinch of salt under other circumstances, but added to Sam's report, it was too coincidental for comfort.

The question was, what to do now?

Even with the two corroborating stories, he was not about to call headquarters and suggest that they launch a sea monster hunt in his town. They would be laughing at him until he retired. His name would become a byword for histrionics in the force. He could imagine some of the officers he had worked with in London having a good laugh at his expense. *"Oh, you've just seen Prince Phillip riding naked down the strand, you've got Seaton's Syndrome, mate!"*

The question was though, where should he go from here? He could not just ignore what the girl had said. After all, she might not be the most reliable of eyewitnesses, especially without her glasses, but the fact remained that she saw something, and whatever it was had carried off her boyfriend.

Seaton decided that his first port of call was to verify whether or not the boy in question was missing. After all, it might just have been a silly prank orchestrated by the lad and his mates.

Seaton glanced at his watch; it was still too early to make inquiries at the Grange, and as Amy could not remember the exact name of the guest house he was staying at, that was his best and only option to verify the story.

It would be several hours yet before his team started arriving for work, so he decided to make the best use of the time by typing up the girl's witness statement. He would get one of his constables to take it back tomorrow for her to sign. He wondered now if he should get old Sam to sign his, just in case. He had not bothered about it before, but he was glad now that he had taken to the trouble to formally log it.

His mind could still not get to grips with the two reports; *giant sea monsters*, what next? King Kong climbing the local shopping centre and being shot down by the RAF?

He thought for a moment. As crazy as it sounded, he wondered if it might be worth his while speaking to the curator of the local maritime museum. He had met her in the pub the other night; in fact, now he came to think of it, it was she who had found *Cappy's* old hat on the beach, so maybe he should take an official statement from her. Just in case. At least he could use that as his excuse to go and see her, before slipping into the conversation the bit about sea monsters.

His mind made up, Seaton walked into the kitchen and made himself a strong coffee to help him stay awake while he was waiting for his constables to arrive.

He decided that in view of their reactions when he told them about what Sam had said, he would tell them about Amy's account first thing.

He needed the reassurance of having them on his side with this one.

***

Dan was quite proud of himself for remembering to set his alarm for 5:45am. Now that it was beeping loudly in his ear, the idea did not seem so wonderful. He had been disappointed the previous evening for not seeing Caitlin in the bar. After his third pint, he decided that it was probably too late for her to put in an appearance, so he returned to the boat, starting to feel drowsy.

Tammi was already fast asleep by the time he climbed on deck. The cool sea air had perked him up on the way back from the pub, so typically now he was not feeling tired. He decided to sit up on deck for a while and gaze out to sea with another beer for company. He had always loved the calming effect the sight of the open water had on his spirit. He could not imagine living anywhere – should he ever decide to swap his boat for something more substantial – that was not within easy reach of the open water. The thought of being cooped up in some vast sprawling town with too many people crammed in on top of each other and no sea to escape to, was his idea of hell on earth.

He may not have been cursed with the ambition of some of his peers, but he was content for now. He had his own boat, his own business, an excellent crew member of one, and he could pretty much do what he wanted and see whomever he chose, whenever he wanted.

That brought his mind back to Caitlin. He had decided that he would definitely like to see more of her. That was when he decided to make the effort to rise early enough to catch her walking her dog on the beach.

Now, however, as he switched off his alarm, his late night and accompanying libations made rising from the pit very much like hard work.

With a supreme effort, Dan jolted himself into life and swung his legs out of bed. Pulling on his jeans and working boots, he selected a clean shirt and made his way to the bathroom. He decided that he still smelt fresh enough after last evening's shower, so just through some water on his face to freshen up. He brushed his teeth and gargled with strong mouthwash to eradicate the aftertaste of the previous evening's nightcap.

Looking at himself in the mirror, he decided not to shave. His stubble was only a few days old, and besides, if he shaved whilst half-asleep, there was a good chance he would cut himself, and that was not a good look for him.

He pulled on his shirt, leaving it unbuttoned as he made his way back to his bedroom to find some deodorant.

Ten minutes later, Dan emerged from below deck and gazed out along the deserted beach. His heart sank when he could not see any sign of Caitlin or her dog. All this effort for nothing, he thought despondently.

He decided to brew some coffee to help wake him up. He reasoned that all was not lost and that Caitlin might still put in an appearance before the morning was over. He considered taking a stroll along the beach himself, just in case she might be farther down towards the town road, but decided that even if she was it was a relatively small beach, and if she had taken the trouble to drive this far up from town, she would surely end up on this stretch eventually.

When Dan climbed back on deck with his coffee, his heart skipped a beat. There in the distance was Caitlin climbing the railing to gain access to the beach, her golden retriever Honey bounding along in front of her, chasing a ball.

Dan absentmindedly took a sip from his mug; the hot liquid scorched his tongue first then his throat on the way down to his stomach. He almost dropped the mug as he concentrated on trying not to scream out in pain. He felt the liquid burning his insides as he took several deep breaths to try and dissipate the uncomfortable ache starting to form in his belly.

Just then, he noticed Caitlin looking his way. Blocking the soreness inside, he raised his hand and waved a greeting. Caitlin returned the gesture, and then turned her attention back to Honey who presented her with her returned toy.

Between the dull ache which had now formed in the pit of his stomach and the burning sensation in his throat, both caused by the hot coffee, he now also felt his heart begin to pound as well. He felt like a teenager about to ask a crush out on a first date in front of his mates and admonished himself for it. This was ridiculous; he was a grown man who had never really had any trouble finding women. So why was he suddenly feeling so clumsy?

He considered it might be because he found Caitlin so attractive. Which on the face of it was normal, she was a stunning woman after all. But, in reality, he did not even know yet whether she was available, let alone interested. She might be gay for all he knew.

He waited. He could just sit there drinking his coffee and see if Caitlin made her way past his boat. If she stopped to talk, that would be a good indication. But what if she did not pass his way at all? What if she stayed at the far end of the beach? What if she walked out passed the fishing boats and back without ever coming near him?

Dan checked himself. This was stupid! He had intentionally set his alarm in the hope of seeing Caitlin, and now here she was within striking distance, and here he was and procrastinating.

Enough! He thought to himself. Putting his mug down, Dan climbed down the gangplank and strode purposefully towards Caitlin, his hands shoved deep in his jean pockets to prevent them looking awkward when he walked.

"Hi there," he called when he was within hearing distance.

"Hello again," replied Caitlin, throwing the ball for Honey to chase again.

"I thought it was you," Dan offered, trying to sound nonchalant. "Has that officer been back to you yet regarding the old man whose cap you found?" Not exactly the best opening gambit he decided, but at least the ice had broken.

"No, not yet," said Caitlin, holding up a hand to shield her eyes from the morning sunshine. "Do you know if anyone else has seen him since then?"

Dan shook his head. "Not to my knowledge; I certainly haven't seen him occupying his favourite chair in the pub. To be honest, I was there last night but didn't think to ask the landlord." Then, as an afterthought, he added, "Sorry."

"Not to worry." Caitlin smiled. "I just can't help thinking about what that old tramp on the beach told me. I know it all sounds fantastic, but I'd feel a lot better if the old man suddenly turned up and there was an innocent explanation for everything."

"I can understand that," Dan offered, sympathetically.

Just then Honey came bounding up to them and dropped her ball in front of them. Dan bent down to offer his hand in friendship. The dog barked and backed away, lowering her tail.

"Honey!" Caitlin called, reproachfully.

Dan stayed where he was. "That's okay." He laughed. "Women are often apprehensive about us sailors in the beginning, but deep down we are all wonderful people."

"Really?" said Caitlin, amused. "That big bloke in the pub the other night didn't seem to think you were so wonderful."

Dan laughed. "Big Jake? He and I are old sparring partners, don't you worry about him."

Honey had begun to edge closer to Dan's outstretched hand. Eventually, her wet snout made contact as she sniffed out the stranger. After a few seconds, Dan risked a head rub. The dog reacted favourably, letting him continue. Dan was pleased; this was progress.

He turned his attention back to Caitlin. "See," he said, confidently, "she knows a good man when she sees one."

At that moment, Honey launched herself forward, knocking Dan off balance. As he sprawled out on the ground, Honey moved in and started licking his upturned face.

"Honey, no!" Caitlin grabbed the dog by her collar and pulled her off him.

Dan sat up on the sand, wiping his face with the back of his hand.

The pair of them burst into fits of laughter.

Caitlin tried an apology a few times, but she found it impossible to get the words out properly.

Eventually, Dan rose to his feet and threw Honey's ball into the distance for her to chase.

Turning to Caitlin, he asked, "Does that mean I'm in the 'Honey loves Dan' club?"

Caitlin's laughter subsided. "Most definitely." She began to help him brush sand from his clothes. Dan tried not to make it too obvious that he was enjoying the delicate feel of her soft hands on his body. He wished that he had decided to wear shorts, and then thought better of it. At least the denim of his jeans concealed his growing erection to some extent.

They walked along the beach talking casually. Dan tried his best to find out what Caitlin's romantic situation was without making it obvious. But consciously or not, she was not giving anything away.

In between turns at throwing Honey's ball, they walked to the end of the harbour and back again. The more Caitlin talked, the more Dan liked her. She had a very easy-going nature, and as they both shared a love of the sea, the conversation flowed.

When they arrived back at Caitlin's car, Dan found himself at that awkward moment when he did not know whether it was the right time to ask her out on a date or not.

He chickened out!

As they said their goodbyes and Dan turned to head back to his boat, he did not see the look of disappointment on Caitlin's face.

He listened from behind as she ushered Honey back into the car and slammed the hatchback shut.

As Dan heard Caitlin open the driver's door, he suddenly found his courage. Turning, he called out. "Caitlin, do you like French cuisine?"

"Love it," replied Caitlin, without stopping to think.

Dan walked back a few paces towards her so as not to have to shout too loudly for her to hear him above the distant sound of the incoming tide.

"It's just that I know this wonderful little bistro which serves the most marvellous seafood."

Caitlin stood on the doorframe of her car so that she could see him clearly, holding onto the roof for support. "Sounds gorgeous. Where is it? In town?"

"No, just outside Boulogne," said Dan, with a straight face. "If we leave around five-ish, we should get there just in time for dinner."

Caitlin burst out laughing, again.

Dan kept a straight face, though inside he was killing himself. "Is that a yes, then?" he asked, hopefully.

When Caitlin stopped laughing enough to be able to speak, she thought for a moment before saying. "Lovely and romantic though it sounds, do you think we could start off somewhere a little closer to home?"

Dan shrugged nonchalantly, but he could not stop a huge grin from invading his face. "Okay then, have you got a favourite in town?"

Caitlin smiled back. "Well, now you've got me in the mood for French cuisine. There is a little place not too far from the museum that I have been promising myself I would try."

"Excellent," said Dan, trying not to explode with excitement. "Shall I pick you up at about seven-thirty?"

"Great, I'll book us a table."

They waved goodbye to each other and Dan waited for Caitlin to drive away.

He walked back to his vessel, rubbing his hands together and whistling to himself. He could not remember the last time he was this excited about anything!

CHAPTER NINE

Seaton's constables began arriving a little before eight o'clock. First was Ralph Carmody, whose entrance was signalled by him pushing the main door too hard, causing it to crash into the concrete ledge behind it. The noise stirred Seaton from his doze. She had finally slipped off into slumber just after seven o'clock with his feet propped up on his desk and his police cap pulled down to cover his eyes from the light.

Seeing his governor up and at his desk this early was a definite sign to the young constable that something must have happened during the night. In such instances, Seaton always responded alone, not wishing to disturb his team unless it was absolutely necessary.

While Ralph made fresh coffee, he asked his governor about the previous night's events, but Seaton held off, stating he wanted to tell them all together to save repeating it. In truth, he was still a little hesitant regarding how to proceed, and he was hoping one of his constables might be able to come up with something constructive.

By eight-thirty, everyone was in. Once they had all sorted themselves out and were seated in his office with a brew, Seaton informed them of his visit to see Amy Friar in the early hours.

Seaton watched the expressions on their faces change as he related her statement to them. He knew that they all had the same thought as him. It was one thing hearing this nonsense for old Sam Cleary, but now he had a much more credible witness who people would believe. He could not afford to sit back and ignore this; he had to act before things grew out of hand.

Once he was finished, there was a stunned silence in the room. Seaton looked at the faces of his squad members and asked in general if any of them had any thoughts.

Eventually, Sally piped up. "Well, guv, I'd say first thing we need to do is see if we can locate this Pete character," she offered, hesitantly. "After all, if he is at work this morning, then either the whole thing was a practical joke by him and his mates on Amy, or she has just made the whole thing up."

"Why would she make up such a stupid story though?" asked Joe. "What would she have to gain by it?"

"P'raps she just wants to be the centre of attention," offered Ralph, before emptying his mug.

"Well, if that's the case, she will soon find herself on a charge of wasting police time!" stated Seaton, harshly. "But…" He walked back around his desk and sat down. "I have to say, speaking to her, she didn't sound as if she was making it up, as incredible as it sounds."

"Which leaves us with the possibility that we have some kind of monstrous creature from the deep terrorising our town?" Said sally, trying desperately not to sound flippant.

"Excellent," offered Joe, excitedly rubbing his hands together. "This is just like in those documentaries on the history channel. This could even be an unknown species, in which case we might get to name it."

Seaton sighed. "Yes, yes, well, let's not allow ourselves to get too carried away just yet." He took a sip from his coffee; it had gone cold. He winced as he replaced it in his saucer. "Sally's right. For now, we treat this like any other investigation, with good honest police work." He pointed to Sally. "You and Joe get yourselves up to the Grange and start asking after this Pete whatever-'is-name-is, and if no one has seen him since last night, then take as many statements as you can from his mates. There could still be a logical explanation for everything."

"Right 'o, Sarge," replied Sally, half turning to leave before stopping herself. "And if he is there, do you want us to interview him regarding what went on with him and Amy last night? See if he was in on the joke too?"

"Yes, please," replied Seaton. "But if he is there, don't mention Amy's story when you speak to him; just see what he has to say about it all."

"Gotcha, guv." Both officers left the room, leaving Ralph and Seaton alone.

Once he had heard them close the main office door behind them, Ralph spoke up. "Guv, you don't really put any credence into this girl's story, do you?"

Seaton rubbed his chin with his hand. His early start had meant he had not shaved and he could already feel the beginnings of rough stubble sprouting. "Ralph, in all my years in this job, I have heard some pretty daft tales, especially when I was in London, but this one beats them all." He stood up again and went to the filing cabinet where he had placed Sam's statement. He handed the file to Carmody, who took it gingerly.

"You're not going to ask me to do what I think you are, are you, guv?"

Seaton looked at him with a sympathetic expression which gave Carmody the answer he was afraid of even before his senior officer spoke. "I am afraid so, Ralph. As much as I think this is all pie-in-the-sky nonsense, we had to cross all the T's and dot the I's on this one. Because if there is so much as a smidgeon of truth in any of it, you know the big boys will be getting involved, and they will do anything to discredit us bumpkin folk in our sleepy little seaside hide-a-way."

Carmody opened the cardboard file and looked over Sam's statement. Looking back up at Seaton, he asked, "Do you want me to bring him in to go over this, Sarge?"

Seaton shook his head. "No, not yet. Softly, softly for now, let's not raise too many eyebrows, they'll be plenty of that taking place if that Pete character is actually missing. Just take it up to Skullen Bay and find Sam under whatever boat tarp he's hiding and pray he is sober enough to be able to read over it and sign it."

"And if he's not?" Ralph asked half-heartedly, dreading the thought of having to ferry Sam back to the station in his patrol car. Even with the windows open, it would take a week to get the smell out.

Seaton saw the expression on Carmody's face. "Sorry, Ralph," he offered, sympathetically. "We'll need him back here to sober up; he'll never manage it on his own."

Ralph shrugged his shoulders resignedly. "Right you are, guv."

Seaton smiled as the young officer left his office. He hoped for his sake that Sam would be coherent and at least reasonably sober.

***

Sally and Joe drove up the winding gravel path which led to the main entrance of the Grange. The gold-coloured metal frame above the stone arch claimed that the house had been originally built in 1752. As neither of them were locals, the two police constables had no idea of the place's history, but Joe had heard in town that the latest occupants were not related to the original family who owned it. Instead, they were a very snooty couple from London, with three equally stuck-up children, all of whom attended private schools as borders. He had no idea what they did for a living, but judging by the enormity of the property and grounds, he guessed it paid more than he would ever own.

Sally pulled the patrol car up near the security guard's box. The guard was a local man whom Sally had seen around town. He smiled at the new arrivals as he emerged from the confines of his quarters to greet them.

"Mornin', officers." He smiled, cheerfully, bending down to the level of their car window. "And 'ow may I be of assistance?"

Sally, being the more tactful one, leaned across Joe to speak to him. "Good morning, we were wondering if we could have a quiet word with the owners, please?"

"They're away at the moment, I'm afraid," replied the jovial guard, "won't be back until next Thursday."

Sally thought for a moment, and then she said, "To be honest, we really wanted a word with whoever is in charge of the builders you've got working here at the moment. Would it be possible to speak to them instead?"

The guard stood up. "Of course you can." He pointed to his left. "Jus' follow the road around the front of the lawn until you come to a large tented area; you can't see it at the moment as it's 'idden by the trees. But once you go round 'em, you can't miss it. There'll be a port-a-cabin to one side of the tents. Their boss is usually in there; I've seen 'im this morning so I know he's around." The guard turned back to look at Sally. "Name's Hobson, Rod Hobson, 'e's quite a nice bloke. Er, I 'ope none of 'is lads 'ave been up to no-good?" The guard laughed to himself.

Sally smiled. "Nothing like that, thank you." She drove around the lawn following the guard's directions.

They soon located the manager's port-a-cabin, and both of them entered whilst being watched by around twenty assorted suspicious workmen.

They explained the reason behind their visit to the manager, who made it obvious by his expression that he did not appreciate being kept in the dark when he asked why they wanted to speak to one of his lads.

Begrudgingly, he checked his work rota for the day.

"A Pete...somebody, you say." He ran his finger down the page before flipping it over the top of the clipboard to the next one. Eventually, he announced, "I've got a Peter Dodds working here, hasn't shown up for work today." He looked at his wrist watch. "He's usually in by now." He looked up at the officers. "I dock their pay if they're late, puts them off getting too tanked the night before."

Sally and Joe looked at each, a silent *"This isn't good,"* passed between them.

Finally, Sally asked, "Does this Pete Dodds have a particular friend or group that he hangs out with?"

The foreman stood there for a while scratching his head, thinking.

Eventually, he said, "You could do worse than speak to Reg, I'm pretty sure they are drinking buddies. I put a few of them up at the same guest house in town."

"Is there somewhere we could talk to this Reg, in private?" asked Joe, emphasising the "private" part.

The foreman looked perplexed. "Look, I wish you would just tell me what this is all about. I'm trying to run a business here and the timing on this project is very tight with some extremely large delay clauses."

"We'll be as quick as we can," Sally assured him. "And we do appreciate your assistance in this matter."

The foreman looked at them both for a moment; they could both tell that he was not happy with the situation. Slamming his clipboard on his desk, he stormed out of the port-a-cabin, shoving the door open with force and allowing it to swing back on its hinge, rebounding of the caravan's shell before swinging back and closing.

The officers brought chairs and sat down, placing another single one opposite them for Reg when he arrived.

After a few moments, there was a timid knock at the door and Sally called for the person to enter.

Reg Watkins was a skinny youth of about nineteen, with short, cropped hair dyed blonde at the ends, and a silver earring dangling from one ear only. His face was deeply pitted and it was obvious to the two officers that he had at one time suffered from severe acne. A tattoo of green and red peeked over the collar of his shirt, but not enough to see what it was actually meant to be.

Sally signalled for him to join them and he slumped down in the chair provided, not willing to meet either of the officer's gazes.

Sally took her notebook from her uniform pocket and began. "Thank you for agreeing to see us, Mr. Watkins. We are making enquiries concerning Pete Dodds, we believe that he is a friend of yours?"

At the mention of his friend's name, Reg took notice. "What about 'im? Is 'e alright?"

Sally took a breath to allow the question to hang. "When was the last time you either saw or spoke to Mr. Dodds, Reg? May I call you Reg?"

"What…Yea fine, whatever." The young man was growing agitated and began squirming in his seat. "Last night, it was last night, we went out to the pub then Pete started chattin' up this fat bird in the chip shop. Next thing he ses they've got a date, so we left 'im by the arcades and went home."

"And that was the last time you saw him?" inquired Joe.

Reg looked from Sally to Joe. "Yea, that was it, 'e never came back to the guest 'ouse, at least not while I was still awake. Then this morning, 'e wasn't there for breakfast." He looked back to Sally. "I jus' thought he'd pulled lucky and was stayin' at that bird's place. I expected 'im to be this morning though." Reg signalled with his head to the door of the caravan. Lowering his voice, he said, "That miserable bugger nicks 'alf a day's money if yer more than an hour late…Cheap bastard!"

"And you've no idea where he might be, other than with this girl?" asked Sally, trying to keep the excitement out of her voice. This was going to be her first potential murder inquiry, and though she checked herself for it, she found the idea thrilling.

"No," Reg whined, "I told yer. I even tried his mobile twice when he 'adn't arrived and left messages…Wot's 'appened to 'im? 'as that bitch done some'ink to 'im?"

"No, nothing like that," replied Joe, looking at Sally as if for guidance as to what they should do next.

Sally took the hint. Turning the page over in her notebook, she said, "We are going to need to know your contact details please, Reg, just in case we need to speak to you again."

The young man looked worried. He nervously clasped his knees together and began tapping his feet frantically on the thin metal floor. "Look, can't you jus' tell me what's 'appened to Pete? I am 'is mate after all?"

Sally smiled. "As far as we are aware, nothing has happened to him, we would just like to speak to him, that's all."

Once she had scribbled down Reg's details, they thanked him for his time and asked him to send the foreman back in on his way out.

At the door, Reg turned back. His face was ashen; he looked to Sally if as he might be on the verge of tears. "Pete is my mate, see. I've known 'im since we were at school. He got me this job." He cleared his throat before continuing. "You just find 'im, please." There was almost a pleading quality to his tone.

After he had closed the door behind him, Joe turned to Sally. "What do you think then Sal? It's looking more an' more like that chip shop girl might be telling us the truth."

"I know." Sally gazed over her handwritten notes from their interrogation. "The plot definitely thickens." She looked back at her colleague. "Once we get the boy's details from his boss, I can't wait to see the guvnor's face when we tell him what we've found out here today."

"Poor old guv," said Joe, sympathetically. "What do you think he'll do?"

Sally shrugged. "Well, with two potential missing victims, plus that other bloke old Sam told the guv he saw being sacrificed to whatever it is in the water, he'll have to inform the powers that be."

"Then what?" asked Joe, sceptically.

Sally shook her head, slowly. "Then we sit back and let the circus take over!"

***

Seaton strolled slowly through the town. The early afternoon sun was at its apex and dressed in his heavy cotton uniform and black cap with its tight plastic band, he tried desperately to walk in the shade whenever possible. Holiday-makers and locals were all going about their daily routines. He could hear the yelps of excitement coming from the funfair behind the arcades, which mingled with the cacophony of coins rattling their way down the numerous slot machines that packed each of the arcades he passed.

It did not help that he was not in the best frame of mind that afternoon. After Sally and Joe had come back to the station with their report concerning the missing Pete Dodds, Seaton knew that he was going to have to instigate a formal investigation. Ralph had been unable to locate Sam Cleary, either on the beach or in the seaman's hostel he was known to frequent whenever he needed a shower or fancied a proper bed for the night. This did not happen often, as the hostel would not allow Sam to bring any alcohol onto the premises, so it was usually only when he was at his lowest ebb that Sam would give in and use it as a refuge.

Seaton knew that old Sam would turn up sooner or later. Unless he too had been taken by the monster! The thought made him shiver in spite of the weather, but even then it was not so much the fact that they might have a genuine monster in the midst, it was more the fact that he would have to be the one to explain it to his superiors in order to launch an investigation. He could already hear them laughing at him behind his back, but by the same token, he could not risk leaving the incidents unreported only for the whole thing to blow up in his face further down the line as the number of victims grew.

Before he made that phone call, Seaton needed to have something more concrete to offer than an unseen monster. He needed to know what might potentially be out there causing this mayhem. That was when he remembered that the young lady who brought him Cappy's old hat, had told him she worked in the local maritime museum. She had seemed very pleasant that night in the pub, and he hoped not the type to be indiscreet. Seaton was sure that she could give him some vital information which he could use as evidence that he had considered all avenues before sounding the alarm.

The museum was away from the main hubbub of the town, and located along a quiet mainly residential street behind the old brewery. The brewery had been closed down years earlier when the owners moved their business to the north of England. The remaining land was still undeveloped, but Seaton had heard on the grapevine that a local contractor was bidding to turn the area into holiday lets.

The museum was air-conditioned, and Seaton felt a welcoming blast as he entered. He estimated that there must have been around twenty people or so milling around the two-story structure, most of whom he presumed were tourists. The middle-aged lady at the reception desk smiled when she looked up at him. Her long black hair was tied tightly in a bun, her gold-rimmed glasses perched halfway down her nose so that she looked over them at the officer.

"Good morning, officer," her greeting was practised and professional, "would you like a ticket?" Her finger was poised over the ticket-ejector button.

Before she had a chance to strike, Seaton said, "No, thank you." Removing his cap, he continued, "I am here on official police business." The woman's smile faded. Seaton felt she even looked a little nervous, though as for why he had no idea. She certainly did not appear to be of a villainous persuasion.

"Oh, I see." She moved uncomfortably in her chair, glancing sideways discreetly to see if anyone was watching them. "How may I help you?"

Seaton smiled warmly. "I would like to speak to your curator, if I may?"

The receptionist physically relaxed as if she had been holding in her breath. She picked up the receiver of the phone on her desk and pressed one of the buttons. After a moment she spoke, holding her hand over the mouthpiece as if to stop any loitering parties from overhearing. "Oh hello, Miss Howard, there is a uniformed officer at reception who wishes to speak to you." The receptionist listened for a moment then smiled and said, "Thank you." She replaced the handset and turned back to Seaton. "Miss Howard will be with you shortly."

Seaton thanked her and moved sideways to allow some new visitors to buy their tickets.

While he waited, Seaton began looking at some of the framed prints which adorned the downstairs walls.

Caitlin appeared a minute later and immediately recognised the officer. She approached him extending her hand in greeting. "Hello again," she said, brightly. "Shall we go to my office; it's more private in there."

As Seaton followed her through the crowd, he glanced around at some of the glass-covered plinths which housed various models of ships, flags, mock battles, and busts of famous men and women of the sea.

Just before they entered Caitlin's office, Seaton caught sight of a picture which made him stop in his tracks. Caitlin reached her office door before she realised the officer was not behind her. She walked over to where Seaton was standing, studying the print.

The picture which had caught Seaton's eye was of a large octopus with its enormous tentacles wrapped around a helpless ship. The brass plaque at the bottom of the frame gave the legend "The Kraken" dated: 1801. There was an A5 card beside it covered by a plastic frame which contained more details concerning the picture.

Caitlin stood next to Seaton and said, "Are you interested in marine mythology then, Sergeant?"

Seaton pointed to the picture. "Is that taken from an actual photograph?" he asked, trying to think if had ever learned when photography was first invented. He seemed to think that it was in the nineteenth century, but could not recall if it was at the beginning or not.

Caitlin smiled. "Not that one, no, but we have some examples of photographs of similar creatures upstairs. Would you like me to show them to you?"

Seaton shook his head. "Not for the moment, thank you, but are you saying that this thing actually exists?"

Caitlin wrinkled her nose. "Mmm, that depends on who you are talking to."

"I don't follow," said Seaton, his brow furrowed

"Well," began Caitlin, "if you were asking a marine biologist say, then they would probably say no, because of the lack of physical evidence we have to date. On the other hand, if you were to ask a cryptozoologist or perhaps someone who studied marine folklore, then you might be on the right track."

Seaton scratched his head whilst he thought.

Still staring at the print, he said, "Perhaps we had better adjourn to your office after all, Miss Howard." He swivelled and put his arm out as if for her to continue leading the way. "I promise I'll try not to take up too much of your time."

Once inside her office, Caitlin offered Seaton tea or coffee which he politely refused.

They sat down on either side of her large oak desk which dominated the centre of the room. The walls around them were decked with dark wood bookcases filled to overflowing with all manner of books, charts, scrolls, and folders. The large bay window behind Caitlin's chair afforded a pleasant view of the sea in the distance above the rooftops of faraway houses.

Caitlin began. "I presume your visit is in connection with that old man's hat I found on the beach the other day? Has he come forward yet?"

"I'm afraid not," replied Seaton, placing his uniform hat on the edge of the table. "No one in town seems to have set eyes on him since the day before you found it. In fact," he leaned in closer, "I need to take you in to my confidence and rely on your discretion to keep what we are about to discuss completely to yourself."

Caitlin was intrigued.

She lifted her hands and shrugged her shoulders simultaneously. "You can rely on me."

Seaton took a deep breath. "The fact is, Miss Howard, we have received some rather distressing reports concerning not just old *Cappy* Jackson, but a couple of other residents all of whom have gone missing from Skullen Bay."

"Really!" Caitlin tried to disguise her enthusiasm, but this was beginning to sound fascinating to a lover of crime fiction such as her. "When you say missing, are you referring to them being kidnapped, or abducted maybe?"

Seaton squirmed; the words were not going to come forth from his mouth easily. Finally, he said, "You might say abducted, yes, but it's a question of abducted by what that's causing us the biggest problem."

Caitlin waited for the officer to continue. She could see how carefully he was trying to choose his words, so she did not want to rush him. But by the same token, she caught herself leaning forward in anticipation.

Finally, she could wait no longer. "Abducted by what, exactly?"

Seaton stared down at his interlocking fingers for a moment before looking up embarrassed and slightly flushed. "Well, from the descriptions we've received thus far, it sounds like one of those things from that picture I was just looking at." He signalled over his shoulder with his thumb.

Silence followed.

Caitlin had to think whilst she digested what she had just been told. Her practical, logical mind digested the information, then began to rationale the details as they were.

Finally, she asked, "Are you telling me that you have eye-witnesses to something akin to a Kraken, like the one in that picture, emerging from the sea at Skullen Bay and actually grabbing people from the beach?" The question even sounded incredulous to her.

Seaton nodded, dejectedly. "I am afraid so, Miss Howard. You can see my problem, I trust?"

Caitlin fell back in her seat. "Well yes, naturally, but are these witnesses, credible?"

"Ah, well there you have a sound point," replied Seaton, sheepishly. "They're not what I would call exactly the most credible of witnesses, no, but you must appreciate that with the alleged victims missing, and the witness reports on file, I must investigate all avenues to try and reach a successful conclusion," he winced, "regardless of how barmy it all sounds."

Thinking for a moment, Caitlin rose from her chair and began to scan one of the bookshelves to her left. Bending her head to one side to see the titles properly, she suddenly stopped and yanked out a large textbook from among the others on the shelf.

She brought it around to Seaton's side of the table and started flicking through the pages.

Eventually, she alighted on a chapter, and skipped forward a few more pages before finally stopping and showing the result to him.

"There," she announced, proudly. "Not having come across too much of the folklore side of things during my studies, there are these." She pointed to the open pages of the book.

Seaton looked closer and saw photographs of what looked like short stocky whales with long thin tentacles attached to them. Each picture showed several fishermen trying to haul the animals on board their ships with grappling hooks and lines. Upon closer inspection, the animals all appeared to be dead. Their carcases suspended by the lines of rope, while their lifelessly elongated tentacles draped over the side down into the water.

Seaton turned the pages back until he reached the title of the chapter: Giant and Colossal Squids.

He looked up at Caitlin. "And these are for real?" he asked, trying to keep the incredulity out of his expression.

Caitlin nodded. "Yep, these are the real McCoy, only no one has ever managed to capture one alive, and of course, all the ones that have been captured are far smaller than those that have apparently been seen." She walked back around to her side of the desk, leaving Seaton with the book.

"And just how big do these things actually grow?" he asked, continuing to scan the descriptions under the pictures while he spoke.

"Well, you have to bear in mind that their ultimate size can only be estimated based on the analysis of the much smaller, younger specimens they have found. But if memory serves, they can grow up to forty-six feet in length from the end of their fins to the tip of their tentacles."

Seaton paused for a moment to try and take it all in, before continuing.

On the one hand, he was glad that he had something substantial he could name as a possible culprit, not just a fantasy or a myth. But on the other hand, he could still not quite come to grips with what he was reading and Caitlin was saying to him.

Finally, he asked. "I take it these things are not common to our waters then? I mean, you don't read about such things on a daily basis in *The Sun*."

Caitlin laughed. "No, you are right about that. Evidence of such creatures usually comes from places such as Antarctica, South America, New Zealand or Greenland. And I do recall some findings emanating from somewhere in Japan. But I have never known of any sightings anywhere near the British Isles. Our waters would not be conducive to their lifestyle."

Seaton sighed. "In some ways, that makes my investigation all the more bizarre." He glanced once more through the pages before closing the book. "So in your opinion, is it possible that one of these creatures has made its way here to our shores?"

Caitlin thought for a second. "I would have to say no on the face of it, but then one thing they always taught us during my first year at university was that nature finds a way."

Seaton rubbed the side of his head with the palm of his hand.

"You don't look that convinced," said Caitlin, smiling at him.

"It's not so much that; it's more a question of how I am going to explain all this to my superiors. I need to say something before another body disappears, otherwise, they'll be all over me."

He flicked through the pages once more before holding the book to his chest. He gazed up at Caitlin. "Any chance I could borrow this for some more research? I promise I won't spill any coffee on it?" he asked, pleadingly.

"I'm afraid not, Officer," Caitlin replied, rising from behind her desk. "But if you come to our bookshop with me, I can offer you a discount if you purchase a copy," she beamed, cheekily.

CHAPTER TEN

Dan had found it increasingly difficult to concentrate on anything all day. He chided himself more than once for feeling like a schoolboy with a crush, but the truth was that he had not felt like this about anyone for a long time-if ever! Caitlin had captured his heart, and they had not so much as shared a kiss, yet.

He hoped that they hit it off straight away. It had been a while since he had enjoyed a steady relationship with anyone save Maggie, and he did not really count what they shared as anything more than a casual acquaintance, both filling a need for the other.

In his line of work, relationships were often strained. The odd hours you were forever committed to just to ensure you made enough to keep your business afloat. The seasonal nature of the work and one-up-man-ship you often found yourself embroiled in. The long hauls during the non-touristy months to make ends meet. The fact that you always looked a smelt a little "ripe", regardless of how many times you scrubbed yourself down at the end of the day. None of this was really conducive to a romantic entanglement.

But still, Dan was a realist. The fact that Caitlin had agreed to have dinner with him was a positive start, but as yet, he had no way of knowing what her situation was. She may make a habit of going on a lot of first dates because that was what she enjoyed. But that was where it ended. A polite "I'll call you" which would never materialise.

Dan had estimated that Caitlin was no more than mid-twenties, so he had to account for their age difference. He prided himself in being in good shape for his age, and true, there were an awful lot of women who seemed to prefer dating older men, but that aside, he reminded himself that he was probably still technically old enough to be her father.

That was a depressing thought!

Again, he checked himself for over-thinking the situation and decided just to get the day's work out of the way and look forward to a pleasant evening in wonderful company and to look no further ahead than that.

The day had not started well. When he and Tammi took their diving cylinders down to the local dive shop to have them filled, they discovered that they were both overdue for their five-year hydrostatic test. Typically, the one shop in town with a testing certificate was backed up with work and could not promise anything sooner than a week.

Dan considered hiring some replacements so they could at least check any damage made by whatever had crashed into the underside of the boat, but Tammi told him to save the money. She had always boasted that she had the lungs of a Japanese pearl diver, so she told Dan that she would dive anyway with just a facemask. After all, it was only to survey the possible damage, not to actually carry out any repairs.

Dan was not over the moon about Tammi's suggestion, but he relented, as he knew that she was a competent diver and she was right in that hiring tanks for such a small task was a waste of money under the circumstances.

Dan insisted that she wear a lifeline and they worked out a tugging system so that he could monitor her safety whilst she was out of his sight.

Upon inspection, Tammi was satisfied that there was no damage to speak of, though she could tell that something large had rubbed up against the underside, bruising the paintwork. They had both been down there a few months earlier for a routine inspection, and she was sure that the damage was not visible back then.

Either way, it meant that they were still open for business, and sure enough, within half an hour, they had their first customers of the day ready to go out.

The day dragged, which Dan had half-expected it to. By late afternoon, he convinced Tammi to start clearing up. The tourists were starting to desert the beach in search of alternative amusements, and under the circumstances, he was only too pleased to leave the final pickings to his competition.

Though Dan did not own many smart clothes, he did have one decent jacket, an array of complimentary shirts, and a couple of smart pairs of trousers which could both be matched with the jacket. He had to scrum age under his bed to find the matching pair to his one and only proper pair of dress shoes, which he then rubbed frantically with a dry cloth to try and bring out some semblance of a shine, as he realised too late that he did not own any polish.

He considered a tie, but Tammi advised against it. In her opinion, the smart but casual look made the best first impression. And she was adamant that he un-tucked his shirt from his trousers and let it hang loose, even though he did not have an overhang to try and hide.

Dan assured Tammi that she could ignore their usual arrangement. Regardless of how the evening went, Dan was confident that he would not be bringing Caitlin back to the boat.

Tammi accompanied him to the edge of the beach, giving him a good-luck hug before making her way to the pub.

Dan decided to walk into town. The heat of the day had started to subside as the sun began its decline, and there was a lovely cool breeze coming in from the sea. On his way to the museum, Dan passed a florist which was just closing for the evening. He stopped himself going in, deciding that such a gesture would be too much for a first date. The last thing he wanted was to scare Caitlin off by coming on too strong. Then again, she might be old-fashioned enough appreciate the thoughtfulness.

Dan had to admit to himself that he was too long out of practise to know what to do for the best. He considered calling Tammi for advice.

He stood outside the shop contemplating what to do for so long that eventually one of the staff came out to him and asked him if he wanted any help in making his selection.

Ten minutes later, Dan knocked on Caitlin's door with a huge bunch of mixed carnations.

When she opened the door, Dan had intended to try and gauge from her expression whether or not the flowers had been a good idea or not. But when he saw her, she instantly took his breath away, leaving him unable to do anything other than mumble a few words of greeting.

Caitlin was dressed in a gorgeous powder-blue dress with tiny yellow cornflowers dotted around. It was tied at the waist with a navy belt, which matched the colour of her shoes and handbag. The hem fell just above her knees, allowing her to show off her perfectly muscled calves and ankles. Her hair was left loose, and hung in tresses like a golden robe around her shoulders. Her make-up was light and perfectly applied, enhancing her high cheekbones.

Before Dan had a chance to fully regain his composure, Caitlin had relieved him of the flowers and planted a huge kiss on his cheek.

"Oh thank you," she gushed, "they're lovely." She took a deep breath to appreciate their aroma. "I can't remember the last time anyone bought me flowers." She turned to take them back inside, then stopped and looked back over her shoulder at Dan waiting patiently outside. "You'd better follow me up; these need to go in water straight away."

Dan's legs trembled involuntarily as he followed Caitlin up the stairs to her flat above the museum. Before Caitlin reached the top stair, Honey came bounding out to meet her, barking happily and wagging her tail. Caitlin patted the dog on the head as she walked past her. Honey waited patiently at the top of the stairs when she saw Dan following her mistress.

As he reached the last step, Honey sprang forward, almost knocking him off balance in a repeat performance from the beach that morning. He reached out and grabbed hold of the banister rail built into the wall just in time to stop himself stumbling backwards. The dog was obviously very excited to see him, jumping up at him and barking her delight as he tried to enter the living area.

"Honey, behave!" Caitlin commanded from the kitchen as she attended to her flowers. The dog sat down obediently in front of Dan, her tail still wagging frantically, a low moan barely audible escaped her mouth as she looked up at him with pleading eyes.

Dan bent down and began brushing her long coat with his hands and ruffling her behind the ears. Honey, in response, collapsed onto her back, offering up her tummy to her new playmate.

Dan glanced around the flat whilst he continued to keep Honey amused.

The flat comprised of an open plan reception room-cum-kitchen, which housed a reasonably sized table and chairs for dining, and a corner sofa unit plus two matching armchairs. The two other rooms, which had their doors closed, Dan presumed must be the bathroom and bedroom. He could not help wondering if this was the closest he would ever be to Caitlin's bedroom, and managed to stifle an audible unconscious sigh.

There were two large bookshelves which virtually covered all the wall space on the left of where he sat. The right-hand side of the property housed a huge bay window which along with the one at the back of the kitchen area, bathed the entire reception area in light, making the flat feel much bigger than it actually was.

As he gazed around him, Dan could not help but notice how meticulously clean and tidy everything was. He grimaced at the thought of Caitlin ever walking into his living quarters on the boat, and made a mental note to ensure he had a mass tidy up if that situation was ever likely to occur.

Caitlin came back into the living room with her flowers arranged neatly in a vase. She placed them on a small occasional table in front of the window, moving the vase around for the best effect.

She turned to Dan. "Thanks again for the flowers; they are really lovely."

Dan rose from his haunches, leaving Honey still on her back, looking up at him. "I'll be honest; I wasn't sure how appropriate they would be on a first date. I'm really out of practise with all this."

Caitlin laughed. With her back to the large window with the evening sun shining in and reflecting off her golden hair, she looked even more beautiful than she had when she first opened the door to Dan. "Well, just so you know, you're doing a wonderful job so far," she said, reassuringly.

The walk to the restaurant took no more than a few minutes. Once they were seated, Dan began to relax a little more. Caitlin was very easy to talk to, and Dan loved listening to the sound of her voice.

The meal was superb. They ordered a shared starter, and on the waitress's suggestion, several small main dishes instead of just two large ones so that they could pick and choose as they went along.

Dan asked Caitlin to choose the wine, which she was happy to. She opted for a deep, rich, velvety red which complimented the food perfectly. When Dan suggested a second bottle, he noticed Caitlin's eyebrows lift slightly.

"What's up?" he asked, concerned by her expression.

"I take it you're not planning on driving anywhere tonight, then?" Her tone was still playful and in no way accusatory. But Dan soon picked up on her pretext.

"Oh no," he laughed, nervously, "I walked down from the bay. It was too nice an evening to bother driving. And anyway, it only took about twenty minutes." He looked at Caitlin. He detected a faint glint of mischief in her eyes which made him laugh again, involuntarily. "What?" he added, holding out his arms in submission.

Caitlin was toying with him and enjoying every minute of it. Dan was such easy company to be in, not intense or overly opinionated like most of the students she had dated whilst studying.

She felt totally relaxed in his company and wanted to make the most of the evening. Leaning closer with a cheeky grin, she whispered. "I was only thinking that twenty minutes downhill equals at least thirty back up…And you're not as young as you used to be!"

Dan feigned slight. "Owww that hurt!"

Caitlin put her hand to her mouth to quell her laughter, catching herself just a little too late. A few diners from other tables discreetly looked around. Dan pretended to look embarrassed, but he too was fighting a losing battle with the giggles.

When they finally had themselves under control, Caitlin noticed the waitress hovering nearby. She waved at her to come over and ordered their second bottle of wine.

As they left the restaurant, Caitlin linked her arm in Dan's. As they walked back towards the museum, a full moon was climbing in the night sky just above the buildings opposite. As they passed a break in the houses, a chill wind raced in from the sea and Caitlin shivered in her flimsy summer dress.

Dan immediately unlinked his arm and removed his jacket, placing it around Caitlin's shoulders. "Better?" he asked.

"Much, thank you," she replied, and leaned towards him, closing her eyes as their lips met. Their first kiss was long and passionate, and neither seemed to want to be the first to break away. Finally, the sound of an approaching dog walker became their signal.

Dan put his arm around Caitlin's shoulders as they made their way back to her place. Now without his jacket, Dan too could feel the sharp sea breeze penetrating his casual shirt, but he did not notice, or care. Suddenly, very little else in life seemed to matter other than him being here with Caitlin.

They shared another kiss outside Caitlin's front door. Without realising he was doing it at first, Dan allowed his hand to slide down the back of Caitlin's dress until it cupped her pert buttocks. He squeezed it gently through the fabric, and Caitlin moaned softly before gently easing him away.

"I'm sorry," Dan said, apologetically, hoping desperately that he had not blown his chances with this wonderful lady.

"Don't be," Caitlin smiled, turning to open her front door. "I'm not."

At the sound of the key in the lock, Honey came bounding down the stairs to greet her mistress at the door. Her overwhelming excitement was infectious and both Dan and Caitlin began making a fuss over the mischievous animal as she rolled around on her back, inviting more play.

After a moment, Caitlin slipped Dan's jacket off and handed it back to him. Dan immediately took this as a sign that the evening was over. Not even an invite for coffee. But then Dan knew only too well what "coffee" stood for by today's standards, and he respected Caitlin's obvious reticence, as this was after all their first date. The potential opportunity of more dates to come was enough for him.

As he shrugged back into his jacket, Caitlin asked, "I don't suppose you fancy accompanying me taking Honey for her evening walk, do you?"

Dan beamed, broadly. "Love to."

Caitlin handed him Honey's lead from a coat hook on the wall. "Okay then, you put this on for her. I'm going to change my shoes and fetch a cardigan. I won't be a second."

They took the dog to the beach behind the arcades. Once they found a deserted stretch, Caitlin let her off her lead and the dog scampered along the sand, eagerly hunting out anything which might be of the slightest interest to her canine sense of smell.

Dan and Caitlin walked along the sand hand in hand behind the dog. Caitlin had ditched the ballet pumps she had changed into once they left the stones and shingle behind, and carried them in her other hand, letting them dangle from her fingers as she walked.

It was almost 11pm by now, and the beaches were still littered with a smattering of bodies enjoying the night air and the sound of the waves.

In the distance, they could hear an announcement stating that the fun fair would be closing in half an hour, and that this was the last chance to buy tokens for the rides.

The tide was out, and they could just make out the water's edge in the moonlight. Honey raced down towards it, barking at the encroaching water every time it tried to catch her unawares.

As they walked, they talked and laughed, and hugged, and cuddled. When the opportunity presented itself, they would stop and kiss. Dan could not help holding Caitlin's body close to his as their lips locked. She felt so warm and soft in his embrace. He was delighted when Caitlin responded by thrusting herself even tighter against him, crushing his rising erection with her groin and gently rubbing herself against him.

When they finally pulled apart, reluctantly, Caitlin looked deeply into Dan's eyes and said, "I need to tell you something serious."

Dan frowned, fearing the worst. "What is it?" he asked, his tone sombre.

"I don't believe in one night stands." Dan could tell she was being honest with him. Though her eyes spoke of passion and want, her voice was calm and professional.

Dan was not sure how to respond.

Finally, he said, "Okay, I understand." He tried to keep the disappointment out of his voice, but heard it slipping through.

He took Caitlin in his arms and hugged her, warmly. Looking deeply into her eyes, he continued, "Once Honey has worn herself out, I'll walk you both back home and be on my way." He smiled, in spite of his feeling of loss.

Caitlin kissed him gently on the lips. "That's not exactly what I meant," she said, trying not to lose the moment. She could see the look of puzzlement on Dan's face and kissed him again before continuing. "What I mean is, I would love to be with you tonight, but only if it means we will be more to each other than just tonight,"

It took a moment for her words to sink in.

Dan did not bother responding. He hoped that his actions would speak for him. He smiled affectionately down at Caitlin and held her even tighter as their lips locked again. Their mutual body language informed each other of where their intentions lay.

♦ ♦ ♦

Terry Connaught, fisherman by day and part-time drug smuggler by night, sat waiting in his tiny two-man craft for his contact to arrive. This was the part of the operation he hated the most: the waiting. It always made him feel like a sitting duck, drifting in the middle of the North Sea, hoping he would not be spotted by any of the coastguard patrols searching for people smugglers.

At thirty-five years of age, Terry was finally starting to feel as if he was getting somewhere in life. It had been a rough and bumpy road thus far, but at least the future was looking brighter.

Originally from London, Terry had been taken in by his aunt and uncle at the age of ten when his mother died. They had been Skullen Bay residents all their lives, but after the excitement of London, Terry could not settle down. As soon as he was old enough, he moved back to London. Without any qualifications or specific talent, unless you counted being caught shoplifting on numerous occasions, Terry soon became engulfed in the seedy world of drugs.

His ambitions never amounted to much, so he was happy just to be on the fringes of the game. Taking control of your own piece of turf in

London was dangerous business, and he had witnessed the aftermath of several clashes between rival wannabes.

Naturally, it was not too long before Terry found himself on the wrong side of the law, and this time, it was for nothing as trivial as pinching the odd bottle of vodka from the local supermarket.

When it came to the crunch, Terry turned informer in return for a suspended sentence and a clean getaway. He had considered trying his luck in Manchester or Birmingham but decided to keep a low profile for a bit, just in case the gang members he had grassed on became suspicious when he popped up doing business in another major town.

His Uncle Jack had been a fisherman his entire life, usually working for one of the major contractors in town. But the boat Terry was using now had been his uncle's pride and joy, having built it himself from scratch and lovingly maintained it for years before his death from a heart attack.

Terry's aunt passed away soon afterwards, leaving Terry as her only surviving relative. His inheritance consisted of the run-down little cottage they had lived in throughout their married life, this boat, and what little savings his aunt had left once her funeral had been paid for.

Terry had stripped the cottage of everything he could either pawn or sell on eBay, leaving only the bare essentials for himself. He had initially considered selling on the boat, fishing being far too much like hard work for him, but then he remembered that he still had contacts abroad who he knew were always looking for middle-men to bring gear into the country.

For the last two years now, Terry had been acting as a go-between for a group in Amsterdam and a supplier in Norwich. As far as he was concerned, his part was easy. Just sail out to the coordinates supplied for him and wait for the drop-off. Then take the stuff to the supplier the following day and get paid. No names, no details were ever exchanged, just a nice little earner for very little work. Lovely!

Suddenly, through the darkness, Terry could hear the rumble of an approaching motor. His lights were off – as per instructions – and in the gloom, he could not make out the features of the vehicle as it drew nearer. He checked his watch; the time was about right, it had to be his contact.

As the approaching craft came into view, Terry relaxed, as he suspected this was his contact. Upon seeing him, one of the crew members on board signalled with a flashlight. Terry waved back in recognition whilst he was bathed in the beam.

The craft pulled up alongside and a hook was thrown overboard to moor it next to Terry. The new craft cut its engine, leaving the two vessels strapped alongside each other with just the sound of the water lapping against them.

Terry waited in the still night. From past experience, he knew that there was no need for formal or friendly gestures. The men who crewed these vessels were neither friendly nor appreciative enough to return such a familiarity. In truth, Terry had often surmised that they regarded him as something of a necessary evil. Another hand reaching out helping himself to a cut of their ill-gotten gains.

But despise him or not, Terry knew that they needed him. They could not land on English soil without the appropriate paperwork, the acquisition of which would raise far too many eyebrows back home. And their contacts in Norwich were not prepared to use their own men to do the dirty work for them. So, instead, people like Terry were employed to act as the middle-men.

Through the shadows, Terry saw a large figure emerge from below deck. It was obvious that the person was carrying something in each hand. Terry walked to the side closest to where the figure waited, and was handed the two parcels one at a time.

Each was approximately the size of a small suitcase, and Terry took each one in turn and placed them safely on the floor of his deck.

The figure then handed over an envelope stuffed with cash. Terry took it and placed it in his coat pocket without looking to see how much it was. This too was the way of the business which he had practised. You did not question your fee – it was agreed in advance – and you could not disrespect the other party by daring to check it in their presence.

Without waiting for a signal, the man turned his back on Terry and walked back towards the door from which he had emerged originally.

Terry waited. A few seconds passed then he heard the other craft splutter back into life. He removed the hook and through the rope back over. The other vessel moved away slowly, then turned and moved away, still in darkness.

Terry felt the weight of his two packages. Judging by their weight, there appeared to be more in them this time than usual. Still, it was none of his business, so he took each one and secured it in the concealed compartments beneath his passenger seats, and covered them over with blankets and cushions to avoid suspicion.

Once the sound of the departing engine had faded, Terry decided to check his wages. Switching on a small overhead light in his wheelhouse, Terry thumbed the notes in the envelope. It all appeared in order. Not that there was really anything he could do about it if that had not been the case. In this business, you did not complain unless you had the firepower to back it up. You either got on, or got out!

Terry replaced the envelope in his pocket and turned the key in the ignition, deciding the other vessel was far enough away by now for him to leave – more of their stupid rules.

The engine spluttered into life. Terry turned on his lights and gently eased the accelerator handle forward.

The boat did not move!

Terry checked that everything was in order; it was. He could hear the engine revving and the accelerator had just the right amount of pressure on it, so he knew it was engaged, but still the boat refused to budge.

Annoyed, Terry turned everything off then waited a moment before switching it all on again. Still, the craft refused to move.

Terry forced the accelerator forward to its maximum. He could hear the engine roaring its protestation as the craft stayed put. He left it running for a few moments more before switching everything off again and stopping to think.

He was certainly no mechanic, but the boat was so easy to operate and he had been doing so for years without any problems, so he had no idea what could possibly be causing tonight's failure to launch.

Terry swore to himself as he left the wheelhouse, taking his uncle's old high-beam torch with him, and walked towards the stern of the vessel. He had no idea what he was looking for, but hoped if there was something obvious he might see it and be able to deal with it without calling for help and having to answer a million awkward questions.

Terry leaned over the side and shone the torch directly at the water. The beam bounced on the black water but could not penetrate the depths adequately to afford him any useful examination. He waited, hoping his eyes might adjust to the view, scrutinising the ripples which ran through his torches arc as he moved it slowly back and forth.

Suddenly, without warning, Terry felt a hard slap across the back of his head. The force from the blow sent him over the side and straight into the freezing water.

The shock of the cold water helped him shake off the initial daze he was in as a result of being hit. Treading water, he spun around, searching in bewilderment for the cause of his fall.

There was no one else on the boat; he knew that for a fact. Even if for some reason one of the men from the other craft had hopped aboard, there was nowhere out of sight for anyone to hide, so there was no possibility that they could have crept up behind him. And yet something had. Something with a punch that could knock out an elephant!

Once he had gained his composure, Terry started to make his way around the side of his boat to the small boarding inlet. He hoped he would be able to pull himself back on board, as he had never had to try before tonight.

He was almost within reach of the inlet when he heard a terrific crash coming from the blind side past the wheelhouse. Terry listened, stunned by the noise and unable to fathom what might have caused it. It sounded to him as if another vessel had crashed into his, but that would have caused the boat to lurch towards him and there would have been a huge swell of water in the wake of the impact which he would have felt even from this side.

He waited, listening intently. He could not hear anything other than the water lapping at the sides of his craft.

He tried to hoist himself back in. As he did so, there was another tremendous crash and splintering of wood, but this time, however, Terry did feel the brunt of it as the impact knocked him back into the sea.

Terry slipped under the water momentarily. All sights and sounds were now blocked by the cold water. Terry kicked upwards. As he broke the surface, he opened his eyes and saw a hideous monster suited only to childhood nightmares, clambering over his boat.

For a split second his brain could not digest what his eyes were showing him.

The creature's tentacles enveloped the craft from above, crashing down on masts, wheelhouse, deck, and furniture, destroying everything in its path.

Terry could do no more than watch in horror as the monster tore his vessel apart. Terry began to swim away from the wreckage as the beast's tentacles smashed everything to flotsam within seconds.

When Terry looked back, all he could see was the last splinters of his uncle's boat, but there was no monster to be seen.

For a moment, he continued treading water, trying to decide if he had just witnessed what he thought he had seen. Were it not for the drifting remnants of his craft, he would still have doubted his eyes even now.

As he floated, his mind turned back to his business of the night. The packages were nowhere in sight, presumably sunk beneath the weight of his boat. He shivered as he wondered what he was going to tell his suppliers in the morning. They would never believe this!

He remembered the money in his pocket. He could always give it back as a gesture, but still they would not believe him. Plus, he knew only too well that what they paid him was a fraction of the street value of what he was meant to be delivering.

He felt his pocket to make sure the envelope was still there. Though now completely soggy, the feel of the money comforted him.

Spotting a large chunk of driftwood, Terry decided that he would be better off trying to make it back to shore and worry about everything else later.

After all, he could always disappear. It was not as if he had never done that before!

As he reached the driftwood, Terry felt his whole body being hoisted out of the water. He screamed as a giant tentacle raised him up and held him aloft.

From instinct, Terry began to punch and kick at the rubbery limb which kept him captive, but in response, the creature merely tightened its grip on his body until he could feel the life ebbing away from him.

Eventually, Terry could not scream anymore; the noise would not come. His eyes stayed open, locked in a stare of pure horror. His mouth opened and closed without making a sound as the life slowly left him.

Once it knew that its prey was dead, the Kraken dragged it under the surface to feed.

CHAPTER ELEVEN

Dan was awoken from a beautiful dream by the rhythmic beeping from Caitlin's alarm. He opened his eyes, focusing on the unfamiliar surroundings. Beside him, Caitlin began to stir. Her head rested on his chest, her golden hair cascading around his torso. Her left leg was wound around his, the top of her thigh just nudging his manhood. As she moved closer to him, cuddling him for warmth and comfort, he felt himself starting to rise.

His erection pressed against the soft skin of Caitlin's inner thigh, became more aroused at the feel of her warm inviting flesh.

Caitlin leaned behind her and silenced the clock. As she turned back, she let her hand slide slowly under the duvet and down Dan's hairy chest, her soft playful fingers loitered teasingly around his navel, before slipping gently downwards and circling his throbbing member.

She gave him a gentle squeeze which elicited a soft moan from Dan's lips. Her fingers danced tantalisingly up and down his shaft, stopping every now and then just long enough to squeeze the bulge at the top.

Dan bent down and kissed the top of Caitlin's head. She looked up, bringing their lips together. As they kissed long and passionately, Caitlin continued to stroke him until he had reached a full erection.

Through sleepy eyes, Caitlin said, "Someone wants to come out to play."

Dan smiled down at her; his eyes reflected both his feelings for her and his wanting. He opened his mouth to answer, but just at that second, Caitlin took a firmer grip and began sliding her hand up and down the full length of his shaft.

Dan moaned out loud again. This was heaven. Much as he wanted to be lost in the moment, he was conscious that if he let things go too far, he was liable to explode all over Caitlin's hand, which wonderful though it would have been, he had to consider her wants as well.

He put his hand beneath her chin and gently lifted, rubbing her lips with his thumb. "Baby," he spoke between moments of ecstasy, "slow down, I'm going to come. Have you got anymore?"

He was referring to the previous night when having tantalised each other with their fingers and tongues, Dan was slightly amused when Caitlin opened a drawer in her bedside cabinet and removed a condom which she then handed to him. Dan could not remember the last time he had used one, which was not to say that he was careless, just that the women he usually slept with were generally of an age where they were already using contraception. He knew that his generation's attitude towards sexually transmitted diseases was somewhat outdated by today's standards, but he too had felt the need for extra protection on occasion. Just not tonight!

But he had to bear in mind that Caitlin was of a younger, more aware generation, where sensible precautions were practiced more regularly.

That aside, they both began laughing at his clumsy, ham-handed attempts at inserting himself into the rubber sheath. Finally, he had looked up embarrassed and apologised for his lack of expertise.

Though sympathetic, Caitlin still found the situation hysterical. "Well there's no use asking me," she said, trying to hold back her laughter, "I've never put one on anybody before…Do you want to call a friend?"

At her words, Dan laughed so much he dropped the unused condom on the bed. He had never been to bed with a woman who made him laugh so much just before they were about to make love. Caitlin was poking fun at him but in a loving, kindly manner.

Even so, the anxiety at not being able to deal with the rubber was starting to make him lose his ardour. He would need to regain his composure before attempting the feat again.

Caitlin noticed Dan becoming flaccid and automatically felt guilt for laughing at him, even though he was laughing too.

She picked up the lubricated tube and dangled it in front of him. "Okay," she began, "I think we need to make this a joint effort, what do you say?"

Dan shrugged and smiled, trying to hide his annoyance at his own performance. "You're in charge," he offered. "What's the plan?"

Caitlin handed him back the condom. "Right, you deal with this, I'm taking charge of this!" She pointed down towards his drooping member. Before Dan could respond, Caitlin shifted her body so that her head rested between his legs. As she began to lick and caress his manhood, Dan felt himself immediately respond.

Caitlin ensured that he maintained his erection whilst he slipped the rubber over his erection. She eased it down for him to ensure it was on properly, before sliding back beside him and guiding him gently inside her.

Their lovemaking had been both loving and passionate in equal measure. After a while, the restrictions caused by the condom seemed to be forgotten by both of them.

Dan managed to hold off until he felt Caitlin come twice before he finally ejaculated.

Afterwards, Caitlin gently removed the soggy rubber tube for him, and wrapped it in a tissue before dumping it in the wastepaper basket on her side of the bed. They fell asleep in each other's embrace within seconds, and stayed together throughout the night.

Dan took in several deep breaths as Caitlin continued to torture him. He knew he would not be able to hold back for much longer, but to be honest, he had given her fair warning.

As Dan continued to moan, becoming more and more lost in the moment, Caitlin began to gently kiss his chest, tonguing his nipples through his matted chest hair as she continued squeezing and releasing his throbbing member. She started to work her way down his torso with soft kisses until she finally reached his erection.

Closing her mouth over him, Caitlin began to work Dan into a frenzy with both her mouth and hand in equal parts.

There was no stopping him now. He knew from past experience that most women did not like having men ejaculate in their mouths, but Caitlin was bringing him to a crescendo which he could not stop even if he wanted to.

And he did not want to!

Dan covered his mouth with his hand to stifle his scream of pure rapture as he exploded.

Caitlin did not seem fazed by his sudden gush; she had obviously been expecting it and intended to take the full force.

Once he was spent, Caitlin slid back to her side of the bed and took a tissue from the box next to the alarm and wiped her mouth, spitting the last remnants of juice delicately into the paper, before disposing of it in the bin.

She turned back over. Dan was still exhausted from the exertion, even though it was Caitlin who had done all the work. His legs quivered under the duvet and his entire body tingled.

Caitlin kissed him deeply. He could still taste a hint of salt on her lips.

At that moment, Honey came bounding into the bedroom and jumped up onto the bed. She plopped herself down, making a channel between the two bodies and offered her head up for scratching.

Dan reached out and ruffled the dog's ears. She pushed her snout further forward, inviting more play.

"I see my competition has moved in," said Caitlin, teasingly.

"Never," replied Dan, taking hold of her hand and kissing the back of it.

After a few more minutes of wrestling with Honey, Dan announced that he needed to use the bathroom, and excused himself. He slipped out from under the duvet and pulled his shorts and trousers on, standing to fasten his belt.

As he made his way around the bed, Caitlin called out. "You know the first rule of the house, I hope?"

Dan stopped in his tracks, halfway to the door. Turning, he looked at Caitlin, bemused.

"First one up makes the coffee," Caitlin said, in reply to his look. Honey chimed in with an affirmative bark, receiving another playful rubbing from Caitlin.

"But I'm a guest," whined Dan, piteously.

"And if you want to be a guest again, mine's black with one sugar, Honey takes hers white with two. Her bowl is next to the kettle."

Dan took the hint. He saluted his orders and made for the bathroom.

***

Sergeant Oswald Seaton was not enjoying a particularly pleasant dream when the station phone blasted into life beside him.

He glanced at the clock as he raised the receiver. It was 6:45am. Only forty-five minutes before he usually woke up; that extra time had now been stolen from him and he knew he would never get it back. He knew from past experience that even an early night would not recuperate lost sleep from the previous night.

"Alton Police Station, Sgt. Seaton speaking."

"Have you seen the local paper this morning? What the hell is going on? Did you know about this? It says that you were not available for information? When the hell were you going to let me know?"

The torrent of screaming questions echoing down the line came courtesy of the high-pitched squeak of Sheila Soames, local councillor, captain of the women's golf team, former head of the local branch of the women's institute – but that was another story – mayoral candidate, and wannabe member of parliament.

Seaton rubbed the sleep from his eyes, allowing the woman to continue her tirade unabashed. It was obvious to him from her tirade that someone had gone to the papers to report the monster of Skullen Bay. He suspected either Harry Friar or his daughter Amy. Old Sam Cleary would not have been believed regardless of how convincing he might have sounded. And he knew straight away that none of his officers would have spilled the beans. He trusted their discretion and loyalty completely.

Now it was really going to hit the fan!

Once Sheila had paused to take a breath, Seaton took his cue. "Good morning, Sheila, how are you today?"

"How am I?" she replied, exasperated. "How do you think I am reading this garbage with my morning coffee?"

Seaton lifted himself into a sitting position on his bed. He caught a glimpse of his reflection in the dressing table mirror opposite, and groaned inwardly.

He slipped on his moccasins and began to pull on his dressing gown as he spoke. "Do I take it that there is a story in the paper this morning concerning some strange disappearances over at Skullen Bay?"

"You can bet your sweet Fanny Adams there is. What the hell is all this shit about, Seaton?"

Seaton was used to Sheila's brassy manner and use of profanity. In all her official positions, she always maintained an air of respectability and decorum, but get her alone on a bad day, and watch out!

"Look, Sheila, I haven't had a chance to read the papers yet, so I can't comment on anything they've said. All I can tell you is that we have one, possibly two or three people missing, and so far, two very shaky witness statements both claiming that some monster from the sea is to blame."

"That's ridiculous." Sheila's voice had not lost any of its venom or volume. "What monster? What the hell are they talking about? Has the Loch Ness Monster taken a holiday and booked in locally?"

Seaton sighed. "Sheila, I don't know what you want me to say. I have received two statements concerning missing individuals in our area, and we are treating them as missing person as per the book."

"Two statements, you said you had three missing people, the paper only mentions one, this stupid boy..." Seaton could hear her rustling her newspaper in the background. Someone else was trying to speak to her on her end and Seaton heard her telling them abruptly to wait. Probably her husband, thought Seaton, poor bugger.

Finally, Sheila came back to him. "Pete Dodds. He's not even local for Christ's sake, what do we know about him?"

"Well, not too much. He's working, or was working, as a brickie up at the Grange. We've already spoken to his best friend there, but he couldn't give us much. But –"

"Have you contacted his parents? He might have just got home-sick," Sheila butted in, not allowing him to finish. Seaton could hear desperation starting to creep into her tone.

"I sent the details down to London; they haven't come back to me yet."

"So who else is missing?"

"Well, according to old Sam Cleary..."

Sheila jumped in again. "Who?"

Well, if you'd let me finish for once, woman, thought Seaton. "Sam Cleary, he's our local down-and-out. According to him, *Cappy* Jackson and another man he didn't recognise have also both been taken by...Whatever this thing is."

"You can't take the word of a drunk, what are you thinking? Was he at least coherent when he made the statement?"

"Not as such," admitted Seaton, "which is why I was sceptical at first. Then when Amy Friar gave me her statement yesterday morning, I decided that perhaps there was more to it, so I instigated investigative proceedings as per protocol."

"And what about this monster? What the hell is this silly girl wittering on about? Do we have a killer shark on our hands, a whale, Godzilla, what?"

Seaton had thus far managed to keep the exasperation out of his voice, but he knew he was fast losing the battle. "Well, according to young Amy, and bear in mind, she is blind as a bat without her glasses, she said it was big and black with large tentacles."

"What, you mean like a giant squid or octopus?"

"Possibly. I have spoken to our local marine expert at the museum and such creatures do exist. Although some more in folklore than in reality, but they do have documented evidence. I've got a book which –"

"Forget books, I want to know what you're doing about it!"

Dan groaned inwardly. "As I said, so far I am treating it as a missing persons, I'm afraid sea monsters and legends are a little out of my purvey."

He could hear Sheila breathing heavily on the other end. She was obviously trying to think of something clever and superior to say.

Finally, she came up with one of her staples. "Well, I'll have to call an emergency council meeting. This could all reflect very badly on our family-friendly image, not to mention our tourist trade."

As Seaton had suspected, she was not actually interested in the potential loss of human life, only on the effect it might have on the towns – and indirectly her – image.

Before he had a chance to say another word, Sheila jumped in again. "You need to be here to answer questions. I'll get my PA to let you know when the meeting is." She slammed the phone down without giving Seaton a chance to respond.

Seaton looked at the dead receiver for a moment, then replaced it in its cradle.

He needed strong coffee, and he needed it now!

***

Dan climbed aboard his boat, whistling loudly. Since his date with Caitlin last night, his life had taken on an entire new phase. Everything looked better, smelled fresher, and generally had a brighter hue. Life was good.

After coffee, they showered and dressed and then took Honey for her morning walk on the beach. Caitlin was such easy company Dan just did not want the morning to end. They talked and laughed, and ran along the sand, with Honey chasing her ball. At one point, they just sat on the sand together wrapped in each other's arms, bathing in the warmth of the early morning sunshine.

Their walk built up an appetite so they headed off for breakfast to a local café where they could sit outside with Honey. Caitlin allowed Dan to order the dog two sausages as a breakfast treat when he complained that he would not be able to enjoy his with Honey looking at him with her big brown eyes, making him feel guilty.

Afterwards, he walked them back to the museum. It was hard for him to say goodbye, and he hoped it was the same for Caitlin. He had been in enough relationships to know that mentioning the word "Love" this early on would probably be the kiss of death for any relationship, but still he had to fight with himself to hold back. He was in love, and it felt terrific. He only wished that he could see into Caitlin's heart to find out if his feelings were reciprocated.

Dan called out to Tammi as he wandered around the boat, but she was nowhere in sight. It was not unusual for Tammi to go into town early; she was an earlier riser than he was, but he thought she might have left him a note. Below deck, he put his hand against the kettle in the kitchenette; it was cold. Either she had not had any coffee that morning or she had had it so long ago the kettle had by now lost all its heat.

He changed into some working clothes, carefully folding and placing his good ones in the wardrobe. When he climbed back on deck, he spied Tammi coming across the sand. She waved when she saw him.

Dan waited for her on deck. "Out for an early morning stroll?" he asked, cheerily.

"Not exactly." Dan could see from the expression on her face that she was troubled. She climbed up next to Dan. "I've been to the breakers. I decided to have a wee check this morning just to make sure everything was sound in the engine room. I'm beginning ta wish I had'ne bothered."

Dan's feelings of euphoria took a sudden dive. "What's wrong? Please don't say it's the engine again?"

They had had some engine trouble six months earlier when the boat suddenly cut out and refused to start back up. Luckily, Tammi was able to fix it, but Dan now remembered her saying that they would need to find parts to reconstruct it before it clapped out altogether.

Now that he thought about it, the parts had slipped both their minds.

Dan's heart sank. This could cost him his entire summer profit, including what he was yet to earn for the rest of the season. "It was running fine yesterday." He was almost whining, and so cleared his throat.

"Well, ta be honest, I thought she was a wee bit too sluggish on the way back yesterday, that's why I thought I might tek a wee look today, an' that's when I found the problem."

Dan scratched the back of his head in frustration. "Do you think it was as a result of whatever crashed into the boat the other night?"

Tammi winced. "'aye it's possible right enough; it was a pretty mighty judder whatever caused it." She pointed down towards the engine room. "I know there was no damage to the outer hull, but a collision like the one I felt cud'easy ha' sent vibrations through the outer casing, causing a knock-on effect inside. A bit like when you bang your head and get compression, the results denny show right away."

Dan swallowed, hard. "So what's your diagnosis? Are we still in business?"

Tammi bit her bottom lip. One thing you could rely about with her was that she was not prone to exaggeration, so whatever she said, Dan knew it would be the case, so her reaction did not bode well.

"Come on, Tammi, give me the worst."

"Well, ideally we need ta replace the engine, but we could possibly get away with a decent re-build, that'll save some. It's no' as gude o' course, but I can keep an eye on it."

Dan closed his eyes and looked to heaven for inspiration.

Tammi waited a moment before continuing. "I was hopin' the local yard've had some spares I could use ta patch it up, but they had nothing of use."

Dan looked back at her. "What about Findley's in the next town?" Despair was beginning to creep into his voice.

"Ey, that's what I was thinkin'. Do yer think yer wee truck'll be up to it?"

Dan thought for a moment. His reliable old transit van had definitely seen better days, but he used it so infrequently that most of the time it sat parked behind the pub. Fortunately for him, permit parking had not yet reached Skullen Bay, so other than the tax and MOT, the van was a relatively cheap commodity to maintain.

Dan rubbed his chin. "I think it should be up to the task. We might need to give it a jump, but otherwise, we'll be fine." He sighed deeply, more to himself rather than for effect. "And the day started so promisingly as well."

Tammi laughed. "Aye, when yer dinny come back last night, I suspected things were going well. How was it, a memorable night?"

Dan smiled broadly, unable to contain his excitement in spite of the news about the boat. The thought of Caitlin immediately cheered him up, and he liked the fact she had that effect on him. "I think I may be falling in love," he admitted, openly.

"Wow, that wer quick. Does she feel the same?"

"Don't know, too afraid to ask." He looked a little uneasy with his own answer. "Besides, I didn't tell her how I feel, that would just send her running in the opposite direction, don't you think?"

"Aye," Tammi agreed. "I always venture more towards caution in matters o' the heart. But the fact she let you stay the night is always a gude indication."

"I know," Dan winked at her, "and to say it was a beautiful night would be an understatement."

"When are yer seein' hur again?"

Dan shrugged. "I don't know. That is, we never made any firm arrangements. I'll give her a call later."

"Don't be too keen," Tammi cautioned. "You don't want to come across as desperate."

Dan frowned. "Do you think I should leave it a day or so? I don't want her to think that I don't care."

"Mebbe yer right. She's obviously keen on you so perhaps waiting is not necessary after all."

As it was, Dan did not have to decide. Caitlin called him during her lunch break. They were on their way back from the breakers yard in the next town, and fortunately, Tammi was driving his old van, leaving Dan free to talk.

He mentioned that he was not alone to avoid any embarrassment.

Caitlin wanted to cook him dinner that evening and Dan readily agreed. When their conversation began to stray into "mushier" territory, Tammi could not contain herself. She poked a finger towards her mouth and made an action as if she was about to throw up. Dan poked her in the ribs several times in response whilst still talking to Caitlin.

When he terminated the call, Tammi could tell that his mood had brightened considerably. Because they did not use Findlay's yard that often, they did not get such a good deal. But the vital thing was that they had the parts so Tammi could get to work and hopefully save the day.

They would still be out of action for at least the rest of the day, and being another hot and sunny one, Dan knew that there would have been customers aplenty. But it still beat the alternative of having to buy a replacement engine.

CHAPTER TWELVE

Justin Topplewell sat in his editor's office, swinging himself around on his boss's chair. He was very excited since learning how well the local paper had been selling that morning, as he was sure that it was all down to his story about the giant sea monster that had grabbed Pete Dodds from Skullen Bay beach.

He had graduated from journalism school the previous year, and this was his first full-time appointment. He realised that it was not on par with one of the London dailies, but he was a firm believer in the expansion of little acorns. If truth be known, he was actually quite lucky to have managed to acquire this job in the first place. His grades had not been exceptional by any stretch of the imagination. But that was due partly to his lack of attendance at class, preferring to be out on the streets finding stories – once his hangover from the previous evening had worn off. He firmly believed that hard drinking came with the territory; he insisted it was in his blood.

His true talent lay in him being able to sell himself. And he had to admit that he was on exceptionally good form on the day of the interview. But now he had to prove his worth, and for that, he was willing to go to any length.

Justin was an opportunist for sure. He had left his girlfriend behind in Manchester when this position had come up, not considering her feelings for an instant. He had mainly been with her because her parents were supporting her financially through college, which meant that by moving in with her, he managed to save a packet on rent.

The floods of tears and pleas from the heart which she had blurted out once he told her it was over meant nothing to him. He put them down to Imogen just being a girl and not able to handle harsh reality. After all, how could she expect him to pass up an opportunity such as this just so that they could be together?

She had to understand, Justin Topplewell was destined for big things and nothing and no one could be allowed to stand in his way.

And this story was just the beginning.

From the corner of the glass partition, he saw his editor emerging from one of the smaller offices. Justin knew that he had been in a meeting all morning, and that one of the topics on the agenda was the extension of his contract. After this latest story, he was confident that his chances were very high indeed.

Bernie Coulson burst through the door just as Justin was going for another spin in his chair. "What the hell are you doing in my chair? Get out, Topplewell!" his boss bellowed as he entered his office.

Justin's cocky, over-confident nature was moving at full pelt. He hopped off the spinning leather-bound recliner and stood up with a flamboyant hand gesture, looking like a trapeze artist who had just completed a very difficult series of summersaults.

Coulson barged him out of the way in order to reach his seat. Reclaiming his balance, Justin moved to stand in front of the desk, directly before his editor.

"What's up, Big Burn? Have you seen the noon-day sales figures yet?" Justin picked up a computer printout he had initially brought in with him when looking for his boss. He let the sheets unfold whilst he kept hold of the top end. "Look at these," he gushed. "Seven shops have sold out before lunch, and most of the rest are reporting excellent sales."

"So," replied Coulson, sarcastically, "what do you want, a medal?" He removed his jacket and placed on the back of his chair. Plonking himself back down in his chair, his corpulence caused the hydraulic air pump to make the recliner bounce twice.

Coulson was a large man by any standard. At fifty-five, he was grossly overweight due mainly to a diet of junk food and whiskey, and the fact that the only exercise he took was walking to and from the office toilet. The weight had started to pile on when he stopped playing golf due to a shoulder injury which actually seemed worse since he had had it operated on.

The surgeon had suggested another procedure, but with still no guarantee, Coulson had decided to live with it. The shoulder did not actually cause him any discomfort during his day-to-day activities, but heavy lifting and swinging a sand wedge were definitely off the menu.

Having separated from his wife the previous year after she found out about him visiting escorts whenever she took the children to see her parents – his excuse for not accompanying them had always been that he had too much work on – he had moved out of the family house – or more accurately, arrived home one day to find all his belongings had been thrown in a skip on their driveway – and now rented a tiny bedsit near the papers offices.

It was convenient for work, but that was about all it was good for. He used it mainly to sleep, shower, and change clothes, eating all his meals at local take-a-ways or at his desk. That, and the fact that he still smoked upwards of thirty a day made him a prime candidate for not making it to his sixties.

He had joined the *Alton Gazette* twenty years ago, having been a freelance since leaving college. In truth, he much preferred the thrill of the freelance life, and the potential was always there to make a lot of money if you were in the right place at the right time, which often he had been.

But it was his wife who insisted that his occupation did not offer enough stability and security to take on the responsibility of bringing up a young family, so she nagged him until he accepted the offer at the *Gazette*.

He had worked his way up relatively quickly to deputy sub-editor, then a few years later, when the sub-editor retired, it was virtually a foregone conclusion that the job was his. His final rise to editor had come about as a result of a tragedy when his boss suffered a fatal heart attack at his desk, and did not make it to the hospital before being pronounced dead in the ambulance.

Again, Coulson was the natural successor, though at the time there was some talk of the owners bringing in some big-wig from London, but it never materialised.

Since then, Coulson had run the ship with a steady hand. If any of his staff did not like him, at least they respected him, which in his book counted for a lot more. He had seen young pups like Topplewell come and go, and they all thought that they were going to be next Woodward or Bernstein. It was part of his job to keep them grounded whilst still keeping the fire within them alive.

Topplewell edged his chair closer to the desk for emphasis. "Look, boss, how about this. I've been hearing rumours that there's some old tramp in town who reckons he has seen others being taken by whatever this thing is. So how about I find him and get his version of events, perhaps he knows more about it?"

Coulson looked up at his employee's eager expression. He reminded him of a puppy with a new toy, wagging its tail in anticipation of someone throwing it for them to go and fetch. He glanced at the clock on the wall; it was only 9:35am, far too early for a drink, though after his meeting this morning with some of the editorial committee members, he felt as if he had earned one.

Coulson slammed his hand down on the intercom on his desk. The force of his action caused several files and papers to jump and shift.

"Mary, coffee please, strong and black!" He looked back over at Justin who was still perched on the end of his chair. He thought for a minute, and then grunted in his usual dismissive manner before continuing. "And exactly what kind of plausibility do you think you are going to get from an old drunk who probably sees all manner of things through his inebriation, including pink elephants?"

"Yea but boss, think of how it will look if this actually comes to something? We've got the jump on it right now; we need to keep control before the big boys get wind of it and start to muscle in."

Coulson had to admit to himself that Justin did have a point. Under normal circumstances, he too would have been pushing for a bigger slice of the action.

But a sea monster!

They would be laughed at – if not something far worse! He had the credibility of the paper to consider. Not to mention his career.

He had only allowed Topplewell to run the first story due to the present lack of any viable front page headlines. Though the girl and her father had seemed sincere enough when they came in, the girl was a little flaky, and her dad had not actually seen anything himself; he was just supporting his daughter's assertions, probably through misguided love.

The fact that she could not give an accurate description of what she saw certainly did not help matters. But the fact remained that no one had seen the young lad she was with since that night, and if the police suspected foul play on her behalf, surely they would have arrested her by now.

A crime of passion. Unrequited love. Perhaps she changed her mind at the last minute and he became a bit heavy-handed and forceful. An attempted rape, she hits out with a rock from the beach, catches him in the temple, and out he goes. She realises what she's done and drags his corpse to the water's edge where the tide carries him off. Or maybe she calls Daddy, and he has a boat and takes the body out and dumps it in the sea.

Now that would make a good story. One that the public would be eager to read about, especially as it involves locals. But on top of that, the trial would probably take place in London. The story would go national. There would be television coverage too. Now getting in on the ground floor of a story like that would definitely be worth it…But this!

There was a knock at the door which brought Coulson out of his reverie.

He waved the woman with his coffee in. Mary had been his secretary for a little over a year. She was a few years older than Justin, and had an incredible figure which she loved to accentuate in tight-fitting tops and extremely short skirts.

Coulson knew that as editor he should have had a word with her about appropriate office attire. But if he was honest, he enjoyed watching her move around the place just as much as her male colleagues did. So he decided to let sleeping dogs lie unless someone else made an official complaint to him.

She placed it in front of him and winked at Justin as she turned to leave.

"Thanks, Mary," Coulson called after her, trying to be discreet as he focused on the graceful movement of her perfect behind.

Justin too turned to watch, just catching Coulson out as he spun back around.

They heard the door click shut. "No panties today. What do you reckon, boss?"

Coulson felt his cheeks flush. "That's quite enough of that kind of talk, Topplewell," he blasted. "Need I remind you of our policy on office etiquette?"

Justin put his hands up in defence. "Just kiddin'," but he could not keep the smirk from his face as he spoke. Feeling the air lighten, he decided to press for home. "Come on, boss; just give me another day on this. I'll suss out if there is anything in the old man's story or not. We can't allow an opportunity like this to pass without at least exploring all the leads."

Coulson thought, chewing the tip of his pen. It was true; another day would not be life or death, and if the old guy did see something of value, possibly the girl and her father disposing of the body, then it could lead to something big.

"Okay," he replied, finally, "one more day, but don't waste it. Find the old man and see what, if any, sense you can make out of him." Coulson jabbed in the direction of Justin with his index finger. "And do not go putting words into the old man's mouth. If there's nothing there, leave it!"

Justin sprang from his chair and raced from the office before his boss could change his mind.

Coulson watched the young reporter as he almost ran to the stairs to make his exit. In many ways, he envied his energy and enthusiasm. He reminded him of himself as a young reporter, always on the look-out for the next "big thing".

He took a sip of his coffee and winced at the bitterness of it. Mary sure was a looker, but her coffee-making skills left a lot to be desired.

He checked around surreptitiously to make sure no one was watching. This was the problem with a glass-covered office. Once he was sure he was not being monitored, he opened his desk drawer and took out his bottle of single malt. Pouring a measure into his cup, he stirred in into the coffee and replaced the bottle.

The second sip was far more pleasant than the first.

***

It was a little before 1pm when the call Seaton had been dreading all morning finally came through. The council meeting had been set for 2:30 that afternoon, and Seaton would be expected to provide some answers for some very serious questions.

Having finished his call with Sheila that morning, Seaton had walked down the road in his dressing gown to purchase a copy of the *Gazette*. Whenever he had done this in the past at this hour, he was usually one of the few people about, so nobody took any notice. But today, the shop was half-full with concerned citizens, enthusiastically discussing the story in the paper about the sea monster.

When he walked in, there was a lull in the conversation. Eyes caught his and either looked away embarrassed, or passed a brief acknowledgement. As he walked to the counter to pay, the other customers busied themselves checking prices on items they grabbed randomly from the shelves, or huddled in corners, trying not to be overheard.

The madness had already started, and Seaton walked back to the station house with a deep feeling of foreboding, wondering to himself how long it would be before sightings of sea monsters started pouring in from all over the surrounding area.

By the time his junior officers had arrived, he had read the story three times. As he had suspected, the reporter had managed to prise some altogether new facts from Amy Friar concerning her encounter with the monster, none of which she had mentioned when he took her statement.

She had told Seaton that she had only just met Dodds. According to the paper, it was love at first sight, and he had asked her to marry him just before he was grabbed and swept away towards the jaws of death.

According to the story, the creature now had at least ten arms with huge razor-sharp claws at the end of each one. She was now positively able to state that the thing had a row of eyes which covered the front of its head, each one the size of a saucer and glowing red with hatred and menace.

The picture they had used was of a much younger – and slimmer – Amy Friar, clearly, thought Seaton, before she had begun her love affair with fried Mars bars.

The article claimed that they had asked Amy to take them to the spot where she last saw the monster, but that she was, even now, too afraid to go back there. They had included a shot of the beach at Skullen Bay, but as to whether it was exactly where Amy claimed the incident took place was anybody's guess. Not that it really mattered; a beach was a beach near as dammit.

His team had the same opinion as he did. All day, they could expect to be bombarded with queries concerning the safety of the town and the surrounding beaches. The phones started ringing just after nine, and did not let up for the next three solid hours. The queries were all the same: Is there a monster? Is it safe to go in the water? What are the authorities doing about it? Have they called the army in? Was it from outer space? The list grew more tiresome and ridiculous as the day progressed.

Seaton decided to keep all three of his constables at the station to deal with the onslaught. For those whose patience grew thin when they were not able to get through to the station on the phone, they began to roll up at the door. The tiny station was not designed to deal with such vast numbers, so Seaton himself came out to fend them off with comforting words of encouragement that everything was under control, and that they did not have anything to worry about.

Deep down, Seaton began praying that he was right. His thoughts kept returning to the pictures in the book he had bought from the museum of those enormous squids. But they were only ever found in much warmer waters than those around the north east coast of England. According to the book, even if one had strayed out of its territory, as soon as it felt the water temperature dropping, it would turn and retrace its path back to more familiar territory.

But it was the conviction in old Sam Cleary's eyes, and the look of terror in Amy's when they were relating their stories that made him begin to doubt the reassurances he was doling out.

He knew that he would not be able to live with himself if someone was killed because he had told them that there was nothing to worry about.

But what was the alternative?

By 12:30, things had started to calm down a bit. Sally – who had started to complain of jaw ache from too much talking – volunteered to make a brew to keep everyone's spirit up.

Seaton returned to his office and continued to read from his book. He still had not decided what his tack would be at the council meeting, but he wanted as much scientific information as possible behind him if the conversation swayed in that direction.

By the time the call came in summoning him to the meeting, he was fairly sure that he could at least give those in attendance the assurance that whatever Amy had seen; science said it could not be a giant squid.

He decided to only skim read the chapter about the Kraken for the simple reason that the book – as well as Caitlin – told him that there was no actual evidence of such a creature's existence. The book even ventured that seamen who had claimed to have seen it were if anything, looking at the giant squid. There seemed little point in bringing myth and legend into the conversation.

Seaton decided it was probably best not to take the book with him to the meeting. He arrived at the council offices with fifteen minutes to spare. He used the large wall mirror in the spotless toilet to check his appearance. He removed his uniform cap and patted down his receding hair until it stayed in place. He walked into the meeting with his cap under his arm, not wishing to have his hair sticking up in the meeting.

There were already six people sitting around the grand conference room table. Four he recognised from previous meetings, including Sheila, who gave him the merest of acknowledgments as he entered.

Seaton walked around the table, shaking hands and swapping introductions with those whom he did not know. One of them was an officer from their nearest branch of "Fish and Game", invited to attend by Sheila, naturally. The other was a representative from the council's press office.

Seaton took his seat, purposely putting as much distance between him and Sheila as he could.

Eventually, two more councillors arrived, both out of breath from running. They apologised in unison for their tardiness, and Sheila brought the meeting to order.

To save time – or as Seaton believed, because she liked to show off – Sheila made the introductions around the table.

"Now we all know why we are here today." There was a general nodding of heads. "It is as a direct result of the story in this morning's paper." She held out a folded copy of the *Gazette*. "It's unfortunate that this appeared before most of us were aware of the situation," she shot a sly glance in Seaton's direction, "but there's no point crying over spilt milk. The question now is, what are we going to do about it?" She offered it out to the room. "Any thoughts, anyone?"

The first to speak was a small, balding man with gold-rimmed glasses. Seaton recognised him from previous meetings; he was usually the first to speak up on any given topic. He wore a dark blue pinstriped suit, was painfully thin, and spoke with a broad Yorkshire accent. "Well, speaking as someone who doesn't believe much of what he reads in the papers these days, I have to ask if there has been any corroboration to this story, or is it just the word of this one girl?"

There was a general murmur of agreement.

Sheila removed her heavy-rimmed glasses and used them to point in Seaton's direction. "Officer Seaton has already spoken to one corroborating eye witness, but to my understanding, you aren't very convinced by his story, is that right?"

Seaton cleared his throat. "The second statement, which was in fact the first one I took, came from old Sam Cleary." At the mention of the old tramp's name, voices could be heard groaning. Seaton continued, "Now, those of you who know old Sam will I think agree that as far as being a reliable witness goes, he's not the first person anyone would think of."

"Was he sober at the time?" piped up a young male suit from across the table.

There was a ripple of light laughter in response.

Seaton waited for the noise to abate. "As you can imagine, he was somewhat worse for wear. Though to be honest, he wasn't falling-over drunk," he caught Sheila raising an eyebrow at him, "but by the same token," he continued, "he would not be anyone's first choice as a witness."

"Is that why you initially did not react to the threat?" This came from one of the late-comers, a middle-aged woman wearing a Laura Ashley ensemble.

Seaton looked at her and smiled. "Yes, you could say that."

"But what about when this chip-shop girl gave you her account? Did you not think then that it warranted further investigation?" This accusation came from the representative from the press office. A very attractive young woman, in Seaton's opinion, who seemed to be trying to hide both her good looks and her age by the way she had her long brown hair tied tightly in a bun, with thin oval-shaped glasses perched on the end of her nose. She had been sitting there since the start of the meeting frantically writing down everything that was said. Now her pen was poised, awaiting Seaton's response.

Seaton had a feeling when Sheila first suggested this meeting that it would turn into a witch hunt with him being the most obvious choice for the stake. But he had hoped that he might find a few of them on his side, willing to listen before making hasty judgements. Clearly, that was not to be the case.

Seaton shifted his position so that he was sitting up straighter in his chair, ready to take on all foes. He looked directly at the press representative who had asked the question before answering. "When I first received Amy Friar's account, I think you can all appreciate that without believing in monsters and creatures from the black lagoon, I felt it more important to first ascertain if there had in fact been an incident, or just a prank by a couple of local lads. After all, the girl may not have been a drunk or a down-and-out, but I am sure if you met her, you would agree that she too in her own way was not the most reliable of witnesses."

"So what did you do to try and corroborate her story?" asked Councillor Nugent. Seaton had met him before on a couple of occasions, and he seemed like a reasonable man, certainly not the type to point an accusatory finger before knowing all the facts.

"Well, initially, I treated it as a missing person investigation. My team ascertained the following morning that there was indeed a missing lad, this Pete Dodds, but we still had no way at the time of knowing if anything had happened to him. Therefore, we followed protocol and contacted our colleagues in London to see if they could trace his next of kin. After all, for all we knew, he might have just become homesick and headed back there."

There were a few nods around the table which Seaton found comforting.

"As it is at present, it looks to all intents and purposes as if the lad really is missing."

"So then we come to this girl's story in the paper!" It was Sheila this time. Surprisingly, she did not aim the statement at Seaton but more as a general observation for all concerned.

"Surely, no one actually believes that a monster from the depths has come ashore on Skullen Bay?" It was the bald-headed man with the spectacles again. "After all, we're all reasonably intelligent individuals and we're not living in a Jules Verne novel."

Laughs and nods all around.

"Well, perhaps Mr. Harrington from Fish and Game might be able to cast some explanatory light on our situation?" Sheila smiled at the F&G representative across the table. He was a large-boned, middle-aged man who appeared to be twitching nervously throughout the proceedings. When Sheila aimed her question at him, he began stammering and mumbling his reply, unable to look anyone in the eye he gazed down at the table while he spoke.

He obviously knew his stuff, thought Dan, but it was obvious that their present situation was way out of his remit. The man visibly relaxed once he had finished speaking, apologising for the umpteenth time that his office could not be of more help.

The meeting carried on for almost two exhausting hours. During the proceedings, when they seemed to be making absolutely no progress, Sheila called for a comfort break, and tea and coffee were served. During the break, Dan called the station to check up on how things were going.

That's when Constable Green informed him that they had received a phone call that afternoon from the dean of a university just outside Norwich. Three of their biology students had been staying in Alton making a documentary on over-fishing and the effect it was having on the environment. When they had spoken to colleagues on the phone on their last day in Alton, they said that they intended to hire a local guide to take them out on the sea to film their report. That was the last anyone had seen or heard of them.

Seaton rubbed his face with his hand whilst Joe Green spoke. This was all he needed. Well, perhaps it was fortuitous that the information had come in whilst the meeting was in progress. If there was any connection between the loss of these students and what Amy Friar and Sam Cleary say that they witnessed, then they were – as the councillor had put it – living in a Jules Verne novel, and he was the sheriff in charge of the hunt.

By the time the meeting had reconvened, Sheila had spoken to the mayor who was sunning herself in the Seychelles at the moment. She had given Sheila a list of actions which she wanted instigated in her absence, and Sheila was to take charge of the situation and keep her informed of all developments until her return.

Before Sheila began with her list, Seaton took the floor. "Look, I am not sure if this is the right forum to mention this," he looked at the tired faces around the table, "but something which may be significant had just come to my attention."

Sheila spoke up. "Everyone in this room can be trusted for their discretion. Sergeant, please continue."

Seaton put his hand to his mouth and coughed. "Well, we have received word this afternoon that three students from Norwich may, and I emphasise the word "may" have gone missing in the last couple of days."

Everyone began offering their opinion. Some spoke to the person sitting beside them, others just to the floor in general. Voices crossed over, points were mixed and missed out.

Finally, Sheila called for order. The noise quickly died.

She looked straight at Seaton. "When you say "may" how sure are you, exactly?"

"At this stage, not at all. As I say, we have only just taken the call at the station, so of course, we'll have to instigate an investigation and try and get to the bottom of it."

His words were greeted with mutterings and several heads shaking.

"Where do you plan to start?" Sheila's voice again rose above the cacophony.

"Well, to start with, the caller said that when they were last spoken to, these students said that they were going to see about hiring a local man to take them out on the sea to make some sort of documentary film. So our first port of call will be to see if we can ascertain who this local man is. If indeed he does exist at all."

"What does that mean?" asked the lady from the press office, pushing her glasses back before the slid completely off the end of her nose.

Seaton looked back at her, smiling. "Well, madam, so far we only have hear-say evidence that they actually did arrange a boat trip with a local man. If no one remembers speaking or seeing them, it makes any corroboration virtually impossible."

The woman returned to her pad, writing frantically.

Before the murmurs had a chance to escalate again, Sheila announced that in view of what the sergeant had just told them, it seemed all the more critical that she divulge the mayor's observations for discussion.

The first point was that Sheila should contact the coastguard and make them aware of the situation to see if they could offer any assistance.

The second was that she contacted a marine expert to see if they could shed any light on what it might be that was attacking their Bay.

At that point, Seaton raised his hand politely, and when acknowledged, he told them how he had spoken to Caitlin and about the book he had read. They all sat agog as he opened his notebook and read out some of the approximated sizes that giant squids could grow to. Someone commentated that he would never touch calamari again, and there was a ripple of laughter which Sheila soon put down with one of her renowned stares. She thanked him for his update, but Seaton could tell from her dismissive manner that she had every intention of finding her own expert.

The mayor's third suggestion made Seaton grown inwardly.

"The mayor has decided," began Sheila, "and this is in no way any reflection on our own brave officers," she nodded towards Seaton without conviction, "that I should contact new Scotland Yard and ask for some detective intervention to take charge of this affair." She purposely avoided Seaton's gaze. "After all, as the mayor quite rightly points out, they have experience in most things, possibly even other instances such as ours."

The general consensus seemed to be that action needed to be taken and that Sheila was the best one for the job. In other words, they were happy for her to find the rope if indeed it existed, and hang herself without involving any of them.

CHAPTER THIRTEEN

It took Justin Topplewell the best part of the day to finally track Sam Cleary down. He began by checking out the beach up at Skullen Bay, as he knew that this was a regular haunt of the old man especially when sleeping off the previous day's intake, but having looked under umpteen tarpaulins without success, he decided that he needed to broaden his search pattern.

His second avenue was the old fisherman's hostel, where Sam had a permanent bunk. The caretaker there was an old fisherman himself and knew Sam very well. He said that Sam had been there the previous night to use the washing facilities and to get a change of clothes, but that he had risen early and left before breakfast, the simple bacon and eggs offered by the hostel usually lost out to something more liquid when Sam had a few quid in his pocket.

The caretaker laughed when Justin told him he needed to speak to Sam urgently, and through a mouthful of half-missing teeth, hissed that his best bet was to start with the local pubs, making sure that he looked inside every off-license he passed along the way.

As lunchtime approached, most of the pubs were getting so crowded that Justin had to fight his way through the mass throngs in his search for the old man. By late afternoon, he had virtually exhausted every avenue without success. No one admitted to having seen old Sam that day, and Justin was beginning to feel as if he was on a lost cause.

But his editor had given him one more day to piece together a follow-up story. And the roving reporter in him was not about to abandon ship; not just yet at any rate. A good reporter, once on the sent, never gave up!

To his annoyance, Justin finally located Sam where he first began to look for him that morning: on Skullen Bay. He was sitting on an old deck chair in the shade of the old pier, watching the holiday makers enjoying the sunshine. As Justin drew closer, he noticed a half-empty bottle of wine resting between the old man's legs. He hoped that Sam was not already so far gone that he would not be able to get any sense out of him.

At least he was sitting to one side away from the main hubbub, so it should be easier to question him without interfering eyes and ears. Justin picked up a discarded deck chair from the beach and carried it over to where Sam was sitting.

The old man's eyes did not acknowledge Justin's arrival, until he sat down and introduced himself. Sam looked at the new arrival sceptically through bleary eyes, before taking a long swig from his bottle. He belched loudly before offering it to Justin. Justin declined politely, so Sam shrugged his shoulders and took another gulp.

"I don't know if you aware or not, Sam, but there have been some disappearances reported from this very beach." Justin thought it best to get in his questions as quickly as he could before the old man grew too intoxicated.

Sam eyed Justin suspiciously, then looked towards the sea, nodding.

"Aye," he replied, "an' there'll be more too before she's done!"

Justin ensured that the recorder in his pocket was on before continuing.

"Who exactly do you mean by 'She', Sam?"

Sam glanced back at the reporter; he rubbed his head through his hat, causing the brim to dip below one eye, reminding Justin of those old gangster films his mother used to love watching when he was little.

Sam leaned in closer. "She who commands the sea, boy," he whispered, almost as if afraid that some of the holiday-makers might overhear.

Justin took out his notepad and pen. He decided that he needed to make a hard copy of everything Sam said, just in case he spoke too quietly for the recorder to pick up.

"So you've seen her?" Justin asked, excitedly. "You can tell me what she looks like and where she comes ashore?"

Sam winked and took another gulp before continuing. The bottle was almost empty now, and Justin began to wonder if he should have brought one with him as a way of keeping the old man's interest. He was afraid now that he might wander off in search of replenishment before he had answered all Justin's questions. "Aye, I can show you alright," the old man turned back towards the sea, "but as to whether or not you would ever want to see her yerself, well that's another matter."

Justin fumbled for his wallet. All he had was a £20 note. He begrudged handing over so much to such an unlikely source, but hopefully if his editor went for it, he could claim it back on expenses. He decided it was worth the risk.

He took out the crisp note and rubbed it between his fingers to ensure that he attracted the old man's attention.

Sam looked eagerly at the note, and began to lick his lips in anticipation of how much alcohol it would buy him. He had a deal with one of the local off-license owners who let him have two bottles of his cheapest wine for a fiver, and five bottles for a tenner, so with £20 in his pocket, he would be sorted for a couple of days at least.

Justin quickly realised that he had the old man's full attention. He moved the note closer to Sam. "This is all yours, Sam, if you promise to tell me all you know about this creature, and where the best place is to see her come ashore."

Sam did not need a second to think about it. He reached out and grabbed the money before Justin had a chance to think again. Hastily, Sam shoved it into his inside pocket and then rubbed his hands together. He picked up his bottle and drained what was left of its contents, as if he needed to wet his lips before starting.

"Well now, boy, if I tell you what I know, you'll be the first one to believe me, but old Sam don't lie," he wagged his index finger for emphasis. "I've seen the beastie now on more than a few occasions, and she always comes ashore in roughly the same place." Sam pointed out to his right a little further up the beach. "It's around there where she's most likely to come out, but not during the day, at least I've never seen her during daylight. She knows that her time is when the sun has gone down and only those privileged enough get to cast their gaze upon her magnificence."

Justin wrote frantically, trying to keep up. "And is there a specific time when she likes to appear?" he asked, hoping to elicit some kind of timetable the old man might have worked out from his past sightings.

Sam licked his lips, the taste of wine still sweet from his last swig. "Aye, she always waits until the sea has moved out past the first buoy." He pointed out towards a buoy which bobbed in the water in the distance. Justin held his hand over his eyes and squinted. "Does you see it?" Sam asked.

"Yes, I think so, it's rather a long way out. What sort of time does the tide reach that point?"

Sam rubbed his chin. The growth on his face grated against his calloused hand, making a faint sandpapery noise. "Ooo now, yer talkin' about anywhere from eleven at night until maybe two or three in the mornin'"

"And when it comes," continued Justin, excitedly, "you've witnessed it actually capturing people on the beach and carrying them out to sea?"

"Aye, she took old *Cappy* right in front of me eyes. Waitin' for her he was, he knew his time was 'ere."

Justin was shocked. "What, you mean he actually knew that it was going to take him, and he just waited for it on the beach?"

Sam laughed. "Why yes, why do you find that so hard to believe?" He looked at Justin in astonishment. "When I'm good an' ready, I'll be waitin' for 'er to take me too." He turned back to face the sea, waving his hand in the air following the distant horizon. "An' she'll know I'm there, waitin' for 'er, then she will rise and take me home to glory."

Justin winced. He was beginning to think that old Sam was fast becoming too unreliable to be a newsworthy source. But then on the other hand, he had been the only witness other than that chip-shop girl to the disappearances, and he had seen more than just one according to Joe green down at the station. Justin made a mental note to himself that he must remember to bung Joe a couple of quid if Sam turned out to be a useful story after all.

Justine turned to a fresh page. "So, Sam, tell me about the ones other than old *Cappy* that you have seen being taken by the creature. You saw Pete Dobbs who was with the young girl from the chip shop being taken, didn't you?"

"Aye, if that were the one that Sgt. Seaton were askin' about, 'e tried to get away, left the young lassie alone on the beach, made a run fer it." He gestured towards the top end of the beach past several youngsters running along the sand screaming their joy at being at play. "But she were 'aving none of it. She 'ad come fer 'im and she weren't goin' to take no fer an answer." Sam half stood with his arms raised. "She stretched 'er mighty arms over the girl and grabbed 'im as 'e was scramblin' away. Dragged 'im back to 'er and left the lassie behind."

Justin looked up from his pad. "So in your opinion, the creature only wanted the boy? She could have taken the girl if she had wanted to, but purposely left her behind?"

"Aye, that's right. She knows what she wants an' what she don't."

"That's incredible," mused Justin, still scribbling. "And why do you think she was only interested in the boy and not the girl?"

Sam shrugged. "Dunno." He moved in closer again. "But I tell you this, the one she took 'efore 'im was a human sacrifice to 'er, that's fer sure."

Justin stopped writing and turned again to face the old man. "Human sacrifice, how do you mean?"

Sam smiled to himself. "Aye, I thought that might make' e' take some notice. I told old Sgt. Seaton, but 'e didn't believe me. But 'e will, when the others start to be taken. Then they'll all start believin' old Sam."

Justin held out a hand to stop Sam wandering off track. "Tell me what you mean by 'human sacrifice', Sam." This could make a terrific angle for the follow-up story, thought Justin. Human sacrifices, devil worship, sea-god worship, cults, who knows where it might lead.

Sam cleared his throat. He needed another drink; the £20 note Justin had given him was burning a hole in his pocket. He hoped that this interview would not take too much longer; he was about ready to start his evening session.

Sam tuned in his chair and indicated to an area just beyond the pier, presently under water. "It were about there, yer see?" He waited for Justin to acknowledge his attention. "There was a man, never seen 'im before. He came down 'ere alone an' started digging."

"Digging," interrupted Justin. "What, just digging a hole on the beach late at night?"

"Aye, that were it. 'e digs this dirty great 'ole, an' I'm watching 'im thinkin' what's it fer. Buried treasure? A dead body? I kept me distance so I could still see what 'e were doin', but where I knew 'e couldn't see me, see?" The old man lowered his voice just as a young couple ran past them heading towards the sea. "Then after a while, this young woman turns up, an' she makes 'im climb into the 'ole. Then she buries 'im up to 'is neck in sand, and leaves 'im there when the sea-goddess comes for 'im."

Justin pulled a face. "She buried him up to his neck in sand for the sea creature?"

"Aye." Sam nodded. "Jus' left 'im there like I said, a 'uman sacrifice he was."

"And do you know who the woman was?"

Sam shook his head. "Nah, never seen 'er before; mind you, I were a bit far away to tell fer sure."

"And from what you could see, the man just let her bury him and wait for his attacker to surface?" Justin asked, still stunned by what he was hearing.

"That's about it," Sam said, confidently. "I told you, it were a sacrifice to 'er from the depths." The old man pulled back and swung around to gaze out to see. After a moment, he said, "She'll be back tonight, you wait an' see."

Justin stopped writing. "What!"

Sam turned back to him. "I said she'll be back tonight. I can tell now when she's going to rise. Oh, she'll be back tonight alright; you mark my words, young mister."

Justin could not believe his ears. He had abandoned his pad altogether now to ensure he had the old man's full attention. "Are you telling me that you can state, categorically that this creature will show itself on this stretch of beach tonight?"

"Aye." Sam smiled. "Don't look so shocked, young mister. I told you I knew 'er comings an' goin's."

Justin thought for a while. This might just be the ramblings of an old drunk, but on the off chance that there was actually something in it, he needed to take full advantage of the situation.

Justin checked his watch. It was a little after 4pm. He looked around, making sure that none of the holiday-makers were within earshot before he spoke.

"Listen, Sam," he whispered gently. "I need you to make sure that you do not tell anyone else what you've just told me, okay?"

Sam spread out his upturned hands. "Who am I goin' to tell? No one listens to old Sam no way."

Justin needed to make sure that no one else had a chance to ruin his coup. He stood up and fumbled in his jean pocket. He pulled out a handful of coins which he estimated equalled about six pounds give or take. He offered them to Sam who cupped his hands to receive the additional bequest.

"Now Sam, let's be straight on this," Justin said, emphasising the seriousness of the instruction he was about to deliver. "This means that you do not speak to anyone about what we have discussed today."

Sam looked up perplexed. "But what am I to say if the police come looking for me again? I don't wanna be caught out lyin' to them; they'll lock me up!"

"Listen." Justin calmed the tenor in his voice. A nervous Sam with a belly full of booze might go running to the police because he thought he had done something wrong, and that could scupper Justin's plans for the night. "There's no reason for the police to come looking for you, you've already given them a statement. Just go and find yourself a nice comfortable hidey-hole and enjoy your refreshment." Justin laid his hand on the old man's shoulder as he rose from his chair. "And don't worry about anything; this can be our little secret."

Justin raced back to the news office, arriving back a little after 5pm. Dripping with perspiration, he made straight for Coulson's office, but it was empty. The evening crew had already arrived and Justin scoured the floor trying to locate his boss.

Finally, he spotted Mary disappearing into one of the file storage rooms, so made a beeline for her. The room she had entered was on three levels with metallic racks standing ten feet apart on all floors. Each one was crammed with achieved files, many fit to burst.

Justin looked around but could not see the PA at first, but then he heard the sound of footsteps on the metal staircase at the far end. He walked along the corridor towards the echoing footfalls and spied Mary one floor down, placing some heavy files back on their respective shelves.

Justin made his way down to her. Mary turned around at the sound of his approach. She smiled warmly when she realised that it was him.

"Hey you, did you come down to give me a hand?"

Justin grinned as he sidled up to her. "Afraid not, I'm looking for Coulson. Any idea where he's hiding?"

Mary stopped what she was doing and gave Justin her full attention.

"He's gone to pick up his kids; he's taking them out tonight for a pizza."

"Damn!" Justin kicked out at the shelf in front of him.

"What's up?" Mary asked, concerned.

"Oh nothing," Justin lied, looking away while he tried to think what to do now.

Mary put her files down on the wheelie tray she had been pushing. She stood square up to Justin, her slender, perfectly manicured fingers placed firmly on her hips. She looked over the rim of her glasses straight at Justin. She reminded him of the librarian he had at school when she caught him and his friends sneaking a porn magazine into an encyclopaedia.

Though Mary was about a hundred times sexier than Mrs. Bansby.

"Come on, you can tell me," Mary urged, seductively. Justin was staring at the floor in front of her. His eyes began to wander up her shapely legs, past the hem of her tightly fitting pencil skirt and onto her shapely hips, and finally her magnificent breasts.

He tried not to linger for too long on her chest as he knew she was watching him. By the time his eyes met hers, he could tell by the smile on her face that Mary knew exactly what he was up to, and she openly encouraged it.

Justin could not help himself as he felt his cheeks redden. Embarrassed, he let his gaze drop back down to the floor. His reaction made Mary's smile even broader.

She reached out and cupped his chin in one hand, tilting his face back up towards hers. She felt in total control and enjoyed the feeling of power it gave her.

"Now why can't you tell me what it is you wanted Coulson for. I am his right hand after all. Maybe I can be of some assistance?" As she spoke, Mary moved her body closer to Justin whilst simultaneously edging him nearer by his chin, until finally their mouths were only a few centimetres apart.

Justin could smell her perfume; it was intoxicating. In fact, Mary herself was intoxicating, and under different circumstances, if he was not so pressed for time, Justin would have loved to have discovered how far she was willing to go with him.

"I…I wanted to ask Coulson if he would sanction me hiring a boat for tonight," Justin half-spluttered out.

"Ooohh, that sounds romantic," Mary sighed. Her breath smelled of a combination of strong coffee and fresh mint. Mingling with her perfume and overall body scent, Justin could not help but close his eyes and inhale deeply.

Oh why had she waited until now to make a move on him?

Surely, she had always known that he was hers for the taking?

Perhaps, he pondered, that was all part of her allure. To torture him by giving him the odd wink and occasional glance at her panties as she purposely made a point of bending over in front of him to retrieve something from a drawer or shelf, rather than go down on her haunches like the health and safety poster lady demonstrated.

"So who were you thinking of taking out on the water then, mmmm?"

Justin could almost feel her lips brushing against his. He could not stand this anymore. Opening his eyes, he leaned in and pressed his eager mouth against hers. Mary reciprocated hungrily, and they stood there locked together, arms wrapped around each other, hands searching, probing, investigating unchartered territory, their bodies gyrating slowly against each other's. Each one listening out in case someone else should enter the storage area.

When they finally pulled apart, both of them smiled at the other.

Justin had to forcibly stop himself from saying "Wow," out loud.

Mary let her index finger trace a path down Justin's torso. When she reached the belt of his jeans, she hooked her finger inside it and pulled him closer once more. Her magnetism was overpowering, and Justin felt himself on the verge of foregoing his scoop and just spending the night with Mary.

As she expertly slipped her hand down the front of his jeans and began to stroke him seductively through the flimsy fabric of his jockey shorts, Justin's resolve slipped even further away. To hell with the sea-monster, he thought.

But then he remembered Sam's conviction that the creature would return to the beach tonight. The old man may have been a drunk and a down-and-out, but he was the only one so far who had studied the creature's comings and goings which made him the most reliable authority on it so far.

Justin knew that tonight may be his best – and only – chance to get a decent shot of the monster. He knew exactly how he would feel tomorrow if he let this chance slip by. Especially if someone else happened to be in the right place at the right time and got the picture instead. This could be the kick-start his career needed. A decent shot with his follow-up article was too great an opportunity to let slip by. Even when the alternative was the chance to spend the night with a stunner like Mary.

"Aren't you going to tell me then?" Mary's words brought Justin back to the real world.

"Sorry, tell you what?" She was still fingering him through his shorts, her fingers moving with great dexterity in the confined area caused by his tight-fitting jeans.

"Who it is you want to go out with on the boat tonight?" Mary teased. "Have I got a rival?"

"No, no, nothing like that, I just need Animal to take some pictures for me."

Mary moved her body closer so that her breasts were crushed up against Justin's chest, her lips pursed in anticipation of another lingering kiss.

Just before their lips locked, Justin asked, "Is there any way you can sign a chit so I can rent a boat for tonight?"

Mary stopped moving her fingers inside Justin's jeans.

She took a step back then removed her hand altogether. The suddenness of her exit caused Justin to wince as she caught the head of his penis with one of her rings. Grabbing himself between the legs Justin bent over, the pain inflicted etched on his expression.

Mary was clearly not impressed at his rejection of her advances. Justin wanted to tell her how flattered he was, and that on any other occasion, he would have jumped at the chance of spending the night with her, and hoped that she would give him another opportunity soon to prove it to her.

But he did not get the chance!

Mary's smile was gone. She turned back to continue with the work she had been engrossed in before his arrival. Over her shoulder, without looking back at him, she said, "The requisition forms are in my top drawer, fill one out, and I'll sign it when I finish here." Her statement was so matter-of-fact that Justin knew that there was no chance of winning her round just now.

He smiled weakly, though Mary did not see it with her back still towards him.

"Thanks, Mary, I really appreciate it."

He heard her harrumph as he turned to leave.

Back in the main office, Justin caught hold of Animal just as he was putting his coat on to leave for the day. His real name was Norman Rice, but it was a newspaper tradition that all photographers were nicknamed "Animal" and that most – if not all – of the staff referred to them by that legend.

Justin ushered Animal into a side office and filled him in on his plan. Animal, for his part, was not altogether convinced in the validity of the scheme. For a start, he did not believe in monsters of any sort, at least not the fairy-tale variety. Secondly, he had already worked a full day and been out on three shoots, so he was looking forward to going home, having a shower, and getting ready to hit the pub. And thirdly, there was a certain barmaid at his local who he had been chatting up for the last week, and he finally felt as if she was ready to succumb to his ambition for a date.

After all that he had given up, Justin was not about to let Animal slip away. The paper did have a couple of other photographers on the staff, but Justin liked Animal. He was a one-off original with his ponytail and permanent five o'clock shadow, the dark glasses he always wore even in the winter, and his dress sense which did not seem to follow any known fashion and had a "fuck you, this is how I like to look" quality about it.

What's more, Justin liked the man's work, liked his style, and above all else, liked his ambition to one day work for one of the big hitters in fleet street.

And that, Justin decided, was his best avenue of persuasion.

"Think about it, Animal; if this thing exists and it shows up tonight, you'll be the only one in the world with a picture of it. Can you imagine what we could charge for that?"

Animal was not sold. "Look, man, a sea-monster? Come on, it's ludicrous. You're taking the word of the town drunk and that fat bird from the chippy. And let's face it, she weren't all there to start with."

"Granted," Justin nodded, "but something must be responsible for all these disappearances. You don't honestly think that I believe it's a monster?" he lied, avoiding Animal's gaze. "But whatever it is, if it shows up tonight and we get a shot of it, we're talking front page all the way. We'll have the big boys knocking down the door, and it'll be our names on the by-line."

Justin could tell that the idea was starting to take route in Animal's mind. He wanted to say more, but decided to let Animal mull it over first, and add to his argument later if necessary.

After a moment, Animal gave in. "Alright, man, when and where?"

Justin moved in and gave Animal a camaraderie-style slap on the shoulder, almost dislodging the photographer's sunglasses in his enthusiasm.

"I'll get Mary to sign the requisition for Coulson so I can hire us a boat, then I'll call you. We should be ready to leave by about nine; gives us plenty of time to get far enough out to be able to see the entire coastline."

Animal was about to leave. He had one hand on the door handle then turned back to Justin. "What kind of boat, man? Nothing too big or ungainly, I ain't no sailor you know!"

Justin held up his hands. "Trust me, neither am I. A simple motor boat should do the trick, I've used one of them a couple of times to go fishing."

When Animal had left, Justin found the forms in Mary's drawer and filled one out. He had just finished when she emerged from the storage room.

When he held it out to her with a smile, she ignored him, grabbed the form, scanned it briefly and signed it, handing it back without looking up at him.

Justin thanked her.

He was going to say something about earlier, but decided from her body language that he needed to do some major grovelling first, and that the crowded office floor was not the place for that.

Perhaps he would start with some flowers, he thought as he walked out.

CHAPTER FOURTEEN

Dan and Tammi had worked straight through without taking a break to fix the engine on the *Lady Anne*. It was one of those jobs that you could not leave half completed when your boat was moored on water. The salt in the sea air could cause even further damage if the plates were removed and left off for any length of time.

Dan thanked God for the dexterity of Tammi's dainty fingers. Dan had often been of the opinion that manufacturers purposely made engine parts inaccessible so that you had to either buy a replacement or pay a fortune to a specialist shop whenever anything went wrong. But Tammi had an amazing knack for manoeuvring her arms and fingers into the tiniest, most cramped and awkward to get at spaces, and still manage to slip a wrench or spanner in with her to loosen or tighten cogs and nuts, whichever the instance demanded.

By 6pm that evening, both of them were exhausted and covered in oil, grease, and dirt. Dan had worn surgical gloves once the dirty work had started because he hated getting grime under his fingernails, and worse still, the fact that he never seemed to be able to fully extricate it no matter how hard he scrubbed. Tammi, on the other hand, said she could not feel her way around the insides of the engine without being able to rely on her sense of touch, especially in the parts which were out of sight once she'd snaked her arm in.

Tammi hit the showers first. She had received a text from Geraldine asking if she was free to hook up, so she had arranged to meet her in town at seven. Dan wasn't expected at Caitlin's until eight, so he had more time to play with.

Before she left for her date, Tammi asked, "Do yer think yer might be out all night at Caitlin's?"

Dan shrugged. "I hope so, but I don't want to take anything for granted." The huge grin on his face told Tammi he was more than a little confident that he would in fact be invited to stay over.

"It's just that I was hoping to bring Gerri back here again, if it's okay?"

"Sure," said Dan. "You two are really hitting it off then I take it?"

Tammi smiled. "Aye, she's a bonnie lass right enough, but I know not to get too involved; she is only seeing me on the side."

Dan could tell by her expression and the timbre of her voice that Tammi felt more for Gerri than she knew the other girl was willing to offer. But at least he thought Tammi would keep her guard up, knowing the situation from the outset.

While Tammi was attending to the finishes touches in the mirror, she called back. "What will you do if Caitlin kicks you out? Head back to Maggie's?" There was a smirk behind her question, which Dan thought cheeky, but typical Tammi.

"No, what kind of swine do you take me for?" He could not help but laugh at her innuendo.

Tammi came through into the main living area, attaching her second earring. Dan could not help but notice how attractive she was. She had applied make-up, which was quite a rarity with Tammi, even when she was going out. Her nails had been scrubbed clean and were now painted a deep ruby red. She was wearing sandals which showed that she had also taken the time to paint her toenails to match her fingers. She was really making an effort for Gerri, and he hoped that the other woman appreciated it, and reciprocated.

"I dunny see the problem. If this young lass chucks you over, Maggie always has room for ye."

Dan slumped down on the sofa to pull on his boots. He had decided to dress more casually this evening as they were past the first-date phase. He hoped that Caitlin would do likewise; otherwise, she might think he had not bothered to make an effort.

"If Caitlin chucks me, I'll be severely down in the dumps, and I'll expect you to drop everything and give me a shoulder to cry on."

Tammi laughed out loud. "If I'm in the arms of a beautiful woman, you're on yer own pal!"

"Cheers," replied Dan, feigning hurt.

Dan left his boat for the walk to Caitlin's with plenty of time to spare. He thought as it was such a pleasant evening that he would take a stroll by the sea in Alton before heading for her flat. He considered buying her a box of chocolates as the flowers had gone down so well, but on reflection, decided it might be too much too soon.

Dan could not believe how scared he was of losing Caitlin after such a short time of knowing her. He had to admit that he had never felt like this before, and though the excitement and anticipation of seeing her felt so good, the constant fear of her losing interest denied him any true happiness.

He wondered if perhaps he had been alone for so long that he was now incapable of fully appreciating the thrill of a new relationship. He had never considered himself to the nervous type, or to lack self-confidence in his own abilities. But Caitlin certainly had a hold over him. One which he felt it prudent to hide for as long as he could; otherwise, he would just come across as desperate and pathetic and he knew that that would not be a good look from him.

Wine!

Now that was different. A personal offering to the host from a grateful guest. He already knew what type of wine Caitlin liked from the restaurant; their tastes in that area were very similar. He knew a couple of good off-licenses in Alton so made up his mind that that was a good plan.

When he reached the promenade at Alton, the sun was still emanating a heat more suited to early afternoon than early evening. Being below deck for most of the day, Dan had not appreciated how hot the day was. The beach was still crowded with bathers and the fun fair and arcades looked as if everyone had decided to postpone dinner until later. There were queues for most of the rides, and three ice cream vans parked a hundred yards or so apart we all enjoying a bustling trade.

Dan removed his jacket, allowing the sea breeze to cool him down. Though it was a lightweight jacket, in this heat, it was still enough to cause him to start perspiring after his walk, and the last thing he wanted was to have to worry about body odour.

He walked along the roadside next to the beach until he reached the pier. Checking his watch, he decided a slow stroll back should allow him sufficient time to purchase the wine and reach Caitlin's a little before his expected arrival. He wished he could just turn up early; he could not wait to see her again, feel her arms around him, her warm soft body pressed against his, the smell of her hair, the taste of her lips.

He sighed longingly. He was dead in the water and he knew it!

As he walked, a novelty shop caught his eye. An idea struck him. He would bring wine for the hostess, and a toy for Honey to amuse herself with while they ate. Perfect!

Dan felt his stomach churn with excitement as he stood outside Caitlin's front door. He checked his watch for the third time in as many minutes. He was fifteen minutes early. Close enough, he thought. It has to be; he did not fancy loitering outside in the street being stared at by the neighbours, so he knocked and waited.

After a moment, he heard Caitlin calling as she came down the stairs.

She looked genuinely happy to see him, and made no comment about his timing. She was wearing bright pink denim jeans and a white cap-sleeve T-shirt. Dan felt instantly relieved that he had not over-dressed for the occasion. She had on silver stilettos without stockings, and Dan noticed a tiny tattoo of a dolphin on her right instep which he had not noticed before.

Once she closed the door, Caitlin threw her arms around him and they shared a passionate kiss.

Honey came bounding down the stairs, barking excitedly.

"Oh," said Caitlin, light-heartedly, "I think someone is getting jealous."

Dan bent down and starting fussing over the dog. She rolled on her back playfully while Dan rubbed her tummy.

Caitlin picked up the wine he had placed on the stairs when he entered. Reading the label of the first bottle, she raised her eyebrows. "Fancy." She looked at Dan who was still playing with Honey. "Who are you trying to impress?"

Dan stood up. "You, actually. Is it working?"

She leaned in for another kiss. "Yep!" she replied, winking at him.

Dan followed Caitlin up the stairs. Honey ran past them, stopping at the top to watch them climb, wagging her tail, excitedly.

"Oh, I almost forgot." Dan took the squeaky plastic bone he had bought Honey out of his jacket pocket and waved in front of the animal. Honey went down with her belly close to the floor as if awaiting a command.

Dan threw the toy across the room, and Honey ran after it, barking.

"You'll be doing that all night now," Caitlin called back on her way to the kitchen.

***

Seaton's day seemed to go from bad to worse. After the meeting at the council offices, he returned to the station to inform his officers of the good news concerning a potential visit from New Scotland Yard. He tried to be as positive as he could, but like the others, he too felt as though the investigation was being taken out of their hands before they had had a proper chance of turning up any substantial evidence.

Bringing the coastguard in and asking for some expert advice from a marine expert did make good sense, so that did not bother any of them. But a London detective with their big-time ideas and procedures was the last thing any of them wanted, especially their boss.

Having filled them all in, Seaton retired to his office to read the report phoned in from the dean of the university where the missing students had been from. The details were sketchy at best. The dean had only called because the students had been loaned some expensive camera equipment which they should have returned by now, as there was another group who needed it for their project.

The students had been staying at the local fisherman's hostel, which over the years had become more and more of a student stay-over than a resting place for weary fishermen, as it had originally been intended. Still, the council needed to show a profit to justify keeping the place open, and the semi-regular turnout of visiting students seemed to keep the wolf from the door.

Sally and Ralph had already gone there to see if they could glean anything substantial about the student's movements from the staff. Seaton hoped that it was a simple case of them getting too drunk and still sleeping it off, or forming a three-some and joining a commune, or eloping. Anything really, just so long as they were not actually missing from his town.

He had enough to deal with. He knew that once Sheila had a bee in her bonnet that there would be no stopping her. She took every opportunity, regardless of the circumstances, and tried to turn it into a potential platform from which she could lobby for support further down the line. And these disappearances, whether they turned out to be the work of kidnappers, human traffickers, mad scientists, or Jack the Ripper, would make a fine podium come election time.

As he slid the filing cabinet drawer shut, the phone on his desk burst into action. He snatched up the receiver. "Alton Police Station, Sergeant Seaton speaking."

When Sally and Ralph returned from the hostel, the news was not good. They could hear their boss on the phone through his office door, so they decided to wait for him to finish before bursting in. As it was, he came out to them once he was free.

Sally and Joe were sitting behind the main desk; Ralph had gone to put the kettle on. Sally was checking her notes from the hostel interviews with the staff. She looked up as Seaton approached.

"Hiya, guv," she said, noticing the strained look on the sergeant's face. Whatever the phone call had been about, it obviously wasn't good news. She was not sure if this was the right time to give him even more to worry about, but decided to press on regardless. "Ralph and I went to that hostel to ask about those missing students." She waited for Seaton to acknowledge he was paying attention before continuing.

"And?" he asked despairingly, fearing the worse.

"Well," she continued, "all their stuff is still there." She heard Seaton groan. "They never told anyone where they were going, but no one has seen them for the past couple of days. And one of the cleaners reckoned that she saw them leave with a lot of photographic equipment the last time they were there."

"Brilliant," said Seaton, slumping into an old wooden armchair by the notice board. "So are we now to presume that they are more victims of our maniacal killer fish?"

The others smirked, realising that Seaton was not in a comical mood at the moment.

Ralph appeared with the tea and placed the tray on the desk before handing them out. Seaton nodded his appreciation. In truth, he needed something stronger than tea right now, but under the circumstances, knew that it would have to suffice.

He blew on the surface and took a sip before making his announcement.

"I've just got off the phone to one of my old colleagues from London. It appears that a detective inspector from Scotland Yard has been assigned to this case, and he will be with us tomorrow."

There was a communal groan in response.

"Don't worry," continued Seaton, "there's worse to come."

The others all moved in closer, dragging their chairs across the floor like school children not wishing to miss story time.

Seaton waited until they had all settled before he continued. "The one who has been assigned to us is a Detective Inspector Ian Sharpe."

"Hold on a minute, sir." Sally almost jumped out of her seat as she spoke, then settled back. "I think I've met him. During training, he came down to Hendon to give us a talk."

Seaton leaned forward in his chair. "And what did you make of him?"

Sally looked a little uncomfortable. She shifted nervously in her chair.

"Come on, Sally," encouraged Seaton, "it's only amongst us."

"Well," she continued, hesitantly, "he was a bit of a pratt actually."

Her two colleagues fell about laughing at her response. Seaton smiled but kept his composure. Finally, Sally lashed out at Ralph as he was within range, slapping him on the arm.

She looked at her boss, apologetically. "Sorry, guv, but you did ask. He was right full of himself. Boasting about all the top criminals he'd arrested and how many gangs he's been responsible for breaking up. He even hit on a couple of my friends now I remember."

"That's okay, Sally," said Seaton, reassuringly. "He's done far worse than that from what I've been told." He drained his mug before continuing. "His last team was investigated by internal affairs. Turned out they were all on the take from some people smugglers who ran a string of brothels around London. The rest of his mob all got the push as a result."

"So how come he kept his job?" Asked Joe, perplexed.

"Well now, it turns out our Inspector Sharpe is the chief constable's son-in-law. So all he ended up with was a demotion back down to sergeant. Seems like he's crawled his way back up to inspector again; worse luck for us."

The young constables all looked at each other, shaking their heads in disgust. It was bad enough having a Scotland Yard man taking over their case, but it was even worse when it was a disgraced officer who should have lost his job all being fair.

Seaton could see that his announcement had lowered their morale. He felt guilty, but he was determined that his officers be kept in the picture, regardless of what protocol dictated.

Then he remembered something else. "Oh, I forgot to say," they all stopped talking and looked back at him, "his nickname is 'Razor Sharpe', and he's too bleedin' dumb to realise that everyone is taking the piss out of him because he's so stupid. He thinks it's a compliment."

This time, Seaton joined in with the laughter.

***

The dinner was sumptuous. Caitlin had prepared prawns with avocado for starters, salmon with fresh pasta, and a flavoursome Mediterranean salad for the main and chocolate mousse for after.

Dan could not remember the last time he had eaten such a fine home-cooked meal. Having missed lunch, he did not realise how hungry he was until the first mouthful. Then it was all he could do to stop himself shovelling it down without taking the time to appreciate and savour the exquisite feast.

Caitlin had really gone to an awful lot of trouble and he wanted to make sure that she knew how much he appreciated it.

After winning the argument to help Caitlin load the dishwasher, they retired to the sofa to enjoy the rest of their wine. Caitlin had chosen a compilation of various classical masterpieces to complement their meal, and now they were listening to a Chopin piano concerto which blended perfectly with the ambiance.

The sun had already started to set, and the light reflecting in from the large living area window had a pale orange hue with a hint of deep red. Through the open window in the kitchen, they could just about hear the sound of gulls above the music.

Dan felt so relaxed he could almost feel himself dropping off to sleep. After all, it had been a long hard day's graft and after such fine fare sleep seemed a natural conclusion.

Much as he loved the idea of falling asleep with Caitlin like this, snuggled together on the sofa listening to soothing music, he knew it would seem rude, so fought with himself to stay alert until the fatigue had passed.

Caitlin kicked off her shoes and folded her legs on the sofa as she nestled her head against Dan's chest.

He kissed the top of her head, breathing in the aroma of her hair. She had obviously washed it just before he arrived and it smelled of sweet lavender with a hint of honeysuckle. He did not know what perfume she was wearing, but her overall aroma was intoxicating.

He held her close and she lifted her head so they could share a kiss.

Afterwards, Dan said, "Funny I hadn't noticed that before."

"Noticed what?" asked Caitlin, craning her neck to see what he was alluding to.

"That tattoo on your foot." Dan nodded towards the end of the sofa where Caitlin's feet were resting.

She looked over. "Oh that, that's Donny my little Dolphin." She lay back against Dan. "I've been sponsoring him for years. You know you see those adverts all over the place, sponsor an animal in the wild or in captivity, especially if it's an endangered species."

"Was the tattoo part of the deal?"

Caitlin laughed. "No, silly. I had it done as a dare at university. Several of us had them done."

"Have you got any more I haven't seen?" asked Dan as he slid a little farther down in his seat to make them both more comfortable.

"No, just him. That one hurt enough, let me tell you."

"Odd I never noticed it before, I'm usually known for my keen sense of observation."

"Well, it just means that you haven't given my feet enough attention." She turned back up to face him, a broad grin stretched across her face.

"I promise I'll try harder in future, ma'am," replied Dan, faking an American accent as he bent down to meet her lips.

Suddenly, the doorbell rang, shattering the moment!

Honey, who had been dozing under the table, exhausted after her game of fetch with Dan, sprang into action and ran to the top of the stairs, barking furiously at the front door below.

Caitlin sat up and looked at her watch. "Who on earth can that be?" she pondered. "Honey, calm down," she commanded. Honey sat obediently where she was, her tail swishing in anticipation.

"Would you like me to go?" Dan asked.

But Caitlin was up and already half-way across the room. "Don't worry," she called back, "I won't be long."

Dan strained to listen above the music as she made her way downstairs. Honey went with her, which made him feel more comfortable. Alton was a relatively quiet town so you did not expect any trouble. Still, it was an odd time for a random call.

Dan heard Caitlin ask who it was, then the latch being pulled back and the door being opened. He could not make out the other voice. It was a man, definitely, but other than that, he was in the dark.

After a while, Dan heard footsteps coming back up the stairs.

Two sets!

He jumped up off the sofa and put down his glass.

Caitlin emerged back in the room with Sergeant Seaton just behind her. Dan recognised the officer from the time he first met Caitlin in the pub. He smiled when Seaton entered the room.

"Oh, I am sorry," exclaimed Seaton when he saw Dan. "I didn't realise you

were entertaining." He turned to face Caitlin. "I can come back another day; it's not life and death."

"No, please, don't leave on my account," offered Dan.

"Don't be silly;" assured Caitlin, guiding the officer towards the dining table. "I was just about to make some coffee, would you like some?"

"Oh, no thank you," replied Seaton, apologetically. "I'll only stay a moment." He looked back at Dan, sheepishly. "I really should have waited until morning; I just lost track of time. It's been one of those days."

The two men took their seats at the table whilst Caitlin busied herself in the kitchen. They re-introduced themselves to each other and began chatting aimlessly until Caitlin came in with the tray.

She placed it on the table in front of them. "Are you sure I can't persuade you?" she asked Seaton.

"No, thank you really, I'm fine," he responded politely.

"Could I tempt you to a brandy or a port?" Caitlin offered as a last ditch attempt. She could feel he was embarrassed at having disturbed their evening and wanted to put the officer at his ease.

Seaton smiled. "No, thank you, that's really terribly kind, but I'm still technically on duty."

"We won't tell if you won't," offered Dan.

"No, but thank you again." The officer could not be persuaded.

"How about you, darling?" Caitlin looked at Dan. He was taken aback for a second. It was the first time she had referred to him as "darling" and it sounded so good he nearly forgot the question.

Regaining his composure with a smile, he replied, "Whatever you're having is good with me, honey."

She blew him a kiss behind Seaton's back as she went to the cabinet where she kept the spirits.

Once they were all seated, Seaton began to tell them about the council meeting he had attended earlier that day, and the actions which had resulted from it.

"I take it the two of you have seen today's local rag?" he asked.

Both Caitlin and Dan shook their heads.

"We get a copy in the museum, but to be honest, I've been so pre-occupied today that I didn't get a chance to open it," replied Caitlin.

Seaton told them about Amy Friar's sighting, and what she claimed she saw.

Dan and Caitlin looked at each other in bewilderment.

"I know I mentioned some of this to you the other day in the museum," he continued, "but now with this article and…" he took a deep breath before continuing, "I know that I can count on your discretion." They both nodded. "Well, today, we received another report concerning three missing students who were apparently staying here to complete a university project about over-fishing or something like that. They too seem to have vanished without a trace."

Dan suddenly sat up. "Hang on just a moment; I was approached by three students the other day asking if they could hire me to take them out so they could make some documentary or the other."

"Really?" Seaton was engaged, his policeman's antennae set to automatic pilot. "What can you tell me about them?"

Dan thought. "There was a young girl and two guys, about eighteen maybe twenty. They were carrying a load of filming equipment and said that the information centre had sent them my way."

"What happened?" Seaton had his notebook out now and had already started to write.

"Well, it had already been a long day, so just as I was speaking to them, Jake Johnson happened passed, so I called him over and he agreed to take them out instead."

"Jake Johnson!" Seaton's expression grew more wary. He had suspected Jake's involvement in all kinds of nefarious activities without being able to prove anything, so if he was involved in the student's disappearance, Seaton thought that he might finally have something on the man.

"But wait," Dan held up his hand. "I spoke to Jake the following evening to ask how things had gone with the students, and he said that they started to mess him about concerning the price, so he told them where to go."

Seaton stopped writing and looked across at Dan. "Did you believe him?"

Dan shrugged. "To be honest, Jake and I don't see eye-to-eye at the best of times, as you witnessed in the pub that night. I mean, yes he was acting cagey, but then he always acts like that. You never get a straight answer from him regardless of the circumstances."

Seaton sat back. He knew that Dan was right. Jake Johnson was the last one you wanted to speak to if you were looking for an honest answer.

But it still niggled him that Johnson might know something about those students, even if he was telling the truth about not taking them out on his boat.

He knew that Jake would need to be questioned, and he was not about to subject his young constables to the task. A thought suddenly hit him and he smiled to himself when he considered suggesting to "Razor" Sharpe that he should do it instead.

Caitlin brought him back. "So, are you saying that you now believe that we have some kind of sea-monster lurking in the waters around Skullen Bay?"

Seaton sighed. "Personally, I no longer know what to think. Going by the evidence, Amy Friar saw something. And even old Sam Cleary keeps bleating on about something huge climbing out of the sea and grabbing people." He noticed the looks on their faces. "I know how it sounds, but put yourselves in my position. I can't just blatantly deny the facts, especially when I haven't got anything to offer as a countermeasure."

Caitlin and Dan both started to feel sorry for the man. He looked as if he was carrying the weight of the world on his shoulders.

"Anyway," he continued, finally, "the main reason I came around, and apologies again for the hour," Caitlin smiled in response, "was that I wanted your opinion as to what I could reasonably state might be this monster, from a professional point of view such as your own." He gestured towards Caitlin.

Caitlin looked at Dan before replying. "To be honest, I'm at a loss. There aren't that many large predators in the waters that we know of, and certainly none other than maybe a rogue shark, which would swim in waters as cold as ours to begin with." She could see the disappointment etched on Seaton's face. "Sorry," she added, apologetically.

"What about one of those giant squids or that Kraken thing that was illustrated in that book I bought from your museum?"

Caitlin shook her head slowly. "Again as I said before, the sporadic sightings of the *Architeuthis* have all been in places where the waters are much warmer and deeper than any around here."

"And that other thing?" asked Seaton, the last vestige of hope already drained from his voice.

Caitlin tried to sound sympathetic. "That is just a legend, a myth. It only exists in folklore. Sightings of the Kraken, as it was called by sailors, were probably early sightings of the giant squid."

Seaton closed his book and scratched his head. In truth, he had read the same thing in his book. He knew he was clutching at straws coming to see Caitlin, but he had to be able to say that he tried every avenue.

He rose from his chair and thanked them both for their time, apologising yet again for his intrusion.

After he had left, Caitlin and Dan returned to the couch with another brandy each.

Dan suddenly seemed lost in thought, so Caitlin asked him what was wrong.

"It's something I've just remembered," he said, shifting his position to allow Caitlin more room to get comfortable. "The other day, Tammi said that she felt something huge ram against the underside of the boat. But there was nothing visible on the surface."

CHAPTER FIFTEEN

Justin scoured the surface of the water, listening to Animal shovel another handful of crisps into his mouth. The sea was surprisingly choppy, considering how calm it had seemed when they first set off from Alton Harbour.

The motor boat Justin had hired was barely big enough for the two of them to stretch out, and Animal's equipment left them even less room to manoeuvre.

Animal lifted the crisp bag to his mouth and leaned back, letting the last remnants slide down before crunching them. He reached back into his carry-on rucksack and removed a can of Carlsberg from the plastic twine which attached it to the rest of the four-pack.

"Want another one?" he offered, holding the can out towards his colleague.

Justin sighed. "Yeah, why not." He took the can from Animal's grasp and popped the tab. Animal grabbed himself a fresh one from his bag, and they clinked cans before starting to drink.

Justin drank half his can in three gulps, letting out a loud belch once he'd finished. He tapped his phone, illuminating the screen. It was almost 1am. This had been a long vigil without any sign of the creature.

Justin was becoming more and more convinced that Sam Cleary had been pulling his leg. He began to regret parting with his £20, which he honestly believed he would not be able to claim back if this venture turned out not to bear fruit.

Coulson would be mad enough at the cost of hiring the boat, and Justin knew he would vent all of his wrath at him, because even though Mary had signed the chit, Justin knew that in Coulson's eyes, she could do no wrong.

Mary…!

His thoughts returned to her behaviour in the filing vault. She had made it perfectly clear that she wanted him tonight. The thought of those firm supple thighs she loved to show off with her tight little skirts. And those plump little tits, just right for a handful with no waste. He could have been sucking on them right this minute. Instead, he had opted to sit out here in the dark morass of water, searching for a non-existent monster.

He wondered to himself that if he were to call this jaunt off and try phoning her, would she be prepared to give him a second chance. He could always say that he abandoned his task because the thought of her offer was so enticing. He wondered how disappointed she had been when he declined her advances. She certainly gave him the cold shoulder when he went to collect his authorisation for hiring the boat. Perhaps she really liked him. Maybe she had liked him for some time and been too shy to say anything. Perhaps she had taken herself home feeling rejected, humiliated and abandoned.

Perhaps she was thinking about him right now. He imagined her lying there on her bed, soft satin sheets beneath her naked body. Her eyes closed, her tongue sensuously licking her lips. One hand caressing her breasts, feeling the nipples beginning to harden at her touch. Her other hand down between her legs. Her middle finger inside her, feeling the inner wall of her vagina, rubbing rhythmically, bringing her to the height of ecstasy, fantasising all the while that it was Justin on top of her.

Justin noticed himself starting to go hard. Not wanting Animal to notice, he quickly placed his beer can between his legs, holding it there with his thighs.

The reality of the situation was that if he dared to call Mary this late, especially after rejecting her, she would more than likely get a torrent of abuse for waking her up at this ungodly hour, before having the phone slammed down on him.

A sudden high wave struck the side of the boat, almost knocking them overboard. Justin's illusion of Mary shattered.

Both Justin and Animal steadied the boat as it bobbed from the aftershock of the wave. Justin's can was wedged tightly between his legs, but Animal's had toppled from his grasp when the wave hit, and was now pouring the remnants of the beer over the deck of the boat. He bent down and grabbed it once he felt it was safe to do so, cursing at the wasted alcohol.

"What the hell caused that?" asked Animal, scrutinising the surface in the darkness.

Justin shook his head. "I don't know, probably just a freak wave; we are quite far out."

Animal was not convinced. He had tagged along because he knew that Justin had a good eye for a story, and a decent set of prints could bring in some very welcome cash. But this whole scenario was starting to wear a little thin in his opinion. In truth, he had never expected to see a monster per se, but the chance that there might be something odd lurking in the water off the Bay intrigued him enough to accompany Justin.

But as the hours rolled by without any sign of anything worth photographing, he was becoming less and less committed. His mind drifted back to the barmaid from the pub. He had been ready to make his move tonight. Still, never mind, he thought, she would keep. Distance makes the heart grow fonder and all that.

Another large wave came out of nowhere, smacking into their side hard enough to cause Animal's equipment to rise off the ground before thumping back down.

The two men looked at each other for a moment, neither wanting to be the first to voice their concerns. This was getting serious. Whatever was causing the waves to strike might potentially overturn them on the next one.

Justin was the first to speak. "Have you got your camera ready? I think we are about to see something worthwhile at last."

Animal nodded. He fumbled in his bag and brought out his camera with a long zoom lens which he attached and clicked into place. He checked the built-in light meter and re-set it to take into account the surrounding darkness.

They both waited, listening intently, neither waiting to shatter the silence and risk masking the approach of whatever was causing the waves.

The boat slowly stopped rocking, the ripples from the last shock dying out, leaving the surface even once again. Both men scanned the water around them, looking for any sign of movement. There was nothing. The only sound they could hear was that of the water gently lapping against the side of their craft.

Secretly, each had decided that they would prefer to leave the scene and just write it off as a waste of time. But neither volunteered the information to their colleague, so in silence they sat, waiting.

After a moment's calm, Justin could feel his heartbeat returning to normal.

Animal was kneeling on his seat to give him a bit more height without actually trying to stand and possibly capsize them in the process. He gripped his camera tightly, poised to take a picture as soon as something worth shooting broke the surface.

Justin called over. "You'd better be careful with that equipment; if it ends up over the side, Coulson will have both our guts for it!"

Animal shifted, relaxing. "Not to worry," he held up the camera, "this, my friend, is state-of-the-art equipment. Shock-proof, water-proof, it can even photograph underwater; it's the same technology they use for deep-sea exploratory photographs. I talked Coulson into buying it for the paper last month. Being a seaside town, it made sense to have something I could use to film events taking place on the water without having to worry about dropping it overboard."

Justin sighed. "The way tonight's going, you probably won't have any use for it anyway."

"What about those waves we just felt? Something must have made them?"

Justin turned and looked out at the inky blackness. "Probably just a couple of freak waves. The tide might be turning."

Animal shrugged. "What a waste of a night. I was going to make my move with that barmaid as well. Could have been well in there by now."

Justin laughed. "That's nothing, mate. I had a sure thing on the cards and I gave it up for this malarkey."

"Anyone I know?" asked Animal, a knowing smirk starting to spread across his face.

Justin picked up on his colleague's innuendo straight away. "You knew? How?"

Animal fell back laughing. "Oh I just happened to pop into the filing vault this afternoon to drop off some negatives and I came across you and the lovely Mary in the middle of some intense lip-action."

Justin was gobsmacked. "How come we didn't hear you? I was listening out for any footsteps as it was."

Animal hit the side of his nose with his index finger. "I can be very stealth-like when the mood takes me. Had quite a naughty peek at the two of you before I decided to retreat gracefully."

Justin could tell that Animal was very pleased with himself. A little in-house gossip could be worth its weight in gold in the right hands.

"Listen, mate," there was a pleading tone in Justin's voice, "you won't tell anyone, will you? If you do, Mary will never believe that it wasn't me that told you."

"Oh, so you still think you're in with a chance after ditching her tonight?"

Justin felt himself go red. He hoped that in this light his colleague would not notice. It was almost as if Animal had seen into his mind and watched his latest fantasy about Mary.

"Well," he said, with sheer bravado, "you never know your luck. Though to be honest, she was pretty pee'd off with me for refusing her."

"I'm not surprised. Well, good luck to you, mate. If you can win her over again, you're a better man than me."

Justin felt instant relief. "Thanks for keeping stum, mate, I'll owe you."

"No problem, old son," replied Animal cheerily. "Now, shall we have another brew so the night isn't a complete loss?"

Justin retrieved his can from between his legs and drained the last of it. He crunched the can and through it overboard. "Why not," he answered, rubbing his hands together.

Animal put down the camera and turned in his seat to retrieve two more cans from his rucksack. As he fumbled in the bag, he felt the boat tilt back and forth. He presumed that Justin must be standing to take a leak before his next beer.

"Easy there, shipmate," he called back. "You'll make me spill the good stuff." Searching for the beers, Animal came across the half bottle of rum he had packed in case the weather turned cold whilst they were out. "Fancy a chaser with your beer?" he asked, turning to face Justin.

Justin was gone!

For a split second, Animal's inebriated mind did not grasp the situation properly. He began to glance around the small craft as if there was some possibility that Justin had crept into a corner to hide from sight, even though the boat was so small that such a task would have been impossible.

Animal spun around. He dropped the bottle on the deck, fortunately not shattering the thick glass. He started to scan the surface of the water from all angles, unable to pierce the gloom sufficiently to see any sign of his friend.

"JUSTIN!" he screamed out at the top of his lungs. He continued to scream it out as he searched the water. There was no sign of the young reporter.

Suddenly, afraid for his own safety, Animal sat back in the boat. He listened intently for any giveaway noises, but there was nothing forthcoming.

His mind raced. Something must have swept Justin overboard, something quick and strong. Justin was very slim, but he was still a man and not easy to lift out of a boat from the water. Animal looked around in panic for something he could utilize as a weapon. There was nothing suitable, other than the bottle which was tiny, or the camera, which was at least fairly weighty. But both options would only be useful in close to hand combat. And Animal hoped it would not come to that.

Holding the bottle above his head, he called out to his friend again.

There was still no response.

Animal felt tears begin to well up in his eyes. His friend must be dead. Drowned, or worse, killed in some monstrous manner by whatever it was that had taken him.

There was nothing he could do. He was a good swimmer, but the thought of diving in to try and locate his friend passed swiftly from his mind without being given any serious thought. If he went in, he would be dead too. That was a fact about which he was in no doubt.

He had to escape!

No one would ever be able to blame him for getting away. Self-preservation was all he had left to consider.

Leaning forward, Animal felt for the starter. He located the ignition.

The key was missing!

Justin must have it with him, he thought, in which case he might as well be in the water too. Being in the tiny craft, he was a sitting target for whatever had taken Justin. And with nowhere to go, his only option was to hope that whatever it was did not come back for seconds until help could arrive.

Animal stood up, eyes scanning everywhere around him. He groped around awkwardly in his jacket pockets, trying to locate his mobile, all the time watching the water, waiting for something to breach the surface. Something horrible!

He found his phone just as Justin sprang from the water and shot up into the air in front of the boat.

The gurgled scream that emanated from the reporter told Animal that he was at least still alive; therefore, there was a chance that he would survive.

It was then that he noticed that Justin was being held up twenty feet above the boat by something from underneath the water.

The creature's tentacle was wrapped around the helpless Justin, holding him tightly in an unyielding grip.

Animal tried to think, to rationalise. But the scenario before him was not a rational one that his mind could deal with.

Justin screamed, the water no longer interfering with his vocal chords. From down below, Animal heard his friend. The cry spurred him into action. Bending down, he retrieved the bottle and hurled it with all his strength at the appendage from which his friend dangled.

The bottle hit home, then bounced off and was lost in the water.

The creature's grip did not loosen. It swayed Justin tow and fro in the air as if waving comically at the boat.

In his helplessness, Animal instinctively grabbed his camera and began firing off a spate of photographs. The combination of having his mobile in his hand and the boat bobbing in the water was making it distinctly frustrating for him to get a clear shot. But he was suddenly determined that if this thing was going to get both of them, he was at least going to attempt to leave some kind of record behind.

He heard Justin scream out once more, and then he heard a stomach-churning crunch before Justin's body went limp.

Animal knew that his colleague was dead. He stopped taking pictures and squinted up through the darkness at his friend's body as it hung there, held up by the enormous appendage from the water like a piece of meat displayed in a butcher's window.

Animal kept his gaze on his dead work colleague as he fingered the buttons on his phone. He dialled 999. As the operator answered, almost as if it had been waiting for the signal, the Kraken lifted another great tentacle from the water and smashed it down on the boat.

The force of the beast's strike was enough to splinter the wooden sides almost completely. Animal felt himself being thrown through the air. He landed with a thump back inside the craft. He watched from his sprawled position as the Kraken lowered Justin's dead body back into the water.

Animal scrambled backwards as far as he could until his back was nudging against his rucksack. There was nowhere left to go. Animal felt around for his mobile which had been hurled from his hand on impact. He thought he could still hear the operator's voice in the distance, but it was not enough to guide him to his phone.

The Kraken hoisted its head above the water.

Animal stared in horror and disbelief at the huge saucer-shaped red eyes which burned into him. The creature's mouth opened, a great wide yawning maw lined with crooked, elongated, razor-sharp teeth.

As Animal watched frozen with fear, the monster lifted Justin's lifeless body from the depths and dropped it into its mouth. Animal watched the jagged teeth biting down on his friend, chewing his body to a mushy pulp in seconds, before closing its mouth to swallow the remains.

Animal grabbed the camera. His mind and reflexes were now working on automatic pilot. He knew his end was coming. He could tell from the menacing look in the monster's eyes that he was next in line to be chewed up in those hideous jaws. He could almost hear his bones being crunched, feel those rows of jagged teeth shredding his flesh to pulp, before being swallowed whole or in bits. Either way, it clearly did not matter to his slayer.

The camera started to flash in his hand; he was unaware that it was him who was taking the pictures. He could not bring himself to lift the camera up to his eye; he did not want his view of the Kraken distorted by the lens. He had to watch as it approached; he needed to see as well as feel its attack.

His lips moved in silent prayer.

He did not see the giant tentacle as it approached him from behind.

Before he could react, the beast had coiled its limb around him, squeezing the life from his helpless body as it lifted him high above the boat then dragged him underneath to resurface on the other side in front of its great mouth.

Animal could just about smell fetid stench from the creature's breath before, mercifully, darkness came.

***

The knock on the door caused Honey to run to the top of the stairs and start to bark loudly at the front door below.

Both Dan and Caitlin opened their eyes simultaneously, woken by the animal's signal that something was wrong.

Bleary eyed, Caitlin looked at the face of her bedside clock.

She turned back to Dan. "Who on earth can that be at 5:30 in the morning?" she asked, perplexed.

Dan rubbed his face with both hands, trying to shake off the remnants of his sleep. His mind focused. "I don't know, but it's never good news at this time of day. Would you like me to go?"

Caitlin considered his offer. Finally, she said, "Yes please."

Dan swung his legs out of bed and pulled on his shorts and jeans. He walked barefoot out of the room, pulling his T-shirt over his head as he went.

Honey met him at the top of the stairs. She barked up at him, her tail wagging excitedly. "Okay, girl, don't worry, I'm going." Dan patted her head gently as he passed by.

Caitlin listened from the bedroom, still under the covers. She was so glad that Dan had been here, as she could think of no reason whatsoever why someone should be knocking on her door at this ungodly hour.

She chided herself for being so afraid. After all, she had Honey, and she did not have to answer the door had she been alone. She could have called out through the window to see who it was. The door was double locked and bolted.

Even so, there was something unnerving about a knock at the door at such an unusual time of day.

She heard the door open and the sound of Dan speaking to someone. There were no raised voices, which she decided must be a good sign.

Next, she heard feet running up the stairs. She tensed involuntarily, pulling the covers up further over her naked body. She hoped the legs reaching the top of her stairs belonged to Dan and not some crazy psychopath who had knocked him out and left him lying in the doorway before coming for her!

Honey barked twice.

Caitlin tensed; she wanted to call out but was too afraid to.

The feet approached, nearing her bedroom door. She hated the fact that she could not see anything from this angle; she should have manoeuvred the bed when she first moved in to allow a clear view into the lounge.

Just then, Dan walked in. Caitlin heaved a huge sigh of relief; she could actually feel her heart pounding in her chest.

Dan walked around the bed and sat down on the edge reaching for his socks and shoes.

Before Caitlin could ask, he said, "It's Sgt. Seaton. He's very apologetic, but it appears that someone phoned the emergency services from off the coast early this morning. They didn't say anything, but the operator heard some strange noises and decided to trace the call. They triangulated the signal and matched the coordinates, so a search and rescue helicopter set out a couple of hours ago, and they've reported an abandoned boat which looks as if it has been attacked by someone, or something."

Caitlin sat up, not bothering to cover up when the sheets exposed her naked breasts. "Oh, that doesn't sound good. But why is he here?"

"Well, apparently their protocol now is that if they can get a local sailor to take them out to the site, it's cheaper to pay them than to call out the coastguard. So he thought of me, apparently."

Caitlin looked concerned. "So what, he wants you to take him out to where the abandoned boat is?"

"Basically." Dan finished tying his laces and leaned back so he could kiss Caitlin.

She held onto him, tightly. "Dan," she asked tentatively, "what if this boat was attacked by whatever attacked those people, and it's still in the vicinity?"

Dan sat up so that he could wrap his arms around her. Her body felt so soft and inviting his initial eagerness to assist Seaton was beginning to wane. But he had already agreed to, and besides, the money would be very useful after yesterday's expenses.

He pulled back and looked her deeply in the eyes. He could see her fear reflected in them, and it gave him a warm feeling inside to know how much she cared.

"Listen," he said, reassuringly, "whatever this thing is, it won't attack a vessel the size of the *Lady Anne*. Besides, Seaton says we will still be in touch with the rescue helicopter and I've got a shark gun on board in case of trouble, and Tammi is a pretty fine shot, believe it or not."

Caitlin knew that she would not be able to talk him out of it. And in a way, she felt foolish for worrying so much. Dan could take care of himself, and it was not as if he was going to be alone out there in a dingy.

But she was worried. Even though, on the other hand, the marine biologist in her wanted to go along too. Being with him would make her feel better.

She sat up. "How about you take me along too?"

Dan blinked in surprise. "What, what for, I mean –?"

"Well, you said yourself that it is perfectly safe on your boat." Caitlin jumped in before he had a chance to find the words to rebut her idea. "And you'll be there to protect me, and there's Tammi with her shark gun and Officer Seaton –"

"No, no, no." This time, it was Dan who cut her off. He pushed himself off the bed and stood over her. "That's just crazy, Caitlin, I need to be able to concentrate on negotiating my way there, how can I do that if I'm worried about you standing out on the deck?"

"You said there was nothing to worry about!" There was an edge of accusation in Caitlin's tone, almost as if she was challenging Dan to admit that he was worried about what he would find.

Dan could feel himself being backed into a corner.

He walked around the bed towards the door to collect his coat. Turning back, he was met by Caitlin standing naked in front of him. With her hands placed firmly on her slender hips, and the way she appeared to be biting her bottom lip, she was telling him there was no easy way out of this conversation for him.

Dan sighed and moved forward towards her, allowing his hands to rest gently on her shoulders. He gazed into her eyes. He thought he saw her starting to tear-up so he held her close to him and kissed the top of her hair. She smelt so good.

Holding her back he bent down to kiss her. Caitlin turned her head away, avoiding his mouth. He almost relented. The battle inside him raged on. She was right, of course. If he genuinely believed that it was safe, why could she not accompany them?

After all, he was taking Tammi!

But he knew the truth. As much as he would not put Tammi in any danger, Caitlin meant far more to him than anyone else in the world. He wanted to tell her, desperately. But the moment was not right, and Seaton was waiting patiently downstairs for him.

Dan kissed Caitlin softly on the side of her temple, and whispered that he would call her as soon as he reached dry land. He also told her not to worry, but he was not sure that she was listening. Or if she was, she did not respond.

Caitlin did not follow him out of the door.

Instead, she waited by her bedroom window and watched him climb into Seaton's patrol car.

As the car drove away, she felt the tears brim over.

CHAPTER SIXTEEN

Dan thought it prudent to call ahead to Tammi, on the off chance she was still with her new lover. He was right. A very sleepy Tammi answered the phone, and Dan could hear someone else in the background frantically moving around.

Once Tammi had recovered her senses, she told Dan she would splash some water on her face and have the boat ready for launch in time for his arrival.

The journey to the boat only took ten minutes. They only passed a handful of cars on the road, which, considering the hour, was not altogether surprising.

As the patrol car pulled up at the beach, Dan saw a young woman standing outside the pub, looking agitatedly at her wristwatch. When she saw the police car, she turned away, as if afraid she would be recognised.

Tammi had fired up the engine and put the kettle on before Dan and Seaton arrived on deck. They were both met with steaming coffee and a very un-coiffured Tammi.

Tammi noticed Dan's grin when he saw her.

She pointed an accusatory finger at him. "An' you can take that wee daft grin off yer face for a start, matey!"

Dan held up his hands in surrender, and gratefully took hold of one of the mugs. He formally introduced Tammi to Seaton, and they cast off.

Dan pinned up the piece of paper Seaton had given him with the coordinates of their objective on the notice board in the wheelhouse. He estimated it would take them approximately an hour and a half to reach their destination. The sea was calm and stretched out before them towards the horizon from which the sun had already begun its ascent into the cloudless sky. It was going to be a fine day, Dan thought, weather-wise at least. He still felt uneasy about the way he had rushed off and left Caitlin. He hoped that she would come around to his way of thinking, and if she did not, then at least be willing to forgive him. It was far too early in their relationship to be having a fight. In his experience, if you haven't set the foundation of the relationship beforehand, something like this could ruin the whole thing.

The thought of losing Caitlin caused a pain to lodge deep inside his chest.

His thoughts turned back to the previous night. How perfect everything had been. After Seaton had left, they lay on the sofa, drinking their brandy, listening to the music and just holding each other. He had never been so content. He wished then that they could have just stayed together like that forever.

When they finally moved to the bedroom, both of them were yawning so much that neither expected the other to settle for anything other than a good night's sleep. But once they were both naked between the sheets and began kissing and cuddling, their passion took over. Their comical fiasco with the condom the previous night was eradicated by Caitlin pushing Dan back on the bed and taking charge of the application herself.

They finally fell asleep in each other's arms an hour later, exhausted, and slept soundly through the night.

Until Seaton rang the bell!

Dan looked out of the window at the policeman who was holding tightly onto the railing with one hand and his coffee with the other. Tammi came out with a refill, which the officer accepted gratefully.

Dan knew that it was not Seaton's fault that he and Caitlin had fallen out this morning. But, at the same time, he almost wished that the officer had knocked on someone else's door to ask for help. Because then, he and Caitlin would probably be running along the beach by now, laughing and joking with each other with Honey in tow, instead of them being miles apart with him feeling like crap!

As they neared the coordinates, Tammi stood up on one of the seats on the main deck and searched the horizon through a pair of binoculars. Seaton for his part held his hand up to shield his eyes and did likewise, though without ocular assistance.

Dan slowed the boat down. The new fittings which Tammi and he had fitted the previous day were holding well, but he still detected a faint shudder whenever he tried to slow the craft down. He made a mental note to mention it to Tammi later.

"There she is!" It was Tammi who alerted them to their quarry. She pointed out to the west, leaning against the back of the seat she was standing on to keep her balance.

Dan manoeuvred the boat to follow Tammi's signal. Soon after, he could see what looked like the smashed remnants of a small speedboat bobbing on the water a couple of hundred yards ahead of them.

As Dan drew beside the abandoned craft, Tammi leaned over the side and managed to hook the smaller vessel with a line. Dan came out and the three of them looked over the side to see what, if anything, there was left to salvage. There was no sign of life in the vicinity so presumably whoever had made the emergency call was now either dead and lying at the bottom of the sea, or their remains had been taken by some predator before Dan and his crew arrived.

The sides of the small craft had been crushed and splintered, leaving gaps so deep that sea water was lapping over the edges and filling the bottom. Dan surmised that it would not take long before the remains sank altogether.

Tammi used her binoculars to focus on the inside of the craft. "Hey," she cried, "there's somethin' there in the bottom." She pointed. "Look there, under the seat!"

Both Dan and Seaton strained to see, but neither could make out anything substantial. Dan fetched a telescopic metal pole with a hook on one end from below deck. Extending it to its full length, he managed to snag what it was Tammi had alluded to.

As he lifted it clear from the wreckage, they all saw that it was an old rucksack. Dan brought it on board and searched through its contents. Inside, there was a couple of unopened cans of beer, some empty food wrappers from sandwiches and crisps, and what looked like an assortment of lenses in a box with a cushioned interior.

"They look like camera lenses to me," said Seaton, leaning over Dan's shoulder. "I wonder if the person out here was a photographer."

Dan turned to him. "You haven't managed to trace the owner of the mobile that made the call?"

Seaton shook his head. "Not yet, but the boys are on it."

Dan held up the empty cloth bag. The sea water had saturated the material, making it feel as if there was still something else inside. Dan checked again just to be sure it was empty.

Tammi returned to the side and searched the wreckage again with her binoculars. She was about to give up when something metallic caught her eye just under the water. "Hey, come here!" she called to the men, excitedly. "Look down there, there's something else under the seat."

Dan dropped the pole back over the side and moved it back and forth close to where Tammi had indicated. He could still not see anything there himself and relied on her to guide him. Twice, he hooked what was left of the seat frame by mistake, the second time having to fight with it to release the hook.

Eventually, Tammi called, "That's it, yer got it, skipper, bring 'er on board."

He lifted the pole out of the water and turned his body around to carry on board whatever it was that he had hooked.

Tammi walked passed him and relieved the find from the hook.

"What is it?" asked Seaton, moving in for a better look.

"It's a camera," replied Tammi, turning it over in her hands. "Looks like a posh one too."

Having checked once more to make sure that they had not missed anything else, they secured the floating wreckage to their boat and headed back for Skullen Bay.

As they approached the beach, Dan took out his mobile and called Caitlin as he had promised. When her phone went to voicemail, his heart sank. He had so wanted to hear her voice again it hurt. He considered ringing off and trying again later, hoping that the missed call on her phone would result in her calling him back. But he decided to leave a message after all, hoping that it might still cause her to call him back when she received it.

Just before he heard the beep, he looked up and saw Caitlin and Honey running along the sand, chasing a ball.

The sight of Caitlin lifted his spirits immediately, and he cancelled his call without speaking.

Once they had moored up, Dan left Tammi to help Seaton retrieve the damaged craft while he went to meet Caitlin. He hurried towards her then stopped just within arm's reach. He felt he needed to apologise, but he just was not sure what to say or how to start the conversation.

From the look in Caitlin's eyes, he could tell she had been crying, which made him feel happy and guilty at the same time. As he opened his mouth to attempt some kind of reconciliation, Caitlin threw herself into his arms and held him tightly. They stayed like that for several minutes with Honey yelping excitedly at the dropped ball she had left on the sand in front of them.

Finally, they pulled apart and Dan picked up Honey's ball and threw it as far as he could for the dog to retrieve. They walked with their arms around each other's waists along the beach, both apologising to the other for the way they had behaved that morning, and both of them insisting on taking the blame.

By the time Dan had seen Caitlin back to her car and returned to the Lady Anne, Seaton and Tammi had dragged the busted boat onto the beach. Seaton had managed to soak his uniform trousers right up to the knee in his endeavours, but Tammi looked as dry as a bone. Clearly, the officer was not familiar enough with the waves to know when to jump out of the way.

Seaton removed his cap and slid the back of his hand across his forehead, clearing away the perspiration before replacing it back on his head.

They surveyed the wreckage together. It was barely recognisable as any form of craft, more closely resembling the contents of a skip outside a builder's merchants. Where the engine had once been, there was just a hole covered by a few bare strips of wood. The seats were mostly gone, torn away by the look of it. What was left of the hull was mangled with more incomplete sections than anything else.

Dan was amazed that the craft had stayed afloat long enough for them to salvage it. "What happens now?" he asked Seaton, curious as to what the officer might be able to make from the derelict boat.

Seaton rubbed his head through the material on the top of his hat. "Well, first thing now is to get that rucksack and camera over to one of our labs for analyses, and to get this baby hauled away in case it is needed for evidence."

"Have you any idea yet who owned it, and whether or not it was them who made the emergency call?" asked Dan, scrutinising the remnants of what had once been the bow. There was a faint marking, almost an outline which for a moment he thought that he recognised.

Seaton shook his head. "Not so far. The mobile number is being traced, but it might be an hour or so yet before the details filter their way down to us." He turned to both Dan and Tammi with a half-smile. "We're not quite NCIS, but we do usually get there, eventually."

Seaton asked Dan and Tammi if they could watch the ruined vessel until he could arrange to have it collected. He promised Dan that the extra time would be added onto his fee for his services.

Seaton headed back to the station with the rucksack and camera. Both were damp, and now that the water had begun to dry, the particles of salt were starting to show through. They both looked as if they had been under water for some time. He wondered if their laboratory in Norwich would be able to glean anything useful from the camera after the salt water had flooded it.

When he arrived at the station, Sally Poole and Ralph Carmody were already there. They both greeted their superior officer and were eager to hear what he had been up to that morning.

Seaton began to tell them about the call he had received earlier when Constable Green arrived looking somewhat dishevelled, as if he had been running. He apologised for his tardiness in between catching breaths.

Once they were all together crowded around the front desk, Seaton began his tale again for the benefit of the late arrival.

When he was finished, Sally asked, "So what do you plan to do with the camera, guv?"

"Well," began Seaton, thoughtfully, "first off, I'm going to call Norwich and see if they want us to take it to them for analysis; I know they have a lab there. They can look at the rucksack too, while they're about it." He turned to Joe. "Thanks for volunteering to drive them over Constable Green." Joe almost objected, then realising his boss was making a point regarding his lateness, said nothing.

Both Sally and Ralph looked at each other and smiled, making sure that Seaton was not looking in their direction when they did so.

"Ralph?"

"Yes, guv," said Carmody, standing up straight almost as a reflex from his sergeant's voice.

"Arrange to have the remnants of the boat collected from Skullen Bay."

"Right you are, guv," replied Carmody, already looking through the book he had retrieved from under the desk for the number of the local haulage firm they were contracted with. "And where do you want me to tell them to take it? On to Norwich with the camera and rucksack?" He turned to Sally. "Joe could hitch a lift with them on the back if he likes."

Joe produced his middle-finger for his colleague, lowering it the second he thought Seaton might see.

Just then, there was a loud crash as the main station door swung open and slammed against the wall behind.

They all looked up in unison. There, framed in the doorway was a short, balding man with a stocky build, wearing a fawn raincoat and a pair of gold-rimmed sunglasses. They all watched in silence while the new arrival gazed around the room as if casing it.

Eventually, Seaton spoke up. "May we help you, sir?" he asked, in his most commanding voice.

The stocky man removed his sunglasses with both hands and folded them carefully before slipping them into the breast pocket of his jacket. He surveyed the team for a moment, then moved forward towards them with his hand outstretched towards Seaton. "Detective Inspector Sharpe," he announced with a hint of smugness, which caused Seaton to take an instant dislike to him. "Scotland Yard." The two men shook hands, Seaton with less enthusiasm than the inspector.

Seaton introduced the rest of the team. Sharpe acknowledged the two male constables with a nod of his head, but made a point of shaking Sally by the hand.

Sally looked uncomfortable as the man held her hand for longer than seemed necessary.

Seaton noticed her expression so butted in. "Well, Inspector Sharpe, if you would like to accompany me into the back office, I'll bring you up to speed thus far."

Sharpe relinquished his hold on Sally, but not before giving her a sly wink. Sally did not return the familiarity.

The inspector walked around the desk to access the back office. Before leaving the area, he lobbed a set of keys in Joe's direction. "My car's parked out front, Constable; it's the silver Merc. Do me a favour and park it round the back somewhere safe. I don't want any seagull shit corroding my paintwork." He did not wait for an answer before turning to follow Seaton.

Once Seaton closed the door behind them both, Sally looked at the others and mouthed, "What a prick!"

Seaton brought Sharpe up to speed on their progress, or lack of it, so far. Sharpe took notes, nodding and sighing without actually speaking. Ralph knocked and came in offering tea; they both accepted. Seaton had not had a chance to make one after receiving the early morning call, so he was very grateful for the young Constable's offer. Plus, he knew that Ralph made his tea just the way he liked it.

Once the briefing was over, Sharpe flicked back through his notebook and re-read some of what he had written, underlining certain sentences as he went.

Eventually, he said, "Right then. Judging by what you've told me, this Sam Cleary seems to know more than he's letting on. I think we should get him in for questioning ASAP."

Seaton looked up in surprise. "Old Sam, he doesn't know what day of the week it is more often than not; he won't be of any credible use to our investigation."

Sharpe closed his book and looked across the desk, directly at Seaton. He took his time putting his pen back in his pocket before speaking. "Now listen here, Sergeant, I appreciate that you don't like the idea of the big boys coming down here and trampling all over your territory, but that's the news, get it?" Sharpe rose from his chair hastily, causing the wooden legs to screech along the floor as he did so.

Seaton was taken aback by the harshness of the inspector's tone. He was temporarily lost for words as he watched his superior officer coming around his desk towards him.

When Sharpe was within reaching distance, he stopped. He stuck his index finger out, aiming it directly at Seaton for emphasis. "For your information," he continued, his tone equally as severe as before, "I did not exactly turn cartwheels when I received this assignment either, but that's the job." He relaxed his hold, shoving both hands in his trouser pockets as he turned away to walk towards the window. "Now I know there's no 'I' in T.E.A.M, but someone has to take charge here, and that's me." He turned back to face Seaton from across the office. "So I would appreciate a little cooperation, and just a smidge of dutiful respect from those officers answering to me, and that includes you!" The finger came out again for emphasis.

Seaton could feel his temper bubbling below the surface. He was not known for his anger, but this man was definitely pushing his buttons.

He took a deep breath to calm himself before answering. "Listen, Inspector, all of my team, including myself, will be at your disposal, naturally." He could still feel his temper rising, so had to make an even bigger conscious effort to relax and keep it out of his voice. "But that does not mean that you should expect us to act without question every time you snap your fingers." Seaton stood up and leant forward, letting the knuckles of his closed fists rest on his desk.

The two men stared at each other in silence for a few moments before Sharpe took the initiative. Holding his hands up, he said, "Fair point, Sergeant, I'm not an awkward man to get on with, ask anyone who's ever worked with me. But we have to maintain discipline, and that means we maintain a structure of rank." He pointed to himself with his thumb. "And that means that I am now in charge of this investigation and all decisions must go through me. Now, do we have an understanding?"

Seaton knew that it would be pointless to argue with the man. The service was full of his ilk who bullied their way through the job, throwing their rank in the faces of all those below them whom might object.

If only you knew what I know about you, old son, thought Seaton.

Seaton began to calm himself down. He knew that this man was not worth the effort. And besides, once this business was over, he would be going back to London, doubtless boasting about how he had managed to knock some order into this little town's police force.

Just then, there was a knock at the door. "Come in," Seaton responded before Sharpe had a chance.

Sally entered the room. She glanced in the direction of Sharpe without acknowledging him, then turned to her sergeant. "Sarge, we've just had a call from a woman who claims that her husband has been missing for at least two days."

"What does she mean by 'at least'? Doesn't she know?" Sharpe butted in, his nose clearly out of joint at being ignored by the young constable.

Sally felt obliged to respond to the inspector's question, even though having heard part of the argument between him and her superior through the door, she already wanted to punch him out for upsetting Seaton.

She looked directly at Sharpe, her manner conveying her lack of respect which was bordering on contempt. "She's just returned from holiday. The last time they spoke was three days ago." She turned back towards Seaton, her tone immediately softened. "By the sound of it, they weren't the most devoted of couples."

"Show me a married couple who are." Sharpe laughed cynically at his own joke. The two did not respond.

"I just thought with what you told us about what old Sam said about seeing that bloke being sacrificed," Sally continued, somewhat unsure now whether she should have mentioned the possible connection she had considered. "Well, the time frame seems about right. It's a long shot I know, but –"

"But nothing," Sharpe cut in again. "See, I told you we need to get that old bloke in here and interrogate him properly." The self-imposed authority in his voice and body language were aimed directly at Seaton, though Sally did wonder if Sharpe was putting on this little show for her benefit. If he was, he was waiting his time. Her loyalty to Seaton could not be tarnished, especially not by a jumped-up little twat like him.

"Right," Sharpe continued, straightening his tie and re-shuffling his raincoat so it sat squarely on his shoulders. "You come with me, luv," he said, thumbing the command in Sally's direction. "Sergeant, you find that old tramp and bring him in here, I want a crack at him myself." He was almost out of the door as he called out the instruction.

Sally looked at her boss, pleadingly.

Seaton gave her a sympathetic smile, then shrugged his shoulders and signalled for her to follow Sharpe.

Seaton followed them out of the office. Sharpe stopped at the front desk to ask Ralph for the address of the lady caller. Before he left the station, he called back to Constable Carmody. "Oh, and by the way, I need somewhere to stay. Find me something close to the station with a king-size bed, en-suite of course. And make it decent, it's on expenses."

With that, he was gone with Sally reluctantly in tow.

CHAPTER SEVENTEEN

Bernie Coulson sat behind his desk, his head resting in his hands. His hangover had not dissipated despite him swallowing four Paracetamol with his first coffee of the day, and walking the half mile to the office instead of driving in, which was his usual routine.

The phone on his desk had rung twice since he arrived, but both times he waited for it to switch to voicemail. He clearly was not ready to face his day yet.

His overindulgence the previous night, though not altogether uncharacteristic, was due to his evening out with his two daughters...if you could call it an evening. His eldest daughter, the brains of the family as he had often referred to her, was studying for her "A" level finals, and thus far too pre-occupied to fritter away an entire evening having dinner with her dear old dad.

She had made her intentions perfectly clear as soon as he had arrived to pick them up. Though she was apologetic for having to let him down at such short notice, Coulson could tell right away that no amount of pouting or pleading was going to make her change her mind.

He resigned himself to the fact that he should be grateful that at least she was putting something as important as her studies before his visitation rights, rather than wishing to spend time with some waste-of-space lout whom she had allowed to pick her up in a nightclub, but it still hurt. Next year, if she earned the grades – of which he had no doubt – she would be packing her bags for Edinburgh University. Why she insisted on travelling so far away from home, he could only surmise. But he knew it would result in him seeing even less of her for at least the next three years, and that thought alone made him hurt inside.

His youngest daughter was at least willing – if not over the moon – to spend the evening with her dad. That was if you could call her looking up from texting her mates long enough to take in a mouthful of food spending the evening with him.

By the time he drove home, Coulson was deeply depressed, and as usual, sought solace from his old friend Jim Beam. He knew that drinking was not the answer, but had decided that it would have to do until something better came along.

His ex-wife who, if he was honest with himself, he missed far more than he had anticipated, had decided that formal communication of any description with him was wholly unnecessary. Even when he dropped by to collect the girls, she always elected to stay out of sight until he was gone.

Theirs had not been a bad marriage all told. In fact, in the early days, they had made quite a successful team. She had been ambitious for him, and coaxed, guided, and bullied him onto the correct path. She had always been the perfect hostess whenever she thought it prudent for them to hold one of her candle-light dinners. And when the offer was reciprocated, she always made sure that she presented herself as the perfect accompaniment to an up-and-coming leader in the news industry.

Their sex life had been quite exciting in the early years, surprisingly. His wife never failed to amaze him at how eager and willing she was to satisfy her husband whenever she saw the glint of apprehension or lack of drive begin to rear its ugly head. She would whisper lovingly in his ear how excited and turned on she was by his business acumen, and speculated teasingly what wonderful things she planned to do to him so long as he kept his focus.

But after the birth of their second daughter, the bedroom side of things began to dwindle, and before long, Coulson had taken to satisfying himself in the shower out of frustration.

Eventually, with no end in sight, he had started to procure the use of escorts whenever his wife was away visiting her parents. Fortunately, he always had work as an excuse not to go, but over time, he found himself becoming less and less cautious, until finally she caught him literally with his pants down, and that was that!

He had hoped initially that his unmasking would have resulted in them seeking guidance or counselling from a marital relations expert. But it soon became apparent that his wife had no feelings for him whatsoever, and in truth, he believed that she was delighted that he had finally given her an excuse to call their marriage to a halt, without making her the antagonist.

Coulson gently lifted his head. Even such a slight movement caused him to wince. From across the office, he saw Mary his secretary arriving for work. She was late, again, but he did not care. He waved frantically in the air with one hand until she noticed him, then he signaled her over.

She opened his office door with a bright and cheery, "Morning, boss." But when she saw the pallor of his complexion and his general disheveled appearance, her initial cheerfulness receded. "Oh dear, a little worse for it this morning?"

Coulson barely managed a half-hearted nod.

"Coffee?" Mary asked, knowing the answer. "Strong, black, and lots of it?"

The sympathetic tone of her voice was very welcome, and Coulson managed a

weak smile. "Oh, and Mary," he managed to catch her before she left the room, "could you see if there's any of that Alka-Seltzer left? My mouth feels like they've been filming Lawrence of Arabia in it."

Mary laughed. "Will do."

While he was waiting for his coffee, Coulson decided to start working his way through the myriad of papers which he had allowed to pile up on his desk. He began by separating what he considered to be the most important, which usually meant those that would cost the paper money if he did not action them. This was followed by a "get to later" pile, which he shoved towards the end of his desk. And the final pile which all promptly went into the bin under his desk.

By the time Mary arrived back with his refreshment, Coulson was sifting through the expense sheets from the last few days. It never ceased to amaze him how, with such a small paper, they managed to pile up so quickly.

Mary put the fizzing antacid in front of him. He took it gratefully and downed it in one, covering his mouth with the back of his hand after he had swallowed, to stifle a loud belch. The action did not succeed as planned, and Mary pulled a face at the loud noise which emanated from his mouth.

He looked up by way of an apology for his behaviour.

Leaving the coffee within reach, Mary turned to go. She was just about to close the door behind her when Coulson called her back.

"What's this for?" he asked, one arm extended with a piece of pink paper in it, whilst the other hand lifted his mug to his mouth.

Mary saw at once that it was the carbon copy of one of their office chits. Moving closer, she bent down the corner of the sheet while Coulson still held it to see what it was for. She recognised it immediately. "That was one I signed last night for Justin. He said that you okay'd it for him to hire a boat."

Coulson looked surprised. "A boat," he spluttered, whilst trying to blow on and take a sip of the hot liquid, simultaneously. Giving up the ghost, he slammed the mug back on his desk, splashing hot coffee onto his hand as he did so. "Ouch!" he screamed, loud enough for those sitting on the first two banks of desks directly outside his office to look around.

Mary's response was as always flawless. She had his hand wrapped in a wad of tissues in seconds.

Coulson's attention, having momentarily been averted due to his accident. went straight back to the pink slip. "What on earth did he want to hire a boat for?"

Mary, still holding Coulson's burnt hand between the tissues, shrugged. "He said that you said it was okay," she replied, in her defense. "Something to do with the story you had him working on," she offered, easing away the tissues having served their purpose.

Coulson thought for a moment. Then it came back to him. He looked past Mary out into the main office. "I still didn't say that he could hire a bleedin' boat. How much was the chit for?"

"Up to £500," replied Mary, taking a step backwards now, her assistance was no longer required with the tissues.

Coulson stood up quickly, immediately regretting it. Holding his hand against his forehead, he slipped back into his chair moaning softly. He waited for the dizziness to disperse, then asked rhetorically, "£500 quid. What was he hiring, the bloody QE2?"

Mary stifled a laugh behind her hand. She knew that Justin would be for it when he arrived. Coulson would never blame her for signing the chit, he never did. He always took it out on the requester, and they all knew that, which generally prevented them from taking the Mickey when the boss was not around to ask.

"Where is he? Is he here yet?" Coulson demanded, his hand still up at his head as he looked out through the glass panels to see if he could spot Justin himself.

Mary looked behind her, scanning the office floor. "I don't think so, boss. Shall I see if he's left any messages at the front desk?"

"Yes please, Mary," Coulson's tone had softened. "And if he hasn't, call him for me and tell him to get his backside in here sharpish!"

"Will do." Mary turned to exit. "And don't forget to drink your coffee," she called as she left.

***

Oswald Seaton could still feel his blood boiling as he toured the streets of Alton in search of Sam Cleary. He knew that it was a completely fruitless exercise bringing old Sam in for questioning, but his hands had been well and truly tied by Sharpe. There was not even a senior officer for Seaton to complain to, unless of course he wanted to follow the official route. And being a pain in the backside was not considered reasonable cause for a formal proceeding.

The sergeant was aware that many of his colleagues who he had remained friends with over the years had had to put up with similar circumstances in the past. He had always been lucky. Being in such an out-of-the-way area such as Alton did not usually attract the hot-headed, fast-stream big shots who wanted to climb the ladder as fast as possible regardless of what carnage they left in their wake. That was usually the type who came in unwanted and made a nuisance of themselves in this line of work.

Sharpe was a little different in that respect. He had already raced ahead thanks to nepotism, and then, because of his own greed, had been dropped. Now, he clearly wanted to make a name for himself so that he could scramble back up the promotion ladder. And for now, it looked as if he wanted to use Seaton's little problem as his springboard. Just his luck!

Having checked out the hostel Sam usually stayed at, plus all the pubs and off-licenses he passed which he knew Sam frequented, without success, Seaton decided to make his way back up to Skullen Bay. He had found Sam there last time, and plus, it would give him a chance to see if the wreckage of the boat had been collected. He checked his watch; it was a little after 1pm. He estimated that Constable Green should have arrived at Norwich by now to hand over the camera and rucksack he and Dan had found this morning. He wondered what, if any, evidence they might provide once they had been examined by the experts.

Hopefully, something concrete. He still was not satisfied with all this nonsense about creatures from the deep coming on land and attacking his townsfolk. What next, aliens landing on the beach?

He wondered if he might be able to introduce Caitlin to Sheila Soames. She was insistent at the council meeting yesterday that she was going to bring in an expert. Well, Caitlin certainly had the qualifications, and what's more, she spoke sense. She would not be the type to jump to fantastic conclusions without first seeing proper evidence. He made a mental note to himself to mention her name to Sheila later on that day, if he had the chance.

That was, of course, unless Sharpe thought it was pointless. Unlike wasting all of this time trying to find old Sam!

Seaton pulled his squad car up at the Skullen Bay beach. The afternoon sun was at its height, and all around him people were relaxing in various degrees of undress. Never much of a sun lover himself, he was still jealous of those who were able to strip off in this heat and cool down with a refreshing pint. He tugged at the collar of his uniform shirt absentmindedly. It was far too hot for all this in his opinion.

In the distant, he could just make out Dan's boat coming back in to port. There was no sign of the wreckage anymore, so at least that had been taken care of before a bunch of sightseers and inquisitive locals started asking too many questions.

That would doubtless wait for another day.

Carefully, Seaton weaved his way down amongst the sun loungers, deckchairs, and towels spread across the roasting sand, on his way to meet Dan.

He knew that he should have made finding Sam his priority, but he felt the need for some intelligent conversation, and he had decided that he liked Dan Savage. Unlike many of the fishermen and pleasure-boaters, Dan seemed to be honest and upfront, with nothing to hide. He was the kind of man that Seaton felt confident he could put his trust in without being betrayed. That was one of the reasons he had asked Dan to help him out this morning, though he still felt guilty for knocking on Caitlin's door so early. It had obviously caused an argument between her and Dan.

Seaton could hear raised voices from downstairs while he was waiting for Dan to get his things.

Still, from what he saw later that morning on the beach, they had made up, so that was something good at least.

As Seaton approached the launch barriers, Dan saw him and waved.

Tammi held out her hand and helped the officer on board, once she had assisted the touring party to exit.

"I see the wreck has been collected," began Seaton, as Dan joined them on deck. "Did you have to wait long before they arrived?"

Dan shook his head. "Not really, not even a full hour."

Seaton removed his cap to allow some sea breeze to tousle his hair. "Well, I think that we can call that an extra two hours of your valuable time, what do you say?"

Dan and Tammi both grinned at each other. "Thanks for that, Sergeant, much appreciated," Dan responded.

"My pleasure." Seaton smiled. "I'll make sure that I send the necessary paperwork off this evening."

"Have you hurd anything back abute the camera and the wee rucksack yet?" asked Tammi, clearing up the remnants of used Styrofoam cups and empty sweet wrappers left by the last group before the wind swept them overboard.

"Not yet," replied Seaton, "but they should be at the lab by now, so hopefully it won't take too long."

"Have you any idea yet who made the call from the boat?" asked Dan, as he wiped away a stream of perspiration with his shirt sleeve.

Seaton shook his head slowly. "Nothing as yet. Again, I am hoping that the film in the camera, if it is salvageable, might give us some clue. Other than that, it's just a question of waiting for them to trace the mobile, or wait until someone reports someone as missing. Either way, until we know for sure, there's nothing else we can do at the moment."

"How's the rest of the investigation going?" Dan asked, turning to check that Tammi did not need any help with her task.

Seaton looked around to ensure that no one else had come within earshot of where they were standing before he continued. "Well, it looks like we may have a possible name for one of the victims old Sam Cleary reckons he saw being gobbled up by whatever is out there." He indicated to the open sea. "But if you know Sam, you'll appreciate that he might not be considered the most reliable of witnesses."

"Yer mean old Sam the wee drunk who sleeps on the beach?" asked Tammi, rubbing her hands against her grimy overalls, as if it would help to clean them.

"That's him," replied Seaton.

"He were right here before we set off," offered Tammi. "I gave him a couple'a quid and he headed for the pub, pleased as punch." She pointed towards the Fisherman's Arms, the sign of which was just visible beyond the sand.

Seaton turned to follow the direction Tammi was pointing in. "Really? That's excellent. Thanks, Tammi."

"Speaking of questioning people," Dan interrupted, "have you managed to find out any more about those students?"

Seaton turned back to face him. "No, not yet. In fact, I was going to speak to Jake first thing this morning." He looked out along the harbour to where Jake moored his boat. It was not there. He suspected that Jake was out on a job. Not to worry; he could keep. He turned back to Dan. "But then as you know things took a sudden turn this morning, and now I have to dance to the tune of a visitor from New Scotland Yard, no less, so Jake will have to wait until later."

"New Scotland Yard?" asked Dan, obviously taken by surprise by Seaton's revelation.

The officer looked around him once more to check that no one else was close enough to hear. He moved in, lowering his voice. "Yes, but please keep it to yourselves for now. Sheila Soames, our local mayoral candidate, sees this as an opportunity to get her name recognised for being the one who took decisive action to save our little community from whatever's out there." Seaton signaled out to sea with a wave of his hand. Dan and Tammi could tell by his tone that he was less than impressed with Sheila's intervention.

Just then, Seaton's radio mike burst into action. It was Constable Carmody calling him from the station.

Seaton answered. "Go ahead, Control."

"Sorry, Sarge. Sheila Soames has been on the phone; she wants you to call her at her office ASAP."

Seaton looked at Dan and Tammi and raised his eyes to heaven at the mention of Sheila's name. "Thanks, Control, will do. Out."

"Speak of the devil," offered Dan.

Seaton smiled. "Never was a truer word spoken in jest."

He found Sam Cleary sitting at the back of the Fisherman's Arms' beer garden. The tramp was slouched on an old picnic table with a half-empty glass of ale in front of him. Seaton smiled at the groups scattered around the garden enjoying their lunch as he made his way towards Sam. He surmised that most of them probably thought that he had been summoned by the landlord to move him on. He hoped that Sam would be in an amiable mood and not too far gone; otherwise, he might take umbrage at being taken away from his liquid lunch and start causing a scene.

Though confused by Seaton's request, Sam was only too willing to accompany the officer back to the station, but only after he had finished his pint, which he did so in one swift gulp.

Seaton did not apologise for opening all the windows of his patrol car. It was a scorching day, and though the vehicle had a very adequate air-conditioning system, Seaton needed the ventilation to disperse his companion's ripe odour.

Sam was in a particularly chatty mood, which Seaton anticipated would make things easier when Sharpe questioned him. Hopefully, the inspector would soon realise that old Sam was far from perfect as any kind of witness and let him go back about his business.

As he pulled his car into the car park at the back of the station, he noticed that Sharpe and Sally had returned from interviewing the woman who had called that morning concerning her missing husband. Seaton hoped that it was nothing more than a coincidence and nothing whatsoever to do with their other disappearances. He could just envisage Sharpe and Sheila getting together to make a career out of all this.

He took Sam in through the back entrance and sat him in their one and only interview room. At the mention of a cup of tea, Old Sam just pulled a face, but Seaton decided that he needed one even if the old man did not appreciate the gesture.

As he left the interview room, he bumped into Sharpe coming out of the toilet. Sharpe looked past the sergeant just in time to see old Sam in the room before the door closed completely.

"Is that my suspect?" asked Sharpe, still adjusting his zip.

Seaton nodded. "Yes, that's old Sam Cleary. I'd better warn you, he's a little worse for wear as usual, so we might not be able to get much sense out of him."

Sharpe shrugged back his shoulders and straightened his tie. "Just you leave him to me; I'll see he makes sense."

The inspector started to walk towards the interview room when Seaton held up his hand to block his path. Sharpe looked at Seaton's hand then straight at the officer himself, a look of disbelief on his face that Seaton would dare to have the cheek to stop a superior officer in the course of his duty.

Before Sharpe could speak, Seaton said, "Look, he's an old man as well as a drunk, but he's completely harmless. Now I need to make an urgent call, but I'll be back in five minutes so perhaps you could make him a nice cup of tea, then we can all sit down together and see what else he can remember."

Sharpe's expression changed from one of disbelief to one of pure malevolence. "You do not tell me how to conduct my interviews, Sergeant!" He almost spat the words out, his eyes widened in anger, his nostrils flared as he took a step closer to the officer. For a moment, Seaton actually believed that Sharpe was going to strike out, but he soon realised it was all part of the inspector's bluff and bluster, which had doubtless worked on countless subordinates in the past.

But not on an old hand like Seaton.

Seaton stood his ground. The two men were only inches apart. Seaton, the taller of the two, held his superior's gaze without wavering.

Eventually, Sharpe looked away, the battle lost. Ignoring Seaton, Sharpe turned and walked into the interview room, slamming the door behind him.

Seaton sighed. Much as he wished to be present when Sam was interviewed, as much to make sure that Sharpe played by the rules as to hear what the old man had to say, he knew that he had better not keep Sheila waiting too long; otherwise, she might turn up at the station, and he could not bear the thought of her and Sharpe kissing each other's backsides in front of him.

On his way to his office to make the call, he stopped at the desk and asked Ralph to take Sam a cup of tea.

CHAPTER EIGHTEEN

Seaton waited on hold whilst her personal secretary tried to trace Sheila down. The music which echoed through the earpiece was classical in nature, but Seaton was not enough of an expert to know the composer.

Eventually, Sheila came on the line. "Sergeant Seaton, thank you for returning my call so promptly."

Seaton almost felt that he detected a note of sarcasm in the woman's tone, but he decided to let it pass regardless. The last thing he needed now was another argument. "No problem," he responded, casually. "What can I help you with?"

"A couple of things," Sheila retorted, her business-like manner remaining constant. Seaton could hear papers being shuffled in the background and the faint hint of someone else talking very quietly, as if to avoid disturbing Sheila. Probably Sheila's poor secretary apologising for something which wasn't her fault as usual, thought Seaton.

Sheila came back to him. "Firstly, has that New Scotland Yard official arrived yet?"

"Oh yes," replied Seaton, trying not to let the anguish in his voice give him away.

"How's it working out? Have you made any progress yet?"

"Well, it's still early days, Sheila, but Inspector Sharpe is following a line of inquiry he seems most confident about."

"Well, that's something at least; I thought that might make the wheels start to turn."

Seaton chose to ignore the obvious dig she was having at his expense. At the end of the day, if Sheila stuck her nose in too far, he could just pull the plug and tell her that the investigation was confidential from now on. And if she did not like it, she could argue it out with the big boys. Chances were, she would get her way eventually by wearing them down with her constant complaining, but even so, he would at least derive some pleasure from being able to tell her 'No' for once.

"Make sure you keep me fully up to date with any new developments?" Sheila continued. "I do not want to read about them in the press without fair warning!"

"I'll do what I can, Sheila, but remember, the press publish whatever they learn straight away, and they have resources that we don't. Plus, if they receive information, they are not obliged to tell us before they publish unless we agree on an embargo, and quite frankly, I can't see them agreeing to one on this case. Sea monsters sell papers. And who would believe that we are taking all this seriously in the first place?"

Seaton could hear Sheila release a huge sigh on the other end. He waited for her retort in silence. "Well, that brings me on to the other reason I asked you to call me." Seaton relaxed, she had obviously decided to drop her original argument. "Do you remember at the meeting we had that I mentioned finding an authority on different species of marine life?" She did not pause long enough to allow Seaton to answer. "Well, I managed to get a professor of cryptozoology to agree to visit us in the next day or so. He sounded very excited on the phone when I explained to him about the reported sightings we've had so far, so he's agreed to drop what he's doing and come straight down."

"Oh," replied Seaton, with obvious disappointment.

"What does that mean?" Sheila obviously picked up on his response.

Seaton sighed. "Nothing really, it's just that I was going to suggest that you might talk to the curator of our local marine museum. She's a qualified marine biologist and seems to be quite an authority on what forms of ocean life there are, and where they can be found."

"Is she a professor of some kind?" The question sounded more like a statement, accusing Seaton of daring to question Sheila's decision.

"Er, I don't think so." He could imagine what would doubtless follow.

"Well exactly, I think you should just leave such decisions to me and continue with your investigation, don't you?" The patronising tone was one of her favourites. Seaton knew that she used it whenever she could.

He did not bother to answer her.

"Now, Professor Garrett Warminster is an eminent expert in the field of underwater sea creatures. He's even written a couple of books on the subject, and from what I understand, he lectures quite extensively on the subject at various universities around the world. So I think I am safe in saying that he is probably the most eminent choice to go to for advice."

"As you say, Sheila." The fight in him was gone. Seaton did not have the energy or the inclination to continue on this subject. He had decided it was far more prudent to back down and see where the pebbles fell.

"Good, well I'm glad that's sorted." She sounded eminently pleased with herself. "Right then, well I will get on with arranging accommodation for the professor for when he arrives. Meanwhile, please let me know the minute there are any developments, you have my mobile number if it's out of hours?"

"Yes, thank you, Sheila." I keep it close to my heart, he thought to himself, and stifled a chuckle.

As he replaced the receiver in its cradle, Carmody knocked and opened his door without waiting for a response. As soon as the door was open, Seaton could hear shouting coming from down the corridor.

He looked at Constable Carmody. "What the hell's going on, Ralph?"

The young Constable looked embarrassed to be there. He quickly looked over his shoulder as if to ensure that he had not been followed, then turning back said, "It's that Inspector Sharpe. He sounds like he's having a right pop at poor old Sam. We didn't know what to do, but it's not right, Sarge."

Seaton pushed back his chair without answering. Sharpe's roar could be heard reverberating down the corridor and probably carried into the street, thought Seaton. What was the man playing at? Old Sam was about as harmless and docile as they came; screaming at him was going to achieve nothing but cause the old man more upset.

Seaton pushed past Carmody and saw Sally and Joe waiting in the foyer. They both looked at him, perplexed, each afraid of what their boss might do, but neither feeling the urge to voice their suspicions.

As Seaton reached the door of the interview room, he could hear wooden chairs being scraped along the tiled floor. As there was no glass panelling on either side, he was unable to see what was going on inside, but by the tone and volume of the inspector's voice, he knew that he did not care for proprieties.

Seaton turned the handle and thrust his weight behind the door, swinging it wide open.

Inside, Sharpe was holding old Sam against the wall by the lapels of his raincoat. The old man looked at Seaton with a pleading stare which caused Seaton's temperature to rise to boiling point.

"Let go of him, now!" He managed to keep his voice steady and under control. Underneath, he could feel the anger welling up.

Sharpe looked at him, his brow furrowed with confusion. How dare a junior officer burst in on him like this! And then have the audacity to give him orders!

Seaton took a step inside the room. "I said, let go of him, now!" He was staring directly at his superior officer. Challenging him, defying his authority. It was almost as if he was daring Sharpe to retaliate.

The three constables shuffled into place just outside the door. Support for their superior officer, unvoiced but distinctive. Their eyes too were burning into the inspector, Sally's especially.

Sharpe realised that he was on a losing wicket. He let Sam slip slowly from his

grasp. The old man almost crumpled to the floor once he was released. Seaton shot forward and grabbed him, knocking Sharpe out of his way en route. His young constables surged forward as one and joined him in helping the old man to his feet, none of them acknowledging the senior officer in the room.

"Come on, old son," said Seaton, comfortingly. "You go with young Sally here and she'll get you a nice cup of tea, go on."

"Yeah, come on, Sam, you come with me," Sally said, cheerily. "There might even be some chocolate biscuits left if the Sarge hasn't polished them all off."

Together, the three of them escorted the old tramp out of the door. Once he was in the corridor, Seaton could hear him pleading with Sally. "I told him that I don't know anything else, only what I told your guv'nor, but that bloke wouldn't listen."

His voice trailed away before Seaton turned to shut the door behind them.

When he turned back to face Sharpe, the inspector was already sitting back in his chair, a know-it-all smirk stretched across his chubby face.

Seaton held himself in check. Regardless of what he had witnessed, and how he really felt about the man before him, he had to remember that he was still a senior officer and though he was not deserving of any respect, it was still Seaton's place to show a modicum of deference as befitted his rank.

Seaton moved closer to the desk in silence, his gaze burning into Sharpe's eyes. As Seaton approached, Sharpe's expression changed. The smirk disappeared and was replaced by a look of disappointment which quickly changed to concern the closer the sergeant came.

Before Seaton had a chance to speak, Sharpe held up his hands as if afraid that the officer might suddenly walk straight through the desk and be at his throat in an instant. "Now look here, Sergeant. I know that my methods may not be your cuppa tea, but we need to see results and that's what I do; I get results."

Seaton leaned against the back of the chair on the opposite side to where Sharpe was sitting. His stare was unwavering and the inspector could not hold his gaze.

Finally, Seaton broke the uncomfortable silence. "And you do that how exactly? By threatening and assaulting an old man who can't fight back?"

Sharpe made some pretence of having to reshuffle papers on the desk. He still avoided Seaton's gaze as he replied, "Look, I wasn't going to hurt the old bloke. I just needed to make sure he was telling us all he knew." His attempt to justify his actions did not hold any water as far as Seaton was concerned, and Sharpe knew that as soon as he had finished speaking.

Keeping his voice steady and remarkably under control, Seaton spoke through gritted teeth. "Just remember this. When old Sam there decides to make an official complaint, he will have me and my constables as witnesses to back him up!"

Sharpe shot out of his chair. His face suddenly drained of colour. His initial reaction was to shout Seaton down, but he quickly managed to rethink his position before making that mistake. He knew that what Seaton was saying was true, and he knew that last time it had only been through his uncle's intervention that he was still on the force.

But he needed a defence, and attack was the best form of that. He tried a half-smile but relaxed his expression, deciding that it would not help him in this situation. He hated these small town mentalities.

"Look here, Sergeant. The old bloke was going bonkers; I thought he was going to go for me, so I just held him back to defend myself, that's all. You weren't here; you didn't see what he was like!"

The accusation caused Seaton to smile in spite of himself. He shook his head and patted down the hair at the back of his head. "Well, I'll tell you what, Inspector," he began, perfectly in control, "in all the years I've known old Sam, I've never known him to so much as raise his voice to anyone, regardless of the circumstances. And no one, including a police complaints commission board, will ever believe that a hulking brute like you could possibly feel threatened by a harmless old man like Sam. But if that's going to be your defence..." Seaton trailed off as Sharpe, spurred into action by the officer's words, came around the table rubbing his hands nervously.

"It won't come to that, surely?" The question sounded more like a plea. Seaton had him on the run and it felt good.

Sharpe stood to one side of Seaton. He started to lift his hand to touch his fellow officer on the shoulder, but thought better of it and stopped himself.

Seaton stared at the man's face. There was genuine fear in those eyes. Seaton imagined that Sharpe could see what was left of his not-so-distinguished career about to flush itself away forever, and the thought was clearly not a pleasant one.

As much as he deserved to suffer, Seaton suddenly felt pity for the man. Seaton could not reason why; it certainly was not respect for his rank and the inspector did not possess any likeable qualities, or if he did he had made a very credible job of hiding them.

But something in the pathetic way Sharpe was looking at him like a drowning man begging for a lifeline, made the sergeant want to proffer the man some hope.

Seaton sighed, deeply. "Knowing Sam as I do, if you were to apologise, sincerely," he put emphasis on the word, "and make a generous contribution to his evening's entertainment, there's a chance he might be willing to forget the incident. After all, he is a forgiving sort of chap."

Sharpe thought for a moment, then without saying anything, he rummaged in his inner jacket pocket for his wallet.

He took out a £20 note. "Will this do?" he asked Seaton, almost beseechingly.

Seaton frowned. "No!" he answered, categorically.

Sharpe made a moaning sound then pulled out another twenty. He held both notes up together. "Is this enough, it's all I've got on me?"

Seaton shrugged. "You could try."

This time, Sharpe did pat Seaton gently on the shoulder as he thanked him and quickly left the room.

Seaton followed behind. He was going to enjoy this!

**

Mary knocked and entered Coulson's office, carrying a batch of draughts for him to survey. As she placed them on her boss's desk, he looked up from the report he was reading and asked, "Any word on Topplewell or Rice yet?"

Mary shook her head, solemnly. "Sorry, boss, no. I've left messages on their home numbers, but both their mobiles seem to have been switched off. I've tried them both a dozen times already." She waited a moment while Coulson thought about what she had told him. Then she asked, "Do you think I should call the police?"

Coulson looked up. His initial shock at her request turned more to understanding as he considered the option. He looked at the clock on the opposite wall. It was just coming up to 3:30pm with no sign of either of them, and not so much as a phone call to say they had overdone it the night before and just woken from a drunken haze.

Like his secretary, he too was beginning to worry.

His hangover had finally cleared, and his head had stopped thumping by the time the second glass of Alka-Seltzer did its thing. He had missed lunch and now he was starving, and when he was this hungry, his brain refused to work properly.

He gazed up at the clock again as if by some miracle the last few seconds might make some difference. Mary was still standing in front of his desk. She was obviously growing more concerned as the afternoon drew on. He watched her start to bite her lip.

Finally, he asked, "Would they do anything now? After all, it's only been a couple of hours, and don't they have to wait at least twenty-four before taking any action?"

Mary shrugged. "I don't know, I've never had to report anyone missing before." She hesitated before adding. "Should I just call the local station and make inquiries?"

Coulson considered her suggestion. He had met the local sergeant in charge of the Alton constabulary before at civic functions, and he seemed like a reasonable sort of chap and certainly not the type to start ranting and raving about wasting police time if you happened to be wrong about something.

But on the other hand, both his missing staff were grown men and able to take care of themselves, and it did seem to him a little premature to start involving the police at this stage.

Looking back up at Mary, he could see the concern etched into her face. She was clearly worried for the two men, or at least for one of them in particular. He had noticed the way her eyes followed Justin around the office when she thought that no one was watching. Still, it did not do any harm; so long as they kept their private lives separate from the workplace, he did not have a problem with it.

He felt a sudden pang of jealousy which he quickly tried to quash. Mary was a stunning woman, but far too young for him. At least, that would doubtless be what she and everybody else would say. Mind you, his paper had a run a story only last month about a twenty-four-year-old actress born locally, who married a seventy-six-year-old retired stock broker.

Still, he had something to offer which unfortunately Coulson did not. Money, and lots of it. That girl knew what she was doing. A couple of years and she could either divorce him for a huge slice, or perhaps if he had a dodgy ticker, she intended to wear him out and inherit the lot. Lucky sod, what a way to go!

Coulson brought himself back down to earth so he could attend to the matter at hand. He glanced at the clock for the third time in five minutes, and planting his elbow on his desk, he rested his chin in the palm of his hand.

Tapping his nose in thought, he finally said, "Let's leave it for a bit longer, Mary. If we haven't heard anything by 5:30, check through their personal files and try contacting their next of kin. They might be some perfectly reasonable explanation for all this."

He could see the disappointment in her face. She needed something to keep her occupied, take her mind off things for a while. Unfortunately, her work was not that engrossing for it to fit the bill.

Then he had an idea. He sat half-way off his chair and removed his wallet from his back pocket. He held out a £10 to her. "Tell you what, it's a blisteringly hot day; why not take yourself to that coffee place round the corner and treat yourself to one of those monstrous iced coffees you love? You know, the one with all the cream and stuff oozing out over the top."

Mary smiled, warmly, and took the note. "Thanks, boss. What about you?"

"A double espresso, if there's enough change."

Mary tutted. "That'll be your fifth today, at least!" She raised an eyebrow in mock admonishment.

Coulson put on his best bashful face. "I know, I think I might have a problem." He grinned.

***

Having watched Sharpe make a very grovelling, almost credible, apology to Sam, Seaton asked Ralph to drive the old man back to his hostel for a rest. As it turned out, Sam asked to be taken back to the Fisherman's Arms instead, so Ralph complied without putting up too much of an argument.

Sharpe decided that he had had enough for one day, so he took the address of the hotel Ralph had booked him into and left. The others were glad to finally be left alone.

Joe related to Seaton and Sally what had happened at Norwich that morning when he had dropped off the camera and rucksack. Once he had explained the circumstances to the desk sergeant, he was promised a response as soon as time allowed. Their laboratory technicians were all working the evidence from a major drug bust which had taken place the previous morning. They were still holding the alleged culprits in custody, and the DCI in charge wanted to make sure that all the charges would stick, so that was their priority for now.

Once Carmody returned from dropping Sam off, Seaton filled them all in on his conversation with Sheila earlier. He had already resigned himself to being summoned to another scintillating meeting at the Town Hall once the professor arrived. Joe made a joke about sending Sharpe in his place, and they all enjoyed a laugh which helped to dispel the bitter taste of Sharpe's earlier behaviour towards old Sam.

The mood remained jovial when Sally revealed that Sharpe had invited her up to his hotel room for a drink whilst they were out that morning responding to the missing person's report. The three officers roared with uncontrolled laughter when she revealed that she had told Sharpe that she was a black belt in karate, and that she could snap his neck like a twig if the occasion called for it. Apparently, he had dropped the subject after that, and did not revisit it again.

The lady who had reported her husband missing was a Mrs. Lucy Hardcastle. According to Sally's notes, she had just returned from a holiday abroad with her children, her husband having stayed at home because he had too many business meetings which needed his attendance.

Mrs. Hardcastle had spoken to her husband on the phone three nights ago and he seemed fine. But when she arrived back and he had not arranged for a car to pick them up from the airport, she contacted his office and was told that he had not been into work for a couple of days, and that no one was able to reach him on any of his contact numbers.

According to Sally, the wife had been quite explicit when they were alone that she and her husband shared an open marriage, and that they mainly stayed together for the sake of their children. But that this was completely out of character for him, which was why she had contacted the police.

Seaton felt a sense of foreboding deep in the pit of his stomach at the prospect that this latest report might concern the other man old Sam said he saw being 'sacrificed' on the beach. He hoped that this would result in a simple case of the husbanded absconding with their cleaner, having emptied the company's bank account, but somehow, he knew that it would not be that simple.

He needed a drink! A very big one!

Just then, the phone in his office started to ring. Instead of walking through, Seaton signalled to Carmody who picked the call up using the desk phone, and handed the receiver across to his sergeant.

The constables watched as Seaton listened intently to what he was being told from the other end of the line.

While he listened, he began writing on the desk pad in front of him, before finally thanking the other party and replacing the receiver back on its cradle.

Holding up the pad, he turned to address his team. "Do any of you know a Justin Topplewell?"

Seaton noticed Green's face redden. The young officer shot up from leaning against the desk and almost stood to attention. "Er, I do, Sarge, sort of." The others turned to face him, causing him to look even guiltier than when the name was first mentioned.

Green cleared his throat before continuing. "Well, I don't exactly know him; more like I know of him. He's a reporter with our local newspaper."

The silence which followed his statement made Green's cheeks flush again. He knew he had been stupid taking bribes from the reporter in exchange for information, but he had never given him anything too confidential. Just the odd name or address, or on occasions minor details of on-going investigations which could not possibly be traced back to him.

At this moment, the weight of the accumulated guilt which had been bubbling under the surface ever since he first met the reporter quite accidently in the pub, felt like it was about to explode.

Green was in a corner. As much as he wanted to come clean to his governor and his colleagues, he knew that he could not bear the shame of such a confession. But then, worse still would be the disgrace of keeping quiet and the truth being revealed by someone else.

Either way, for now, he was going to keep quiet. This was not the time for confessions, and he would decide himself if and when the time arose.

"Why do you ask, Sarge?" Sally broke the silence. Luckily for Green, no one seemed interested in knowing how he knew who Topplewell was. And he was grateful for that.

"It appears," replied Seaton, "that it was his mobile that made the call in the early hours to emergency services from that boat we fished out of the sea this morning."

Seaton turned his attention to Green. "How do you know him, Joe?" The constable had just begun to relax when the question was fired at him. Everyone turned to look at him, awaiting his reply.

"I met him once in a pub and got talking. That's how I remember him because he had a weird surname." Green complimented himself on his recovery. He even sounded convincing to his own ears.

He felt confident enough to knock the nail home. "Mind you, that was a while ago. I'm not sure if he still works there."

Everyone seemed to accept the plausibility of his statement. As much as he hated having to lie to his colleagues, he made a mental promise to himself that this would be the very last time that he put himself in this kind of position.

"Right then," Seaton continued, looking at Joe. "As you're the only one who at least knows what he looks like, get yourself down to the paper's office and make discreet inquiries. But don't say anything for now about our suspicions, or why we're looking for him. The last thing we need is a media frenzy."

"Right you are, Sarge." Joe grabbed his uniform hat and exited the building. Once outside, he heaved a huge sigh of relief before setting off on his duty.

CHAPTER NINETEEN

The sight of the young uniformed officer entering the premises made everyone in the newsroom look up from what they were doing. The general hubbub which buzzed throughout the normal working day simmered to the level of a barely audible whisper as all eyes turned to Joe Green.

Mary, fearing the worst having spent all day trying to reach both Justin and Animal without success, immediately put both hands up to her mouth as if to stifle a scream, before pushing back her chair and rushing to greet the young constable.

Putting on her most professional demeanour, Mary escorted Joe to Coulson's office. Coulson shook Joe's hand and ushered him in, holding the door open for Mary to leave. He could see that she was reluctant to go, obviously anxious to hear if there was any news about the reporter and photographer. But Coulson thought it best to hear whatever the constable had to say alone, and then he could decide what to tell the rest of his staff.

He squeezed Mary's hand gently as he guided her out. When she looked at him, he could see that her eyes were beginning to well up, so he gave her a sympathetic wink and a smile, as if to let her know that everything would be okay.

Once he was sure that the door was securely locked, Coulson took his place behind his desk opposite Joe. He offered him tea or coffee which Joe politely refused.

"How may I help you officer?" Coulson braced himself for bad news. In all his years in the newspaper business, the only other time he had witnessed a uniformed police officer entering the office was when he had come to arrest one of the reporters on a charge of harassment.

Joe took out his notebook. "Does a Justin Topplewell work here?"

Coulson sighed; it was as he had feared. "Yes, Officer, he's one of my best reporters." He needed to cut to the chase. "Has anything happened to him?"

Joe felt himself starting to flush. He made a perfunctory gesture to stall for time by turning the pages of his notebook back and forth. Seaton had instructed him not to let on about their suspicions, and foolishly, Joe had not thought to think up a plausible story on the way down.

Eventually, he cleared his throat and said, "Nothing that we're aware of, we were just trying to trace him." He looked back up to meet Coulson's glare. Joe could see the look of suspicion in the editor's eyes. He obviously did not believe him, but Joe would have to remain constant or face the wrath of his sergeant when he returned to the station. He took a deep breath to relax his vocal chords before continuing. "Do I take it that he hasn't reported for work today?"

"I'm afraid not, Sergeant."

"Oh, it's just plain constable actually." Green smiled.

"My apologies. Yes, I'm afraid both Justin and one of our photographers, Animal…oh sorry," Coulson corrected himself, though he had to think for a moment to remember what Animal's real name was. Everyone called him Animal so it just rolled off the tongue. Finally, he remembered. "Norman Rice. Animal is just a newspaper folklore nickname we give to our photographers." He could see that Joe was frantically scribbling while he was talking.

Coulson waited for Joe to stop before continuing, eager to see which bits he made a note of in case it gave him a clue as to what the police already knew, as the officer was clearly under instruction not to divulge anything at this stage. "The pair of them set off yesterday evening to hire a boat." He watched Joe's pen moving swiftly across the page. "They were planning a follow-up to our story on the Pete Dodds disappearance; you know the one where that young Amy from the fish shop stated that her boyfriend was killed by a large creature which emerged from the sea at Skullen Bay?"

Joe Green seemed to be writing down everything Coulson said. The editor sat back in his chair, leaning his elbows on the arm rests, his fingers joined together under his chin in the shape of a church steeple.

The young officer was oblivious to Coulson's game plan. When he finished writing, he quickly re-read what he had put down so far, then asked, "Do you knew where or who they were hiring this boat from?"

Coulson shook his head. "Sorry, no, I wasn't here when they acquired the requisition form," he signalled outside his office, "but my secretary Mary signed it off in my absence. I don't think they told her exactly where they were going. Would you like me to ask her to come in here?"

Joe looked up in mid-sentence. "No, that's fine; I'm getting all I need for now." He returned to his scribbling.

Coulson looked out towards the main office. People were clustered in small groups, obviously discussing the officer's presence and doubtless speculating on the reason behind it.

Mary was sitting behind her desk alone. Coulson watched as she snatched another tissue from the box on her desk and daubed her eyes. Her actions spurred him on; he had to try and find out something from the constable before he left.

Leaning in, as if to give the impression that anything said would remain between the two of them, he asked, "Can you please level with me, Constable; obviously something is wrong otherwise you wouldn't be here, right?"

The editor's words stopped Joe's train of thought dead in their tracks. He was the one who was meant to be asking the questions, not the other way round. He tried to imagine how his governor would handle the situation. There was no point losing his cool and trying to sound all authoritative and official; that would only hack the editor off and probably cause him to clam up.

Joe remembered his training. Keep calm and in control at all times. Apologise for the official nature of the interview but stress that the law required it of investigations at this early stage. He knew that Coulson was no idiot. There would be no point in trying to concoct a story; better to just come clean and adhere to procedure for the moment.

For a brief second, Joe wondered if Coulson knew that he was one of the missing reporter's informants. Did reporters keep some kind of file or computer log listing the details of those whom they paid for information? The thought made Joe feel very uneasy, and he found himself squirming in his chair involuntarily.

He had to remind himself that he was better than that. At least, he was now. After the earlier scare at the police station when he thought he was about to be unmasked, he made a promise to himself that he would treat his office with more respect. He had made mistakes in the past, foolish ones due to greed and stupidity, but all that was behind him now. If Coulson suddenly produced an envelope stuffed with notes and shoved it across the desk to Joe in exchange for telling him all that the police knew concerning Justin and Animal's disappearance, Joe would refuse to take it and threaten to charge the editor with trying to bribe an officer of the law.

Joe remained steadfast. He straightened himself in his chair and addressed Coulson directly. "I'm very sorry, Mr. Coulson, but at this stage of our inquiry we just need to know Mr. Topplewell's whereabouts for the purpose of elimination. I'm afraid that am not at liberty to divulge anything further at this stage."

Coulson gazed out of the glass partition at Mary again, as if he was trying to send her a psychic apology for failing to find out anything concrete for her.

Joe followed Coulson's gaze. Several journalists looked away when they noticed the police officer looking in their direction. A very natural reaction, thought Joe. He had seen it a hundred times before from people who genuinely had nothing to be afraid of, but still they could not meet an officer's gaze.

He did feel some empathy for them. After all, Justin and Animal were probably close to some of them, but his duty was his duty and he had to deal with the situation abstractly.

Turning back, he asked Coulson, "Could you possibly give me their home addresses and the contact details of any next of kin?"

Coulson tensed. 'Next of kin'? That could only mean one thing. He had been in this business long enough to know that much.

He excused himself and left the office. Joe watched as Coulson was suddenly surrounded by a mass throng as he entered the main floor area. Coulson waved them all away, patted some on the shoulder as they turned away, dejected.

He returned a few minutes later with the details for Joe.

As Joe was adding to his notes, Coulson suddenly had a thought. "Officer, supposing for the sake of argument that Topplewell and Rice did eventually rent a boat last night as they had indicated."

"Yes," replied Joe, eagerly.

"Well, and I'm only surmising now," he clarified his point before continuing, "sooner or later, the boat hirer will probably turn up here demanding to know where the vessel is. That is, if they never made it back to shore, don't you think?"

Joe was about to answer, then realised that if he did so he would be giving away more than he should. He thought for a moment, before replying. "If either Mr. Topplewell or Mr. Rice returns, could you please ensure that they contact us immediately at the station?" He took out a card from his uniform pocket and handed it over to Coulson. "Likewise, if anyone else should show up claiming to have seen them, please also let us know."

Coulson looked at the details on the card absentmindedly. He resigned himself to the fact that he was not going to make any more progress here today.

***

Dan and Caitlin sat themselves down at one of the tables furthest from the bar at the Fisherman's Arms. It was Caitlin's idea to go for a drink after work, and though Dan would have preferred a cosy night in to make up for their minor disagreement that morning, to be honest, he was just happy to be in Caitlin's company.

Dan could feel the eyes of some of the patrons following them back from the bar. Caitlin had a figure that could stop traffic, and he knew that it was not just him being biased. Tonight, she had opted for a tiny pair of denim hot pants, with a white shirt tied at the waist, and a simple pair of white plimsolls to complete the look.

Simple, elegant, and incredibly sexy all rolled into one neat package. Dan still felt the need to pinch himself every so often just to make sure that he was not dreaming.

Usually in those American science fiction films, they tried ensured that the role of the female scientist was always played by a drop-dead gorgeous actress. But they never managed to pull off the part of a serious academic as well as being a cute babe. But Caitlin was the real thing. How could someone so intelligent be so beautiful? Not to mention kind, sweet, thoughtful and caring?

He really was a lucky man, and he intended never to let that fact slip his mind.

Caitlin chose the chair against the wall so that she could see the bar from where she was sitting. Dan placed her drink in front of her before pulling out his chair to sit. They clinked glasses and said, "Cheers."

After taking a long sip of her white wine, Caitlin asked, "Have you heard anything yet about those things you'll found this morning?"

Dan shook his head while he swallowed his beer. "Nothing yet. Mind you, I doubt the sergeant will tell us anyway, seeing as they are part of an ongoing investigation."

"What do you think could have happened to whoever was in that boat?"

Dan raised his brows. "Well, I have to admit, the only time I've ever come across a boat in that state, was when it had been smashed against the rocks during a storm. But this one was out in the open sea, no rocks for miles."

Caitlin played with the rim of her glass, circling it with her fingertip. She had painted her well-manicured fingernails a dark shade of pink. Dan wondered momentarily if she had matching toenails. He suspected she did. He hoped to find out later for sure.

Caitlin brought him round from his reverie. "Could another boat, a bigger one, have crashed into it and caused the same amount of damage?"

Dan nodded. "It's always possible. But it's hard to fathom why someone would do that on purpose. And if it was an accident, then why didn't they stop and pick up the crew from the water?"

Caitlin thought a moment. "Feuding drug gangs perhaps. People smugglers maybe, not wanting to leave any witnesses behind."

Dan laughed, softly. "You have a very vivid imagination, Miss Howard."

Caitlin smiled and kicked him gently under the table. "I realise it's a little outlandish for this kind of territory, but don't you think it could even be a possibility?"

Dan took another quick gulp of beer. The gassy liquid slipped down too fast and he was relieved when he managed to suppress a belch. "Anything is possible where the sea is concerned. We get checked randomly when we're out by officials looking for drugs, or guns, or even people. They're all a huge trade and some runners think they stand more chance of getting away with it if they use a small insignificant looking boat like mine, so it's perfectly plausible."

Caitlin's eyes narrowed, suspiciously, but there was still a trace of a smile on her lips. "You're not just saying that to humour me, are you? I can kick harder you know."

Dan held up both hands, defensively. "Honest, guv'nor," he said, in a mock cockney accent.

Caitlin laughed out loud at his antics, putting her hand to her mouth to lessen the volume. She was glad that she had not been in mid-swallow; otherwise, she might have choked.

Dan waited for her giggles to pass before he leaned in closer. The nearest patrons to them were two tables away and doubtless unable to hear their conversation above the overall din of the drinkers, but Dan felt it was better to be safe now than sorry later. "What's your opinion concerning the possibility of some kind of Loch Ness Monster being out there?"

Caitlin thought for a moment before responding. "Well, I certainly wouldn't rule anything out. There's more water than land covering the world, and even with all our modern technology, we haven't been able to build a machine sophisticated enough to take us right down to the depths."

"So you think that there might be something down there lurking in the deep?"

Caitlin shrugged. "Some thing, or many things. That's just it; we scientists like to keep an open mind, especially when you consider that new species of wildlife are forever being discovered."

"But something big enough to take out a boat, admittedly a small one…What about that girl's story about something coming out of the water and grabbing her boyfriend? Do you think that the two are connected?"

"Mmm, it's not so much what we think, as what we can prove."

Dan looked confused. "How do you mean?" he asked.

Caitlin pushed her glass to one side so that she would not risk knocking it over. She leaned forward with her elbows on the table, using her hands to help her elucidate. "You know for example that all the sightings of the Loch Ness Monster were of it in swimming the water?" Dan nodded. "Well, interestingly enough, one of the first sightings was by an old couple who swear that they saw something large and slimy, slither across the road in front of their car before diving into the water. So if their story is true, the monster can move on land as well as under water.

"Likewise, all the sightings of, let's say, the giant squid, have always been in particular parts of the world with the squid in the water, because that's where squid are found. Now, if there is another type of creature, a hybrid or even a completely as yet undiscovered abnormality, then who's to say it cannot move about on land as well as in water."

Dan frowned. "And be big enough and mean enough to somehow slither up on land and capture people? Not to mention, smash a boat to a pulp in the water?"

Caitlin wrinkled her nose. "Well, a giant squid could certainly cause some damage if it wanted to. I've met colleagues who have seen them, albeit only fleetingly, and they've all said that they would not want to be on the water regardless of the size of the craft if one of them decided to attack."

Dan rubbed his chin. "You're making me feel like I should consider a change in trade now."

Caitlin lowered her hand and grabbed one of Dan's fingers. She began to massage it playfully as she spoke. "And what would you do instead?" she asked. "Any plans?"

"I could become a writer. Tell the story of my many adventures on the high seas."

Caitlin squeezed his finger before letting go. "Now that sounds like the making of a bestseller."

They both laughed together.

***

Seaton pulled up in the pub car park. Today had been one of those days, and he needed a drink desperately.

After Joe had reported back from the newspaper, it seemed a foregone conclusion that the victim in the wrecked boat had been the reporter Justin Topplewell. What's more, it seemed like there was a good possibility that he had an associate with him in the boat too, now also unaccounted for. Seaton would show Sharpe his report in the morning; no point in disturbing him right away as there was clearly nothing that could be done for the two men. And besides, Seaton had had enough of the inspector for one day.

Tomorrow, they would doubtless be contacting the local constabulary from wherever the two men's next of kin's lived. As neither was local, it would be down to them to break the news to their families. Seaton had performed the task himself in the past, not a very pleasant job. You never knew exactly what to say or how to say it. You tried to show empathy without being condescending or trite. And you never knew how the recipients were going to react until they did so.

He had to admit that he was glad that the duty would not fall to him.

As he was about to enter the pub, Seaton suddenly caught sight of Jake Johnson walking up the path. Exhausted though he was, he had been meaning to speak to Jake for a couple of days now, and this might be an ideal opportunity.

Seaton waited at the pub's garden entrance for the fisherman.

When Jake saw the officer standing there, he quickly altered his course, trying and failing to make it look natural. He was now starting to move away from the pub and down towards a side street.

Seaton had to call out twice, the second time louder than the first in order to get Jake to stop.

Seaton had long suspected Jake of getting up to all sorts of illicit activities over the years, but so far, none of the man's actions had warranted official investigation. Somehow, he always seemed to remain one step ahead of the law, but his luck had to run out soon.

Jake did not turn back, but simply stood in place waiting for Seaton to come to him. Seaton wondered if Jake knew why he wanted to speak to him, or was it his natural shiftiness and fear of discovery which made him always act so suspiciously.

Seaton took his time walking slowly towards the big man. Let him sweat; do him good, Seaton thought.

As he heard the officer walk up behind him, Jake swung around to confront him, his face demonstrating his usual scowl of loathing and contempt which he reserved for representatives of the law as well as anyone who he suspected was capable of crossing swords with him.

"What is it, Sergeant? I've got a lot on tonight." Though the big man's voice was level and under control, Seaton still detected a hint of malevolence in the undertone.

Johnson towered above the sergeant, and as usual, tried to use his posture and body language to intimidate. But Seaton was not flustered in the slightest. He had been in the job a long time and knew only too well how to deal with the likes of the Jake Johnson's of the world.

"Well, if you're in a hurry, Jake, we can always do this down at the station tomorrow, if that's more convenient for you?"

Jake's eyes widened in horror. His initial belligerence died away within seconds and was replaced by the 'Jake' version of politeness. "No, there's no need for that, what can I do for you, Sergeant Seaton?"

Seaton pretended not to notice the sudden metamorphosis. "Am I right in thinking that you were approached by three university students a couple of days ago who wanted to hire you to take them out at night to film a project they were working on?"

Seaton watched Jake's eyes narrow. The friendly façade drained from his face in seconds. Jake knew what Seaton was talking about, that much was obvious. The question now was how to find out everything he knew.

"Was that bloody Dan Savage shooting his mouth off? I'll have 'im!"

Seaton held up a restraining hand. "What are you getting so irate about, Jake? No one's accusing you of anything. I just want to know if you remember the incident, and if so, what happened."

Seaton could tell that Jake did not want to talk. He knew straight away that the big man had something to hide; he just was not sure what as yet.

Jake's mind raced. He felt like a rabbit caught in the headlights of an oncoming car. It was one thing to lie to someone like Dan, but lying to a copper, especially one who knew him, that was another matter.

Jake cursed Dan beneath his breath. This was all his fault, and one day, Jake would get even with him. The question now was what to tell Seaton. He was no fool, so Jake could hardly fob him off with any old rubbish. There was no going back; he could not afford to blurt out the truth. Even though he did not kill them himself, he did pawn their equipment, and did not report their deaths to the authorities. He was not sure of the technicalities were for acting the way he had in the eyes of the law, but he suspected that the result could mean prison.

"Well?" Seaton was starting to get impatient. Jake was taking far too long to come up with a plausible story for it to be the truth.

Jake shrugged. "I don't know what you want me to say. I told Savage that they started arguing over the price, so I told them to piss off. Last I saw of them, they were walking back along the beach, probably to try and find someone else."

Seaton watched Jake's eyes as he spoke. They darted about rapidly, looking in every direction possible but never at Seaton.

"So you never actually took them out on your boat?"

Still avoiding the Sergeant's gaze, Jake continued. "No, like I said, they tried to mess me about so I told them where to go. It's been a long day; I didn't have time for no timewasters." Suddenly, Jake felt more in control. His story seemed innocuous enough not to need embellishing. Unless the copper had a witness who had seen Jake take them out, no one could prove it. He waited for Seaton to bring his ace out of the hole. When the officer stayed silent, Jake felt confident enough to push his defence home a little further. "Why, have they put in a complaint about me because I gave them the sharp edge of me tongue?"

Seaton looked up at Jake. He was still acting very shiftily in his body language, but now there was also a hint of cockiness in his mocking tone. It was almost as if the big man knew that Seaton was only going on Dan's word, and Dan had not seen anything conclusive.

Seaton knew in his gut that Jake was lying about something.

But what exactly, he could not be sure.

"No, nothing like that, Jake, don't worry." Seaton knew there was no use in pressing the matter further at this stage. He stared at the big man for a few more seconds; Jake still could not hold his gaze. "If you remember anything else which might be pertinent, let me know, please?"

Jake's whole demeanour relaxed, visibly. A half-smile spread across his hairy face, which Seaton thought could just have well been a cock-sure smirk.

Jake saluted the officer as if he was one of his subordinates and turned to walk away, whistling a tuneless monosyllabic tune as he went.

Seaton watched the man leave, feeling a little helpless and ineffective. He considered that perhaps this was not the right time to question Jake. After such a long day, he was tired and exhausted. He needed food, drink, and sleep. If he had interviewed Jake when he was fresh and rested in the morning, he might have been able to prise something more worthwhile out of the man.

Feeling somewhat dejected and cross with himself, Seaton headed back to the pub.

He ordered a pint of strong ale and a shepherd's pie for his dinner. While he stood at the bar sipping his drink, a familiar voice spoke to him.

He turned and saw Dan standing next to him at the bar. "Oh, I'm sorry Dan, I was miles away then. How are you?"

"Doing better than you by the look of things," Dan joked, "what's wrong?"

Seaton sighed. "Oh you know." He glanced around him, but there were too many people within earshot. "This business!"

Dan took the hint. As the barmaid brought him the drinks he had ordered, he asked if the officer would like to join him and Caitlin at their table.

Seaton accepted, grateful for some congenial company.

Not wishing to act like a gooseberry, as he took his seat, Seaton announced that he would only stay until his dinner was ready, joking that he knew what it was to be young and in love. The comment made both Dan and Caitlin exchange a sly smile with each other.

"So how is your investigation going?" asked Dan. "Any more sightings?"

Seaton shook his head. "No, thank God. Oh, by the way, I just cornered Jake Johnson outside, he denied all knowledge of taking those students out on his boat that day after you introduced them."

Dan nodded. "Yes, that's what he said to me too. Not that I believed him, he's hiding something."

"That's for sure," agreed Seaton. "Trouble is, without any witnesses, he knows he can get away with it."

"What do you think he's hiding?" asked Caitlin, curiously. "I mean, I know that he has a bit of a reputation around town, but do you think he is capable of murdering them and disposing of their bodies in the sea? What would be his motive?"

The sergeant took a long drink from his glass before considering his answer. He knew that officially he could not say too much, but the fact was that he liked Dan and Caitlin, and he felt he could trust them both to be discreet.

He leaned in a little closer. "Motives have a funny way of presenting themselves when you least expect it."

Dan and Caitlin both looked at each other quizzically. "How do you mean?" asked Dan.

Seaton put down his glass. "Well, and I'm purely speculating now," he emphasised, "suppose Jake did take them out on the sea with the intention of just letting them make their film, then bringing them in home. Then say something happened, and as a result, Jake ended up hurting or even killing one of them, even by accident. What's he to do now? He panics, has to get rid of the others as they are witnesses, so he kills them too, and chucks all the bodies over the side."

Dan and Caitlin were both agog. "Seriously?" asked Caitlin, mesmerised by Seaton's assumptions.

"Well, as I say, I am only surmising. It may sound fanciful, but it's an old story which had cropped up on numerous occasions in the past." He could tell from their expressions that he was causing his fellow drinkers undue concern. So he added, "Not around these parts, I hasten to add, but the scenario is a sound one, nonetheless."

Dan took a swallow of beer. "Look, I know Jake can be a bit of a nut-job, but murder, just like that? Do you really think he's capable?"

Seaton shrugged. "In my line of work, we have to consider all possibilities, but as I say, I'm only surmising." He moved his glass to one side. "Knowing Jake, he's probably up to his armpits in all kinds of nefarious activities, so he has a hundred reasons to be cagey. But that doesn't mean that he isn't telling the truth about those students."

They all thought for a moment.

Then Caitlin added, "If not Jake, then have you any idea of what might have happened to those students then?"

Seaton sighed and shook his head. "Nope. I'm hoping that they decided to go off on a student jaunt and are all lying together in a muddy field somewhere still sleeping it off." He laughed, good-humouredly. "Now that would make me very happy."

They chatted in general for a while. Seaton was beginning to feel much calmer and more relaxed now. Whether that was due to the company, the beer, or both, he did not care. It lifted his spirits and that was much needed.

Eventually, the barmaid called over that his dinner was ready. Seaton stood to leave, thanking the couple for their delightful company.

"Oh by the way," he remembered, "we've got one of your distinguished colleagues joining us tomorrow." He looked at Caitlin, smiling.

"Really?" she replied, mildly surprised. "Who's that?"

Seaton thought for a moment, then answered. "It's a Professor Warminster, I think."

Caitlin almost choked on her wine. Dan went to pat her on the back, but she held up a hand to say she was okay. Once her throat had cleared, she asked, "Not Garret Warminster, please?"

Seaton frowned. "Yes, that's the one. Why, do you know him?"

Caitlin nodded. "Unfortunately, yes," she replied with obvious loathing in her voice. "He taught me once at university. 'Garret the groper' we called him, a nasty little creep. What made you ask him of all people?"

Seaton held out his arms in defense. "Nothing to do with me, that was our town mayoral candidate Sheila 'bloody' Soammes." He smiled warmly at Caitlin, then said, "I take it from your last comment that you would not be interested in joining me at the next town meeting to discuss developments concerning whatever is out there?"

Caitlin winced. "I'd love to, under normal circumstances, but if 'Garret the groper' is in attendance…"

"I'll make sure that I seat you far away from him," Seaton assured her. "I'll be there to protect you remember."

"Was he really that bad?" asked Dan, trying to hide his amusement at Caitlin's expression.

"Well, put it this way, one of the girls in the year above mine grew so fed up with is wandering hands that she kicked him in the shin and left her stiletto buried in his leg. He had to go to hospital to have it removed."

"Didn't anyone make an official complaint about him?" Dan asked, comfortingly.

"I think a few did, but he managed to talk his way out of trouble; he's a real charmer when he wants to be."

"Well, I'll keep you informed either way," said Seaton. "And just see how you feel about getting more involved, I won't push the issue."

He left to have his meal, leaving Dan and Caitlin to enjoy their evening.

CHAPTER TWENTY

When Seaton finally returned to the station house that night, it was almost mid-night. Instead of just having a couple of pints as he had initially intended, he finished the night on four pints of strong ale, washed down by two large stiff whiskeys.

Naturally, he left the patrol car there and walked back to the station. The night was cool and welcoming after such a hot day, and Seaton felt thoroughly deserving of his bed by the time he reached home.

The stroll from the pub should have taken him no longer than twenty-five minutes, but as it was such a calm night with barely a soul about, the policeman decided to take a stroll along Skullen Bay.

There was only a quarter moon tonight, but the stars were out in their glory, which afforded him a panoramic view of the sea from the beach. He stood there for what seemed an age, just watching the water and the way the light caught the waves as they rolled along.

The tide was still quite far out, so he decided against walking right up to the water's edge. Instead, he stayed back far enough so that his feet were still on hard sand and not slush. With the peaceful tranquillity of the moment and the gentle lull of the sea, it was hard for him to imagine that there might be some great monster lurking in the shadows below the waves, waiting hungrily for its next victim.

If such a creature did exist, then by and large, the investigation would be out of his hands. Doubtless, the coastguard or the Navy would bring in their people to try and capture, or kill it. It was just his luck that whatever it was had decided to pick his remote little town to surface and start a killing spree.

Before turning in, as was his nightly habit, Seaton poured himself a shot of single-malt whiskey from a bottle which he kept locked away in his desk's bottom drawer. The frustrations of the day and the annoying Inspector Sharpe were becoming nothing more than a memory.

Noticing that his computer was still switched on, Seaton decided to check his e-mails before retiring. As expected, there was one from Sheila confirming the professor's arrival tomorrow – or today as it was now – and setting the time for the council meeting for 2:30pm.

Seaton made a mental not to remember to inform Sharpe in the morning.

Amongst the miscellaneous jumble of information messages, he noticed one from the laboratory at Norwich. Ignoring the others, he clicked it open, and sure enough, it was the report regarding the rucksack and camera.

He skim-read the first few pages which covered when and where the articles had been found and at what time they were brought in to the lab. He moved through until he reached the summary regarding the camera. The report stated that the camera had been badly shock-damaged, and that the outer water-proof skin had been pierced, allowing salt water into the digital chamber. Unfortunately, this meant that most of the photographs which had been taken were now inaccessible, but there were a few survivors that had escaped corrosion and they were attached to the e-mail.

Seaton eagerly moved his cursor to the attached icons and clicked each one in order. The first showed what looked like an egg with a large red stain across it. The second resembled a crocodile or alligator's skin close-up. The third image was of something splashing down in the water, but it was too indistinct to actually make out what it was, and the angle gave it the illusion of being something small in a shallow area of water.

The fourth frame made Seaton slump back in his chair. Though there was nothing in the shot to give any idea of size, it looked like something long and thick was wrapped around a dead man. You could not see his face or make out any specific characteristics, but from certain angles, it did not take too much imagination to see that it was a full grown man and not some toy soldier being staged to look like a human being for the picture.

The body was being suspended by whatever was holding it, as it lay slumped in the thing's clutches.

Seaton stared at the picture for a long time. Finally, he began to believe that there was something out there lurking in the waters off Skullen Bay.

He poured himself another shot. Suddenly, he needed it. The calm solemnity which he had felt moments earlier had now been shattered by what lay before him.Gingerly, he clicked on the last icon.

The last frame chilled his blood!

It was a close-up picture of a hideous open mouth, with row upon row of mangled pointy teeth, far too many to count, which faded into darkness at the far end of the shot, leading to…God knows what or where.

Seaton ended up staring at this last shot for even longer than he had at the previous one. He cringed inwardly at the prospect of this being the last thing the photographer might have seen before being chewed on and swallowed up by that cavernous maw.

He wondered how someone could keep hold of a camera long enough to take the final picture, knowing that your life was about to end in such a monstrous fashion.

Seaton felt a sudden admiration for whoever had taken the picture, and he automatically raised his glass to the screen in salute, before emptying it in one swallow.

***

Seaton rose early the next morning. His sleep, when it finally came, had been fitful and sporadic, peppered with nightmares of large jaws chomping down with sharpened yellowing fangs.

His head thumped as a result of his alcohol consumption the previous evening, and he sought solace in a hot shower and a strong pot of coffee.

Having printed off copies of the pictures sent to him by the Norwich laboratory last night to take with him to the council meeting that afternoon, he struck upon an idea. He wanted to show them to Caitlin first. He would appreciate her opinion far more than he would Sharpe's or this professor with the wandering hands.

He did not want to go to the museum too early in case Dan was staying over again. He already felt embarrassed that he had had to wake them up yesterday to go on their little fishing expedition. But by the same token, he did not want to leave it too late, as he wanted to be back at the station without Sharpe knowing what he had done. Otherwise, he felt sure that Sharpe would kick up a fuss about letting anyone else see them before he had made a decision.

He knocked on Caitlin's door a little after eight. There was no answer. He decided that they must still be asleep, so he waited, intending to try again in ten or fifteen minutes.

Just then, Caitlin and Dan came around the corner. Caitlin was carrying what looked like a shopping bag with the top of a French stick poking out from it. Dan held Honey on her lead; in her excitement, she was almost pulling him over in her haste to get home.

Seaton waved and they responded likewise. He waited on the doorstep for them to arrive.

As they approached, he made a point of speaking first. "I'm sorry about this, you two must think that I'm a stalker or guilty of police harassment or something?"

They both laughed. "No, that's okay." Dan smiled. "We've decided you're one of the good guys."

Seaton moved to one side to allow Caitlin to insert her key in the lock.

"I know it's early," the sergeant continued, "but I would really appreciate your opinion on something."

Caitlin raised her eyebrows. "I'm intrigued. Good thing you're just in time for breakfast, come on up."

The three of them went inside with Honey leading the way up the stairs.

Caitlin put on the coffee while Dan busied himself making them bacon sandwiches with the French stick and real butter. They had decided they deserved it whilst they were taking Honey for her morning walk.

Once everything was ready, they all sat at the dining table. Seaton had initially refused the offer of breakfast, but now looking down at his thick French stick lavishly spread with golden butter, and the mountain of fried crispy bacon on the centre plate waiting to be devoured, he was glad that he had changed his mind.

"What was it you wanted to show me?" asked Caitlin, biting into her baguette.

Seaton automatically went for the envelope, then stopped himself. He looked at both of them eating. "Actually, you might want to wait until after you've finished before seeing these," he advised.

Dan put his hand over his mouth still chewing. "Are they something disgusting?"

Seaton paused for thought, then said, "I'd say more disturbing than disgusting, but even so, I don't want to put you off your breakfast."

They finished eating, and Dan prepared a fresh batch of coffees.

"Here we go then," said Seaton, spreading out the photos on the table. "These are what escaped damage from the camera we found on that wrecked boat yesterday. I just wondered what you might make of them."

Dan and Caitlin both scrutinised the pictures avidly amidst murmurs of shock and disbelief. As Seaton expected, they paid most attention to the last two depicting the dead man suspended and the mouth with the rows of ugly teeth.

Finally, Caitlin spoke up. "Well, bearing in mind the quality is not so great, if whatever this thing is really killed those two newspaper men, and all the others, then from a scientific point of view, we have some kind of phenomenal creature using our bay as a feeding ground."

"So you think it might be real, then?" asked Seaton, almost goading her into an alternative solution.

Caitlin shrugged. "Well, as I said, the pictures aren't great, but as they are all the evidence we have," she looked at Seaton, "and you do have several missing people all of whom disappeared in roughly the same place, this is one obvious solution."

Dan glanced over at her. "The alternative being…?"

Caitlin looked back at the pictures before her. "Search me."

***

The town hall meeting started promptly at 2:30pm. Seaton had arrived earlier with Sharpe as arranged to show Sheila the photographs. She gazed at them furtively, as if afraid someone else might creep into her office unannounced.

"And these are the genuine article?" she asked, to neither man in particular.

Sharpe stayed quiet, so Seaton responded. "As far as we know, it's hard to verify anything with the camera having been destroyed, and of course, no witnesses."

Sheila switched back and forth from one copy to the other. As with Caitlin and Dan earlier, she focussed mainly on the last two. "This could be big," she announced, excitedly. "Very big!"

"What, you mean the creature?" asked Seaton, quizzically.

Sheila looked at him over the rim of her glasses like an exasperated school mistress staring at a dim-witted pupil. She continued speaking only after she had stopped staring and went back to concentrating on the pictures. "No, I mean the event itself. If we are fortunate enough to have our very own certifiable monster…Well, I don't have to tell either of you gentlemen what that could do for the town. Look at Loch Ness, for example; their entire tourist industry depends on a monster which no one has any evidential proof of. And here we are with photos and witnesses. This is all very exciting!"

Seaton could not believe what he was hearing. He had long thought that Sheila Soames suffered from a general lack of empathy, but this was too much, even for her.

He took a deep breath to control his rising anger. "With people being killed around us in what must be an unimaginably agonising manner, I hardly think that 'exciting' is the most appropriate adjective to use, do you?"

"Steady, Sergeant," Sharpe jumped in, feeling a kinship with the council official's status. "There's no need to be rude. All the lady meant was that this could be very exciting for the town, which will benefit everyone. Recent tragedies aside, naturally."

Sheila smiled her appreciation at Sharpe, and gave Seaton a flash frown.

At the main meeting, Sheila introduced all those in attendance to Professor Garret Warminster. Seaton found him a very flamboyant, extroverted, almost eccentric individual. He was dressed in a white three-piece linen suit with an open-neck shirt. Around his neck, he wore a multi-coloured cravat, and perched at an angle on his head a wide brimmed fedora-style hat, which he only removed after he had been introduced to the group.

Sheila circulated the copies of the photographs Seaton had brought around the table, while she brought everyone up to date with the latest developments. The new arrivals began to stir and mumble as they surveyed them.

Professor Warminster withdrew a large magnifying glass from his inside pocket and studied the pictures enthusiastically.

Once everyone had seen them, Sheila asked the professor if he would care to address the gathering. For a moment, Seaton thought that she was going to burst into applause as the man stood to make his address. Fortunately, she did not.

Looking around him, the professor spied a blackboard behind where Sheila stood, so he decided to position himself in front of it before beginning.

"Well, thank you, ladies and gentlemen," he began, "and thank you Miss Soames for that marvellous introduction." They smiled at each other, embarrassingly.

Seaton looked at Caitlin who raised her eyes to heaven.

The professor continued. "As Miss Soames mentioned, my area of expertise is cryptozoology, so I have many years in the field as it were, studying sightings of creatures of this ilk. However, I must say that this is the only time that I have come across an established sighting of a cephalopod of this size anywhere near the British Isles. From a scientific point of view, local tragedies not withstanding, this is a very exciting find."

The professor droned on for over an hour, detailing his many expeditions around the world and the frustration at all the 'near misses' he had encountered. Seaton had to force himself to stay awake, catching himself stifling a yawn more than once. Surveying the faces around the table, it appeared to him that he was not the only one fighting a losing battle.

Seaton wondered how someone who had been invited to lecture on his chosen subject to gatherings all over the world – according to him – could possibly possess such a monosyllabic voice.

Finally, the torture was over, and the professor opened the floor.

The petite lady who had been at the earlier meeting was the first to put her hand up. As with the first meeting, she had spent the majority of this one writing frantically in her notebook. Seaton seemed to remember that she worked in the council press office which would explain her constant scribbling, but he could not be positive.

The professor invited her to speak.

"What, in your opinion, is this creature in our waters most likely to be, or is it an as yet undiscovered aberration?"

The professor began to move around the table as he spoke, as if for emphasis. Remembering what Caitlin had said about him earlier that day, Seaton noticed with interest how he hovered behind the lady who had asked the question the longest. Leaning gently on the back rest of her chair, he peered over her head as if watching what she was writing. Seaton wondered if that was all he was looking at. When he glanced over at Caitlin, he quickly realised that same notion was going through her mind as well.

"Taking everything thus far into account," the professor continued, "I am firmly of the opinion that what we have here is by far and away the best sighting of the legendary Kraken." He spelled the name out for the benefit of the lady who asked the question. "Though our waters are much colder than those one might usually associate with such a creature, the mere fact that we know so little about it suggests that perhaps we've been looking for it in the wrong places before now."

"So where does it come from, and why is it here now?" asked a squat man with a receding hairline and glasses who Seaton thought he remembered from a previous meeting, but could not be absolutely sure. The cut of his suit and his general demeanour gave the appearance of someone important and influential, but then Seaton's experience of such people in his line of work meant that looks could be very deceptive.

The professor continued his tour around the table as he continued talking. Seaton could see Caitlin physically stiffen as he approached her chair. At the last second, Seaton put his arm across the back of her chair and leaned in as if to ask a question under his breath, like a protective father warning off a potential suitor.

Caitlin, realising his game-plan, smiled her gratitude as the professor quickly moved on.

Professor Warminster answered all the questions put to him in the same affluent manner, exuding a confidence that doubtless came with the fact that the majority of people around the table would have to take his word for whatever he said.

Eventually, Sheila adjourned the meeting, stating that she would contact everyone individually to arrange the next one.

Once the others had left, only Sheila, Seaton, Sharpe, and the professor remained. Seaton had wanted to let Caitlin stay, but Sheila had made it quite clear that her presence was not needed. Seaton walked her to the door and apologised for Sheila's behaviour, speaking quietly, though not really caring if Sheila could hear him or not.

Once they were alone, Sheila asked Professor Warminster for his plan of action.

Taking the floor once again, the professor continued to expound his philosophy on the origins of the Kraken, and why it so imperative that no action was taken that might harm it or cause it to move away from the area.

While Sheila and Sharpe listened intently, Seaton sat with his elbow on the table, resting his cheek against his fist. All he could think of was how they were going to explain to the families of the victims that they were not planning to take any action against the creature that had killed their loved ones.

Furthermore, what were they planning to put into action by way of a preventative measure to ensure that there were no more victims in the future?

Eventually, the professor divulged his plan of action.

"I have already contacted the British Oceanographic Institute, and they have agreed to lend me the equipment to undergo an expedition to try and film the Kraken in action."

Seaton could not bite his tongue anymore. "When you say in action, I take it you don't mean devouring his next victim, which is what is likely to happen if we don't take immediate action to warn people of the danger."

Sheila's lips went thin in anger. She yanked her glasses from her head and before speaking. "No one is suggesting that we do not take precautions, Sergeant, but first, we need to hear what the professor recommends before making any hasty decisions."

"Hasty decisions!" Seaton rise to his feet. "There must be thirty to forty vessels all from our shores out on the sea right at this minute, full of fishermen and holiday-makers, any of whom could end up being this thing's lunch if we're not careful."

"Sit down, Sergeant!" ordered Sharpe, noticing the growing antagonistic expression on Sheila's face.

Seaton stayed on his feet for a moment, then realising that his was the voice of reason in the wilderness, he shrugged his shoulders and slumped back in his chair.

Sheila shot Sharpe a grateful smile, then turned back to the Professor. "I'm sorry, Professor, you were saying?"

The professor had maintained his rigid posture throughout Seaton's outburst. He nodded his appreciation to Sheila before continuing. "Well, as I was saying, once the equipment arrives tomorrow, I hope to undertake an expedition that will give us the evidence we need to prove the creature's existence, categorically. Once that has been established, we will then have full backing from the institute to launch a full-scale operation to try and catch the beast."

The professor looked from Sheila to Sharpe for accreditation for his plan. Their simpering smiles gave him all the reassurance he needed. When he saw Seaton's expression was unchanged, he added. "Of course, in the meantime, I would strongly advise that we ground all other vessels in the area, save the one I will need to use tomorrow, until we have the creature safely ensnared and ultimately removed to one of our research aquariums."

"How long do you think all that will take, Professor?" Asked Sheila, tentatively.

"Oh, no time at all. Let's see, if I go out tomorrow to film the Kraken, then once I have shown the evidence to the institute, it should not take them longer than a day or two to supply me with what I need to capture the creature, so shall we say four days, tops?"

Sheila clapped her hands together. "That is good news. I'm sure that the mayor will be only too happy to give your plan her full support." She made some notes in her file before continuing. "So, for the moment, we need to secure you a vessel to use for your expedition tomorrow, is that correct?"

"That's right," replied the professor. "It doesn't have to be enormous, just big enough to carry the underwater equipment, including the winch which will have to be bolted into the floor."

Sheila turned to Sharpe, ignoring Seaton completely. "Perhaps you would be so good as to allow Sergeant Seaton to take the professor down to the harbour to see if he can negotiate the use of a craft for tomorrow?"

Sharpe smiled. "No problem at all." He gave Seaton a half-glance, not actually waiting for his agreement.

"And in the meantime," continued Sheila, starting to get to her feet, "I will speak to the coastguard regarding your suggestion, Professor, to ground all the vessels in the bay until further notice." She purposely avoided Seaton's gaze as she spoke. "It'll cause quite a stir, I imagine, amongst the local boys, but hey-ho, they must realise that we are only acting in their best interest."

"If they can't appreciate that, then they can lump it, I say," Sharpe added, hoping for, and receiving, another winning smile from Sheila for his troubles.

***

Seaton took Professor Warminster in the patrol car up to Skullen Bay. He decided that it made sense to give Dan first refusal to take the professor out to photograph the Kraken. He surmised that whatever the institute were willing to pay for hiring a boat would help compensate Dan for the money he would lose when the coastguard grounded all the boats until the creature had been captured.

The professor spent the journey up to the Bay on his mobile, clarifying his specifications for what he needed to be sent down for the expedition. By the time he had finished his conversation, they had arrived at Skullen Bay.

Seaton could see that Dan's boat had docked; so on their way down the beach towards the harbour, he explained to the professor why he thought that Dan was the obvious choice for his excursion.

When they arrived at the *Lady Anne*, Dan and Tammi were on deck. Seaton made the introductions and explained briefly to Dan what the professor needed. The professor took over from there, describing how he would need his launch to be bolted to the deck of Dan's boat, and that he would need at least one member of crew to act as a diver in case the winch became entangled on something and needed to be freed.

Dan listened, taking in everything the professor had to say.

Just then, Caitlin appeared from below deck. The professor's eyes immediately alighted on her, and he lost his train of thought. Staring at her for a moment, he suddenly announced. "I know I saw you at today's meeting, but we've met somewhere before, I'm sure of it."

Caitlin came forward, holding out her hand. "That's right, Professor, you lectured at my university when I was studying for my post-graduate qualification. Caitlin Howard."

The professor took her hand and squeezed it gently, but firmly. "That's right, I never forget a face, it was bugging me all through today's meeting." He was still holding her hand, reluctant it seemed to let go. "And what are you doing here, exactly?"

Caitlin withdrew her hand. "I'm the curator of the local maritime museum. The sergeant here thought it might be useful for me to attend the meeting earlier this afternoon."

"Quite so," agreed the professor, seemingly oblivious to the fact that they were not alone. "In fact, you must accompany me tomorrow on my little expedition, I'm sure that you can offer some valuable insight, and as a fellow student of all things marine, I dare say you'll find it as fascinating and exciting as I will."

Caitlin looked shocked to receive such an offer. She looked at Dan, momentarily, then back at the professor. "That's very kind of you, I would love to come along, thank you."

The professor smiled. "Perhaps we could finalise details tonight over a little dinner? They've put me up at the best hotel in town, or so I'm led to believe."

Caitlin felt her cheeks go red. "Oh, thank you very much for the offer, but I'm afraid that I am already spoken for this evening." She moved next to Dan and put her arm around his waist. He reciprocated with his arm around her shoulders before bending down to give her a quick kiss on the lips.

Seaton smirked whilst trying to be as discreet as possible.

Tammi, on the other hand, had to turn away to stop her laughter from blaring out.

The professor cleared his throat, suddenly embarrassed by the realisation that there were others around him who had heard his proposal being denied.

He strutted off towards the bow of the boat and pretended to inspect the wheelhouse. He leaned in closely a few times and rubbed away fictitious scratches before he stamped his foot several times as if to test the sturdiness of the deck.

Next, he gazed up at the masts and then counted his steps from one end of the vessel to the other.

Finally, looking at Dan, he announced, "I'm very sorry, Captain, but I'm afraid that your vessel won't do."

Everyone else looked at each other with their mouths open, speechless.

Professor Warminster, pretending not to notice their expressions, thanked Dan for his time and went to exit the craft. Before he did, he turned back to Caitlin and said, "I will ask the good sergeant here to let you know when and where to meet for tomorrow." With that, he strode off the boat.

Seaton felt he had to apologise to Dan. Dan reassured him it was okay, and the sergeant followed the professor down the beach in search of an alternative craft.

When they were out of earshot, Caitlin turned to Dan, her eyes starting to well up. "That was my fault, I'm so sorry. He would have hired you if it wasn't for me."Dan put his arms around her and pulled her close. He gazed deeply into her eyes and kissed her nose. "It's not your fault, don't be silly. The old devil probably thought he was in with a chance and blames me for ruining it."

Caitlin gagged. "Oh please, I think I'm going to throw up!"

CHAPTER TWENTY-ONE

Seaton dropped the professor back at his hotel. Against Seaton's better judgement, the academic had opted for Jake Johnson's boat Reaper's Revenge to take him out for his excursion to try and find the Kraken the following day. Initially, as usual, Jake was very sceptical when the professor approached him. Seeing Seaton with him only helped to put Jake even more on his guard.

Eventually, the professor persuaded Jake to take him below deck to discuss the proposal in private. While they were out of sight, Seaton remained on the jetty. Jake's crew were all on board, swabbing the deck and clearing away the debris from the day's outings. In Seaton's opinion, each of them was as dodgy as their captain.

Stan and Gerry Clive were only kept in line by their mother, Maggie, who ran a local guest house. Without her guiding hand, the pair of them would certainly have spent most of their adolescence in juvenile detention, but as it was, she had always managed to keep them on the right side of the law, which was a continuous battle for her even now. Fortunately, they had both inherited their father's knack for all things mechanical. Not that either of them had bothered gaining any qualifications in spite of the fact that Maggie had fought tooth and nail to get them both signed up to apprenticeship schemes when they left school. Their only other talent lay in the fact that both brothers were excellent swimmers, and keen divers, though again, frustratingly, neither could be bothered to earn qualifications which would have allowed them to pass their skills on.

Ray 'Hammer' Hodges was Jake's only other crew member, and he had certainly seen more than his fair share of the inside of Her Majesty's prisons. At thirty-five, he had spent over a third of his life behind bars for various offences, ranging from breaking and entering to grievous bodily harm. He stood six feet tall and was almost as broad as he was tall. A stooping, slouching figure, combining hard muscle and fat in equal amounts. With his shaven head, which seemed to sit directly on his shoulders without any room for a neck, massive arms covered in tattoos, and thick course hair covering his entire upper torso, it gave him the all over appearance of a bald gorilla, which was exacerbated by the fact that his general form of communication consisted of grunting and mumbling incoherently.

When Jake and the professor finally surfaced from below deck, Seaton knew from the self-satisfying look on the professor's face that they had struck a deal. Jake, for his part, was rubbing his hands together and smiling broadly.

205

On their way back to his hotel, the professor informed Seaton that he intended to set sail tomorrow evening at 8pm. As the Kraken had not been spotted during the day, it made more sense to be on the water during the hours of darkness, and the eight o'clock start would give them ample time to reach a location which the professor deemed as best suited to watch for their prey.

Seaton promised to pass the details on to Caitlin the following day.

When he arrived back at the station, Seaton found Sharpe holding court. He was excitedly telling the constables that Sheila was setting up a press conference for the evening, and that he would be in attendance to represent the police. This suited Seaton, as he had never had the stomach for all that pretence and false affability.

Seaton stood at the back to let Sharpe continue.

"So then what Sheila…er Miss Soames and I thought," Sharpe quickly corrected himself, almost as if trying to hide any familiarity the two might share, "that what we could do was have a wall of pictures of the victims so far, at least the ones we know about, so that she could send out a heart-felt message of condolence to their relatives, then we…"

"Hang on a minute!" Seaton butted in. "How can you state that we have victims when half of their families have not been officially informed yet?"

Sharpe stopped dead in his tracks, his brow furrowed. "Wh-What do you mean? I thought we had been in touch with all the relatives already?"

Seaton moved forward and indicated to his open office door. "If you had taken the time to read the reports, you would know that we have not confirmed yet that the three university students are dead, let alone victims of our sea creature. Same thing with those two men from the newspaper. Or, for that matter, that bloke who ran the meat plant whose wife you and Sally interviewed"

Sharpe opened his mouth but no words came out. He looked at the constables as if trying to gain support, but there was none forthcoming.

Finally, he turned back to the sergeant. "Well, why not? Why haven't we confirmed that they were victims of this…thing, whatever the Professor calls it?"

Seaton seethed, through gritted teeth, he replied, "Because of a little thing called proof, evidence, and lack of it thereof!"

Sharpe himself looked ready to implode. His face flushed bright pink, and for a second, Seaton feared the man might be having a heart attack.

The inspector looked at his watch, then at the station clock as if he needed confirmation of the correct time. "Right," he bellowed, "you have just over two hours; make sure that all the next of kin are contacted before the conference." He looked back at Seaton. "Call all the local stations and make sure you emphasise the need for haste, mention my name if you have to, but get it done. The last thing we need is for the grieving relatives to find out about their loved ones in the papers, or worse still, on the radio or TV tonight."

Sharpe was not prepared to look Seaton in the eye once he had finished speaking. Looking at his watch for the second time in thirty seconds, the inspector grabbed his coat and made for the door. "Right, I've got to go back to my digs and get ready for the conference." He moved past Seaton without acknowledging him. "Make sure you make those calls!" he shouted behind him as he walked through the main station door.

Seaton and his constables watched the door swing shut behind Sharpe in silence. While Seaton was looking away, Sally signalled surreptitiously to her colleagues. They both nodded their assent.

"Don't worry, guv," she said, reassuringly, "we'll stay back with you until all the calls are made. Fancy a cuppa?"

Seaton turned back slowly at the sound of her voice. He looked at his team and smiled, thanking them all and reminding himself how lucky he was to have their support whenever he needed it.

***

Stan Clive drained the last dregs from his glass then brought it crashing down on the table, almost shattering it in his anger. His younger brother, Gerry, glanced about to see if anyone else reacted to the noise. Satisfied that no one had noticed, he drained his own glass, but placed it somewhat more gently in front of him.

"Bloody thievin' git," said Stan, more to himself than to his brother. But Gerry knew exactly what he was talking about. After his meeting with the professor below deck, Jake sat down with his crew and told them about tomorrow night's little adventure. Upon hearing the details, neither of the Clive brothers were enamoured by the idea of having to spend the night on the water, especially as they would not be allowed to drink as it was the professor who was paying their wages. Hodges did not complain, but then he never did. He was devoted to his mate Jake who was the only operator for miles who gave him a job when no one else would entertain the idea.

Jake had sweetened the pot by telling the boys that for the night's work they would each be paid £500 in cash. That had put a completely different complexion on the subject, and at first, the boys set off to the pub to celebrate their good fortune.

That was until Hodges had come in for a pint and let slip that Jake would be earning £10,000 for the hire of his vessel for the night.

That information suddenly brought the Clive brother's spirits crashing down, especially Stan the eldest. He knew that it would be him and his brother doing most of the work as usual, while Jake just took the wheel and played at being captain. And they would only receive a lousy grand between them, leaving Jake to pocket eight and a half grand for himself after he had paid off Hodges. And furthermore, Stan was convinced that Hodges would get something extra just because Jake liked him, but Hodges would never let on how much.

As far as Stan was concerned, he and his brother were being screwed over, big-time.

If they had an option, Stan would tell Jake to shove his job. But he knew that with their reputations, it would be hard for him and his brother to find alternative employment, and their mum would hit the roof if they ended up unemployed, especially when it would be their fault for leaving. And knowing his mother, she would probably drag the pair of them down to Jake by their ears and make them beg him for their jobs back.

Stan could still remember when he was ten years old and his mother was called down to the school because he had been bullying some younger kids and stealing their lunch money to buy comics and sweets. Having spoken to the headmistress, Maggie strode into the playground with thunder on her face. She found Stan and grabbed him by the scruff of his neck, then marched him over to an old tree stump they used to use as a make-shift bench. Removing her shoe, she flung him across her knee and paddled him, much to the amusement of his peers who all gathered round to watch the spectacle. He had been the butt of many jokes from that day on, his hard-man image permanently tarnished.

But now his pride had been severely dented. He expected Jake to make more from the deal – after all, it was his boat – but this was just taking the Mick.

Gerry stood up and went to the bar for a refill. He did not bother asking his brother, as he knew what the answer would be. Stan was intent on getting wasted tonight, and Gerry, as the younger sibling, would be obliged to keep up with him, or die trying.

"You know what we should do?" Stan muttered when Gerry returned, not stopping to make sure if his brother was paying attention to him or not. "We should go out there ourselves and find this bleedin' thing, and drag it back to shore for that professor bloke, then 'e can pay us the ten grand instead of Jake."

Gerry took a slug from his glass, consuming a third of the beer before resting.

He wiped the foam from his mouth with the back of his hand before responding. "Ha ha, that would really piss Jake off; that'd teach him to try shafting us."

Stan nodded, smiling to himself and then started drinking, more slowly this time.

"But 'ow would we go about it, Stan?" asked Gerry, furtively checking the area for eavesdroppers.

Stan continued tipping back his glass. Gerry knew that his brother was going to finish his pint in one. He had seen him do it a hundred times before and always when he was hacked off about something or someone.

Gerry took another big gulp from his own glass, forcing the beer down faster than he would have liked, but not wanting to fall too far behind his elder brother.

Stan slammed his empty glass down on the table and released an enormous belch which even those at the back of the bar heard. But he did not care. His mind was working overtime. An idea had taken route and he intended to cultivate it to fruition.

Just then, an idea took hold. Stan turned around in his chair, half-rising, and started to scope the other patrons in the pub.

Gerry finished his pint, but managed to quell the rising gas inside him, just allowing enough to escape to please his big brother. "What you lookin' fer, Stan?" he asked, quizzically.

Stan slumped back down. "Not what, 'oo?" he replied, lifting his empty glass as if to double check that he had consumed the entire contents. He slid the glass back across the table towards his brother. "Right," he said, "get 'em in again, an' a double whiskey each as chasers; we're going to need them tonight."

Gerry complied, as he always did, especially when his big brother was in a bad mood, as he clearly was now.

As he stood to head for the bar, he asked, "So 'oo was it you wus lookin' fer jus' now?"

Stan gazed up at him and tapped the side of his nose with his finger. "I'll tell yer when yer get back. An' don't ferget the whiskeys!"

Having finished their drinks complete with chasers, the brothers left the Fisherman's Arms and staggered across the forecourt towards the beach. Gerry tucked the carrier bag with the two bottles of single malt they had purchased from the landlord of the pub under his jacket and zipped it up for safety. The bar owner had been only too willing to charge them per bottle rather than by the glass as he would have done had they been on the optics. The loss of the extra revenue was a small price to pay rather than have the Clive boys kicking off, especially Stan who was clearly half-cut already.

They stumbled across the road and onto the beach. Stan stood there, taking in huge lungfuls of sea air in an attempt to try and clear his head. They had work to do!

Stan had relayed his plan to his brother when he returned from the bar. They needed to track down old Sam Cleary and get him to show them the best spot for the creature to appear. By all accounts, he seemed to have witnessed the creature's appearance more than anyone else in town, and therefore should be in an excellent position to put them on the right track.

Once they had their starting point, they would procure a boat. Several of the fishermen left their vessels in dry dock when not in use, so it would be easy pickings for two experienced seamen like Stan and Gerry.

Next, they planned to steal aboard Jake's boat and help themselves to ropes, hooks, poles, and anything else they guessed they might need, including, just in case, his secret stash of guns and ammo he kept hidden under one of the bunks below deck. It made the whole event taste even sweeter to Stan knowing that he would be using Jake's equipment to catch the creature and do him out of his ten thousand pounds.

They found Sam half-asleep underneath one of the moored boat's tarps, holding onto a half-empty bottle of cheap wine for dear life. Stan roused the old drunk by rocking the boat violently on the sand.

Sam woke with a start, much to the brother's amusement.

"Come on, old Sam," said Stan, bending down to lift him by the arm. "We're goin' on a little adventure, thee an' me."

Sam pulled back, reluctant to leave his shelter, until Stan called to Gerry to give him a hand in hoisting the old man up. In their haste to move him, Sam lost his grip on his bottle and it fell back into the boat, smashing on one of the oar locks. The remnants of the red liquid quickly seeped into the wooden frame.

Sam, unable to pull himself free of the brother's grip on him, let out a cry of despair. "What d'you 'ave to go an' do that for?" he yelped. "That was me dinner gone to waste."

Gerry carefully removed one of the bottles of whiskey from inside his jacket, and removed the stopper before passing it to the old man. "'ere, 'ave some o' this; that'll keep yer quiet."

The old tramp squinted to read the label, before taking hold of the bottle neck and pouring the fiery liquid down his throat.

Gerry kept his hand on the bottle so it would not fall and end up like the wine. Both he and his brother laughed as the old man gulped down the contents, ravenously.

"That'll do fer now," said Stan, after a few seconds, and Gerry, taking the hint, carefully removed the bottle from the tramp's mouth, laughing again as he watched Sam suck at empty air as the bottle left his lips.

"Now then," said Stan in his friendliest voice. "You won't mind showing me an' me brother where we could find this sea monster thingy of yers?" He grabbed Sam around the shoulders and held him tightly as if he was a long-lost friend.

Sam looked from one brother to the other, concern etched on his face. He did not like the Clive brothers. They were bullies and had often shouted abuse and made fun of old Sam when he had been minding his own business. A couple of times, they had even tipped him out of a boat when he had been sound asleep, just for their own amusement.

But at least this time they had given him a drink. And it was good stuff too. Hopefully, there would be some more before the night was out.

Reluctantly, Sam left the comfort of his chosen place of slumber and took the brothers down the beach and across to where the remnants of the old ruined pier still stood.

Once there, Sam stood facing the sea with his eyes closed, swaying slowly back and forth as if in a trance. The brothers looked at each other and Stan shrugged, reaching out for one of the bottles. They stayed there for a few minutes, the Clive boys taking it in turn to swig from the bottle, Sam almost oblivious to their presence, lost in a world of meditation.

Finally, Sam stopped swaying, raised his arms out to his sides, and threw his head back. Gerry moved in for a closer look. He could see the old man's lips moving, but there was no sound emanating from them.

After another moment or two, Sam lowered his arms and turned to face the brothers. Before speaking, he reached out to Gerry for the bottle, and took a long drink before handing it back. "She's out there tonight, don't you worry. She's about two miles straight ahead." He looked at each brother in turn to ensure that he held their full attention. Both men were staring straight at him, mouths open.

He had them!

Sam laughed. "Not to worry though, she's fed for the nights, so you'll be quite safe." He took hold of the bottle again and enjoyed another long swig.

"How do you know all this, old man?" asked Stan, suspiciously. "Are you takin' us fer idiots or some'ink?"

Sam managed to keep a straight face. He stared deeply into the older brother's eyes, and said, "Old Sam knows because she speaks to him, always has. That's 'ow come I've seen 'er so many times. But she won't be 'ere for much longer." The two men moved in closer, their curiosity peeked.

"What d'yer mean?" asked Gerry.

Sam shrugged. "I don't know, she just tells me she will be moving on very soon, maybe tonight, who knows."

Stan and Gerry immediately began making arrangements to get out on the water. It was as if Sam was no longer there. He waited a moment as the two men planned their strategy, lost in their own little world.

Eventually, they moved away towards the harbour; neither bothered to thank old Sam for his help, both engrossed in their conversation.

Sam waited for a moment then moved off. The half-empty bottle of single malt held tightly in his grasp more than made up for the remnants of his cheap plonk which the brothers had caused him to drop.

He giggled to himself, amazed that they could be so stupid as to have fallen for his little rouse. He decided to find a quiet place to enjoy his 'earnings' further down the beach, away from the harbour altogether. That way when the Clive boys came back in, furious with him for sending them on a wild goose chase, there was less chance of them finding him and taking their revenge.

Within half an hour, the Clive boys had collected the equipment they needed from the *Reaper's Revenge* and had procured the use of Greg Thornton's boat. Greg was a retired bus driver who kept the boat in dry dock for most of the year, taking it out only on occasion when the mood took him. Just like several other residents of Skullen Bay, Greg had bought the vessel second hand dreaming on long summer afternoons spent on the sea fishing, or just relaxing and enjoying the calm serenity. But the reality of the situation was never quite the same as the fantasy, so Greg's, just like several other residents' crafts, lay covered for most of the year.

Having dragged Greg's boat into the water, Gerry pushed off while Stan exposed the starter wires trying to get the engine to catch. After much shouting and swearing, he finally achieved his goal, hit the starter button, and the craft set off into open water.

Gerry cracked open the second bottle of single malt which they had purchased earlier. His thought process already hazy due to the mixture of alcohol he had already consumed that night, he was unable to remember what they had done with the first bottle. Though he had always maintained that he could take as much as his brother, in truth, Gerry was nowhere near being the alcoholic his elder brother had spent a lifetime achieving.

They both took it in turns to take slugs from the bottle. As they drifted further from out from the shore, leaving the mechanical glow of the fluorescent street lights behind them, the enormity of their undertaking started to dawn on Gerry. It had seemed like a great idea back in the pub in the warmth and convivial atmosphere created by the other patrons around them. But now, out on the water, in almost pitch darkness, in a craft so small it barely held their equipment, the thought of coming up against the this unknown creature face to face caused a shiver to course through him which even the whiskey couldn't prevent.

Stan noticed his brother's sudden frisson. "What's up wi'you?" he asked, laughing to himself. "Feelin' the cold? 'ave another drink."

Gerry did as his sibling suggested, shrugging off the feeling of isolation and fear that had crept in.

Once they were far enough out, Stan killed the engine and they waited in silence. Low clouds scudded across the sky, masking the starlight and increasing Gerry's feeling of isolation.

They passed the bottle back and forth, though in the dim light Gerry only pretended to take huge mouthfuls, hoping his elder brother would not notice.

After half an hour, Stan was beginning to grow restless. They had primed all the weapons and attached the hooks to the lines, ready to ensnare the creature once it showed itself. There was nothing to do now but wait.

Gerry wished they had brought torches. Neither of them considered it back at the *Reaper's Revenge* and there were several on board they could choose from. Also, stopping to make a flask of hot coffee would have been a good idea, not to mention some sandwiches, as neither of them had eaten since lunchtime.

Gerry often marvelled at how focused his brother could be on certain occasions like this, to the extreme of not being effected by human conditions such as hunger, cold, or tiredness. Yet he seemed to have the attention span of a goldfish when it came to anything which he found tedious or dull, such as reading a book.

As time moved on with no sign of the Kraken, Stan grew more fidgety. Gerry wanted to suggest that they turn back and give it up as a bad idea, but he was afraid of his brother's backlash, so stayed quiet. He hoped that Stan would make the offer himself before too long. The night was drawing on and the air was growing colder. Neither of them had thought far enough ahead to consider bringing warm outer clothing, and Gerry could feel the dampness seeping into his bones as he sat there, waiting for something to happen.

Suddenly, they heard a splash somewhere in the distance. It was too dark to see what had caused it, but both brothers tensed inadvertently. Stan picked up Jake's shark gun and checked that the safety was off. Gerry grabbed hold of the sawn-off shotgun and the two of them scanned the water through the darkness.

It was impossible to see more than fifty feet in front of their eyes, and even then, the dark sky and black water blended to form a uniform hue, which made it impossible to distinguish which was which.

They waited, poised.

Gerry could feel his legs starting to go to sleep, so he manoeuvred himself gently to a kneeling position. As careful as he was, his action caused the small craft to list and tilt, almost to the point of capsizing.

Stan turned on his brother. "Stay still!" he demanded, before turning back to squint into the darkness.

In his efforts to move stealthily, Gerry realised that he had managed to trap the shotgun under his ankles. He knew that retrieving it now would cause his brother to react again, so he left it where it was. Unarmed, he grabbed hold of both sides of the small craft to steady himself.

They continued their vigil. The gentle lapping of the water against the boat was the only sound to break the silence. The low clouds made it almost impossible to distinguish any shapes in the water.

After what seemed to Gerry an eternity, his brother turned back around to face him.

"Bugger..." was all he had a chance to say before an enormous tentacle broke the surface and pulled him overboard.

The shark gun snagged the exposed engine wires as Stan exited the craft. His cries died as he was immediately dragged under the water.

For a moment, Gerry was too stunned to react. He glared at the empty space which his brother had occupied seconds earlier as the realisation of his predicament set in.

Gerry scrabbled to retrieve the shotgun, his mind still unable to comprehend what had just happened. His eyes remained focussed on the swirling water beside the boat which signalled his brother's swift departure. He tried to position himself in such a way that when his brother resurfaced he could grab him and pull him back on board.

He lifted his knee to release the shot gun. As he did so, the whiskey bottle rolled under his leg without him realising it. When he tried to re-settle himself, his shin slid along the rounded glass and it moved beneath his weight, causing him to topple over backwards.

The back of his head slammed against one of the seat panels as he blindly let off a shot into space.

He stayed down for a second, trying to collect his wits. He could feel something wet in his hair and realised that he must be bleeding, the force of the blow having caused his skin to rupture.

He groped his way back up to a kneeling position. His head spun, the pain from the contact clouding his vision. Without realising it, he released his grip on the shotgun and it fell to the deck, discharging its final round which discharged straight into his ankle.

Gerry screamed out in agony. The searing pain in his ankle now superseded the throbbing pain in his head. He could feel himself starting to black out. He fought against the inevitability of it, straining to control his agony.

With a tremendous effort, he lunged forward to take control of the motor, any thoughts about saving his brother now gone. Chances are, he was dead already, and if not, there was no saving him from whatever had grabbed him, so why waste his life in a futile effort.

As he leaned forward, his body weight moved to his injured ankle. He felt a crack and fell back immediately in agony, shrieking. The pain was intense; his ankle was on fire, and even without putting pressure on it, the pain did not yield.

He slumped forward, relieving all weight from his legs, and tried to drag himself along the deck towards the motor. He realised that he no longer had a weapon to defend himself with, but he did not care; now his only priority was escape. If he could start the boat and head back to shore, he might be able to stay conscious long enough to call for help.

He reached the motor and managed to pull himself up enough to reach the wires his brother had jimmied to start the engine. As he fumbled trying to lace them together, he listened intently for anything which might resemble something surfacing outside the boat. Whether it was his brother or the creature, he wanted to know.

His fingers seemed devoid of any dexterity as the brass strands kept slipping from his grasp. He tried to sit up further, pushing himself back with his good leg, but the rocking of the boat on the current left him sliding back before he could make purchase.

Seconds seemed like hours before he finally managed to link the wires together sufficiently to hold. He hit the starter, and mercifully, the engine roared back into life.

With a supreme effort, Gerry hoisted himself into an upright position, fighting against the pain in his ankle and the throbbing numbness in his head, until he was in a fit position to steer the boat back to shore.

He allowed one final glance around for any sign of his brother, but not seeing anything, he moved the rudder to turn the craft around.

Before the boat could settle from the acute turn, it was thrown up into the air by a force from below. The boat capsized, sending Gerry and all the equipment, guns, and whiskey bottle crashing into the water.

Gerry screamed involuntarily as he flew through the air, the black water silencing his cries as they had so to his brother's moments earlier.

He surfaced long enough to clear his throat and catch his breath, before something wrapped itself around his torso and squeezed the breath out of him.

Before he slipped under the water, he felt his ribs crack and splinter. The salty taste of blood filled his mouth, and he felt himself losing consciousness as he was pulled below the surface.

CHAPTER TWENTY-TWO

Seaton rose even earlier than usual that morning. The previous evening, once he and his team had contacted all the constabularies which were local to the next of kin of their known victims, and tasked them with informing the parents, partners etc. of their loved one's demise, he sent his team home and drove to the town hall to catch the tail end of the press conference.

By the time he arrived, most of the excitement was over. The press photographers were all packing away their equipment, and several reporters stood huddled in corners talking on their mobiles, explaining to their editors how much space they would need for their story.

Seaton found Sheila in her office along with Sharpe, the professor, and an Inspector Seale from Her Majesty's Coastguard, whom Sheila introduced to him.

Once they were all seated, Sheila confirmed the plan of action for the following day. It had been decided to still allow the town's fishermen to still go out first thing, though the coastguard would be posting warning signs up and down the beach at Skullen Bay and the main beach at Alton.

The tourist fishermen and sightseers, however, would not be allowed out on the water, mainly because the mayor did not want to risk the lives of any visitors. Though the Kraken had not so far – to their knowledge – attacked any of their local vessels, it was known that several tourists used the tours specifically to go diving and swimming out at sea, and that was a risk the mayor did not wish to take. To that end, the coastguard volunteers would be patrolling the beaches to ensure that no one went out.

The equipment the professor had requested from the institute was due to arrive at noon, and Sheila had agreed with Sharpe that a police presence was needed to keep the curiosity seekers at bay whilst it was being installed on Jake's boat.

Finally, Sheila had arranged for a coastguard rescue helicopter to land on Skullen Bay to remain on stand-by just in case the expedition team had problems and needed rescuing.

When Seaton enquired how many passengers the helicopter could carry, he could see Sheila's facial expression cloud over. She was obviously aware that the rescue helicopter could not carry all those on board Jake's boat, but she emphasised that it was more precautionary than anything else. It still made no sense to Seaton, who considered it on par with the Titanic not carrying enough lifeboats because the owners said that they would not be needed.

He could tell straight away that it was not an argument he was going to win, but he had made his point, so he left it there.

After the meeting, he phoned Caitlin as promised, to let her know what time the expedition was planning to set off the following evening. As he could hear Dan in the background, he asked her to let him know about the vessels being grounded the next day.

As Seaton left the station house, the sky was just beginning to brighten. There was no sunrise to speak of as such; the weather forecast for the day was cloudy for the most, with a chance of thunder by the evening, but fortunately, no rain. It was a complete contrast to their recent spate of baking sun and cloudless skies, but not uncommon for the British summer.

He drove up to Skullen Bay. The fishing boats were already out and the beach was packed with men and women in uniform, setting perimeter boundaries and erecting the 'Danger' signs which Sheila had arranged for.

In many ways, thought Seaton, it was a good thing the weather was going to be miserable; otherwise, there would be an awful lot of unhappy sunbathers voicing their protest.

Seaton watched the coastguard volunteers from the road for a while before returning to his patrol car and heading back into town. On the way, he stopped to buy a paper. Sure enough, the lead story was about the eminent Cryptozoologist Professor Warminster braving the elements to capture the first ever live footage of the Kraken. There was a picture of the professor and Sheila standing side-by-side, shaking hands and smiling.

Seaton also noticed a smaller caption below the lead story in tribute to the two local newsmen who were both now suspected victims of the beast.

Seaton decided to treat himself to breakfast at a local café. One way or the other, today was going to be a very long one.

When he returned to the station house, Sally was waiting for him.

"Hello, Sally," Seaton said, pleasantly surprised. "You're in early. What's up, wet the bed?"

Sally laughed. "No, guv, actually I wanted a word before the others got in."

Seaton was intrigued. Sally was not usually this secretive. "Come in then," he said, indicating towards his office. "Shall we talk in there? More private?"

Once they had taken their seats, Sally began. "You know this expedition thing they're doing today? Is there any chance that I could go along?"

Seaton was taken aback. "Why would you want to go? You know it may be dangerous?" Seaton knew that Sally brought out his protective side, though he had always taken care to mask it.

Sally leaned in closer, as if afraid someone else might come in. "I was thinking last night, they probably already have divers on stand-by, but you know that diving is my hobby and I've been doing it for years. I've got all my certificates, and…Well, to be honest, I am quite excited at the prospect of being in the vicinity of an adventure like this. I would really love to be a part of it."

She was looking at Seaton with her big puppy-dog eyes, a little girl begging her daddy to let her go and play on the swings with the big kids.

Seaton was at a loss for what to say. He had never imagined that Sally – or any of his constables – would actually want to go on the venture, let alone be practically begging for the chance.

He was conscious about not making promises he could not keep. After all, the expedition was actually nothing to do with him, so his word did not carry any specific weight. But he did remember overhearing the professor asking Jake if he had any divers on his crew in case the equipment became entangled underwater and needed to be freed. Jake had told him that one of his crew could do that, but knowing them, Sally would be far more professional and trustworthy and easily the better choice.

He looked at her across the table. Big as she was, she could always turn on the little girl act if she needed to.

Reluctantly, he said, "I can't make any promises, it's not my call, but I'll ask the professor if he can use your services and we'll see what he says."

Sally ran around the table and hugged him before he had a chance to move.

Seaton laughed and half-hugged her back. Much as he wanted to return the full compliment, it somehow did not seem appropriate. As it was, anyone walking in on them now might well jump to the wrong conclusion.

"Come on now, I said I would ask. There's no guarantee what the answer will be."

Sally pulled back and touched him playfully on the end of his nose. "Aw you'll persuade him, guv, how can he refuse you?" And with that, she skipped out of the room, turning at the door to give him one last affectionate smile.

***

Having taken Seaton's call the previous evening, Caitlin did not bother to set her alarm clock. Dan would not be able to take his boat out, and she did not intend doing a full day at the museum, as she suspected the night was going to be very long.

But she was still excited at the prospect of the venture. It had awakened her thirst for knowledge which she had noticed waning since she had finished studying. It had always been at the back of her mind that one day she would embark on her PhD, and she wondered if this might provide her with the grist to kick-start the process.

She and Dan had stayed up later than they intended, talking, listening to music, drinking and cuddling on the sofa. By the time they finally dragged themselves to bed, neither had enough energy to contemplate anything other than sleep. So they drifted off in each other's embrace.

Dan had the more fitful night of the two of them. Deep down, he harboured concerns about the expedition, but he was reluctant to voice them to Caitlin. She was obviously quite excited about the venture and he did not wish to dampen that. But all the same, he would have been far happier if the professor had elected to use his boat instead of Jake's. Admittedly, Jake's was far bigger and better equipped, but it was the captain and crew that worried Dan more. The idea of them having to take care of Caitlin should anything happen was akin to allowing a drunk to hold your family's priceless porcelain vase.

Honey granted them an extra couple of hours in bed before reminding them that she needed her morning exercise. They walked along the beach hand-in-hand while the Labrador exhausted herself chasing her ball, then they re-visited the café they had discovered on their first morning together for breakfast.

Dan bought papers for both of them so that they could read the professor's article simultaneously. They both ordered a full English plus two sausages for Honey. The waitress, obviously an animal lover, cut the sausages into small bite-size pieces to allow them to cool before Honey devoured them, hungrily.

Once they had finished eating, they both ordered another coffee while they re-read the article. Honey placed her head on Dan's lap, looking at him longingly while he stroked the top of her head. As Caitlin seemed engrossed in the article, he surreptitiously slipped a piece of bacon he had purposely kept back to Honey. The dog chomped it, gratefully.

"I saw that!" said Caitlin, from behind her newspaper.

"It fell," Dan lied, very unconvincingly. Caitlin glanced at him over her paper with a knowing look. Dan pulled his best 'Did I get away with that' look, which made her laugh.

Over coffee, Dan asked, "So what do you fancy doing today before your excursion tonight?"

"Well," replied Caitlin, "I was thinking I would like to go and see the equipment being unloaded on the beach. See what the professor has ordered, and see if I can be of any help in constructing and affixing it."

Dan's face dropped. He had hoped that they would spend the day together, but he understood Caitlin's enthusiasm for being an integral part of the whole process. This was her 'thing'. She could not disguise the excitement in her voice when she spoke about it, and Dan, for his part, wanted to be as supportive as possible. Even though deep down, he still wished that she was not going.

After breakfast, they returned to Caitlin's to shower and change. At Caitlin's suggestion, Dan had started leaving a couple of changes of clothing at Caitlin's for when he stayed over, which was becoming a far more regular occurrence.

Caitlin dropped in to the museum to inform one of her staff that she would not be in for the day, then she drove them both up to Skullen Bay.

She had never seen the parking area so full. The beach was crowded with a combination of coastguard volunteers, disgruntled fishermen, and tour guides annoyed by the fact that their boats had been grounded. Die-hard sun worshipers hoping for a break in the clouds to top up their holiday tans and miscellaneous families scattered around the temporary perimeter cordons just trying to enjoy themselves amidst all the chaos.

The institute's vehicles had already arrived, and they could see the professor by one of them, taking charge of the decampment.

Dan walked Caitlin over to where he was standing. At first, he appeared to be ignoring them, so Caitlin cleared her throat loudly to announce their presence.

The professor turned and looked at them over the rim of his glasses.

"Good morning, Professor," offered Caitlin, politely. "I was just wondering if I could be of any assistance with the equipment."

Warminster half-smiled, clearly pre-occupied with his present task. "Oh, right, excellent, yes if you could..." he began, absent-mindedly. He pointed in the direction of Jake's boat. "Would you please go and help sort the assembly on deck? Just until I get there? I can't be in two places at once."

"Certainly, no problem." Caitlin did think to ask if he wanted her to pass on any specific instructions as the men on board might not take kindly to her trying to take over, but she decided that he was far too involved with his present task to concentrate on specifics.

Caitlin and Dan walked down towards the *Reaper's Revenge*. Dan kissed her and left her on the jetty, knowing that his presence would probably not be appreciated by Jake. Caitlin waved goodbye as she climbed aboard.

As he was about to leave, he suddenly saw Tammi waving to him from the deck. He stood there for a moment in shock, wondering what she was doing on Jake's boat. He waited while she climbed down to where he was standing.

"What's all this?" he joked. "Jumped ship?"

Tammi took him by the arm and walked him away out of earshot. "Listen, skip," she began, "I know this looks a wee bit strange, but Big Jake came calling an hour ago. He can't seem to locate those Clive boys and he's panicking because his engine was sticking yesterday, and he doesn't want anything to go wrong tonight."

"And he asked you to help him; I hope he's paying you?" asked Dan, still astonished at finding her on Jake's boat.

Tammi looked back behind her to make sure no one was listening. "Aye, believe it or no, he offered me £500 to help him, but I told him where to stick it. Twenty minutes later, he comes back with £1000, in cash no less, and virtually begs me to help him out."

"A grand?" said Dan, his eyes wide in amazement. One of the many reputations Jake had around town was that of being tight-fisted. So for him to be willing to part with so much money, and in cash, must have meant that he was really in trouble.

"Aye, I know," replied Tammi. "I couldn't afford to say no; that could pay for our engine overhaul with some to spare."

Dan was visibly touched by Tammi's generosity. Her earning this money had nothing whatsoever to do with him. After all, it was not even as if she was working for Jake and not with Dan; he could not even take his boat out if he wanted to.

He put his hand on her shoulder. "You don't have to spend your money on the boat, much as I appreciate the gesture; you're earning it, not me."

"Ah rubbish. That boat gives us both a living, and it's the least I can do for all you've done for me."

"You know," Dan sighed, looking into her eyes, "I'm going to miss you."

Tammi looked back in surprise. "Miss me! Why, where am I going?"

"I'm sacking you at the end of the week!" Dan managed to keep a straight face until Tammi clicked on to his wind-up and punched him on the arm.

***

Seaton pulled up at Skullen Bay in the patrol car with Sally beside him. He was surprised at how busy the beach was considering the lack of sun and general activity on the water. But then considered that the professor's piece in the paper this morning may well have spurred on several onlookers, eager to see what all the commotion was about.

They spotted the professor by one of the institute's vans, and both made their way along to it. As they neared it, Seaton said to Sally, "Now don't go building your hopes up too much; all I can do is ask. It'll be his decision in the end."

Sally nodded. Desperate as she was to be a part of the expedition, she knew that what her sergeant said was true. She let Seaton walk in front of her as they reached the professor, not wanting her eagerness to cause her to blurt something out by accident while Seaton was trying to secure her a place.

The professor was obviously pre-occupied with what he was doing, so Seaton excused himself, recognising how busy the academic was, and offered Sally's assistance as a way of lightening his load for later on. Expressing his own opinion that a police presence on board might also assist in keeping the crew in line.

Warminster appeared to only be half-listening to the sergeant. He turned and glanced towards Sally standing smartly, almost to attention, behind him.

He looked her up and down, making no effort to disguise his admiration.

He removed his glasses. "Are you an experienced diver, Constable?" he asked, chewing on one stem of his frames.

Sally took her queue and moved forward. "Yes, I've been diving for over five years now. I have all my certificates up to date and I'm a member of several dive schools throughout England." She checked herself for sounding far too eager, almost desperate to be included.

She waited, biting her bottom lip for the professor to make his decision. He was still sizing her up, and under normal circumstances, she would have said something about it, but on this occasion, she was willing to put up with a little ogling.

Eventually, after what seemed to Sally an eternity, the professor conceded.

It was all Sally could do to restrain herself from jumping up and down and clapping her hands.

"Do you have all your own equipment, and can you have it ready in time for the off tonight?" the professor asked, conscious of the short notice.

Sally nodded, energetically. "Yes, I just need to get my tanks checked, which shouldn't take long. There's a place I know in town who can do it on the spot. The rest of my equipment is all in order."

The professor raised an eyebrow, but thought better of making a juvenile remark.

Once back in the patrol car, Sally could not resist giving Seaton another big hug.

***

Tammi sat outside the Fisherman's Arms with her lunch and a pint of beer. It had been a long day so far and there was still the trip tonight to get through. Jake's boat was in an awful state. Some of the bearings had ground down to dust, and it appeared as if several of the filters had never been changed or even cleaned since the boat left the factory.

The Clive brothers had not shown up, so Tammi was working below deck by herself. *Hammer*, Jake's other crew member, was trying to be as helpful as he could, but it was obvious to Tammi that he did not know much about the inner workings of the vessel. He was obviously more a hands-on-deck sort of crew member.

By 3pm, she had the engine at least sounding healthier, but her warning to Jake that it desperately needed servicing was met with a disgruntled shrug. Either way, after tonight's little adventure, it would not be her problem. She had only been paid to keep the craft going until they returned to port tonight, and that was all she was willing to take responsibility for.

Having finished her lunch, Tammi contemplated having an afternoon nap to recharge her batteries before the evening's events. As she finished her pint, she felt her mobile vibrating in her pocket.

It was a text from Geraldine. She felt her heart skip a beat as she opened it. She hoped that she was not going suggest seeing her tonight. That would just be typical. Unless she asked her to wait on the *Lady Anne* for her until after the excursion was over. But then that would not be fair on Geraldine, as Tammi had no idea how long she would be out for.

She opened the text. Geraldine was asking Tammi to give her a call when she had a moment. Tammi called her straight away. She could feel her legs physically starting to shake. It concerned her how much of an effect Geraldine was having on her without even knowing it. Tammi had not felt this way about another girl for a very long time, not since Scarlet. But it was all happening far too quickly. She wanted to tell Geraldine how she felt, but she knew that she could not; it was way too early for anything like that.

But she did adore her; there was no getting away from it. Whether or not Geraldine would reciprocate her feelings was yet to be seen. For now, Tammi had no intentions of telling her.

The phone was answered on the second ring. "Hiya," said Geraldine. Straight away, Tammi felt the hairs on the back of her neck bristle. The usual cheerfulness was gone from Geraldine's tone. Something was wrong!

"What's up?" asked Tammi, trying to sound as if she did not suspect that there was a problem.

There was an uneasy pause on the other end before Geraldine spoke. Tammi could hear her clearing her throat and taking a deep breath; the wait was agonising.

Finally, Geraldine began. "Tammi, I'm really sorry about this, but I'm afraid that I can't see you anymore."

The words hit home like a jackhammer. Tammi felt a dull ache starting in her stomach, creeping up her body until she thought she might choke.

She had no idea how to respond. Her heart was breaking, but what could she say? They had known each other for less than a week, and Tammi had no right to expect Geraldine to have fallen for her as quickly as Tammi had for Geraldine.

"Are you still there?" asked Geraldine, tentatively. She could obviously tell from Tammi's silence that the news had not gone down well. But then these things were never easy. "Tammi?"

"Yes, I'm still here," Tammi sniffed, fighting back tears. She chided herself again, determined to get a grip.

"I'm really sorry about this; I really do like you…A lot." Geraldine's voice took on a comforting, soothing quality; it was as if she was trying to explain to a child why they could not do something or go somewhere, when it was out of their control.

THEN WHY? Tammi wanted to scream down the phone. Instead, she took a deep breath and tried to maintain a dignified facade. Something had obviously happened, and though she was desperate to know what, Tammi decided to let Geraldine explain if she wanted to; otherwise, she would just accept the inevitable with good grace and try to move on.

"Okay, darling," said Tammi, trying to keep the hurt out of her voice. "Well you take care of yerself, and if you change yer mind, you've got my number, don't be afraid to use it."

Geraldine gasped on the other end. It sounded to Tammi as if she too was fighting back the tears. God, she was desperate to know what was going on, but she was not going to force Geraldine to tell her; she had to do so of her own accord.

"I'm really sorry," was all Geraldine came back with.

"Me too, darling." *You'll never know how much!* "Bye."

The line went dead.

Tammi put her head in her hands. She could feel the tears welling up in her eyes, but she refused to let them go. Not here, out in the open for the world to see. She had always been the most private of people, and when she cried, she cried alone.

She rubbed her eyes with the heels of her hands, took a napkin off the table, and blew her nose, hard.

Just then, she noticed one of the bar staff coming outside to clear away glasses. She signalled and waved her glass in the air. The waitress, having served her earlier, understood.

Tammi decided another pint was what she needed more than sleep right now.

***

Dan and Caitlin had enjoyed a pub lunch by the front and then taken Honey for a run along the beach, before returning to Caitlin's flat and making love. Caitlin had set the alarm just in case they overslept.

When the beeper went off, she awoke to see Dan lying propped up on one elbow, gently tracing patterns on her bare skin with the tip of his index finger. She smiled and pulled him down on her so that they could enjoy a long, slow, passionate kiss.

When they pulled apart, Caitlin looked deeply into Dan's eyes. She knew instinctively that something was wrong. The expression on his face told her that his mind was not there with them enjoying the moment.

She did not ask him what it was!

She had already guessed. He did not want her to go out on the expedition tonight. They had talked around the subject during lunch, and even then, she had the distinct impression that Dan was not willing to push the issue. It was almost as if he was afraid that they might have another argument which, after the last one, neither of them wanted.

She could understand his concern from the point of view that whatever it was out there had killed. But even he had to admit that on a boat the size of Jake's, they should be quite safe. It was more the fact that he was not going to be on board to protect her, and she loved the fact that he felt so protective towards her, without trying to mollycoddle her.

True, he had refused to take her with him when he took Sergeant Seaton out to look for those reporters, but that had all been decided in a matter of minutes just after they had woken up, so she had to take into account that fact that they were both still a little groggy from sleep. She felt sure that if they had had time to discuss the situation properly, she would have talked him around.

She had not let on that she knew Dan had asked Jake if he could be on board tonight. She had overheard the conversation when Dan thought that she was out of sight on Jake's boat. Jake had been completely dismissive of Dan's request, even when Dan offered his services for free and told Jake that he was captain and would still be giving the orders. She knew that that was not an easy thing for Dan to swallow, but he did it anyway.

Jake had still refused. Dan had not pleaded, but he had come close, and Caitlin had to fight the urge to run down and tell Dan not to belittle himself, but that would mean admitting that she had overheard their conversation, and there was no way she was going to embarrass Dan in that manner.

Looking into his eyes, she felt as if she could read his thoughts, and wondered if he felt the same. It was almost as if the conversation she was running over in her mind was one they were actually having with each other through some kind of telepathic connection. She knew that Dan did not want her to go because he loved her, and she loved him because of it.

Neither of them was brave enough to give the words utterance, but the feelings remained nonetheless.

Caitlin was actually feeling guilty for putting Dan through this torment. She could sympathise, remembering how helpless she felt when he went out with Officer Seaton. She had waited on the beach with Honey, her mind in turmoil until she finally saw him retuning to port.

But how could she save him the anxiety without giving up her place tonight? There was no way that she could think of. She was not putting the venture before Dan's feelings, and she was sure that he understood that. But she needed to go; it was more than just a want. This could turn out to be the discovery of a hitherto unknown species of sea life, and she had the chance to be in on the ground floor. Dan would never deny her such an opportunity, but at the same time, she did not want to put him in the awkward position of asking him if he was alright with it. Even if he was not, he would lie, because he knew what this trip meant to her.

"Dan?"

"Mmmm."

"I love you." The words had flowed from her mouth before she had a chance to stop them, but she did not regret saying them. They were the truth, regardless of his response; she suddenly needed him to know.

Dan looked at her quizzically, as if her words were still sinking in. His reply took him less than a few seconds to utter, but somehow to Caitlin, it felt interminable.

"I'm so glad you said that," he replied, smiling.

"Why glad?"

"Because I've wanted to say them since we first met, but being a man, I was too much of a coward." He paused a moment, gazing down on Caitlin's smiling face. He followed the contour of her lips with the tip of his finger. "I love you too, darling. Just in case you were wondering."

CHAPTER TWENTY-THREE

Dan and Caitlin pulled up at Skullen Bay at 7:30pm. The parking area was full, so Caitlin managed to squeeze her car in behind the Fisherman's Arms.

The coastguard had cleared the beach in anticipation of the arrival of the helicopter Sheila had arranged. Coastguard volunteers lined the perimeter ensuring that the mass crowd that had gathered were kept back at a safe distance.

A make-shift entrance had been erected to allow those taking part in the evening's events access to the beach, so Dan and Caitlin made their way through the crowd towards it.

The young volunteer monitoring the entrance flipped through his list of names provided. He found Caitlin, but not Dan. After checking again, he looked up, embarrassed, and announced that he was under orders not to allow access to anyone who was not on his list. Caitlin, who was by now feeling slightly more anxious than excited about the evening ahead, started arguing that Dan was with her and that if he was not allowed in then she would not enter either, and if she was not there, the launch would have to be postponed. Dan was incredibly impressed by the way she embellished her position without wavering. Had he have not known better, even he would have believed she was telling the truth.

The young volunteer, still apologising to them, fumbled with his walkie-talkie trying to contact his superior.

At that moment, Dan spotted Seaton making his way towards them from the beach. Dan pointed the approaching officer out to the young volunteer, who put down his radio and waited for Seaton to arrive.

"What's the trouble?" Seaton asked the volunteer whilst acknowledging Dan and Caitlin.

"I'm sorry, sir, but this gentleman is not on the list, and Miss Soames gave explicit orders that only those listed could enter without her say-so." The young man was clearly embarrassed with his office, but desperate to prove himself steadfast.

"That's okay, lad," said Seaton, comfortingly. "I'll take responsibility for Mr. Savage."

That was good enough for the volunteer, and he waved both of them through, his face still slightly flushed from the encounter.

Seaton accompanied them down to Jake's boat. It appeared as if they were the last to arrive; everyone else who was going out had already had their picture taken by the newspaper photographers invited by Sheila. Now that Caitlin had arrived, they were ready for a group shot which Professor Warminster quickly arranged.

Several reporters were gathered on the sand, and once the pictures were all taken, they began firing questions off. Sheila Soames stepped forward with her hands raised and called for order, insisting that all those with questions raised their hands and did not interrupt their colleagues while they were talking.

Dan stood back out of the way. When he caught Tammi's eye, he waved and she walked over to him. Dan could tell two things about her straight away. One was that she had obviously been drinking; the other was that she had been crying.

She smiled half-heartedly as she drew near. "Hiya, boss, what d'yer think of their wee circus?"

Dan put his hand under her chin and lifted her face up. She could see from his expression that he was worried about her. He did not have to ask her if anything was wrong; he obviously knew that something was.

"It's okay," she reassured him, before he had a chance to speak. "Plenty more fish in the sea, an' all that rubbish."

"Oh, that's it," replied Dan, sympathetically. "Her loss." He gently nudged her cheek with his closed fist. "So are you looking forward to your little adventure this evening?"

"Can't wait...For it to be over." She pointed behind her to Jake's boat. "That's if that old rust-bucket makes it back, that is."

Dan looked concerned. "Is it really that bad?"

"Well, put it this way, I'll be spending the majority o' my time below deck just keepin' the pistons working. Those Clive boys obviously hav'ney the first clue about maintenance."

"Have they still not turned up?" Dan was concerned now more for Maggie than her tearaway offspring. He knew that if they were sleeping off hangovers at home, she would have dragged them back to work by now.

"Nope," replied Tammi, shaking her head. "Gude thing too, or Jake would have 'em for dinner; he's well pissed off with them."

Tammi looked back to the group behind them. Sheila and the professor were still answering questions. Sally, already in her diving gear, was standing talking to Seaton on the jetty. Jake and Hodges were already back on board. Hodges had been especially reluctant to have his picture taken, and could not wait to return to the safe haven of the boat.

Caitlin had obviously been collared by the professor after the group shot, and he seemed to be keeping her by his side whilst he spoke to the reporters.

Tammi turned back to Dan. "How's yer wee lassie doin'? She up fer this?"

Dan pulled a face. "Sort of, but to be honest, I'll be happy when it's all over."

Tammi smiled. "Don't worry, skip; I'll take gude care o' her for yer."

Dan pulled her to him and kissed the top of her head. "You make sure you take care of yourself too. I want you both back in one piece."

She hugged him back. "Deni worry; if that beastie comes near me, I'll give it one o' these." She held up a clenched fist. "That'll send it scuttlin' home."

Whilst the last few questions were being answered, in the distance, Dan could hear the distant whirring of a helicopter. Everyone seemed to stop whatever they were doing to watch its approach. The photographers all rushed forward to record the landing, jostling each other for the best angle. The propellers created a cloud of sand as the craft neared the beach, causing the crowd to turn away and cover their eyes.

Once it touched ground, the excitement was over, and Dan watched as Sheila ushered everyone away from the professor in order to allow him to board Jake's boat.

Dan looked for Caitlin, but Warminster seemed to have her by the elbow and was guiding her towards the ramp. Dan felt his heart sink as the professor's body blocked his view of his girlfriend; he decided to wait until she could see him before trying to wave goodbye. He felt a sudden urge to rush forward and give her a goodbye hug, but was afraid he might cause Caitlin unnecessary embarrassment.

Just then, he saw her break free from the professor's grasp and run down the ramp straight into his arms. They hugged tightly for a moment. When they released, Dan could see Caitlin's eyes were moist. He wondered if deep down the little girl inside her did not want to go anymore. But the mature, sensible, professional marine biologist side of her was winning the battle.

"I'll be waiting right here for you," he said reassuringly, holding her face in his hands. "Please come back to me in one piece."

Caitlin's tears spilled onto her cheeks. Dan wiped them away with his thumbs, and they hugged once more. Caitlin walked away, still holding Dan's hand, not letting go until the last moment.

Dan watched her board. She turned back and blew him a kiss from the top of the ramp before being called away by Warminster to assist him with the submersible camera.

As the boat pulled out, the crowd from behind him cheered and waved. It reminded Dan of those scenes in films where a ship is leaving the dock destined for some faraway land; except here, there were no streamers.

***

After an hour, Tammi turned off the engines as instructed and released the anchor. The boat had been handling pretty well so far, and

Tammi prided herself on the fact that that was mainly due to all her preparation work on the engine earlier in the day.

Hodges stuck his head down to offer her her third cup of coffee since they set sail, and she accepted, gratefully. The effects of the four pints of beer she had consumed at lunchtime were starting to wear off, and the coffee helped stave off the dryness in her throat.

Tammi climbed on deck to join the rest of the party. The professor was busy tampering with the remote controls for the underwater camera, leaning over Caitlin as she pressed buttons and turned knobs at his instruction, trying to get the screen in front of her to focus.

The control panel had been set up in a make-shift Perspex cocoon which reminded Tammi of a fish bowl.

Jake was in the wheelhouse, monitoring their position. He was in direct contact with the coastguard on a special frequency they had set up for the occasion, and had agreed on a half-hour check call just to confirm that they were not in trouble.

Sally was tinkering with the submersible camera's outer shell, ensuring that the cables were all properly cleated into position so that they would not become tangled when the craft was lowered into the water.

Hodges arrived with the coffees and starting handing them round.

Tammi took hers and thanked him. He gave her a toothless smile in response. Tammi guessed that his missing teeth had all been knocked out in fights, which made her wonder what shape his opponents were left in.

She took one for Sally and carried it out to her. The police constable thanked her and the two of them sat out on deck, gazing at their surroundings.

The cloud cover had been low for most of the day, never allowing the sun to completely penetrate through. Now, as darkness was looming, the sky had taken on a dull, uniform greyness which was verging on black in the eastern sky.

Suddenly, a huge streak of lightning lit up the night sky. Everyone saw it and reacted. The weather forecast had threatened thunder and lightning before the day was out, and as if to verify the reports, a loud rumble of thunder slowly rolled across the heavens.

At least there was no sign of rain, for which they were all grateful. The expedition would not have been called off because of a sudden downpour, but nobody wanted to be standing about getting soaked in the cold night air.

The professor appeared from the cocoon, a broad smile across his face. He clapped his hands together like a school teacher calling for order from an unruly class as he walked over to where Tammi and Sally stood drinking their coffee.

"Okay everyone," he announced. "We're ready to drop the sub overboard." He turned around him to usher Jake and Hodges to his side.

"If I can ask you all to take hold of one edge of the craft." He waited until the two men came and joined Sally and Tammi, and watched while they each positioned themselves around the submersible to even the load. "Right now," he continued, "I will operate the winch. If the four of you could ensure that you guide the sub gently over the side, once it's clear, I will give the signal for you all to stand clear, then I'll lower it into the water, okay?" He waited for everyone to confirm they had understood his instructions before taking up his position behind the winch.

With the help of the four of them, the submersible was lowered safely into the water. Once it began to dive beneath the surface, Caitlin called out that she was receiving a perfect picture on the monitors.

The craft was equipped with four angled lenses, which allowed the viewer a 360-degree view of the vessel's surroundings.

Once Warminster was satisfied that it was down far enough, he switched off the winch and hurried back into the cocoon to join Caitlin. Caitlin was not at all comfortable being in such a confined space with the academic, and wondered to herself if he had chosen this exact model because it would give him an excuse to have to squeeze in so close to the operator. She remembered his reputation from university, so she made a point of keeping her legs closed and her shoulders hunched forward away from his looming figure.

Due to the cramped enclosure, both Sally and Tammi agreed to take turns with Caitlin to watch the monitors.

For two hours, there was nothing much of any interest showing up. It was now almost midnight and the initial excitement for the anticipated venture had started to wane for everyone.

Both sea and sky had blended into a black abyss, upon which the only light came from Jake's boat. The clouds had not let up, but at least the thunder and lightning had stopped, and the air did not feel cold enough for rain.

Tammi was in the cocoon gazing at the monitors, when one of them suddenly went blank. Immediately, she started twisting the knobs on the view finder and when that did not have any positive affect she began pressing the reset button to try and bring the picture back.

When that did not work, she called out to the professor. He had been sitting alone at the stern of the boat, reading.

By the time he reached the cocoon, another of the screens had gone blank.

"They just went dead," explained Tammi as he reached the entrance.

Without answering, he ushered her out and took her seat. He began playing with the same knobs and buttons which Tammi had tried, becoming more and more frustrated with the lack of response.

231

He tried turning all the monitors off from the main switch. Left them for thirty seconds, then switched them all back on again together. Now only one screen came on; the others all remained in darkness.

Muttering loudly to himself, Warminster slid out of the cocoon to address the others. "Well, I think it's safe to say that either the batteries need boosting, or the cables have somehow become tangled on something and been pulled out of their sockets." He turned to Sally. "Looks like you're on, young lady."

While Caitlin and Tammi helped Sally on with her air tanks, Jake and Hodges just stood watching from the bow. As far as Jake was concerned, he had already earned his money for the night and did not intend putting himself out any more than was necessary. Hodges naturally took his lead from his mate. Which was not in itself unusual, as Hodges usually only did something if Jake told him to.

While Sally checked the gauges on her breathing apparatus, Warminster explained on a diagram how to operate the battery boosters. He specified that if the cables had become entwined, she must disconnect them first before untangling them, and then re-plug them in one at a time.

Sally nodded her confirmation and moved to sit on the side of the boat, before waving and dropping backwards into the water.

There was no sign of her once she slid beneath the surface.

Caitlin returned to the cocoon to monitor the screens. Everyone else stood waiting on deck.

After almost five minutes, the professor was growing impatient. "What on earth is she doing down there?" he said, rhetorically. "She should have managed to re-connect at least one of the cables by now!"

Tammi looked across at him. "Do you think she might have gotten into trouble?"

Warminster looked over the side, as if he was able to pierce the depths and see down to the bottom. "No, she should be fine for a while yet, probably just tinkering with the boosters."

Tammi was not at all convinced. "Should I suit up and g' down after her, just in case?" she asked generally, but still looked in Warminster's general direction.

No one answered straight away. Jake and Hodges just glanced over the side. Jake shrugged his shoulders; Hodges just kept on staring down.

Before the professor could answer, there was a huge eruption of water in front of them as the Kraken broke the surface.

They all stayed still for a moment, frozen to the spot.

It was far larger than any of them had imagined. Even Jake who had previously seen one of its tentacles was not prepared for what had just risen before his eyes.

The Kraken's head, a gigantic hump which took on the appearance of a small island sitting above the surface, opened its saucer-shaped, blood-red eyes with tiny pinpricks of black in the centre of each one, and stared malevolently at the four people on deck.

Before they could react, a gaping black maw opened below the creature's eyes and it emitted a piercing a cry so blood-curdling that it felt to those on board as if the boat rocked.

Caitlin, having heard the commotion, ran out of the cocoon and stopped dead in her tracks when she saw the cause.

The sight before them would have been the ideal shot the professor was hoping for, had the circumstances not been so dangerous, but the camera equipment set up on deck was now lying forgotten and unmanned at the other side of the deck.

From out of the water, a huge tentacle shot out and came crashing down on the far deck with such force that the side of the boat where the Caitlin and the others were standing rose out of the water high enough to send them all sprawling onto the deck.

In quick succession, three more limbs emerged from the depths, smashing into the boat from different angles, draping over the sides like massive pythons invading the deck. One of them swept across the top deck, knocking over the camera equipment and shattering the cocoon.

There was a mixture of shouts and screams as the five of them scrambled to try and evade the searching feelers. Hodges rose to his feet to try and make it to the wheelhouse before the radio antenna was smashed, but he was cracked across the back by an attacking limb before he managed to make it halfway.

The professor crept along the deck on his belly, manoeuvring past broken Perspex and splintered wood. His initial trepidation had apparently left him as he tried to make it to the camera equipment before it too was destroyed. This might be his only chance of obtaining evidence to establish the existence of the creature he had for so long championed as a viable entity, often at the expense of ridicule from his peers.

As he reached out to grab the tripod the camera was affixed to, he felt a searing pain in his left ankle. He turned back to see one of the Kraken's tentacles wrapping itself tightly around him. Warminster screamed and kicked out simultaneously, the heel of his shoe making contact with the creature's limb as he lashed out.

He managed three good shots before the tentacle wrapped itself tightly around his leg and hoisted him off the boat, dangling him upside down above the water.

The professor continued to scream and struggle, kicking and punching wildly in a vain effort to free himself from the monstrous hold the creature had on him. His mind rebelled; why would it want to hurt him? He was the one who would introduce it to the world. He had been championing its cause all these years, and here it was; attacking him, of all people. He wanted to scream out loud, *No, not me, take them!*

But the words never had a chance to form themselves as the creature held him directly over its mouth for a second, before releasing its hold on him, dropping him directly into the cavernous mass which was lined with row upon row of misshaped fangs.

Warminster managed one more scream before the mouth closed, severing his body in half.

No one on board had seen the professor's last moment of life. They were all still huddled at floor level. But they heard his screams, and all made intelligent guesses as to the manner of his end.

They all stayed motionless, crouched down as if the sides of Jake's boat could protect them. They had already witnessed how much damage a single swipe from one of the beast's mighty limbs could make, and none of them were under any illusions as to how this evening could end.

But there was always hope!

They waited in silence. The thought crossed Caitlin's mind that the creature was too busy devouring the professor right now to concern itself with them. The thought made her stomach turn, and she put her hand to her mouth to prevent herself from gagging and spewing up on the deck.

True, she had never liked the man, but no one deserved such a horrible end.

"Hammer...Hammer..." Jake called to his mate who was still lying motionless, having been struck by the swinging tentacle. Hammer moved slightly and groaned, obviously still dazed.

Jake groaned to himself. Hodges was obviously not going to be able to make it to the radio right this minute, and this might be their only chance.

Caitlin was actually closer to the wheelhouse than Jake, but he decided he would only be satisfied if he made the call himself. Looking around him, Jake started to crawl slowly towards the wheelhouse.

He passed by his friend, pushing him harshly as if trying to wake him from a lie-in after an all-night bender. Hodges still only groaned, but he was starting to come around, slowly.

Jake grunted, obviously not happy with his crew member, and manoeuvred around him to get help. He passed by Caitlin without acknowledging her and crawled through the open doorway, only rising high enough to reach the radio with his outstretched hand.

They heard him calling the 'Mayday' message, demanding that help be sent immediately. The radio crackled into life, the operator on the other end asking for their present situation.

"Present situation!" Jake almost screamed in response. "Two are dead and we're just waiting to be served as the fucking main course, now fucking move your arse and get us some help, NOW!"

Almost as if in response to Jake's screaming, a tentacle lifted over the side and crashed down next to Tammi, cracking the deck beside her.

She reacted immediately, crouching into a ball and pushing with her feet to propel herself away from the exploring limb.

Caitlin watched in horror as Tammi's foot skidded on the wet floor, and the feeler almost instinctively realising that she was in trouble, wrapped itself around Tammi's outstretched leg.

Tammi screamed as the creature's grip tightened.

Without thought for her own safety, Caitlin lunged forward and tried to grab hold of the tentacle to pull it off Tammi. The creature's grip was so tight and its outer skin so slimy, that Caitlin could not get enough of a grip on it to make any difference.

Tammi screamed as she struggled to break free. Each time she fought, the creature instinctively tightened its grip, until Tammi no longer had any feeling in her lower leg.

The Kraken heaved several more of its limbs over the side of the boat, until one whole side of the deck appeared covered. The creature began to rock the vessel from side to side, causing Caitlin to roll further down and crash into the discarded camera equipment.

Regaining her balance, Caitlin grabbed a tubular metal extension from the camera's tripod and edged forward back towards Tammi. Once she found her balance, Caitlin swung the metal rod above her head and brought it crashing down on to the limb that held Tammi captive.

It was to no effect. The Kraken did not loosen its grip on the stricken woman. Caitlin swung the pole down again, and again, each swipe making contact with its target, but always to no avail.

Caitlin looked down at Tammi, helplessly. Out of desperation, Caitlin fell to her knees and sunk her teeth into the beast's tentacle. Her mouth filled with the taste of acidic, salty rubber. Closing her eyes, she pressed down hard, but her jaw would not close; the outer skin of the monster was far too tough.

Just then, another of the creature's limbs swung round and knocked Caitlin over onto her back. She landed hard; the wind was knocked out of her. Lying on the deck, trying to catch her breath, she could hear Tammi still screaming. She managed to lift her head slightly and could see Tammi being dragged towards the bow of the vessel.

Suddenly, Hodges shot out of nowhere and lunged past the stricken Caitlin, grabbing hold of the tentacle which was pulling Tammi away. He managed to get his meaty arms around the limb, and squeezed and pulled and jerked at it with all he could muster. But still, the creature would not yield.

Scrambling forward, Hodges managed to find the end of the thing's tentacle and shoved his hands between it and Tammi's body, trying desperately to prise it off her. The struggle lasted mere seconds without any sign of Hodges making purchase, before the creature swung another limb round from the back of him, which sent him sprawling to the floor.

Before he could recover, the limb wrapped itself around his enormous frame, managing to trap his arms against his side.

It hoisted him into the air, his legs kicking frantically into space, his grunts and groans as he tried to wriggle free emphasising his wasted effort.

In that same moment, the thing released its grip on Tammi, spurring Caitlin back into action. She threw herself forward and grabbed hold of Tammi's ankle, then tried desperately to pull her to veritable safety before the Kraken could regain its composure.

Tammi began to slide down the deck in the direction Caitlin was pulling her. As she moved closer, Caitlin grabbed hold of the women's jeans by the belt and tugged even harder. Just as she was making ground, the Kraken let loose another attack on the boat which tilted it back in the other direction, sending both Caitlin and Tammi crashing against another of its protruding limbs.

This time, the creature caught Tammi in a full body hold, wrapping its tentacle around her waist and lifting her up towards the still-struggling Hodges before Caitlin had a chance to react.

Caitlin screamed out in frustration as Tammi was yanked out of reach.

Jake witnessed his friend and Tammi being taken by the creature from the comfort of the wheelhouse. He had remained there in relative safety having delivered their SOS. Now, he realised that the beast was not going to be content until it had taken them all, and destroyed his boat.

Jake slipped out of the wheelhouse on the other side of the deck and ran towards the entrance to the cabins below deck. Once inside, he closed the swing doors behind him and bolted them. He was not concerned with Hodges and Tammi; they were already fish food, and Caitlin was sure to be next. What he needed was an equaliser of some description. One of his guns or his spear gun should hopefully be powerful enough to pierce the creature's skin and send it packing.

As he walked down the wooden staircase to his cabin, the boat was rocked by a massive thud on the port side. It was followed by another, and another straight after.

The force of the blows sent vibrations through the hull, knocking over everything which was not nailed down of rooted in place.

Jake held his balance by gripping the banister tightly. He lost his footing momentarily, but managed to right himself and stay on his feet.

Once the thumping on the side of the boat had ceased, he ran down the last few stairs and along the corridor into his personal cabin. He made straight for the hidden compartment under his bunk where he kept his illegal firearms and ammunition, secreted.

It was empty!

For a moment, he just stared vacantly, his mind trying to focus on where else he might have put his weapons, but he knew that there was nowhere else; he had always kept them in the same place and only he and his three crewmates knew of their location.

In frustration, Jake started throwing anything he could lay his hands on around the cabin, frantically trying to uncover his armoury's new location. But it was futile; they were nowhere to be found.

He stood in the middle of the floor, shaking his fist to heaven and yelled, loudly.

Another tremendous crash from outside the hull sent him reeling backwards, and this time, he could not maintain his balance. Falling back, he cracked his head against the corner of the upturned bunk. He swore, venomously at the piece of furniture as if it had feelings of its own, while he rubbed his head, trying to reduce the pain. He could feel a lump starting to rise at the back almost immediately.

Swearing and cursing, he made his way through to the tiny galley and retrieved a large carving knife from the cluttered remains of fallen pots, pans, and cutlery mingled together on the floor.

He held the knife tightly in his grip as another hefty smash from the outside cracked open the protective outer layer of the hull, and water started to seep in.

Kicking recalcitrant bric-a-brac out of his way, he made it back to the stairs and climbed back to the top deck level.

Tucking the knife into his belt, he unlocked the doors and crept back out on deck. He saw Caitlin cowering behind the wheelhouse, but there was no sign of Hodges or Tammi. Jake presumed that they were both dead by now and no longer his concern.

He edged slowly along the deck until he was next to Caitlin.

Two of the Kraken's huge tentacles were still wrapped around one side of the boat, whilst two more circled in the sky above them.

From below deck, a tremendous thud caused the boat to lift completely out of the water and slam back down. Both Caitlin and Jake were lifted off the deck with the force of the impact. Caitlin came back to earth with a hard thump on her behind, causing her to yelp as she made contact with the hard wooden deck.

Jake was flung to one side, but luckily, he managed to grab hold of the side railing to stop him going overboard.

Within seconds, the Kraken shot forward another tentacle which smashed what was left of the masts and ripped the top of the wheelhouse clean off.

It seemed to Jake that the beast was determined to destroy his craft, leaving him and Caitlin without protection in the water, and then they would be easy pickings.

He had to think of something to save himself, never mind the girl. If he made it out of here as the soul survivor, he could make up any version of the story he liked; no one would be around to dispute it.

He wondered how much longer the coastguard would be in sending help. It seemed to him an age since he sent out the distress call; surely they must be here soon.

Another loud crash from the bow caused that part of the deck to splinter and crack. The Kraken, sensing the frailty of the craft, brought its massive tentacle down again in the same place, completely destroying the wooden covering. Now there was a gaping hole leading down below deck where Jake knew water was already beginning to seep through.

Caitlin struggled to her feet, holding onto what was left of the wheelhouse to steady herself. Her backside ached from the last fall. Hot tears streamed down her face, caused by a mixture of witnessing the pointless deaths of her fellow travellers as well as the certainty of knowing that her life too would soon be extinguished by the hideous jaws of the monster which was swam only feet away.

She knew that Jake would not do anything to help her, but then she knew that there was probably nothing that he could do anyway.

In her mind, she sent a message to Dan, telling him she loved him and that she was glad now that he had not been able to accompany them; otherwise, he too would soon be dead if he was not already. Doubtless, he would have been slaughtered by the beast whilst heroically trying to save her or Tammi, or even one of the others.

She opened her eyes and saw Jake standing before her.

He was staring right at her wide with a mixture of terror and malice in his eyes, as if his present predicament was all her fault.

Caitlin felt the sudden urge to move away from him, but what would be the point? They would both be served up to the beast before too long.

But clearly, Jake had other ideas!

Without saying a word, Jake lunged forward and lifted Caitlin onto his shoulders. At first, she could not imagine what his plan of action might be, but given his size in comparison to hers, she was in no position to supplicate with him.

In one swift movement, he pressed Caitlin's tiny frame above his head, and walked purposefully to the edge of the deck.

Caitlin screamed as she came face to face with the repugnant aquatic gargoyle with its eyes portraying a look of menace and evil, staring straight back at her.

Jake held her aloft for several seconds, before flinging her overboard directly towards the yawning maw of the Kraken.

CHAPTER TWENTY-FOUR

Dan edged the accelerator lever forward gently to its maximum. The engine screamed in protest. He left it there a few more seconds to see if the noise would die down, but when it refused, he lowered the handle gently until the high-pitched screeching abated.

As desperate as he was to reach Caitlin and the others, he knew full well that there was no point in blowing the bearings, leaving him adrift on the water, anxiously worrying about the fate of his girlfriend and his best friend.

In the distance, he could hear the whirring of the chopper blades as the coastguard helicopter drew closer overhead. Finally, they must have received their orders to attend to the emergency call.

Dan had almost come to blows with the pilot back on the beach. He had been standing within earshot when Jake's call came through. Dan had expected the helicopter crew to burst into action and charge to the rescue. Instead, the pilot calmly explained to him that they had to wait for radio confirmation from their HQ that it was appropriate for them to attend.

APPROPRIATE FOR THEM TO ATTEND!

What was the point of them being there if they were not going to race to the scene now that the team were in trouble?

They were not just there for the scenery!

Dan had begged them to attend, but the two pilots just sat calmly, waiting in the cockpit reiterating their position as if reading it straight form a textbook. Meanwhile, Caitlin could be in direct danger, and these two were accepting cups of tea from one of their volunteers.

Dan knew that he was more concerned for Caitlin than any of the others, including Tammi, and part of him felt guilty for it. Naturally, he did not want any of them to come to any harm, but Caitlin was his priority; there was no way to deny that.

Finally, the waiting had become too much for Dan. He knew that the chopper would get there much faster than his boat, but he couldn't stand around, twiddling his thumbs, idly waiting for the heroes to decide if they would attend or not.

He told them he was going after Jake's boat, and they could what they wanted.

At that point, the pilot became very indignant, and started shouting at Dan that he would only get in the way and make matters worse. Against his better judgement, Dan lost his temper and flew at the pilot, gripping him tightly by his uniform lapels and almost wrenching him from the cockpit.

At that moment, several of the coastguard volunteers became involved, grabbing hold of Dan and pulling him away from their colleague.

Dan struggled with the men, but there were too many of them to break free.

This was wasting more time, he should have just left and jumped on his boat, at least then he would feel as if he was doing something positive.

Fortunately for Dan, Seaton saw the commotion and came to his aide. The police officer ordered the men to release Dan immediately, which they did. Dan quickly explained the situation and even Seaton questioned why the pilot was not in the air already.

The argument was getting them nowhere, so Dan announced to Seaton that he was going to set off in his boat. He had overheard the pilot mention their exact co-ordinates when Jake's message came through, so he was confident that he could find them.

This time, it was the supervisor in charge of the volunteers who spoke up.

"I'm sorry, sir," he announced in a very dogmatic manner. "No one is allowed on the water without express permission from Miss Soames!"

Dan could feel his temper rising to the surface. He took a deep breath and turned to Seaton for support.

Seaton ignored the supervisor and called his two constables over. Carmody and Green were only a few feet behind and both came and stood by their superior, awaiting instructions.

"Officers, I want you to escort Mr. Savage to his boat straight away, please." He turned and looked directly at the volunteers who had gathered behind their supervisor. "And if anyone tries to get in your way," he continued, still looking at the supervisor and his team, but obviously talking to his own men, "I want you to arrest them for obstructing a police officer in the course of his duty!"

The two constables answered their affirmation in unison.

Dan gave Seaton a nod of gratitude and turned to leave with the officers.

Seaton watched the three men approach Dan's boat. His demeanour cast an air of authority that he had cultivated over his many years in the force, which ensured that no one else present dared to challenge his authority on the subject.

Dan was making good headway, but his frustration at not being able to push the engine any further was still making him anxious.

Jake's SOS message may well have been an exaggeration on his part, but regardless, they had to be in danger for Jake to make the call. Though Dan's opinion of the fisherman was not exactly high, from what Dan knew of him, he was too cocky to call for help unless he absolutely needed it.

The helicopter passed overhead and soon disappeared behind the horizon. Their presence gave Dan a modicum of hope. They would certainly reach the scene long before him, and they were trained to deal with emergencies at sea.

Though probably not the kind they were about to encounter!

***

Jake held onto what was left of his wheelhouse with one hand, for balance. In his other hand, he still clutched the carving knife he picked up from the kitchen-area below deck.

He knew that he had made contact with the creature on several occasions as it swiped at him and what was left of his craft, but it did not seem to make any difference. The Kraken's skin was too tough to penetrate, even with such a sharp implement being wheeled with great force.

The boat was listing badly at the stern, part of it now under water. The constant barrage of blows being dealt by the monster seemed to Jake to be causing more damage with each strike. Soon, he knew the vessel would be taking on too much water to stay afloat.

His options were minimal, but he refused to go down without a fight. Before he succumbed to those jaws with their uneven rows of razor-sharp fangs, he was going to plunge his knife in the damn thing as many times as he could. Even with his last breath, he would fight.

Just then, he heard the distant whir of the propeller blades from the helicopter.

He strained to look behind him in the direction from which the noise was coming. He could see the chopper just coming over the horizon, heading straight for him. At that moment, another tentacle came crashing down in front of him, obliterating what was left of his safe haven.

Jake sprawled forward across the deck. His body rolled a couple of times until he managed to stop himself, just before he tumbled down a huge crater caused by one of the beast's earlier attacks.

Jake scrambled to his feet, slipping several times on the soaked wood before he managed to gain purchase. Miraculously, the carving knife was still in his hand, and he swung it wildly at an approaching limb as it swept the deck in front of him.

The chopper hovered overhead. Jake looked up and signalled wildly for them to drop him a rope ladder, or something similar to allow him to reach safety. He was finding it harder with each passing second to keep his balance. The boat tilted dangerously to one side as the sea started to pull it down.

The Kraken, now aware of the chopper hovering overhead, lifted itself as far out of the water as it could and angrily waved six of its tentacles in the air as a warning to the new arrival.

The chopper stayed where it was, its whirring propellers goading the Kraken as if making fun of it for not being able to catch them.

The Kraken let out an ear-piercing screech of frustration at its inability to reach any higher. Jake put his hands to his ears, the noise was unbearable. His predicament was growing worse by the second as his boat continued to take on more water. It would not be long before the entire craft was underwater and him with it at the mercy of the creature.

He looked up at the chopper in despair. There was still no sign of anything to grant his access. What were they waiting for? They were after all, his one and only chance of survival.

Just then, the Kraken gave a loud snort as if trying to empty its lungs. Jake looked back at the creature and saw its eyes were once again fixed on him. Evil, menacing embers which glowed red, so much so that he imagined he could actually feel heat emanating from them.

But there was something else in their stare. Dan soon realised what it was. It was determination, a refusal to admit defeat. The aggressor was unable to access its prey, like a cat whose paw was not long enough to reach the mouse under the cupboard.

The beast had already claimed the lives of the rest of the expedition, but it would not be satisfied until it had taken the last one standing.

The boat still held, bobbing gently on the water, but there was no way of knowing for how much longer. They were in stalemate. The creature could not reach Jake; he could not reach the chopper, and the chopper could not reach him.

But even so, whether it knew it or not, the Kraken still held the winning hand. Mere patience would be enough to win in the end, for Jake knew that another strike at his boat would mean its demise, and with it his too, unless he somehow managed to get to the chopper first.

Everyone stayed still for a moment.

Then the Kraken snorted another mountain of spray, and slowly began to sink beneath the waves, those evil penetrating eyes unblinking as they disappeared beneath the surface.

Within seconds of its disappearance, the surface of the water calmed. The helicopter used its powerful beams to check the surface for any undue ripples, but nothing was evident.

Even so, the pilot waited what seemed to Jake an eternity before lowering the bird close enough to make it worth dropping the rope ladder.

Jake was already soaked, but now because of the boat's tilt, he was standing in a foot of water.

He reached out and grabbed for the ladder, and missed. The effort of the lunge caused him to lose his balance, and once again, he found himself sprawled on what was left of the deck. This time, he lost hold of the knife and he watched it slide away until it ran out of floor and plunged into the sea.

Jake forced himself upright, the ladder swung teasingly in front of him. He knew that the pilot must be doing his utmost to keep the bird steady, but the frustration was still raging inside him as he grabbed for it once more and missed, this time his fingers brushing one side of the rope, but not leaving him enough to make a grab for it.

"Fucking come 'ere!" he demanded of the obstinate object, as it dangled tantalisingly just out of reach.

The boat began to lurch dangerously to one side. Jake knew that this was it; the craft would not recover this time, and it would continue to tilt until it was finally swallowed up by the sea. And him with it.

Jake watched the rope swing to and fro. Timing his chance, he threw himself forward in one last desperate attempt at salvation. At that precise moment, the rope changed its rhythm and swung away from him as he fell, causing him to miss it once again. As he felt himself toppling over, he groped the air and just managed to make contact with the last rung.

Jake held on for his life. The boat swayed and rocked with Jake holding onto to the ladder with one hand, swinging with it.

Using what was left of his strength, he managed to pull himself up enough to grab the ladder with his other hand as well. He waited for a second to catch his breath, and then he began to haul himself up until he managed to finally get a foothold on the bottom rung.

Steadily, he began to climb the ladder. Once he had a secure footing, he wished the bird would just fly away and carry him back to safety; there was no point in hanging around. All the others were dead and the beast could still be lurking beneath the waves.

Jake held on tightly, ensuring that each time he climbed another rung. his position remained secure. The last thing he needed know was to fall from such a height.

The chopper hovered steadily, the beams of its search light still skimming the water looking for survivors or the beast returning.

Now Jake felt his confidence returning. He was past the halfway mark and growing steadily more positive with each step. The helicopter's foot stand was only a few feet away, and once he reached that, he would be secure.

His future looked very bright indeed. *Jake Johnson: The Hero of Skullen Bay.* He could just imagine the headlines. To hell with his boat; the old rust-bucket was way past its best anyway. The insurance would sort that out. He would sell his story to the highest bidder. The papers loved something like this. And sod the local rag, his story needed to go national; he wanted the big boys bidding for him.

And who knew where it could lead? Television interviews, a book deal, maybe even a feature film about the incident. Now who would he agree to have playing his part, he wondered.

Without warning, the surface erupted as the Kraken broke the surface at speed and shot out a tentacle which wrapped itself around the chopper's foot stand.

Jake screamed, involuntarily. The creature's limb had brushed past him and was now between him and the safety of the chopper.

The pilot responded immediately, trying to manoeuvre the bird to shake loose the limb which held it down.

But it was futile. The Kraken held fast and began to pull the chopper down towards it. The pilot tried desperately to lift the chopper higher to force the Kraken to release its grip, but the bird did not respond. The power of the beast was far too much for the craft.

A second tentacle sprang from the water and wrapped itself around the same stand. Now its hold was unyielding. The chopper leaned over on one side as the creature yanked on it, proving it was in control.

Jake tightened his grip on the ladder and still tried to climb higher, as if in denial that the Kraken was winning the struggle. Before he managed the manoeuvre, he was grabbed from behind by one of the beast's massive limbs, as it curled it slowly around his torso almost egging him on to fight back.

Before he could even scream, Jake was yanked off the ladder and held high in the creature's vice-like grip. Each time he let out a breath, the pressure exerted by the beast squeezed him tighter, making it almost impossible for him to breathe.

Jake could no longer draw breath. The restriction imposed by the tentacle would not allow his chest to rise and fill with oxygen. He felt himself starting to black out, his whole body going limp.

He was barely conscious when the helicopter propeller sliced his head clean off.

***

Dan watched in horror as he saw the helicopter in the distance being wrenched down into the sea. The initial eruption of water as the chopper's blades made contact with it soon died down as the vehicle disappeared beneath the surface.

Dan wanted to cry out. He could just make out what looked like the last vestige of Jake's boat jutting out of the water, but there was no sign of life whatsoever.

Dan reached down beneath the dashboard for his binoculars. Holding onto the wheel with one hand, he scanned the area for some trace of survivors, but he could see nothing other than water and debris.

The monster had slipped below the surface with the helicopter, and Dan could only surmise at the gruesome scene which was taking place below. He suddenly felt guilty for arguing with the pilot earlier, but he knew his feelings would serve no useful purpose now.

The voice of reason in his head advised him to turn back. There was nothing he could do, no survivors to pick up, everyone was dead, included his Caitlin.

Dan felt his heart lurch in his chest and a lump clogged his throat.

He would not believe it until he saw it for himself. She could not be dead. She was waiting for him, bobbing on the waves, praying he would reach her before it was too late. And he would!

Dan slowed his boat down to a crawl as he neared the last part of Jake's boat which was still above water. He scanned the water for some sign that Caitlin or Tammi or one of the others might still be alive, but there was none. He angled his search lights to see further afield and swooped across the area as far as the beam would allow. But still, there was no sign.

Dan climbed onto the top of his wheelhouse to try and obtain a better view. Desperation was beginning to set in, and deep down, he knew that his efforts would be fruitless; but still, he was not willing to accept the situation that his world had just collapsed.

Suddenly, there was a cry from somewhere in the distance.

Dan froze, listening intently. Had it been his imagination? Was his mind playing tricks on him, taking cruel advantage of his weakened constitution?

He waited, concentrating, still unable to see where the call came from, if indeed there had been one at all.

He lifted the binoculars to his eyes once more and searched the water.

There it was again; he definitely heard something from further ahead.

Dan jumped back down from the roof and took the controls, edging the boat forward slowly in the general direction he felt the call had come from. With one hand on the wheel steering and the other sweeping the search beam across the area before him, he strained to make out something moving in the water.

Then he saw it!

About two hundred yards ahead, an arm waving, no two, three, there must be at least two of them still alive. With his heart in his mouth, Dan edged closer, spotting the search light directly at them.

As he drew nearer, he recognised Caitlin. She had both arms in the air while someone in a wetsuit was holding her up with one arm and waving frantically with the other. Dan could not make out the face because of the face mask, but he surmised that it must be the police constable as she had been the only diver on board when they set off.

Dan's heart skipped several beats, and he forced himself to steady his nerves and concentrate. The last thing he needed now was to become careless and flood the engine or crash into one of the floating ruins from Jake's boat and spring a leak.

The closer he came to the women, the faster his heart beat. He was all too painfully aware that the creature might still be in the vicinity, and judging by what he had witnessed it do to the helicopter, his little boat would not stand a chance.

Once he was close enough, Dan cut the engine. Caitlin and Sally both started to swim towards him. Dan went out on board and threw them a lifebuoy. Once they had both grabbed hold, he began to gently pull them in.

He prayed silently that the creature had left the vicinity, satisfied and satiated by its earlier conquests that it no longer felt the need to stay in the area.

Both the women reached the side of the boat together. Dan automatically reached down and grabbed Caitlin's hand. He helped her into the boat and left her standing on the deck whilst he helped Sally. As much as he wanted to hug Caitlin right now, he knew that getting Sally out of the water was his priority, and Caitlin would realise that.

Once they were both safely on board, Dan hugged Caitlin for the longest time, then pulled Sally in too and they crowded in for a group hug.

When they released, Dan could not resist holding Caitlin again.

He looked deeply into her tear-stained eyes. "I thought I'd lost you for a moment back there," he said, trying desperately not to let his own tears of joy show.

"You almost did," Caitlin agreed. "If Sally hadn't found me underwater and shared her mouthpiece with me, I'd probably be dead by now."

Dan hugged her again and mouthed a "Thank you" to Sally over Caitlin's shoulder.

Sally smiled back, her cheeks flushed.

After he and Caitlin had separated, he looked at both of them. "Any chance anyone else survived?" he asked, already knowing the answer.

Both women looked at each other, neither wanting to state the obvious.

Finally, Caitlin shook her head. "I'm really sorry about Tammi."

Dan smiled. "I bet she went down fighting?" He turned away from them, resting his hands on the side of the boat, and looked out to sea.

After a moment, he turned back, his eyes moist. "Right then," he began, "I think the first order of business is for you two to get below stairs and dry off, and get into some warm clothes. There's plenty of coffee and tea in the kitchenette, so help yourselves."

Both women nodded, gratefully. "Do you think it will come back?" asked Sally.

Before anyone could answer, the Kraken raised itself above the surface of the water a few feet in front of the boat.

Four gigantic tentacles emerged from the sea and waved about menacingly in front of the three of them. Dan instinctively put his arms out to the sides as if to protect the women, even though he knew deep down that if the beast struck, there was little chance of any of them surviving.

The creature's eyes squinted at the three humans, like a spider savouring the terror of a stricken fly caught in its web.

It waited and watched, almost as if it was tensing before striking the killer blow.

Dan could not think fast enough. He speculated several scenarios through his mind in rapid succession, but none of them had a happy ending.

The three of them waited, poised for the attack which would surely follow when the creature was ready. Time was on its side. It could just sit there torturing them for as long as suited it; they had nowhere to run!

The Kraken spewed out a shower of water which covered the boat and all those on it.

Then it slowly slipped back beneath the waves, and was gone.

They waited, frozen in place for what seemed an eternity before Dan whispered for the women to follow him into the wheelhouse. He did not want them below deck, just in case the beast struck and they became trapped. Better to be on deck and at least in with a fighting chance, though the conclusion would still be inevitable.

Dan started the engine and accelerated as gently as he could, trying to keep their movements as surreptitious as possible.

Slowly, they headed back to Skullen Bay, and safety.

When they disembarked on the beach, Seaton ran forward and hugged Sally, unashamedly. She reciprocated, and then took a turn with her two colleagues.

Warm blankets were provided by the volunteers for the women, which they accepted gratefully.

The reporters and photographers were still in attendance and flashes went off from all angles as Dan and Caitlin began their walk up the beach.

Microphones were thrust at them as they pushed their way through the mass throng, until some of the volunteers managed to get the situation under control and created a gauntlet for them.

Once the news people realised that Dan and Caitlin were not in the mood to talk, they turned their attention to Sally who was still being embraced by her colleagues.

Finally, Dan and Caitlin made it back to the car. Once inside, he hugged and kissed her again, oblivious to the noise and flashes of those stragglers who had followed them back, not willing to relinquish the chance of a last minute comment or picture.

When they pulled apart, Caitlin could see two streaks rolling down Dan's cheeks. He could not hold his tears back anymore. His expression was still one of being strong and in control, but his eyes gave away his true feelings for her.

"I love you so much, Dan Savage."

Dan wiped his eyes. "That's good, because I was wondering if I could tempt you into marrying me, sometime soon."

Now it was time for Caitlin to cry, with tears of joy.

NIGHT OF THE KRAKEN – EPILOGUE

The Kraken had been swimming for several days since the attack on the boat. The urgency of its situation had warranted a retreat. Instinctively, it had known that survival was paramount and the risk to itself of attacking the boat again just to access those on board was not worth it. After all, it had already despatched most of the crew that had been involved in trying to destroy it; the others could wait!

Now it headed into warmer waters, its great tentacles propelling it forward at speed, watching as some of the fiercest predators of the deep moved swiftly out of its path. It had been here before; not exactly in the same spot, but the region was familiar to it. It knew that it would soon reach the perfect spot, and once it had, it would wait for its time.

It had fed well during the last attack, which afforded it more than enough sustenance to complete the task at hand. Since then, it had not needed to eat. Indeed, to try and consume more at this stage, it felt would only be counter-productive.

It knew what was happening to it. Had no idea why or how, just that it was the way of things, a new beginning.

As the temperature of the water increased, so did the clarity of it. This felt cleaner, safer, and far more conducive to life – far less threatening than where it had been recently.

The creature revelled in the feelings which coursed through it. They were all new experiences and most welcome, building in intensity with each mile covered.

Eventually it stopped.

It had arrived.

The creature allowed itself to drift slowly to the ocean floor, where it lay motionless. It surveyed the area around it. There was plenty of fish in the immediate vicinity, plenty of food for the operation.

The Kraken looked up, its perfect vision piercing the water above it, gazing miles ahead to the surface to ensure that no craft passed overhead.

Raising two of its great tentacles slightly off the ocean floor, it waited. The moment was almost here.

Within minutes, the first creature shot forth from the mighty Kraken. It was closely followed by another. Then another followed. And another. And still more, until finally there were a dozen miniature versions of the beast darting back and forth in front of it.

Within seconds of emerging, each creature knew instinctively what it must do to survive. Blinking to take in their new surroundings, the creatures honed in on whatever sea life was within striking distance, gorging themselves on their first taste of solid food.

The Kraken looked on with pride.

The new cycle had begun.

THE END

CHECK OUT OTHER GREAT
DEEP SEA THRILLERS

PREHISTORIC BEASTS AND WHERE TO FIGHT THEM
by Hugo Navikov

IN THE DEPTHS, SOMETHING WAITS ...

Acclaimed film director Jake Bentneus pilots a custom submersible to the bottom of Challenger Deep in the Pacific, the deepest point of any ocean of Earth. But something lurks at the hot hydrothermal vents, a creature—a dinosaur—too big to exist.

Gigadon.

It not only exists, but it follows him, hungrily, back to the surface. Later, a barely living Bentneus offers a $1 billion prize to anyone who can find and kill the monster. His best bet is renowned ichthyopaleontologist Sean Muir, who had predicted adapted dinosaurs lived at the bottom of the ocean.

MEGALODON: APEX PREDATOR
by S.J. Larsson

English adventurer Sir Jeffery Mallory charters a ship for a top secret expedition to Antarctica. What starts out as a search and capture mission soon turns into a terrifying fight for survival as the crew come face to face with the fiercest ocean predator to have ever existed- Carcharodon Megalodon. Alone and with no hope of rescue the crew will need all their resources if they are to survive not only a 60 foot shark but also the harsh Antarctic conditions. Megalodon: Apex Predator is a deep-sea adventure filled with action, twists and savage prehistoric sharks.

 **SEVERED**PRESS

facebook.com/severedpress
twitter.com/severedpress

CHECK OUT OTHER GREAT DEEP SEA THRILLERS

HELL'S TEETH
by Paul Mannering

In the cold South Pacific waters off the coast of New Zealand, a team of divers and scientists are preparing for three days in a specially designed habitat 1300 feet below the surface.

In this alien and savage world, the mysterious great white sharks gather to hunt and to breed.

When the dive team's only link to the surface is destroyed, they find themselves in a desperate battle for survival. With the air running out, and no hope of rescue, they must use their wits to survive against sharks, each other, and a terrifying nightmare of legend.

MONSTERS IN OUR WAKE
by J.H. Moncrieff

In the idyllic waters of the South Pacific lurks a dangerous and insatiable predator; a monster whose bloodlust and greed threatens the very survival of our planet...the oil industry. Thousands of miles from the nearest human settlement, deep on the ocean floor, ancient creatures have lived peacefully for millennia. But when an oil drill bursts through their lair, Nøkken attacks, damaging the drilling ship's engine and trapping the desperate crew. The longer the humans remain in Nøkken's territory, struggling to repair their ailing ship, the more confrontations occur between the two species. When the death toll rises, the crew turns on each other, and marine geologist Flora Duchovney realizes the scariest monsters aren't below the surface.